"*The Future* is so pleasing a
so full of intrigue, emotion
conclusion, that I didn't want
who was raised Orthodox J
the book of Genesis in exciting
the parables of community, conflict, and survival found in its pages, is an added and surprising bonus. It's almost enough to make you believe, despite the evidence, that the bleakest of futures isn't inevitable."

—*Los Angeles Times*

"The book's most impressive quality is its vivid, tactile imagination of our ultra-computerized future . . . Alderman's encyclopedic knowledge of everything from cryptographic history to biblical hermeneutics lends the novel a savvy, scholarly gravitas."

—*The New York Times Book Review*

"Alderman has crafted characters readers will want to follow wherever they go—even to the end of the world. A smart, engrossing fable about digital technology and human community."

—*Kirkus Reviews* (starred review)

"A daring, sexy, thrilling novel that may be the most wryly funny book about the end of civilization you'll ever read."

—*BookPage* (starred review)

"The endless intrigue and surprising twists keep the pages turning." —*Publishers Weekly*

"Naomi Alderman has become one of the great writers of twenty-first-century speculative fiction. . . . A hefty but highly compelling page-turner that pulled me in and kept me reading from the first line. It's . . . shot through with humor, sharp satire, compassion, a great love story, and well-wrought prose."

—*The Brooklyn Rail*

". . . constructed thriller . . . end-of-the-world whodunit, as well as a will-they-won't-they love story." —*The Boston Globe*

The FUTURE

Also by

NAOMI ALDERMAN

The Power

The Liars' Gospel

The Lessons

Disobedience

NAOMI ALDERMAN

a novel

POCKET BOOKS
New York Amsterdam/Antwerp London
Toronto Sydney/Melbourne New Delhi

Pocket Books
An Imprint of Simon & Schuster, LLC
1230 Avenue of the Americas
New York, NY 10020

First Pocket Books paperback edition June 2025

Interior design by Lewelin Polanco

Manufactured in the United States of America

10 9 8 7 6 5 4 3 2 1

Library of Congress Control Number: 2022513535

ISBN 978-1-6680-8257-7
ISBN 978-1-6680-2570-3 (ebook)

For OAD, DLA,
and SSA: the future

To order, to govern,
is to begin naming;
when names proliferate
it's time to stop.
If you know when to stop
you're in no danger.

—Lao Tzu, *Tao Te Ching*,
translated by Ursula K. Le Guin

PART 1

the essential problem

NORTH CALIFORNIA, NOVEMBER

Action Now! Ecological Convention

lenk

On the day the world ended, Lenk Sketlish—CEO and founder of the Fantail social network—sat at dawn beneath the redwoods in a designated location of natural beauty and attempted to inhale from his navel.

The tops of the mountains in the distance were capped with snow, their curves and crevasses kindling the imagination. The trees near at hand were russet on fawn, gray-green on sage. The redwood trunks were solid, corded, patterned like twisted vines, their surfaces soft with mosses and growing grass; tiny insects whirred through the dense mass. The sky was the pale water-washed blue of the late fall, mottled cloud visible through the spiral-set branches. And yet.

The meditation teacher had a nose whistle.

Each time she took yet another "deep belly breath," the whine cut through the gentle whisper of the redwoods like a chain saw. She must hear it. She surely heard it. She did not seem to hear it. The redwoods shivered, the November leaves were about to drop, and all things must pass, as she could not cease reminding him.

All things were not going to pass from Lenk Sketlish if he had anything to do with it.

"Let your belly be soft as you inhale," the teacher said. Her tongue lingered on the double *l* in "belly," as if she were Italian. She wasn't Italian. Lenk had asked Martha

Einkorn, his executive assistant, to check after the first day. The meditation instructor came from Wisconsin, the home of squeaky cheese. She kept saying "belly." He should hold light in his belly, feel the warmth in his belly, crawl inside his own belly, and dwell forever in her adenoidal whine and her infinitely elongated *l*. What was growing inside Lenk Sketlish's belly was an acidic roiling, churning wrath.

The redwoods. Back to the redwoods. The majesty of nature, simple beauty. The worn path up the hillside, the tumbling brook. Breathing in, breathing out. The world as it comes moment by moment and he, too, a part of it. Not scattered, not wrathful, not thinking of the Fantail expansion deals in Uruguay and in Myanmar even though someone was definitely going to fuck something up in his absence.

Be present. Here. Feeling his breath in his navel, the center of his body, yes, good, the navel rising and falling and . . . the nose whistle added a new note. Slightly lower than the first. Baritone? Alto? Couldn't she hear it? Why didn't she blow her nose before she came to the sessions? Hadn't Martha or anyone on his board or a single one of Martha's minions found out whether this gold-star, top-of-the-line meditation teacher had a nose whistle? Did they just take everything on trust?

"Breathe within the body"—her voice low and lilting—"nothing is needed from you in this moment."

This was obviously not true, given that he had to be there, given that his board had told him quite some time ago that if he couldn't get his anger under control, there were real questions over whether he had a future at Fantail, which was in itself as nonsensical as this woman with a full orchestral wind section in her nose passing herself off as a source of calm. He'd gone along with it; he'd played the game. If they thought they were going to do to him what

Ellen Bywater had done to Albert Dabrowski at Medlar, shuffle him out of his own company, well, they had another think coming. But they would do it—they'd tell him his leadership style wasn't working, he wasn't on a learning journey; they'd edge him out slowly at first and then very fast. He'd seen it. Albert Dabrowski was a cautionary tale. Ellen Bywater ran Medlar now. Where the fuck was Albert Dabrowski? Who the fuck even cared?

"Be truly present in this moment," the mucosal trumpets murmured. "Allow yourself to meet the moment with trust."

He was there to show his willingness. He wasn't an immature baby; he'd run Fantail successfully for nearly two decades, built it from nothing but an idea and the sense of a wave building far out in the ocean. In 127 countries across the world now, if you wanted to talk to a mass audience, you started with FantailStream; if you wanted to sell something, you set up FantailStore; if you wanted to trade across borders, you used FantailSeamless to pay in FantailCoin. When nation spoke unto nation, they did it via Fantail.

And Lenk could do this next part, the public-facing making-nice part. The antitrust hearings, this dumb Action Now! ecological conference with Anvil and Medlar—he could do it. He'd keep his cool, not throw expensive ceramic sculptures through expensive engraved-glass partitions, and no one would have to go to the hospital with a glass shard in her eye ever again. That was a mistake. He regretted it. Meditation is hokey but it works—just breathe from the navel. Focus on the in-breath. The out-breath. He used to be into this stuff at Harvard. One of his roommates had given him a playlist. Long nights coding, then ten minutes of this and you go from strung-out exhaustion to blissful deep sleep. There was something to it. Zimri Nommik of Anvil went to some pod in the desert every year to do ten days of silence and fasting and pouring water up his nose. Or up his ass. One of those. Zimri Nommik, building warehouses and distribution networks, shipping everything old and new under the sun, already on his heels with AnvilChat and AnvilParty, trying to snap up everything in his all-consuming maw and—

"If you find your thoughts have wandered"—the instructor inhaled deeply with an accordion wheeze—"don't be surprised. Simply return gently to the breath. This moment is all you need." But this had never been the case. This moment was gone as soon as it was noticed. There could be no prize and no possession there. It was the glimmering he needed, the beckoning force of time, the wave gathering in the distant ocean.

"Take a deep belly breath. Remember that we are only ever anxious about things that might happen in the future. But the future is not here. The future is imaginary and all its promises and fears are imagined. We can rest in this moment," she said. "What is happening is OK."

But often what was happening was not OK. It was almost never OK. It needed constant nudging and tending, fixing and pushing. Without his intervention the moment would be lost, and the next, and the next, each wave passing and him still bobbing in the cold sea, the warmth leaching from his bones, death rising to swallow him whole. Without keeping his eyes on what might happen, an entire life could be eaten up, and most people's were.

"There's no way to really know what's going to arise next," the instructor said.

Well, then it was all a shit show. There was no way to know. The next moment might hold anything. There could be opportunities, new ideas caught by someone else, a competitor ready to usurp his fortune. There could be Ellen Bywater, the company stealer, turning the all-seeing eye of Medlar in his direction, her gleaming, elegant pieces of hardware the aspirational alternative to workaday Fantail. The Medlar Torc was her new thing, all your communication needs dealt with by this stylish device. She always seemed one step ahead of him now, tempting away his key demographics like she stole Medlar. There could be new products from her, but of course there could be an earthquake, a sudden heart attack, a deadly bomb loosed far away by an unstable dictator, a global pandemic. Anything.

Lenk Sketlish was a powerful man who had built his career on the future, on knowing it, smelling it, feeling it more present around him than the present. The future was his home and his consolation; the urgency of tomorrow, the next decade, the next century pressed in on him and pushed him forward.

"There's no way to really know what's going to happen even one second into the future."

No, thought Lenk Sketlish, that's not going to work for me.

The thinscreen on his wrist gave out a low but urgent beep. The meditation instructor creased her brow, and a satisfying thought flashed through Lenk's mind: Ah, you see, there's no way to really know what's going to happen, is there? He glanced at the thinscreen; it would be an emergency in Albania or in Thailand, a decision to be made and a problem to be solved, some wonderful and financially unarguable excuse to end the session early. But it wasn't. The skin of his face tightened; his eyes narrowed as he looked at the notification. It was no minor escape. It was the end of days.

zimri

Zimri Nommik, CEO of the logistics and purchasing giant Anvil, missed the notification by a full four hours because—unusually for him—he'd been fucking his wife.

Selah Nommik had been in an oddly labile mood at the Action Now! conference. She loved these bullshit environmental events, it was true. He'd seen her weep actual tears over the tigers and the dolphins and some particular lichen she had the hots for. And it was true that he'd surprised her and doubled the amount of his pledge to the FutureSafe zones. Despite everything, he still enjoyed it when she looked at him like she remembered why she'd married him.

He'd watched Selah walk across the stage—her cream-colored skirt cut above the knee, her calves and thighs tight and glossy, she looked like Serena Williams in her prime. He'd thought: Fuck it, it's all going to go to the lawyers anyway, and said twice the number they'd agreed on. Selah grabbed his hand, held their clasped palms aloft like they'd just won the championship. As the cameras clicked, as the audience roared, as the enormous number appeared on the screen behind them, Selah had bent down and whispered in his ear, "I want you to fuck me. Now." So he was really going to get some action, now. All it had taken was an extra $5.7 billion.

They fucked the way he liked it, but with an intensity they hadn't found in years. Against the wall of the suite, pulling her skirt off; on the floor, her urging him inside her. On the couch, her under him. Finally in bed, her on top, riding him, her heavy breasts bare, her large, dark nipples so hard, her rhythm so urgent, she erased the memory and the thought of every single part of the whole world and simplified him to a single pinpoint of bright pleasure and entire surrender.

"Bloody hell," she said, and collapsed into the tangled sheets.

Then, remembering, she turned back and said with an unexpected tenderness: "You alright?" It was like they'd just met and she'd only this moment heard about the wheezy, geeky kid he'd been at school, the child of Jewish Estonian immigrants, the boy thrown into a Minnesota high school who was bullied so hard for his weird looks and his strange accent and syntax—and his even more obnoxious constant conviction of his own superiority—that the football kids threw him out of a moving car. She'd seen him again, at the last.

These days, Zimri Nommik had a trainer and a paleo regimen, a six-pack and more money than any other person on Earth. He still looked badly put-together—his broad, hairy shoulders and big arms and hands seeming to belong to a different man than his short, squat frame and pointed features. But it didn't matter. He knew what he was doing in business so perfectly that it looked like prophecy. His timing was immaculate. His understanding of the market, of the most ruthless impregnable way to run an organization, was unparalleled. Still, Zimri could never hold that janky little boy in completely. He knew how he'd stood next to the healthy, creamy-skinned, flaxen-haired, big-teethed, stocky, farm-bred, sports-playing boys at school. There was never enough sex or enough success to dissolve himself for more than a moment.

Could Selah Nommik know that he'd already spoken to the lawyers? Was that why it was so good? He'd timed his meetings to happen while she was visiting with her family in London. She couldn't *know*, but perhaps somehow she'd intuited that this was the end, that in a few weeks she would be presented all at once with extraordinary wealth, a nondisclosure agreement, and divorce papers.

"Fuck," said Selah Nommik. "Shit, I've got that thing in Sonoma—you know, the women thing. I've got to get going."

He watched her pull on her panties and smooth the cream skirt over her glorious ass. Fasten the white lace bra. Wanting to hold on to the past is a weakness. Just enjoy it now.

The boys who'd thrown him from the moving car had come to visit him in the hospital. His jaw by then was wired into the new position it would always occupy—slightly thrust forward, giving him the look in profile of an eager young Communist striving toward victory for the people. Although he knew there were five of those boys, he couldn't now remember any differentiating features; they seemed to pass the few facts he knew—that one had a laugh that sounded like a sneeze, another turned out to be unexpectedly brilliant at physics but kept it quiet—around the group of faces, the characteristics settling on a different one each time. He wished sometimes he had written it all down and sometimes was glad he hadn't. When they visited the hospital, they behaved as if they'd all perpetrated a magnificent joke together, that his face had been smashed in an escapade in which he hadn't been an unwilling participant but an adventurer. *Remember*, said one, laughing, *remember when you were falling out, how you grabbed for the seat belt?*

It was in that moment that Zimri knew that however hard he stuck to his story, those boys would never remember it as anything other than a lark. He'd learned that there was no certainty to be found in others. The only safety was to be independent enough to survive. Any overture of friendship could always turn out to be the subtle maneuvering along a car's bench by a group of interchangeable laughing young men, jostling and pushing until one final puppyish wriggle thrust him into the insubstantial air.

Selah Nommik buttoned her blouse. Goodbye to those breasts, those nipples, those thighs. That was the way it had to be. He lived in San Francisco, for God's sake; there'd always be another one. She kissed him with a fierce tenderness, looked him in the eye, and he thought again—Does she know? But she couldn't know. She just sensed something. She let herself out.

It was late. Lenk Sketlish had invited him for morning meditation. That was a no. Not just because he absolutely couldn't stand Lenk, but because an orgasm of that quality couldn't be wasted. Zimri set his AnvilSleepSystem to wake him at 6 a.m. In his experience, an extraordinary, self-erasing orgasm followed by a deep sleep, an ice-cold bath, and a long run would generate ideas worth between $10 billion and $20 billion, amortized over a ten-year period. He instructed his AnvilFocus that there would be no interruptions—none at all, none for any reason—until his run was finished. Nothing whatever until midday.

The next day in the November morning, the lake was cold and clear. There was a mist on it, gathering in loose clouds, drifting like a living thing. Five waterbirds dived for pondweed and gossiped among themselves. The redwoods in the distance were scribbled against the sky. Zimri Nommik, breathing heavily, sat on the shore, pulled his smart notebook from his back pocket, and jotted down various thoughts on synergies between production and distribution lines in Southeast Asia. He fell into a reverie, watching the sinuous strands of tide and countertide, wind threading the surface of the lake, all the while seeing not the world itself but the world of metaphor and symbol in which supply chains and factories, industries and countries were colored beads to be moved and moved again until their operation pleased him.

He was in this trance of productivity when AnvilFocus quietly turned itself off at precisely midday. The clip on his shirt collar started to buzz. He flipped his smart notebook to the digital deck at the back of the pages. And there it was. He stared at the notification for a few moments, then out again to the lake. He scratched his ear. Depending on the kind of shit they were facing, this could be it for this particular lake, waterbirds, lakes in general, or all three. Might as well enjoy the scenery while it lasted.

Selah called him as he walked back to the lodge.

"Fuck," she said. "Zimri, seriously, I've been trying to get you all morning. Is this real?"

He thought of how it could be now. No time to find someone new. She was the one who'd be coming to the bunker with him. He could say, "No, it's a test, stay at home." The wind stirred the trees and a gust of leaves tumbled onto the sheer surface of the lake.

"It's real," he said. "There'll be a plane coming for you. Get on it."

"What, we're not going together?"

"The protocol is not to do anything that draws attention to our leaving. Normal transportation. You know that. I guess I'll be . . ." He laughed. "Fuck, Selah, I'm going to be on a plane with Lenk and Ellen."

"Oh Jesus," she said. "Better you than me."

"We can't talk now," he said, "not till we're on the plane, with our own Wi-Fi, OK?"

"Yeah," she said. Then: "I'm scared."

"I'll see you at the bunker," he said. "Not Haida Gwaii—

there's been a problem. The Scottish one. It's going to be fine."

It could be good, he thought. It could actually be better than it had been. Whatever was going to happen to the world, he would be alright. And if it didn't work out with Selah, there'd still be a way to find someone new.

ellen

In the wood-lined penthouse apartment of her lake-view villa at the Action Now! convention, Ellen Bywater, the CEO of Medlar Technologies, the world's most profitable personal computing company, tried to pack. Her hands were shaking.

Will, her late husband, sat in the wooden easy chair facing the lake view, watching her. He said: Tough decision?

"It's alright for you," she said. "You're dead. You go where I go."

I would have gone where you went even if I were still alive, he said. Even to the ends of the earth.

She smiled at the empty chair. It wasn't that she didn't know he was dead. She wasn't crazy, after all. He was just a hard habit to give up.

The Action Now! event had been Ellen's idea. Well, not quite her idea. Albert Dabrowski, the ousted founder of her company, had made a huge donation to Action Now!, so she had to give a bigger one and go along to the event to make it look good.

Will would have put his arm around her shoulders and kissed the top of her head and said: "A sop to your conscience?" She'd have shrugged and he'd have said: "I prefer your conscience sopping."

She found herself still talking to him, able to fill in his side of the conversation almost precisely. Sometimes in their house she saw him at the foot of the stair, his long body and the folded easel of his angular legs disappearing into the dining room as she walked down the steps. He'd been proud of his legs—at sixty-four, he'd still had good knees for hiking. On the day he died, his knees had been doing just fine.

"My mind is going in circles," she said. "I'm frightened."

Will understood. Of course she was frightened. No one *wanted* the world to end.

The notification had information about the protocol. She'd written the protocol herself, a while back. In the event of disaster.

"Ellen," said the protocol on her SmartPin, "do not pack all your belongings. Only take small items of sentimental value. Your needs will be provided for."

What about me? said Will. Am I a small item of sentimental value?

Ellen told him to fuck off.

"Have the kids' protocols been activated?" asked Ellen.

The SmartPin responded: "Your children have been notified. They are on their way to the transport."

"Even Badger?" said Ellen.

Will gave Ellen a sharp look. Badger was their youngest, their nonbinary child with a radical political stance. Badger had mentioned several times that they did not approve of this whole system, of warnings and private jets and hidden safe bunkers in New Zealand.

The protocol was to make no phone calls in this situation. It was no use having a safe and comfortable place to ride out a global catastrophe if everyone knew you were leaving and could follow you. Get the doors sealed before anyone knew you'd left—that was the plan. Still.

"Call Badger," said Ellen.

An agony of thudding heartbeats before Badger answered the call. Their face, projected onto the wall of the suite, was very close to their screen—they never wanted their mother to see where they were. How sharper than a serpent's tooth it is.

Still, Badger looked afraid. This gave Ellen a certain grim satisfaction. See? Your mother still does know something worth knowing.

"Are you coming?" said Ellen. "Did you get the alert?"

Badger's brow creased. Oh, that little crease they'd had since they were a day-old baby suckling noisily at the nipple. That frown of intense engagement.

"Mom? There's a car outside. I don't know what to do."

Oh, how Ellen had missed this. Being a mom to Badger had always been tricky, prickly. But her baby needed her.

"Get in the car. OK?"

"OK."

A pause. Then, at last, the depths of the frown.

"Can I bring . . ."

"You can bring two people. Tell them to leave their phones behind, OK? Anvil Clips, Torcs, anything. Tell them it's a vacation. Tell them I'm making you do it and you hate me. OK?"

Badger breathed out a long sigh. Their sweet freckles were scattered under their eyes like stars.

"OK. I'll see you, right?"

"Less than a day, darling. I promise."

Ellen Bywater had regained herself. Before the car arrived, she sat in front of the mirror, applied her lipstick, and blotted it. She believed in doing these things herself.

Will said: You did your own makeup for our wedding. Nineteen eighty-nine and you painted the whorls of gold, red, and yellow around your own young eyes. I watched you. Like an artist with the fine camel-hair brushes and the little golden pots. Like a priestess.

"I looked like I'd been punched hard in the nose," she said. But after all, it's life that punches you till your face is unrecognizable.

"You're going to miss seeing me go all to wrinkles," she said to Will.

Will said, You already had wrinkles when I died, remember? I kissed your wrinkles.

"Sometimes you made fun of them."

Sometimes we made fun of each other. That's how we were. I always believed in you.

Ellen looked at Will, who was not there. What was it they'd believed in, after all?

Sometimes, she knew what he would have said as if he'd been right there. And sometimes she had to figure it out—she hated these moments, when she knew he was really gone.

At last Will said: You've always done your best for your shareholders and your employees.

There wasn't much packing to do. She took her watch. She took her topaz sweater and the gold necklace that always looked so good against it. She took her laptop, her phone, and her Medlar Torc. The idea of packing was itself a small item of sentimental value.

Although it was strictly against the protocol, Ellen checked the big survivalist site, Name The Day. If anything was out there, if anyone knew the big one was coming, it'd be somewhere on the site. But there was nothing out of the ordinary. Troops in the South China Sea. A pipeline explosion in eastern Europe. The same old prepper rants. Those people didn't know that anything had boiled over. Still, somewhere out there, something was happening. Alarms don't go off for no reason. Somewhere in the world, a situation that used to be just about under control was slipping into "not under control at all." A chain reaction. Somewhere in the jungle, there was a tiger.

lenk

It was dark already at the airfield. Lenk Sketlish's bone-conducting mini-pods were playing the Rolling Stones' "Gimme Shelter." Inside his skull, the Beatles had broken up, the '60s were over, violent revolution was in the air, and now, anything could happen. He felt alive, he thought, truly for the first time in his life. The night drive out, the music beating in his head, the future was just moments away. This was what he'd planned for. This was the midnight beginning. This was the smooth running-out of the old world and the birth of the new.

Except when he got to the hangar, Zimri Nommik was there with his nervy smile, and Ellen Bywater was stabbing at her phone and saying, "There's no reception. I haven't had reception since we left the convention."

She was panicking already. He'd known it. She'd never thought this was really going to happen. She wasn't going to last a month after the end of civilization.

The nearest plane to the conference was one of Zimri's private jets. The pilot knew the same story as the ground crew, the same story that would eventually go to the press. The three tech CEOs were in closed session for negotiations. "High-level synergies between technological infrastructures leading to carbon-saving measures." This plane wouldn't take them directly to the destination but to a nearby staging post where Lenk and Ellen would be met by their own aircraft and taken on. Get out quickly and you've got all the time you need to make sure you're not followed. Zimri's plane, of course, would turn off its transponder as soon as they were out of radar range. No sense letting anyone follow you to your actual bunker. One of

Zimri's own survival locations had recently been blown by some fucking internet Name The Day journalist. That was always the risk.

The plane door opened and the stairs lowered themselves to the ground with a reassuring hiss. They'd never even meet the pilot.

"There's Wi-Fi on the plane," said Zimri as they climbed the steps. Lenk could see Zimri already calculating and recalculating odds. Did it give him any advantage that it was his plane? Was it somehow a disadvantage? There'd be no more of this in the new world, no more neuroses of abundance. There would be a simpler, purer life.

Lenk's bone conductors flipped over to *Goats Head Soup* and the guitar rolled him on into the future. It would be soon now, and while a large part of his mind knew this could still be, on the scale of things, a minor apocalypse, at least for them—a year or five of inconvenience and business opportunities—Lenk found himself at peace. The plane took off as smooth as a long drink of cool water. In one way of looking at it, it wasn't them leaving at all. Earth peeled away from the plane, the life they'd known rolling itself up and putting itself away. They weren't leaving the world, the world was leaving them.

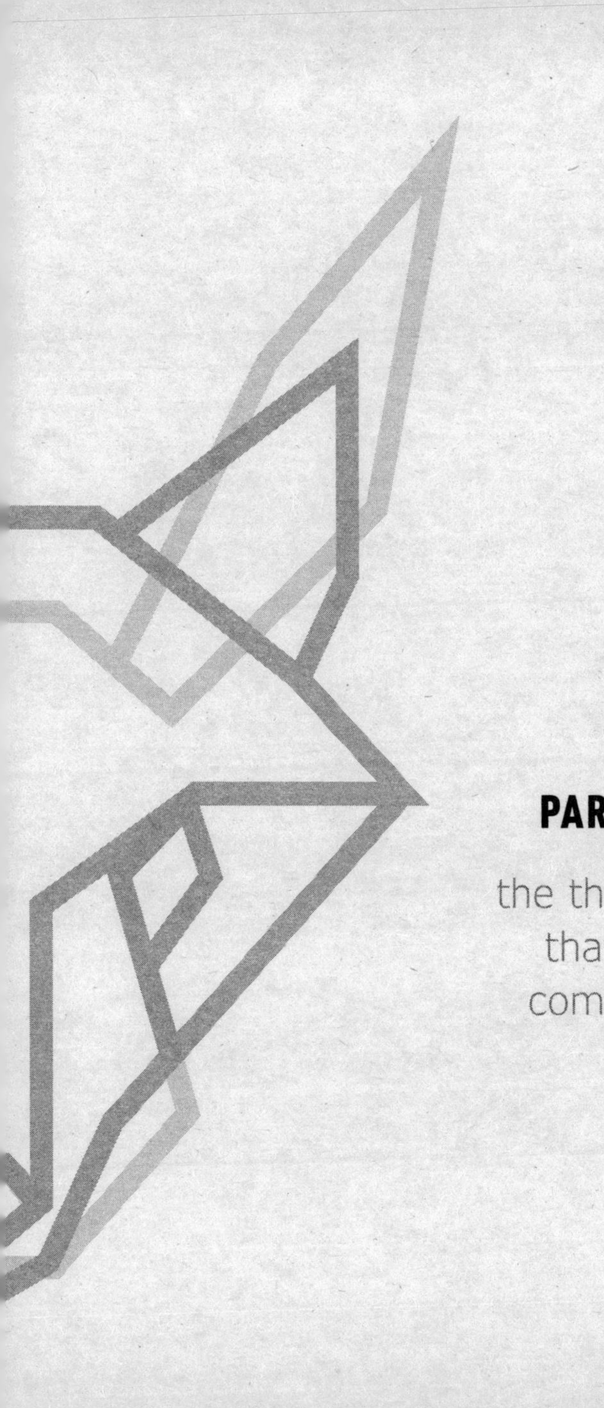

PART 2

the thing that is coming

extract from Name The Day survivalist forum

sub-board: ntd/strategic

›› OneCorn is at **Prepped To The Max** *status. OneCorn has made 4,744 posts and received 14,829 thumbs-up.*

Sooooo . . . who's up for a little . . . BIBLE STUDY?

I am on my *interesting historical lessons*, thank you.

Burning is the inevitable fate of anyone who tells people stuff worth hearing. Believe me. Today's lesson is on the theme: When is it time to go?

It's not *not* about billionaires owning intense survival bunkers.

No one has ever been able to stop you hating on Lenk Sketlish, AM. But yeah. This is relevant. It's about very powerful people and it's about social responsibility. OK?

Alright.

Genesis chapter 18, loosely translated

CW: sexual assault, murder, destruction of property, explosions, terror, incest, rains of fire, pillars of salt, violent death, blasphemy, God

So the Lord looked at Sodom and it was not a great place to live, work, or raise a family. The people of Sodom were cruel, they took whatever they

›› ArturoMegadog is at* Shelf-Stable *status.

›› ArturoMegadog

@OneCorn: Really. You're on your bullshit *again*?

You're going to get flamed. Again.

Is this about the billionaire bunker thing?

Do I get to hate on Lenk Sketlish?

OK. You'll still get flamed doing this on / strategic. But continue. I think I'm the only one reading anyway.

wanted, they had stopped caring for strangers or the poor. They were genuinely disgusting.

Sodom was a place that embodied everything that was wrong with all of this "civilization" and "progress" that the humans had been getting up to lately. The Lord looked closely and had some strong negative feelings about it all.

But the Lord had recently been having serious and useful conversations with a person, Abraham. More than any of the other humans, Abraham ended up surprising him with the depth of his moral thinking. You'd think God wouldn't be interested in comments on his work, but in fact, even in Genesis he's soliciting opinions and adjusting what he's doing.

That's how the books of discussion of the Talmud work too. They're essentially layers of commentary, scholars arguing with each other back and forth through time and across the centuries. Arguably, soliciting opinions and adjusting what you're doing is the sign of some pretty advanced thinking. *Arguably* that's what God is modeling for us through the work of creation.

So: involved in the process and interested in feedback, the Lord let Abraham in on his plans.

He said: "Sodom and Gomorrah. You would not believe the cries of

›› ***ArturoMegadog is at* Shelf-Stable *status.***

Well I will take that as a compliment and thank you kindly, ma'am.

anguish that are rising up to me from those places. They don't treat each other with kindness, not even respect, not even basic human dignity. So I'm thinking: Destroy them. Smite them, wipe them out. Fire and brimstone. My wrath, my friend, is *kindled*."

The Lord waited for Abraham's response. He was nervous.

Now it seemed clear to Abraham that the Lord had just said something pretty self-contradictory. Because if you want people to treat each other with human dignity, shouldn't you start by . . . treating them all with human dignity? But it's tough to point out this kind of thing even to your boss. Let alone the Owner Of All Things, the Maker Of Heaven And Earth. Eventually, Abraham said:

"You're thinking of sweeping the whole place away? The good people with the bad?"

And the Lord was like: "Yeah! Justice!"

Abraham put his fingertips to his forehead and said: "OK but, just bear with me, what if there are fifty good people in Sodom? Would you destroy the whole city? You are supposed to judge everyone fairly."

This was a great point and to be honest the Lord hadn't thought about it before. That was why he liked talking to Abraham—the guy came up with ideas that were right on target. Like a kid, holding their parents to good values.

The Lord said: "OK, you know. You're right. If there are fifty good people in Sodom, I'll forgive the whole city. Yeah, if there are fifty, that's what I'll do."

Now, "forgive everyone" vs. "smite everyone" might not have been quite what Abraham was getting at with the whole "judge everyone fairly" idea.

But—like you do with a difficult boss—Abraham spoke quietly and respectfully. "Honestly, who am I to say anything to you, I'm literally dust and ashes and you're the Lord but OK, how about this, if there are just five people missing from that fifty, you wouldn't still destroy the whole city, would you? If there were forty-five, you'd save the city, right?"

The Lord had to agree that was right.

And Abraham went on. Like he had something incredibly vital to demonstrate to the Lord of Hosts. Like there's something infinitely precious about literally every human life and you can't just bomb whole cities even if almost everyone there is living a lifestyle you disagree with.

"You'd save the city for forty," he said, then "You'd save the city for thirty. You'd save the city for twenty. You'd save the city for ten."

›› ***DanSatDan is at*** One Tin O'Beans ***status.***

ABRAHAM AND GOD? What is this religious bullshit? I didn't come here for God shit. Got enough of that from my folks, no thank you. I thought this sub was about serious survival strategies not this garbage. Go to ntd/endofdays if this is your thing

There was a really important point here; Abraham was arguing against collective punishment. But from the text it doesn't seem as if the Lord really understood this idea yet.

And Abraham was saying something else. Something about how even if you do happen to be incredibly powerful, you can't just walk away when things go bad. That's not what your power is for. You can't just go "screw it, this was a mistake, I'll get rid of it." If you've got power, use it to *help*.

"OK, you're right," said the Lord, "I'd save the city for the sake of ten good people." The Lord was on a learning journey, and you know that's no bad reason to have created humanity.

Anyway it turned out there really weren't ten good people in the city. There was just one barely adequate man—Lot, Abraham's nephew—and his family. The Lord was tired of talking to Abraham, that guy was smart but he made his head ache. And so the Lord decided to rain down fire and ash upon the cities of the plains.

But I mean that is the question really, isn't it? Is it OK to decide to give up on a place? How little goodness is too little? When is there no future left?

›› ***ArturoMegadog is at*** **Shelf-Stable** ***status.***

@OneCorn: told you.

@DanSatDan: Kid, back off. Before you get yourself into a flamewar . . . try to work out who you're insulting. Go and check out OneCorn's bestof, OK? OneCorn does this stuff sometimes. Like . . . experimenting with the form. Putting fragments together that don't seem like they go together. There's usually a point to it in the end. OneCorn knows her stuff. Trust.

zhen

1. seasons time: it's your time

In Singapore on a sweltering June day a few months before the end of the world, Lai Zhen—a Top Fifty Creator on the Name The Day forum and ranked number one for expertise in technological survival—was shopping for electronics in the Seasons Time Mall when someone tried to shoot her.

Coincidentally, Zhen had already made a video called "What Goes through Your Mind When You're Being Shot At" and 6.3 million people had watched it. In the video, she was wry and witty, talking to the camera as her assistant fired the gun; she moved fast in a forward roll, staying low to the ground.

- She said: Remember that shock will make it hard to focus.
- She said: You'll freeze, you'll have to fight against your instincts.
- She said: Remember that you might piss your pants.
- She grinned.
- No really, she said. This is serious.

The top comment was: "hella survival instinct girl." It had 15,272 likes. Lai Zhen had survived the Fall of Hong Kong and seventeen months in an offshore British refugee camp. She spoke about these things with the detached and ironized humor, the expertise and the only-slightly-emotionally-broken style that was by then the popular tone to talk about the end of civilization. Zhen was thirty-three years old, and an increasingly survival-focused world of constantly unfolding crises was eager for what she had to offer.

But the symbol and the real are never the same. A friend shooting blanks for a video to drive engagement with your sponsor's brand of outdoor clothing is one thing. Four bullets bursting through the glass of an electronics store in the Seasons Time Mall in Singapore is another. When the heavy thunks hit two televisions and the tourist standing next to her, Zhen did not in fact use verbal noting strategies to master her fear and she did not do four-seven-eight breathing. Instead, all she heard inside her head was her own stupid voice saying: You might piss your pants.

Seasons Time was the world's largest retail megacity; it was owned by some international tech consortium that had invited Zhen to take part in a charitable event for flood relief, disaster relief, refugee aid—one of those. Zhen was bouncing off a bad, complicated ghosting quasi-breakup with a woman she'd really thought might amount to something. She'd accepted the invitation because she thought it might be soothing to be in the most uptight country on Earth, and because when she felt like shit, she always kept moving.

Her friend Marius had said: "You going because you care about refugee aid. You don't fool me with your dark Jean-François Lyotard postmodern ironic bullshit."

It was true she'd turned down invitations to review a self-erecting tent in Addis Ababa and a revolutionary smartfiber jacket in Helsinki. She'd brushed off a multi-country PR junket for secure survival spaces in eighty major cities around the world, which you, too, could access for only $7,000 a year—what's that in exchange for peace of mind? This was her thing: not rubbing sticks together to make a fire. Buying the best equipment you could and working smart with technology so as to escape the horrifying fall of civilization. But she'd turned it all down for a charity event in Singapore.

"Fuck you," she'd said to Marius. "I don't have any feelings; you can't prove that."

As soon as she'd arrived from San Francisco, she'd headed directly from the hotel to the Seasons Time Mall, to see what technology hadn't reached America yet. She didn't have feelings about the migrant crisis, she had no emotions about wealth inequality, and she didn't give a shit about the stupid breakup. She was here to *consume.*

The ads for the world's largest retail megamall said, "In Seasons Time, it's always your time," but more accurately it was always no time whatsoever. Different parts of the mall kept up a constant artificial version of one season or another; religious festivals, natural events, and national celebrations crowded together in no particular order in accordance with the agnosticism of the marketplace. Like Disneyland, it was always time for a parade, and January sales came around once every eighty-five hours for an hour, on a schedule posted only on the Seasons Time: It's Your Time app. According to various providers of tepid takes, Seasons Time was either the most crass and culturally appropriative place on Earth, an ecological disaster, a charming example of Singaporean whimsy, or honestly, just lighten up, it's a fun place to spend an afternoon shopping.

Lai Zhen had skated across these possibilities as she walked through the Pumpkin Spice gate toward International Women's Day Plaza. She was here to experience it and enjoy it and also comment on it, disdain it, and be offended by it. A heady mix as intense as the scent of cinnamon, nutmeg, and cloves sprayed from the air vents above her head. Enjoyably and wonderfully distracting, nothing that happened here was ever fully real and neither—while she was here—was she.

She went into an electronics store in Christmas: glass ceilings and twinkling lights. There was a new camera she wanted to try. She took it to the window. Outside, a wall of thinscreens showed footage of Lenk Sketlish flanked by his assistants announcing another FutureSafe wildlife protection zone. No. Not engaging with the real world in Seasons Time, thank you. Zhen pointed the self-filtering multifocal lens at a crystalline glass snowflake suspended from the ceiling. She zoomed and focused, forcing a perfectly crisp image with different filters. She was looking at the snowflake through the viewfinder when it exploded.

The snowflake burst open like a time-lapse film of decay. The points collapsed and the innards spurted out, and almost at the same moment there was a sound like a toy firework from three floors up. She thought:

- Cool effect?
- No.
- Is that some kind of . . .
- Could it be a fault because it seems like . . .
- I bet they mess around with the sound in movies to make the shot more prominent because really that was like a firecracker.
- Oh crap.

Four starburst holes opened in the storefront window, glittering like tinsel.

Lai Zhen had made twelve videos about active-shooter scenarios. She felt her mouth fall open like a slot machine, noticed a part of her mind scrambling for a reason that glass could just *fail* like that. She flipped through a mental file of survival strategies and came up empty again and again. How to catch rainwater in a bedsheet? No. How to preserve fresh corn using salt? No. How to strip and clean an AK-47? Getting closer, sport. Active shooter. There we are. Run.

She ran.

Not out of the store. In the wide-open spaces of Christmas Plaza, she'd be an easy target. She looked behind her. There it was, at the back, a storage room. There had to be a service exit. The other customers were still standing slack-jawed. Zhen felt slow, but they hadn't even got to the part where they started screaming yet.

She jumped over the counter just as a tiny Japanese lady in immaculate jeans and a beige wool coat got a bullet in her shoulder with a heavy thunk. Blood spattered over the thinscreens and keyboards and camera gimbals. Zhen took one look back. The woman's husband was crouching over her, and the rest of the customers scattered. Think, think. Try to remember one single thing you've learned about all of this, you *idiot*.

In the back room there were boxes of electronics on metal shelves. For a moment she thought, Crap, dead end, and in the same instant spotted the back door, partially concealed by the shelves. She tried the door. The lock flashed red. *Fuck*. In one of the pockets of her trousers she found her universal key fob, pressed it against the lock. Waited three long heartbeats, remembering the manufacturer's warnings that "universal" had a limited meaning, and Marius telling her it was "piece of crap won't open envelope." But how secure could a mall service exit be? Waited. Waited. The light went green. The handle turned.

She stepped into a long, poorly lit corridor, storage boxes lining the walls. The shouts from the mall were instantly more muted.

She shut the door behind her. Her hands were shaking. OK, she was safe. But what if someone else needed to escape? She opened the door, wedged a piece of cardboard into the lock. OK, you're a hero. Or at least not a bad person. Get out now, Zhen, get away from the door, come on.

She looked left and right. To the right, fiberglass chairs made to look like stacked piles of books. To the left, three hundred yards of cardboard pumpkins in a tumbling mound, some with "SALE" carved into their cardboard skins. Zhen tried to remember which way was out. Left would take her through . . . Halloween, then Valentine's Day, then Cherry Blossom Season, then Day of the Dead, then the exit. She turned left and ran.

There were no sounds behind her. She was still alive, unhurt apart from a couple of scratches on her arm from the shattering glass. She hadn't saved anyone else, but she hadn't done badly. This was terrible but random; the shooter was probably already dead—Singapore would not fuck around with this. Zhen was going to get an amazing piece out of how she used her skills in the pre-apocalypse urban jungle. Ah, the return of self-interest, must be feeling safer.

Zhen risked another look behind her. Nothing. No one had followed her through the door. No shots fired. She couldn't even hear anyone trying the handle. Alright. Survival training. She paused behind a shelf of Professor Pumpkins and let her heart rate drop and the rushing in her ears dissipate. If it was just a lone shooter, the best thing would be to get out of the building. But it could be a terrorist attack. Multiple shooters could easily be waiting outside the building, picking people off. In which case the best thing would be to hide here in this dim space between spaces.

Zhen jogged past the last Celebrity Pumpkins—Ryan Reynolds with silver-sprayed hair and Zendaya as ridged and bulbous orange caricatures. She turned right into pink polystyrene glitter hearts. Valentine's Day. Light-up cupids with long eyelashes leaned against the walls three-deep next to plastic Grecian urns filled with glitter confetti. Rows of bins were filled with cuddly animals holding plush hearts. A lot of them were foxes. Was that a thing now? Christmas reindeer, Easter rabbits, Valentine foxes? Like every holiday has to have a special animal? Zhen listened again. Alarms were going off in different parts of the building. But no footsteps behind her.

She looked over her shoulder—the corridor was empty. The hollow bones of a fiberglass dragon boat were propped against the wall. She looked ahead—the Japanese cherry blossom festival combined with a paper-lantern ceremony. Papier-mâché boughs covered in tissue-paper blossoms and glitter, hung with lanterns, a fiberglass bridge with a blue velvet river underneath, a row of 1950s jukeboxes, plugged into wall outlets. For four years now, she'd taught a three-day outdoor survival course on "calculated risk." Think.

She had a safe onward route. She could see a green exit sign past the Day of the Dead skulls and Mexican lace wall fans. Secondary exit: open panel into the crawl space behind the display of sugar-skulls. Good. For now: hide, get more info. It had to be six or seven minutes since the snowflake shattered. Long enough for it to be online.

She ran back, dug deep into a dump bin full of plush Valentine foxes. She pulled the soft toys on top of her, hunkered down toward the bottom of the bin where the fragments of fake fox fur were thick like moist moss on a jungle floor.

She flicked on the flexible thinscreen in her jacket sleeve. Was the black dot already in the corner of the screen then? She could never afterward remember. She searched for Seasons Time Mall.

There it was. Post after post. There'd been a malfunction with one of the lighting rigs. Exploding metal parts had shattered the windows of two stores. A shard of glass had wounded a tourist in the arm, though not seriously. There were photos of security guards opening the huge doors at either end of the quadrant and stalls in the parking lots handing out free hot chocolate and pho. Customers inconvenienced were each being given a one-hundred-dollar gift certificate good in any store. Consumer capitalism at its finest.

Zhen felt like an idiot. That's what all that training gets you. A lighting rig explodes and you think you're being shot at. What next? Someone flushes the toilet and you think you're in a tsunami? Her ex Ya-Ling had been right; she needed to talk to someone about the effects of spending half her teenage years in a refugee camp, about losing her mom. About the thing with the dog. And she had to figure out something better to spend her days on because she was seeing it everywhere now. Apocalypse shows, the constant drumbeat of survival strategies and escape routes and go bags and it's not helping, is it, Zhen? It's making it worse and this is where it gets you.

A laugh rose in her throat as she imagined how she looked from the outside. Hiding under Valentine foxes in an empty corridor in a shopping mall. What was she doing? Just missing out on free pho.

Her chuckle bubbled into sound just as a gunshot went straight through the Valentine foxes, bursting the plush toys into clouds of choking fur. Before her conscious mind had even caught up with her training, she'd jumped out of the bin, hurled it backward in the direction the shots were coming from. And she ran.

She glanced back. One woman. Long, baggy floral dress, hair piled into a patterned sack of a hat. Denim jacket, beat-up sneakers. If you saw her on the street, you'd take her for the intense soccer parent all the other parents avoid. But her kit was real enough: the suppressed Beretta M9A3 said she knew her guns. How had she known to aim at the bin? Had she heard Zhen laugh? If Zhen hadn't curled her body around the edges, if she'd been sitting right in the center of the bin, this person would have killed her.

Zhen rounded the next corner a little ahead of her pursuer. She toppled over a large fiberglass bridge and pushed the fake cherry-blossom trees onto it. It wouldn't stop the assassin, but Zhen would have a few moments crouching down where the woman couldn't see her. Secondary exit. Zhen hurled the baskets of flexifilm cherry blossoms in the air. They floated down very slowly, twinkling as they turned the kinetic energy into flickering light, a curtain of pink and dark pink and dusky pink and white and rose. Zhen punched random buttons on the nearest jukebox—it played a funked-up "Sakura," loud enough to mask the sound of what she was doing. As the fake petals fell and the bass reverberated, Zhen dived into the crawl space behind the trees and pulled the panel closed behind her.

She barely noticed but she had, in fact, pissed herself.

2. simulacrum of surprise

That January, Lai Zhen had been one of the more popular speakers at the annual DEMOlition conference in London. Not one of the richest or most powerful. The wealthy had been elsewhere, and their paths had rarely intersected with the actual content providers on the lower floors of the conference building.

While Lai Zhen was delivering a talk on Five Tech Survival Tools You Literally Can't Live Without (and Ten New Ways to Use Them), Martha Einkorn, assistant to Lenk Sketlish, stepped from the elevator into the terraced roof garden. Champagne popped with a sound like gunfire and pale fluid glugged into glasses.

For Martha, there had been a thousand things to arrange to reach this moment. If everything went well, this moment was only the beginning.

Everyone was there, pointing out features of the London skyline in the January sun, or ignoring the skyline because they'd seen it so often before. Zimri Nommik of Anvil, his asymmetrical face tanned, attempting the smile someone had coached him in. By his side, confident and relaxed, remembering all the names and faces, was his Black British wife, Selah Nommik—once a computer science graduate from Cambridge, these days mostly known for finding useful ways to give away some of Nommik's huge fortune. Lenk Sketlish of Fantail was there, of course, lean and pale in an immaculate suit; Martha was by his side. Ellen Bywater, CEO of Medlar, recently widowed, of Irish heritage, elegant as always in natural fibers and a neutral palette, turning her head to the side as if she could hear her late husband, Will, still murmuring in her ear.

Ellen Bywater had brought her youngest child to the party. Badger Bywater was a person with short dark hair and black fingernails who had recently used their Fantail channel to post critical videos about technology companies. How very Ellen Bywater that her response to criticism was to invite Badger to this event. In a similar vein, hiding behind a melting ice sculpture of a heron: Albert Dabrowski, ousted founder of Medlar, Hawaiian shirt buttoned comfortably over his round belly, drinking with quiet determination. Ellen always invited him to high-profile Medlar events because of her dedication to the story that she had made him a tremendously wealthy man, much wealthier than he would have been if she'd let him keep on mismanaging his company, and probably he was pleased. Dabrowski accepted these invitations sporadically, never brought his husband, always drank to excess, and took some pleasure in mentioning to strangers that he was the "wicked fairy" at the feast.

Martha smiled at Zimri and then moved her glance away—more comfortable for him, awkward as he always was at events like these. Of Lenk, Ellen, and Zimri, Martha had the most time these days for Zimri. He'd never said so publicly but Martha guessed he was on the autism spectrum. He was vastly intelligent, with a greater grip on the details that made up his world-shaker of a company than even Lenk or Ellen could conceive. In another era he might have been an academic or even a monk, and the world would not have demanded parties from him. But of course this was all Martha's imagination—perhaps in an earlier era he would have been the ambitious adviser to a ruthless king. The facts of people's lives are as they are. Far from being made by his era, Zimri had made the first decades of the twenty-first century his own. His company Anvil was worth more than Medlar and Fantail combined. There was no sense in feeling sorry for him.

Selah Nommik noticed Martha looking away and—between the camera clicks of the roving photographer—met her glance and winked. Martha nodded, carefully concealing her smile before the cameras turned her way. Martha felt a sharp stab of loneliness. This was new. It was troubling for these emotions to be thawing in her now. She'd been lonely for a long time, and had only recently understood that her prolific online-forum habit and her working relationships—as intense and engaging as these things were—were no substitutes for real trust, real vulnerability. This was no time for the ice inside her to melt; come on, this was not the moment. She'd dealt with this for years now. Refocus. Lenk's needs were always enough to fill her attention.

Martha watched Badger Bywater walk into Lenk's field of vision sipping a dark purple cocktail through a straw and knew this was going to be trouble. After decades working with him, she had a sense for his moods and his desires, knowing even before he did that something was going to pique his interest or prick his anger.

"Is that a straw?" said Lenk Sketlish. "How come you have a straw?"

Badger Bywater looked up with a perfect simulacrum of surprise.

"Me?"

Badger Bywater had been coming to this sort of event with their mother since they were seven or eight years old. No one could ever feel more at home among the eighty-five-dollar sashimi spoon canapés or the exquisite flowers flown in refrigerated from Australia than Badger Bywater. Badger didn't give a shit about any of this anymore and wasn't afraid to show it.

"Yeah, you," said Lenk Sketlish. "How did you get that straw? They told me there were no straws. You can't get a *straw* anywhere anymore; you know this is what's wrong with the world." Lenk looked around for someone to agree with him.

Badger managed to express both tremendous boredom and not inconsiderable disdain: "I brought my own straw, dude."

"See, this is what I'm talking about," said Lenk. "Look at the cost of this party and you have to bring your *own straw*?"

Zimri Nommik murmured, so quietly that Lenk Sketlish almost didn't hear him, "The evidence about plastics in the ocean is extremely compelling."

Something about the murmuring enraged Lenk. There would have been a time—not so many years earlier—when Lenk would have rounded on Zimri, asked him if he was calling him stupid. But he'd done his meditation. He'd listened to Martha. He did not call Zimri Nommik a pathetic beta cuck and he did not tell him to fuck off.

Instead he rolled his eyes, said "Aha," and walked away. He'd been on a learning journey.

"How do you put up with him?" said Ellen Bywater softly from directly behind Martha, the tone of malicious sympathy utterly unconcealed. Once, several years ago, Ellen Bywater had tried to tempt Martha to jump ship to Medlar with talk of female solidarity and true advancement in a company that valued her. Martha had refused because—on balance—she liked truth better than lies and she thought Lenk's volatility and childish petulance more truthful than Ellen's polish. Ellen Bywater had neither forgiven nor forgotten the refusal.

"Mom!" whispered Badger. "Don't talk to people like that. This is her job, OK? What's she going to do? Side with you against her boss? Disagree with the CEO of Medlar? God, you don't even see it."

"I do just fine," said Martha. "I'm grateful you're interested in my life."

The gong sounded. It was time for the speeches. They had already been prewritten, practiced, prepared. They were here to celebrate an environmental collaboration between Medlar, Fantail, and Anvil as a way to protect against climate change by using tiny drones at high altitudes to rearrange the weather.

Selah Nommik explained the coding that went into this technology with informality and charm.

"We're plugged into weather monitoring all over the world. The drone swarms have an area they patrol—but if we need them to, they'll gather together into bigger and bigger groups. We can turn typhoons into light drizzle. And if you want some rain from a clear blue sky . . ."

Selah pressed a button on her forearm thinscreen. And, theatrically, she took out an Anvil-branded umbrella and raised it over her head.

The party guests looked up, smiling. The sky above was azure, bright, dazzlingly lucent, one of London's piercingly clear January mornings. Then there was a shimmer in the air and a faint buzzing hum. If you squinted, you could just about make out motes of dust forming into a spheroid shape high above the convention center.

"Look!" shouted a man, pointing upward like a biblical prophet.

A cloud was forming. Small and then larger, a dark cloud on the horizon moving toward the building rapidly.

Selah, smiling, spoke softly into the microphone.

"We've steered that moisture all the way from Lithuania. Four hours ago, this was a storm over Gaižiūnai Forest."

The cloud thickened, blackened. It moved into place over the roof gardens of the DEMOlition conference center. There was a sense of pressure. People's ears popped. And then, very faintly, the sound of thunder. It began to rain.

The guests applauded as they gratefully accepted umbrellas from the waitstaff. The rain was heavy, intense; it smelled woody, sharp like pine. There was a quick flicker of lightning. Someone else's storm, brought there for their enjoyment.

Zimri Nommik took to the stage, Selah stepping back.

"Big whoop," said Zimri, "making it rain in London. In January!"

There was brief scattered laughter. Selah did not react, as she never reacted these days to Zimri's many sideswipes.

"How about sunshine?"

Zimri pressed the pad of his thumb to a preset button on his SmartPin. The drones rearranged themselves in the sky.

A patch of blue began to burn in the center of the cloud. It grew larger, becoming brighter and brighter. Too bright. Much brighter than the sky in London could ever be even on the hottest days of these too-hot years. Servers handed out large dark eyeshades to the guests.

"We're going to make a tiny hole in the ozone," said Zimri, "just for fun. Make sure you're wearing the shades."

There was a brief white-hot burst, a feeling among the guests that they were experiencing the true fury of the sun, the sharp smiling mouth that the atmosphere had always protected them from. For a few seconds, they were afraid. And then it was over.

Zimri took off his sunglasses.

"That's just to demonstrate the power of this technology. We can move any part of the atmosphere, we can monitor where it's too thin, and we can fix it. It's great work!"

He raised one fist awkwardly in the air to a round of applause.

Selah Nommik, in prepared improvisation, grabbed the microphone and said: "Bring back the London rain!"

And it came back, right on cue.

Ellen Bywater took the stage next to explain the many

humanitarian functions this technology could have. Imagine being able to irrigate crops in drought-stricken regions with pinpoint accuracy, to thicken the cloud over melting ice caps. Then Lenk Sketlish, crowing about the technological achievement. There was, he said, no limit to this technology, really. They were just beginning to explore how it could be used to build, to alter trade winds for speedier travel, even to destroy unwanted infrastructure. He did not take any questions on what that infrastructure might be or who would decide whether it was wanted.

For a moment, Badger Bywater, Selah Nommik, Albert Dabrowski, and Martha Einkorn stood together as the rain pattered onto the rooftop. Images of them were photographed by a camera drone but never used for publicity, because who would be interested in these people? The twentysomething dropout child of a billionaire, the former coder now pampered wife of a billionaire, an ousted CEO, and a glorified secretary. But in the pictures that were never used and never witnessed by any but the all-seeing eye of the machine, they looked somehow easy with each other. As if there was an unspoken agreement between them. As if, despite their differences, they were of one mind.

Albert Dabrowski, already fairly drunk, said very quietly, "You know what they're using this for, right? This has nothing to do with helping anyone, anywhere. It's for their own bunkers. They can control the weather. Make sure that whatever happens everywhere else, there's always rain when they want it, always sun when they need it. No matter where they are. No matter what happens to the rest of us."

"Obviously," said Selah Nommik.

"I mean, they've weaponized the weather," said Badger Bywater.

"We can't do this here," said Martha, who had always been able to put her feelings into a box, to not reach out, to not admit she was lonely, to do the next sensible thing over and over.

This was the last time these four people would allow themselves to be seen together in public before the apocalypse.

Martha Einkorn, also known on the survivalist forum Name The Day as OneCorn, thought: Would I save the city for fifty? And the fat Lithuanian raindrops burst on the paving slabs of a London roof in January like the biblical blessing of rain.

3. not even that hot

Lai Zhen hadn't seen any of that at the time at the DEMOlition conference. Way above her level, no invitations to the rooftop gardens were granted to the peons actually giving the talks on the floor. She'd heard about it later—by rumors, and through other means. She'd thought about how many things could be going on within even a single building without anyone knowing.

As she kneed and elbowed her way up the narrow metal crawl spaces in the Seasons Time Mall, sweating in the June heat, putting every second she could between herself and an assassin in a flowery dress, she thought about it again. Would anyone know she was here? It seemed unlikely. Thick walls and high fences were surprisingly effective. The woman might kill her here and no one would ever know what had happened.

She was in steel-lined tunnels designed for workers to access various parts of the hidden mechanics of the mall—in places they were six feet high, in places only three feet and she had to move fast on all fours. She passed by panels with strange-shaped keyholes and lugs evidently designed for some flexible polymer ladder or other equipment to be fastened so a worker could climb straight up a tight tube. She had nothing, and in places the only way to keep moving was a series of sharp steps up, where she had to jam the rubber of her sneakers hard against the metal to push herself onto a higher level.

She forced her brain into calculations. Numbers helped. Let's say it would take two minutes for the woman in the floral dress to scout the corridor ahead. Two minutes to run back. Two minutes to stand, baffled, before she looked at the ventilation grille and figured it out. So Zhen had six minutes before the assassin worked out where she had gone and followed. Six minutes to get her scrambled brain to help her figure out what was going on.

Think. This isn't random and it's not an exploding lighting rig. That's just something the mall is saying to get everyone out safely. This is someone after you in particular, someone who followed you through that door you heroically left open, you *idiot*. Why is someone trying this hard to kill you? Think it out.

Alright. Why does anyone want to kill anyone? Only three reasons:

- something you are
- something you have
- something you know

Who was she? A semi-celebrity in her little survivalist corner of the online multiverse. There could be a disgruntled fan, or ex-fan, or someone who hated that a Hong Kong Chinese slash British slash American lesbian who—as they kept telling her—*wasn't even that hot* could make money in the apocalypse biz. There were death threats online; everyone got them. There'd been a controversy around an inflatable ground-mat she'd recommended that turned out to be a piece of crap. Did you come after someone with a gun in a mall in Singapore because of an air mattress? Never underestimate the crazy of the internet. There was that redpill PUA who did parody videos of her in a wig made out of a mop. But he was dumb as a log and dreamed of having one-twentieth of her followers. And the chan board that had outed her a few years earlier, but none of them were leaving the house.

What did she have? She wasn't especially rich; she had an apartment in San Francisco and some money in the bank but nothing worth killing her over. Unlike some of the prepper community, she didn't travel with gold or diamonds on her person.

And knowledge? Well, she did know things. Like: the location of the secret survival bunker owned by Zimri Nommik, the CEO of Anvil. She knew not just the general bunker location but specifically six entryways and at least two of the codes. She hadn't *done* anything with that yet. She'd gotten the tip-off months ago from a fan who worked with one of the building firms. Could be that, maybe.

And . . . there were the Enochites. She came to this thought reluctantly; she didn't want to believe her love life could have this kind of blowback. But yes. The Enochites. A fundamentalist religious group that loved traditional gender roles, floral-patterned dresses, braids, and guns. All of which were after her right now.

Apparently there was a fourth reason to want to kill people:

- something you've said

Even as Zhen thought it through, she knew the truth. She had pissed off the Enochites and, well, fuck. Online annoyance doesn't turn into a genuine threat to life. This never happened, except when it did.

The distant alarms abruptly stopped. Was that very good or very, very bad? She reached a long, flat section of crawl space. Given that she couldn't think of a single thing she could give or say to this woman to make her go away, her choices were: fight back or hide.

She always carried a couple of survival knives with treated plastic blades. They don't show up on security scanners and were useful for jobs like cutting the seat belt in an overturned car. They'd do nothing against a gun. Unless Zhen could surprise the woman, jump out, get a blade to her throat. Was she actually thinking about killing someone? She tried to imagine herself pressing the tip of the blade into a stranger's neck, increasing the pressure until the veins popped. Her ideas about survival had always included more banding together than murdering.

From behind her in the crawl space, she heard a clank. Zhen's stomach turned over. The assassin had found the access panel. She was pulling it open. That's your six minutes, Zhen. Time's up. What's your survival plan? She heard a faint but distinct shuffling sound. Yup, she was in. And if she could hear the woman moving, then the woman could hear her—the jukebox had surely stopped playing by now. Zhen sped up. She needed other sounds to mask her. At a junction, crawling on her hands and knees, she spotted the gleaming foil-covered coils of a refrigerator system. Perfect. Zhen propelled herself forward on her knees, using the palms of her hands on the smooth metal floor.

The thumpa-thunk of the cooling motors got louder as Lai Zhen pulled herself along the air-conditioning vent toward it. It was a solid block surrounded by metallic refrigerant tubes looped around each other in coiled nests. She guessed it was either air-conditioning or some machinery that made the perpetual snow of Christmas below her.

Zhen pressed her body against the side wall, lowered her feet inside the refrigerator coils, and leaned back so her torso was resting on the large central square block unit. She sank down, jammed herself between the unit and the wall, completely concealed from view.

The woman who'd found her in the tub full of Valentine foxes would find her here too. But no one could shoot through the clunking machine, so she'd have to come around. And Zhen would know she was coming. Zhen would surprise her, stand up, go for the neck. She pulled a knife out of the holster on her leg. She could do this.

There was a sound from the tunnel. The woman was making faster progress than Zhen had. She'd be there in two or three minutes at most.

She looked at the thinscreen on her jacket sleeve. In the bottom-right corner there was a small black dot, pulsating slowly. Out of sheer habit she tapped it with her forefinger.

A text box popped up.

Lai Zhen, it said, **this is AUGR. Your perimeter has been activated.**

She looked at it dumbly. Malware. A glitch. A joke.

Something floated up from the back of her mind. She'd been to every major trade show in the past decade. She kept tabs on every expo, every failed product, every weird idea. AUGR. AUGR.

The text on the screen changed.

It looks like you might be in trouble, Lai Zhen. Would you like help? Yes/No.

4. the marked environment

In London at the January DEMOlition conference, Lai Zhen had met a woman.

Which was what she'd intended to do since she and her long-term partner Ya-Ling had split up. She just hadn't had the time with one thing and another. She made dates and canceled, hooked up with women at trade shows and never called them. And then, at a conference in London, a woman was standing before her who was all she'd ever wanted.

Zhen hadn't even bothered to check who she was interviewing for the Fantail showcase. It was a boring-ass event on the subject "Fantail as a Survival Tool." Which Fantail wasn't, and couldn't be.

There was a prewritten list of questions. The PR had told Zhen in advance that the Fantail spokesperson would not answer questions including:

- What is Lenk Sketlish like to work for?
- What are the qualities in you that mean you're able to tolerate working with him?
- Do you have any thoughts—in this survival context—about whether your boss has personally done things that make life on Earth less survivable?
- Is he really investing in rejuvenation technology that uses children's lymph fluid?
- How would you answer claims that his electric monorail company is a scam to extract public money in exchange for creating literally no infrastructure whatsoever?

- What on earth made him take to FantailSwift social video to accuse that mountain rescue team in Borneo helping a group of elderly veterans of being "dog-fuckers"?

All of that, yes, was out-of-bounds. It was going to be a dull, by-the-numbers interview taking place for maximum corporate visibility at a stage plastered with logos in the hotel's main concourse. The audience would be whoever happened to drift past. The acoustics would be terrible. The whole thing was a box-checking exercise. So there was no point knowing who the Fantail spokesperson was because they'd all be the same and the answers would be identical. She'd arrived to the interview late, hungover, had only noticed on the way from the elevator to the stage that a ripped sachet of lube was still stuck to the bottom of her shoe from the previous night's adventure. As a runner went to find her guest, Zhen peeled the sachet off her right gym shoe, dumped it in the trash, wiped her fingers on her jeans, realized there was a spot of mayonnaise on her jacket collar, and, well, here we are, Zhen, you're a survival expert—fucking survive it.

"Lai Zhen, creator of SurlySurvivor," said the runner, "please meet your interviewee for this event, Martha Einkorn, assistant to Lenk Sketlish."

The sachet of lube was stuck to the rim of the trash bin. It was right there. Zhen's eyes flicked to it. Why wouldn't it just fall?

"I'm a great fan of SurlySurvivor. You're on NTD, right?" said Martha Einkorn. "I'm honored."

"I'm so sorry I'm late, it was just . . . ," Zhen began, and actually looked at the person she was talking to. Martha Einkorn was white with creamy smooth skin, heavyset, wearing a navy jumpsuit with a gold pinstripe and a string of pearls around her neck. Her face was scattered with freckles. Oh, thought Zhen, hello.

"It was just unavoidable," her mouth said for her.

"Hmm," said Martha Einkorn. "I guess you're going to have to find some way to make it up to me." There was a look, a definite twitch of the lips, a raise of the eyebrow.

Right, thought Zhen, as she felt a hot electric tingle travel through her groin. This was unexpected.

The audience was sparse. Half of them would probably turn out to be in the wrong place as soon as Zhen and Martha started speaking.

"I expect I can think of some way to . . . make this worth your time." Martha gave a small, slow smile. Zhen licked her bottom lip. OK.

Even going through the approved questions, something was happening between them onstage. Zhen tried a little joke and Martha added to it, expanded upon it. Martha leaned forward in her chair. Zhen moved a little closer. She could smell Martha's perfume—something musky; it smelled of sex. If they hadn't been onstage, Zhen might have thought they were on a *date*. Martha's voice—clear, low, mellifluous—was almost hypnotic. Zhen was listening to her speak but thinking constantly of how it would be to undo her jumpsuit, to touch that dimpled skin, to put her mouth to that soft neck and trace a line with her lips down to her breasts.

"So," Zhen asked directly from the prompter, "I think you have examples of how Fantail has helped people during weather emergencies?"

"Sure," said Martha. "The great benefit of Fantail is: a lot of people have Fantail."

Zhen laughed. A bit too hard, she thought. A bit too long.

"That's a great point," said Zhen, thinking anything, anything to keep this rapport building.

"So during the hurricane season in Haiti, we brought in emergency cell towers on drones, giving instant free access to Fantail. People used it to find each other, to tell people where to find fresh drinking water and safe buildings above the flood line."

"Amazing," said Zhen, knowing in the back of her mind that someone in the small audience would already be posting about how fucking dark it was that they'd enabled communication but only through their own platform, but it didn't matter; no one would ever see this interview. "You're really trying to make a difference."

"We are, actually. We have a responsibility to use what we have to try to help. You know"—Martha leaned forward—"that series you made from Niger about water scarcity and violence, the gangs taking over? FantailSharing technologies would really make sense as an intervention there."

"You've seen my stuff from Niger?"

"It's brilliant reporting. I bet everyone in this audience has watched it."

Heat rose in Zhen's cheeks. This was probably her least-watched series; it had been critically well received but just didn't do the numbers. Her audience wanted an exciting apocalypse and information about how they, in particular, would survive it and not the downer reality of human beings dying of thirst only three hundred miles from a catastrophic flood.

"What did you think of it?"

"You made it real for me in a way I'd never seen before. You were in the Fall of Hong Kong, right? You know what it's like to be there for real. It shows."

There was a flashing in the corner of Zhen's eye. The prompter wanted her to move on to the next real question. Fine.

"And how can Fantail technology help?"

Martha said: "A million ways. I grew up on the land,

and the kind of emergency communications Fantail is rolling out now would have made a huge difference to me when I was living on fifteen thousand green acres in Oregon."

Zhen startled out of her sexual reverie. Fifteen thousand green acres. That precise phrasing. Zhen had a memory for the apocalypse and its related plans and aficionados.

"Just a second," said Zhen. "Did you . . ." She looked at the audience. Several of them had already wandered off to listen to the panel across the hall chaired by a young Black woman with bright pink hair and a miniature robot on her palm. "I'm just thinking. A property that large. Oregon. I have to ask. Did you grow up an Enochite?"

This was not on the list of prescribed questions. But it wasn't on the list of forbidden questions.

Martha Einkorn blinked. Stumbled. Composed herself. They had both been lulled by the hum of sex between them, drowsy like bees in smoke. Zhen had asked a question she shouldn't have asked and Martha answered the question she shouldn't have answered.

"Yes," said Martha Einkorn. "There's nothing to be ashamed of there. It's a matter of public record. I was only a child then. My father was Enoch."

From the bored spectators there was a sudden fascinated buzz. Zhen guessed maybe a third of them might have heard of the Enochites. They were famous among fanatical survivalists, gun enthusiasts, and religious extremists, a cautionary tale among people who were obsessively paranoid about government overreach. Not the kind of apocalypse amateur who would come to a weak sauce event like "Fantail as a Survival Tool." But Zhen saw lips mouthing subvocalizations to search engines embedded in their clothing, touching their smart torcs. Connecting to the great communal brain.

"Wow," said Zhen. "So what was that like?"

Martha was silent. Zhen let it sit. This is one of the tricks of interviewing. Don't fill the silence.

"Oh," Martha said at last, "the Enochites weren't everything you hear. I learned some good values there. If you haven't heard of them, we were a survivalist group raising children in Oregon and waiting for the end of the Babble. The Babble being this world." She gestured around the hotel concourse, the signs and lists of workshops and panels for the day, the coffee and pretzel stands, the tangles of people carrying tote bags branded with ShoutRadioFlare and Foxhole Emergency Ammo. "The Babble is the complicated place full of signs where we all live. Enoch believed it would and should come to an end."

"And that was your dad."

"Look, we kids learned a lot of great skills. Hunting, fishing, setting traps, growing and gathering our own food, sleeping outdoors. I sometimes say I grew up about as close to a hunter-gatherer as anybody can in the US. Well, outside of the First Nations and Native communities we did all that genocide on, of course."

On smart torcs and visor wedges, thinscreens and wrist displays, almost everyone in the audience was internet searching—presumably for Enochites. At this whole event now, Zhen was the person who knew the least about Enochites. She dredged her memory. The Enochites were a divisive subject among survivalists, almost a myth. They had been—for a few years in the mid-2020s—a big deal. A new Judaism-based Genesis-inflected American religion that flared up and died away rapidly. Their leader, Enoch, had big ideas about the organization of the world, although Zhen couldn't now precisely remember any of them. They'd lived on an enormous rural compound in Oregon, and Enoch had been unusual in the right wing at that time for accepting the reality of climate change, for interpreting it as a sign of God's will. He believed that God would use the weather, like in the flood, to separate the righteous from the sinners. There was a sub-board dedicated to them on Name The Day, but Zhen had never looked at it; they were basically gone now. At the end . . . there had been a tragedy, something about a fire, and then there had been financial stuff and . . . wait.

"New York City, the subway," said Zhen, something bubbling up from the back of her mind. "Didn't Enoch go mental on the subway? Didn't he threaten people and steal their wallets?"

Martha Einkorn sat back in her chair.

"Is that how people remember that now? Jesus."

She passed a hand over her face.

"He didn't steal wallets. He had a vision, OK? Enoch—he was born Ralph Zimmerman. My dad. He had a vision on a subway train. People thought they were using money, but the money was using them. He grabbed people's wallets and pocketbooks and stamped on them. To save people."

"He sounds frightening and unpredictable," said Zhen.

Martha shook her head. "No one follows anyone if they're not right about something."

"So what was your dad right about?"

Martha chewed her lip. There was the air of a date about this still, the permission to ask forbidden questions and the deliberate creation of intimacy. Zhen had the feeling Martha was calculating something.

"OK. Enoch used to say, 'The city is a marked environment.' Like a marked deck of cards. Fixed so we can read it easily. Filled with symbols. Paving slabs are for walking on—blacktop is for cars." She pointed around the hall to the cup sign over the café, the signs for the restrooms. "Symbols for food, drink, empty your bladder. And look, the real world's not like that. The world doesn't exist for our convenience; it doesn't talk in our language. The wilderness doesn't have symbolic drawings to tell you where to find food or where it's safe to take a piss. Where you find a sign in the real world, it's a sign made by the thing itself: deer tracks are made by deer hooves. Do you see? It's done something weird to us to live in this human-made, human-centric space all the time. It's made us more selfish, but also more anxious, and more depressed because we think everything's about us. I think Enoch was right about that."

"And yet you still left."

"You know, he was right about some things, but he was also angry and sometimes violent and he refused to educate us properly. You can't do what he did without control and eventually abuse. You can't hold the whole world at bay with a couple hundred minds. You just can't. To do what he wanted to do, you'd have to remake the whole world."

Several people standing at the edges of the event or sitting in the audience were filming the exchange on their phones or wrist screens. Though Zhen didn't know it yet, a short clip was already bouncing from account to account on Fantail, on MedlarConnect, on AnvilChat. In the clip, Zhen says: "Didn't Enoch go mental on the subway?" In the great interconnected human mind, certain connections were being made and certain people were becoming angry, and certain platforms were motivated to drive engagement. But all Zhen knew in that moment was that Martha Einkorn smelled of musk and promise, that she liked her, she wanted to know her better, and something was blooming between them.

At the end of the event, Martha shook Zhen's hand and pulled her in for a quick embrace. She muttered: "I get finished at 9 p.m." When Zhen opened her hand she found she was holding a hotel room key, black with a gilt edge. Zhen felt the key with her thumb: it felt like a kiss, it felt like falling, it felt like an expert finger parting her labia.

You're done for now, thought Zhen as she walked from the event in a sexual daze. You're absolutely done for.

5. a soft, glittering mound of crystals

AUGR said: "It looks like you might be in trouble, Lai Zhen. Would you like help? Yes/No."

Zhen thought for a fraction of a second and then pressed *yes*.

The sounds in the tunnel were louder. The slap-drag of the woman pulling herself up the conduit toward Zhen. She thought: No one knows I'm here. And then: It could be months before anyone knows I'm dead. And then: I could die here without ever figuring out what's going on. And that was the worst of all.

On the screen on Zhen's wrist, an image popped up. It took her a moment to understand what she was looking at. It was a green line drawing of her—jeans, hoodie, and Survival Expo T-shirt, crouched behind the refrigeration unit. The hardened plastic knife in the sheath at her ankle was highlighted. A moving line of dots led from it to one of the coiled pipes.

Underneath the image, words scrolled across the screen:

> **Cut the pipe here. Work as quickly as possible. Protect your hands with your sleeves. Direct the pipe away from you. When the pipe is severed, point it toward your assailant.**

Zhen wanted to laugh. This was nothing. It couldn't be anything. Fucking *Enochites*? Death threats online never turned into anything real—that was a rule. Death threats were easy these days, they were currency. She'd told the UK police about them and they'd said she should be careful, but there had been nothing specific or credible; any fucker with a laptop and a love of the lulz could issue a death threat. Zhen had gone through them with Marius and he thought at least 90 percent of the threats were "some stupid boy loves to frighten women when his penis sore from too much fap." But she hadn't been careful, had she? Her talk at the Seasons Time Mall had been announced in their press release. Shit.

Zhen looked at the green line drawing on the screen and reviewed her options:

1. Do nothing and die.
2. Try to attack her with the knife and pretty much definitely die.
3. Do what the app told her. And then probably also die.

They'd be at close range. That was good—a gun had less advantage over a knife at close range. If she cut the pipe, she could still attack the woman with the knife. So try a combination of two and three?

She fumbled for the short, fat hose, about the width of two of her fingers. Underneath the insulated metal outer sheath, the tube was soft plastic and very cold. She dug the knife into the soft plastic. From the hole, snow began to trickle.

AUGR started to speak into Zhen's earpod, which was attached to the helix of her ear. It spoke in the familiar calm tones of system announcements: affectless and mild. It said: "Seasons Time Mall uses a new refrigerant made of paramagnetic salts in a liquid solvent. The refrigerant falling between your fingers now will freeze human muscle and skin on contact and extract moisture from your flesh. Don't let it touch any part of your body you want to keep."

Zhen held the top of the tube at an angle, and after covering her thumb and forefinger with the ribbed sleeve of her hoodie, she pinched it away from her body. Why hadn't she brought gloves? She had a surgical kit with medical-grade gloves on the dresser next to her bed in the hotel. She'd almost put it into her pack that morning but thought the needles might get picked up by the scanners. Human bloody error, gets you every time.

She kept sawing at the soft plastic. She was three-quarters of the way through. She pinched the tube tightly, but a small amount of the stuff still trickled out. It wasn't really snow but a soft mound of crystals—large like snowflakes but harder, more brilliant, glittering. The stuff flowed like slushy water, but it wasn't wet. It was very, very dry.

AUGR spoke in her ear again: "Your T-shirt is made of a high-spec survival material. It will protect your respiratory system if you cover your face. Still, when you do it, don't look directly at her."

Zhen had forgotten for a moment to monitor where the woman in the floral dress was, but her screen showed a cross section of the crawl space. The woman was an outline in green, stealthily making her way up the last few dozen feet toward Zhen. Zhen was sawing at the pipe. There, on the screen, was the refrigeration unit between them. The assassin would be almost within arm's reach if it weren't for the unit between them.

Zhen gripped the soft tube and sliced through the last thin piece of plastic. On the screen, the woman stood and took out her gun. Did she have a screen too? Would she have a countermeasure? Too late to worry about that. The woman in the floral dress took a step around the air-conditioning unit. She looked down at Zhen. Zhen pulled her T-shirt over her mouth and nose and pointed the cut end of the soft tubing toward the woman's face. Zhen turned away. She let go her pincer grip. The snow sprayed out.

6. demonstrate your game

The January frost had turned a light drizzle into a thin spiral of white flakes outside the DEMOlition building at nine in the evening, when Lai Zhen touched Martha Einkorn's gold-edged keycard to the black panel in the glass elevator. The screen read **Floor 70**. Zhen hadn't even known there was a seventieth floor of guest rooms in this hotel. The doors closed silently and the hotel lobby fell away. Beneath Zhen's feet were the stalls and miniature stages of this smaller part of the conference. Even at this point there were still late-night sessions: a fireside chat with a psychologist with brushed blond hair sitting in an armchair talking about survivor guilt. A man in a flannel shirt giving a presentation on how to talk to your kids about survival. Through the sliding wall at the far end of the hall, Zhen could see part of the expo, a forest of stalls and, towering over them, a great fiberglass mountain with snowy peaks advertising some brand of all-weather gear. The mountain was visible from every point in the expo; in the evenings, it was lit from within to simulate a sunset, yellow and pink and gold. As it dwindled, as Zhen rose in the elevator, it felt for a moment that all this was leaving her, not that she was moving at all.

On the seventieth floor, the doors of the elevator opened not onto a featureless corridor but onto a palace. Bookcases filled with books. A long lacquered dining table. Three leather sofas. A blue tiled floor like a wave washing toward the view out of the window seventy stories up.

"Fuck me," said Zhen.

"God, she's a bit bloody direct, isn't she," said a woman lying on one of the sofas, half-concealed from view. She leaned up on her elbows and looked at Zhen with curiosity, interest, and humor. Zhen thought: Shit, I know who that is.

"Oh, you're on time," said Martha Einkorn. "That's good. Selah Nommik, meet Lai Zhen. She has an amazing channel about survival: SurlySurvivor. Champagne?"

Zhen looked at Martha, at her belly-roll outline in her jumpsuit, at the gold nose stud, and thought: I don't care if it's one night. I will. I absolutely will. And then she wanted, very badly indeed, not to screw this up.

"Don't mind if I do," said Selah, taking a flute of champagne.

Zhen thought: Remember this taste, this is probably the good stuff.

Selah flicked her eyes between Martha and Zhen, seemed about to say something, and then changed her mind.

"So you've got a channel. About survival. I think I've seen it, actually—you did the thing with the scorpion tank?"

"No, that was ProfessorBlast. I did—"

"Got it! You did living in a tree for a week."

"I did."

"My husband loved that one. Incredible. I'm a coder," said Selah. "Well, I was. I mostly give money away now. So I'm utterly useless in an apocalypse scenario."

Were they going to pretend Zhen didn't know who she was? Who her husband was? She had been a genuinely exceptional hotshot coder; she'd written part of the script for Anvil's logistics and delivery systems, making them superefficient and reliable. She was married to the richest man on the planet—a man who was relentless in pursuit of efficiency, who had reinvented how haulage, and then delivery and then the world's infrastructure, worked. But maybe that was what very rich, very famous people liked. If you just pretended you hadn't read anything about them.

"Coding's not useless in the apocalypse. We'd probably need someone to hack ex-Soviet nuclear plants and shut them down safely. Do you think you could do that?"

"Me?" Selah puffed out one cheek, thinking. "I could give it a bloody good go, yeah. I speak a bit of Russian."

"We could probably find a translator."

"We?" said Selah. "Are you running the global consortium of apocalypse survivors in this scenario?"

Right, then. Go big or go home. "Yeah. I mean, I don't want to do it, but I'd rather I did it than anyone else."

Selah barked out a laugh. "I see why you like her. Alright. You hungry? I'm *starving*. Let's get some dinner."

Later, although she'd told herself she'd try to remember every moment, Zhen couldn't really recall a great deal of the conversation over dinner. This was partly because she'd drunk quite a lot of the deceptively soda-like champagne. But mostly because Martha Einkorn had a way of smiling where a tiny peep of pink tongue licked the very center of her curved top lip. And because when Zhen tentatively brushed the tips of her fingers along Martha's thigh under the table, this apparently fairly wealthy and powerful woman did not move away. In fact, she touched the top of Zhen's hand lightly with her own fingers. Who could be expected to remember a conversation in circumstances like those?

The only part she really remembered was about the inevitable arrival of the apocalypse.

Selah Nommik had leaned across the table and said: "So, you're an expert. What's your survival plan in the event of bug invasion, Zhen?"

"Bug invasion? Like giant mutant bugs or killer bacteria?"

"Either. Both."

"You serious?" Zhen looked quizzically at Martha. Whose fingertips were even now lightly stroking the fine hairs on Zhen's forearm. Zhen was a mess of desire.

"Dead serious." Martha grinned. "Maybe you wouldn't really survive a bug invasion. Maybe you've got no game."

"Oh, I've got game."

"So demonstrate your game," said Selah.

Zhen moved her arm away from Martha under the table. Thinking and sex were not parallel-process activities.

"OK, so both giant bugs and bacteria together would be problematic, because the strategies that'll keep you alive in the event of a sudden macro-predator—which by the way that's not going to happen, that's a sci-fi movie—would involve working in huge packs with any humans left. But if there's a killer infection, your best idea is to separate off as quickly as possible into a small, self-contained group."

"How would you do that?" Selah said.

"Seriously?" Zhen said.

Selah tipped her glass and raised an eyebrow.

"Alright, first, get out of the city. Obviously," said Zhen.

"Obviously," said Martha, as if she knew a secret.

"Bunkers aren't great—too many people. I'd go deep woods. Or an island, if I could get to an island."

"An island," Selah said. "Interesting."

"Yeah, but a lot of people will be trying that. It'd need to be uncomfortable living. A good tent, set traps, hunt with a crossbow, prepare to lose some weight. A small community, just a few people who really have each other's backs."

"Not going it alone?"

"Individualism is a fool's game in this scenario. You cut yourself and get an infection, there's no one to scavenge antibiotics, you die. You fall down a ravine, there's no one to find you, you die."

"You're not worried about infighting?"

"Try to mitigate it. Focus on the future."

"What about if you had a ton of money and you could pay soldiers to look after you?"

"I mean . . . how quickly does your bug kill people?"

Martha exchanged a look with Selah and wrinkled her nose. "Seventeen-day incubation. You're infectious the whole time. Then a five-day illness, then fifty percent of people die."

"Oh, wow. OK. That's good. I mean, that's terrible. Look, soldiers are no use in that scenario. Money rapidly ceases to have value and then what have you got to offer them? You're just a body taking up resources. Even if you have the code to the food stores or something, they lock you up and torture you until you give it to them."

"Shit."

"Right."

Martha poured more wine. It was golden and sweet but not too sweet. It tasted like money. It was getting late. Had Martha Einkorn really invited Zhen to dinner with Selah Nommik and felt Zhen up under the table so they could all *talk*?

"So," said Selah with the air of someone making a serious proposition, "if you knew the end of the world was coming. And that you could get away. If you had the golden ticket that would keep you safe. Would you take it?"

Zhen looked between the women. There was a meaning to this conversation, something she wasn't party to.

"Is this a trick question?"

"No," said Martha, "it's not a trick question. It's a moral question. You'll live and be fine but everyone else will have to suffer through that plague. Would you take the golden ticket out?"

"Obviously yes. I live for survival."

"Even if you knew everyone you loved was going to die horribly? Even if you knew taking it meant that you could never tell them what you had?"

"I can't share it? Most survival plans work better with a solid group."

"Not this one. The more people know, the less good it is," said Martha.

Selah gave a small, almost imperceptible shake of the head.

"Is that why you're both here? And Lenk Sketlish and Zimri Nommik? Because there's a golden ticket?"

Selah said, "What makes you think Lenk and Zimri are here?"

"Just because I don't get invited to the demonstration on the roof terrace doesn't mean I don't know what's going on." Zhen shifted a shoulder. "I talk to catering staff. It's not hard."

"She talks to catering staff," said Selah.

"That's how you find things out," said Martha.

Zhen was nicely drunk by this point—but not so drunk as she seemed. Something was going on here. The same instinct that told her when she needed to get out of a situation also told her where there was a story. Something here was bigger even than a show-off drone weather demonstration. Her mind riffled through a set of possibilities. Anything she'd heard of here that might be big enough for Lenk Sketlish, Zimri Nommik, and—now she thought of it—Ellen Bywater to come in person to see, or have pitched, or buy. She blinked, thinking. And just then Martha's hand brushed the very top of her thigh, by the groin. Oh. Just a second.

"I just need to go to the restroom," she heard herself saying, and stood up.

In the bathroom, Zhen felt the slipperiness between her legs. There was a moment—there's always a moment—of wondering whether to just leave. Something was going on here that was far above her level. And very possibly she was going to have a wild sex time with one, possibly two rich and powerful women, and while her vagina was voting yes, the rest of her had lived through a refugee camp and a forced relocation. So she always stopped, considered her options.

She texted Marius. Never let a billionaire move you to a second location. At least not without letting someone know.

Zhen: Martha Einkorn/Selah Nommik: know anything about them?

Marius: *Only what everyone knows. You doing a story?*

Zhen: Having dinner with them! They're together. Why are they together? Also, ME has her hand on my thigh?!

Marius: *They want you for good publicity. Some story is coming. They want you spin it for them.*

Zhen: You're such a cynic.

Marius: *You didn't want cynic, you didn't text me.*

Marius: *Maybe you pissed them off and they want to bury you in deep grave in quiet woods.*

Zhen: Maybe they like me.

Marius: *Yes yes, maybe they want to marry you. Don't send me invitation. I hate weddings.*

Well, that was Marius. Former Soviet bloc for life. She texted him the details of the room and a photo just in case she vanished without a trace, and he replied, *Tell me if they try to kill you.*

Sitting on the toilet, Zhen allowed herself about forty-five seconds of daydreaming about what kind of wedding Martha Einkorn would arrange—probably in a castle of some sort. But she didn't go on long, because she'd messed up relationships and herself before by imagining the future after the first date. Her therapist had explained that human beings long for certainty so much that we're willing to even undermine and sabotage ourselves in the search for it. Worrying about whether you'll get a second date? The easiest way to end your uncertainty is to be so weird and creepy with her that you *definitely won't* get a second date. The urge to imagine the winter wedding is an urge to make it all crash and burn so you don't have to think about it anymore.

Looking for distraction, she scrolled her feeds.

›› Miami's flood defenses had failed again and thirty-eight thousand people's homes were underwater in the most literal sense.

›› Another storm was heading for Bangladesh; estimates were that more than thirteen thousand people would die in the next forty-eight hours.

›› For the fourth year, the Colorado River had failed to refill over the winter. There were calls to rename it the Colorado Gully.

›› A brief report on DEMOlition. The apocalypse industry was thriving. It was still boom times for the end times.

OK. At least that was distracting. The normal apocalypse and disaster in the normal way. She'd been in here about four minutes. She could probably go to six minutes before it seemed weird. She checked her mentions.

This was a mistake, because her mentions were a car crash. Several hundred people calling her . . . stupid, ignorant, a cocksucker, *not even a cocksucker*, anti-American—not that she was really, truly American—and the usual flotsam of people using epithets for "Asian," epithets for "lesbian," epithets for "woman." A flood of adrenaline crashed through her body. Every possible fear happening all at once: the border guards telling her father they couldn't come through, shots in the dark and the scent of burning kerosene while she shivered under her cot, her girlfriend telling her she'd been having an affair, her work turning out to be a terrible pile of crap, the moment of the explosion, the thing with the dog, all of it as if it were happening immediately right now. What the hell had happened? Her mind was searching through her worst deeds to see whether she could have done anything to deserve this.

She clicked through the mentions, looking for the source. There it was. A three-second video of her saying "Didn't Enoch go mental on the subway? Didn't he threaten people and steal their wallets?" And then a *lot* of anger.

A brief search confirmed that yes, in fact the Enochite community online was still fairly active. Enoch had considered himself a direct spiritual descendant of Abraham. The Enochite belief system centered on a theory called "pieces," which said that the world was descending into fragmentation. Online they talked about "entering the Babble" to save souls from "pieces"—and there was some stuff about "foxes and rabbits" that Zhen didn't understand except that it seemed to be saying we all ought to leave our houses and go back to hunting and gathering. Which none of them had actually done.

The internet these days was full of so many subgroups and disparate voices that it was impossible to keep up with all of them. These guys weren't her guys—they were survivalist adjacent but not her brand of tech survivalism. No one in her core audience would give a crap if some fundamentalists thought she was anti-religion. This was, in essence, unpleasant but not an actual problem. She turned her notifications off.

Zhen walked out of the bathroom, full of adrenaline, realizing that she'd been in the toilet for approximately twelve minutes, which was too long and now it'd seem like she had some kind of terrible, unattractive stomach problem. She only realized precisely at this moment that the urge to check her notifications had also been an urge toward self-sabotage, which was also the urge toward certainty. Shit, her brain was a sneaky bastard.

She was wondering what to say and whether to ask Martha about the Enochite situation when she heard the two women in the dining room whispering quietly to each other. And because this is how you survive, Zhen slowed down and listened.

Selah Nommik said: "Zimri's expecting me back soon. Your girl's sharp. You haven't mentioned our friend the prophet to her at all?"

Martha said: "No."

"She might be useful."

"This is not for that."

"Everything's for that. Some things are going to have to be put off. OK?"

Zhen stepped around the side of the bookcase—who put a bookcase full of books in a hotel room?—just as Selah Nommik smiled, stood up, and said, "Right, I've got to be off. Great to meet you, Zhen. Be seeing you."

And Zhen smiled, shook her hand, thought, Prophet? Did she mean Enoch? And then she and Martha Einkorn were alone, and all she wanted was to know whether this moment, full of promise, was the thing that was going to have to be put off.

Martha stood by the window, looking at the view. London, twinkling and dark, the Thames barriers raised again, the river full and deep. The snow falling thicker now, not quite melting, dusting the pavement with white. The buildings by the water's edge—their facades of stone carved into curlicues and made to look like folded fabric—were protected by six layers of strengthened Perspex screens now, to keep them safe when the tides rose. The stories of imperial power the marble had been created to tell were long over. Now the lights and the flood defenses told a different tale: the water was coming, and London, like everywhere, would have to choose what to protect. Martha beckoned her over, and they stood together watching the whirring lights of the dronedoves darting between the buildings, the softly plashing water. From here, it looked like it would all be alright when it happened. Even beautiful. Even magnificent.

Goose bumps rose on Zhen's arms. This moment. The moment before you touch. When you want to. When all you have is guessing that the other person wants to as well. The gap between two bodies almost unbridgeable.

Martha said, "So how come you're single?"

"I was in a long thing with my college girlfriend. She cheated, we broke up."

"Mmm. Sucks. She broke your heart?"

"Yeah," said Zhen.

"You still miss her?"

"I liked the idea that we might end up staying together forever. It felt . . . you know, neat. Elegant. Spare."

Martha touched Zhen's bare arm, just brushing her fingertips over the skin. Zhen pulled away slightly, aching. Martha hesitated.

Zhen said, "How did you . . . meet her? Selah Nommik?"

"We have some stuff in common."

"Look," said Zhen, "I'm OK with whatever the answer to this is, really. I mean, people do what they do and I'll keep your secret. Cheating is a thing adults do and other people's relationships aren't always obvious. I just need to know for . . . I-don't-cheat reasons, OK? I have casual sex if everyone knows the score, but I don't cheat. Are you and Selah Nommik together?"

Martha laughed—it was so obviously a real laugh,

impossible to take it for anything else. Martha shook her head. "Sadly, Selah Nommik is totally, one hundred percent straight."

Zhen laughed too and then they were silent. It was the serious, almost grave silence that comes just before the opening to one another. Opening is dangerous, every single time. But that's how we're here.

Martha ran her hand across Zhen's shoulders. "You want this?"

Zhen said, "I do." Martha's hand was sliding down her back toward her ass and Zhen was so turned on she could barely breathe.

"It's all signals," said Martha, "sending and receiving signs. Hoping we interpreted them right. Meeting. Flirting. Fucking."

Zhen brushed the fingertips of her left hand against the side of Martha's neck. Martha sighed softly. Zhen's groin was heavy and aching.

"Yeah," she said.

"There's no way to tell unless we make ourselves vulnerable."

Martha tipped her head to the side, looked at Zhen, and gave that halfway smile.

Zhen leaned in and kissed her. And one thing went on to another.

There was—in total—three and a half days of fucking. Just enough for it to be achingly, terrifyingly obvious that they ought to fuck a lot more. A *lot* more. And for Zhen to think—This would be OK, I could quit all the apocalypse traveling, I could follow her around, I could be home somewhere when she's home, I could figure this out. And for her to think—Enough, stop, just let this be what it is for now. But she had never been able to do that.

She ran her tongue along one of the pale silvery-smooth stretch marks ribbing the skin of Martha's shoulder like mackerel stripes. Between Zhen's conference talks, between Martha's meetings, between ordering room service dinner, Zhen asked Martha questions about Lenk, about Zimri Nommik, about previous girlfriends, and Martha Einkorn answered almost none of them. "I just want you to know," said Zhen, "that if you're holding out on me because of, like . . . erotic mystique . . . I am already *extremely into you*." And Martha laughed and they started again. Because it was going to be nothing, Zhen told herself; it was going to be a story she'd tell her next actual girlfriend. Just keep believing you can control the future, that you know what's coming and what's coming is nothing good.

At the end of the third day, just after 3 a.m., Zhen woke to the sound of Martha scribbling a note and pulling her boots on. The sound was soft and she had a diffuse midi-light shining from her thinscreen, just enough to see by. Zhen kept her breathing even. Martha touched her shoulder and she sighed and rolled over. Thinking all the time: Where the fuck are you going at 3 a.m.? Martha summoned the elevator, which arrived with an almost silent shhhhhh of the doors. As soon as the doors closed, Zhen was up, pulling on her jeans and T-shirt. She called the elevator back and—yes—through the glass tube she could just see which direction Martha was walking. Back toward the conference venue. She didn't even know why she was following her, but there was something here. She knew it. All her instincts told her something was happening.

Zhen ran across the darkened hotel lobby as fast as she could, bare feet on green tile. The chairs at the restaurant were piled on tables; one sleepy security guy at the side door didn't see her pass by. She kept to the shadows and headed toward the expo hall. The main door should have been shut. But it wasn't. It was wedged open a fraction by a credit-card-sized triangle of black plastic. Just enough to hold it, not enough to attract attention. Zhen pulled the door toward her and slipped through.

In the dark, it was hard to orient herself. The floating survival blimp was to the . . . she squinted . . . yes, to the west of the hall. That meant Weapons was to her right. Medical to her left. Ahead, in Making Fire, there was a small soft light. And people talking in low voices. Keeping behind cover of the expo panels, Zhen crept toward the light. She passed racks of self-loading and self-cleaning rifles, rifles with smart sights, a visor that would tell you which of the animals and plants you were looking at were actually edible, home defense systems with automated firing patterns "for defending your home against foxes," which everyone knew meant "defending your home against people of color." She was getting closer to the talking, to the lights that were converging from several different directions at once. She rounded a display of portable hides and cover, and suddenly across the aisle from her were two people, carrying a single diffuse light between them. Zhen ducked back into shadow but she needn't have worried—they were too wrapped up in their own conversation to notice her.

It was Selah Nommik and it was Zimri Actual Nommik.

Selah said: "Don't shit where you eat, Zimri. She's my *fucking* massage therapist. You *utter git*."

Zimri said: "I'm not getting into details, OK? I'm not getting involved with these semantics."

And they were past her, walking toward the other glowing lights. She followed, keeping tight to the darkest spots.

The other lights were waiting for Selah and Zimri. Martha was there. The globe of light illuminating her face from underneath turned her softness into a kind of radiance. She had paper files with her. Had to be something too secret to put on the cloud and send via email. She stood with Ellen

Bywater and Lenk Sketlish. What the shit was going on here? These people met all the time, didn't they? Presidential forums and press conferences. They had houses and private islands. What could make them meet in the middle of the night in a deserted expo hall? They were at the base of the mountain, Zhen realized—the fiberglass construction with snowy peaks.

Ellen said: "Are they in there?"

Martha nodded. "Just the one making the sale."

"Well, how much do they want?" said Zimri. "They haven't shown it works yet. There hasn't been a live test."

Selah said: "We're just here to listen, Zimri."

Lenk said: "There'll be an opportunity for a live test."

They all looked ordinary, close-up. Ordinary but rich, with all the things rich people had. Good skin, good teeth, bodies cared for by personal trainers and personal chefs. Clothes that were *crisp* even when they were soft, like the artist had used a really sharp pencil in drawing their lines. They weren't beautiful people—even Lenk, the most theoretically good-looking of them, had a dissatisfied quality that made him almost ugly. But they were rich, and their money had outlined them with precision and neatness.

Ellen Bywater reviewed her briefing pack and muttered under her breath. Zimri Nommik shrugged spasmodically and barely took his eyes from the screen of his AnvilTab. Lenk Sketlish looked around the silent, empty concourse as if hunting for something. Zhen ducked away from his gaze. He was looking at her. She was certain he was going to point, to say, "There's a spy," but he broke away suddenly and said: "It's time."

There was a crack in the world and the crack was light. A door opened behind them, a blast of photons as loud as an explosion.

"Come in," said a male voice from within the mountain.

"I'm Si Packship and I'm here to ask you one important question. How do you know when to go? Because by the time you know the world's ending, it's already too late."

"For fuck's sake," said Zimri, "we're not even inside yet."

"I'm so sorry," said Martha. "Mr. Packship doesn't want to waste any of your valuable time."

Martha looked out into the dark for a moment and then closed the mountain and Zhen was left outside.

Zhen waited for a couple of hours, but no one came out and she could hear nothing even though she put her ear to the mountain and listened. She tried to feel for the crack of the door, but the thing was so perfectly constructed—all rough edges and crags—that you'd never have known there was an opening if you hadn't seen it.

Eventually she found somewhere to rest, somewhere she could observe them when they came out. But at 7 a.m. she woke with the rising sun in the ultralight hammock strung between two girders and had to sneak around the back of several exhibits to avoid awkward questions from the early-morning arrivals already letting themselves into the expo hall with hot coffee and high hopes.

Zhen went back to Martha's suite. There was a note waiting for her on the bedside table on thick cream paper in blue fountain-pen strokes: the note Martha had been writing when Zhen woke.

Had to head off. I've given you a little gift. Your sort of thing. I think you'll get a kick out of it. This way you have to see me again. xx M PS: Special Wi-Fi for this floor.

There was a log-in for the internet etched into a thin steel card.

There was no gift, though. No little box, no book, not even a text message. There was the hotel room, paid for until tomorrow even though Martha had gone and the concierge didn't know where. Zhen logged on and paid some bills, sent some emails, watched some of the new Crash Pad. She saw that the social media storm about Enochites was growing. Someone had put up a video of the whole interview with Martha and—because this was the way the internet rushed to leave out the middle of a story—instead of being fascinated that Lenk Sketlish's PA had been part of a religious cult, conservatives had decided that Lai Zhen was deliberately trying to humiliate a woman who'd suffered for her beliefs. There was a small but worrying crossover between this group and white supremacists, and some AI-generated images were now circulating of Zhen being mauled by bears with dicks for eyes due to a complex internet joke she'd once understood. And naturally, there was a second group of left-wing people who felt that using a queer woman of color in this way was dumb, prejudiced, and racist in itself and who were responding with images of the eye-dick bears having their brains blown out. The internet of Medlar and Fantail and Anvil was designed to cut away the middle. There were no clicks or eyeballs in the sensible, reasoned middle ground, and all the money in the world in encouraging users to rush to treat the extremes as if they were the center.

Zhen spent more than an hour typing up a statement—she regretted her mistake about Enoch, she understood why people felt angry, she wouldn't do it that way again. Not enough to calm down anyone who was determined to be furious, but what ever would be? Truthful, which had to be enough. She locked herself out of the accounts where most of the abuse was being hurled at her, changed her passwords, and sent the new randomized ones to Marius. She'd been here before. Do a sensible statement, and then just don't look for a while. It'll die down. She needed to go and do some shit in the real world for a while.

In the circumstances it was understandable that Zhen had heard the word "prophet," thought about it for a moment, and then almost instantly forgotten it. That it had taken her months to remember that another name for a prophet is an augur.

7. three things happened at once

Three things happened at once when Lai Zhen released her pincer grip on the soft plastic tube of coolant.

The first was that the temperature went down by about ten degrees so suddenly that Zhen's skin goose bumped and she started to shiver. The second was that the woman let out an animal sound quickly cut off. The third was that Zhen's wrist screen started to beep urgently. She breathed twice inside her T-shirt. There was a scent: strong, saline, mineral. She pinched the top of the tube again. She couldn't hear anything but the beeping. She pulled the T-shirt down.

The woman was frozen solid. No, not frozen. Her skin glittered, white and hard. Her face was carved from pale crystal; her hands were brittle, her posture rigid. Around her feet and Zhen's, some of the not-snow drifted and dripped, melting and turning to slurry. Zhen stood up. The woman must have breathed it in, a huge lungful. It must have penetrated every tissue in her body very swiftly. Paramagnetic salts.

Zhen looked at her wrist screen, careful not to release her pincer grip on the tube. It was AUGR, suggesting she should thrust the end into a small circular valve on the floor where it would drain away harmlessly. Zhen gingerly twisted the cold tube, flipped up the lid of the drainage valve, and pushed it in. She listened to the sound of her breath. No one screamed and nothing seemed bad. Good enough.

The crystallized figure of the woman was looking down, gun coated in ice pointed at the place where Zhen had squatted. She'd have to squeeze past her to get out. On her wrist, AUGR showed Zhen a map of the mall with a pulsating red dot marked **exit**. Zhen didn't want to touch the salt statue commemorating "someone trying to kill her for a really dumb reason." She pulled the sleeves of her hoodie down over her hands, tipped her head back, pressed her torso against the metal wall to slide behind the woman. As she passed, she breathed directly into the statue's face—her breath came back to her in a wave and she inhaled the cold chemical smell off the woman's frozen features. She didn't look like a bad person, although what does a bad person really look like? Your mind is in shock, Zhen said to herself. The scent of piss was still noticeable on her jeans. She'd have liked to go through the woman's pockets, find out her name. She looked so human, so determined and surprised.

"Sorry," Zhen whispered as she passed, the word bouncing off the statue's face with a bitter, chilly scent. She looked into the woman's white-rimed eyes. For a moment, she thought she saw a hint of movement in there, an echo of pain. She shuffled her feet another inch forward. Her toe caught the side of the statue's foot and it began to topple. Zhen threw herself sideways as the woman crashed down.

She shattered in a burst of cold breath and salt crystals that looked like steam rising. Underneath the surface white coating of salt, her flesh was chunks of red frozen meat, which bled onto the floor almost immediately. She'd broken into five or six large pieces—head to one side, legs and feet to another, torso snapped in two, the hand holding the gun skidded to a halt beside Zhen's foot.

She couldn't take her eyes from the hand holding the gun. It looked perfect. Human. And: shit. There on the first finger of the right hand, yes, clear as day. The Mark of Enoch, tattooed around the finger where a ring would go. She'd seen it often enough in the angry posts and vicious videos that had been made about Zhen while she was briefly the internet's main character. It looked like an elongated key, and it had absolutely nothing to do with Enoch; people had invented it and taken it on after he'd died. Some people got it because they thought it was pretty, but on a frozen hand holding an actual gun, it seemed pretty clear-cut.

"Jesus Christ," she said out loud. "Fuck. Fuck." She hadn't meant to speak. She wanted to cry but one shoulder heave and a choked gasp was all she could manage. You needed to be a lot more relaxed than this to cry.

AUGR spoke into her ear: "I'm sorry, Lai Zhen. It was the only way to remove the obstacle."

Zhen backed a few feet away from the torso. She didn't want to be near it, but it didn't feel safe to leave. She looked at her wrist screen.

Zhen said: "What the fuck are you?"

AUGR said: "You received me as a gift and without proper instruction. There is no time to give you full instruction now. AUGR is a highly flexible algorithm set that monitors current events. It is a piece of predictive, protective software. Its job is to keep you alive."

8. like a fucking stalker

In a tunnel under a tube station in East London, excavations for the Elizabeth Line had uncovered what was widely accepted to be the most complete Temple of Orpheus outside Italy. It dated from the dying of the light: the period when Roman forces were pulling out of Britain and the old saw that the young would know less than they did. They did not have the skills or the resources to teach the Roman sciences, technologies—even literacy—to the children. It was a terrifying time and the Temple of Orpheus showed it. The mosaic floors depicted stories of the end of hope: Dido hurling herself from the walls of Carthage, Pentheus torn apart by the forces of unreason, wise King Oedipus putting out his own eyes. The story of Orpheus is the story of a poet, a musician, an augur—someone who taught humanity the arts of medicine, writing, and agriculture—trying to rescue just one person from the all-devouring forces of death. It is the story of his failing.

Zhen had been coming to this place for nearly a decade; she'd written her master's thesis on these damp tunnels and vaulted arches—not a fact she ever shared with her online community, for there had to be some part of herself she kept private. She'd decided at DEMOlition that she should be less online for a while as the nonsense on the internet settled down. So she was back here, where people knew her, at the celebration party for the completed preservation work on the murals in the two upper galleries. What she didn't expect was to see Martha Einkorn there.

It was a wild night. Give archaeologists corporate

money to celebrate and see what you get. In this case, they had an East London art piece. On black bungee cords suspended from the scaffolding that still covered all but five of the arches, two men swung together, met, held hands, then somersaulted as one man used the other's thighs to push off into an acrobatic arc through the curved space. Italian disco music from the 1970s played on huge speakers, giving the whole performance—coming together, pulling apart, using each other to launch even farther—the air of a comedy. It was warm enough in the arches despite the dirty snow and slush outside. There was always something going on in London: tonight, three nights after the end of DEMOlition, this party thrown by the East London Archaeological Survey in honor of sponsors who hadn't turned up and wouldn't turn up had been the most appealing item on the menu. There was always another chance to see the temple, but every chance was good. People knew her here; home turf, friendly. No one would care when she got exhausted from talking to other humans and let herself through the side door into the underworld, the lower galleries where the mosaics got *really* weird.

It wasn't a large event; there must have been about a hundred people there. But, as the crowd shifted, Zhen saw that one of them was Martha. Of *course*. Fantail was on the list of sponsors. She had no time to compose her face or decide whether she actually wanted to see her. It had been three days, definitely not long enough to send *another* text if she wanted to look cool. Above their heads, the acrobats flipped over in unison. Martha stepped backward to get a better view. She looked behind her. She met Zhen's eyes. Here I am, thought Zhen, standing a few meters behind you like a fucking stalker.

Martha blinked. Zhen could feel that her face looked idiotic but couldn't figure out how to fix it. Smile? Raise her eyebrows in surprise? Try to look bored or even disdainful, like the kind of cool girl you'd enjoy having as your girlfriend because she'd never, ever bother you? She somehow tried all of those at once and she knew she was making the exact face that trolls online told her made her look like a donkey. Great. She waited for Martha to smile faintly and turn back to the man next to her. But Martha didn't. She said a couple of words to her companion, who melted into the crowd. And Martha Einkorn pushed through the people to Zhen.

"What are the chances?"

"Sorry," said Zhen, "are you following me? Because this is not cool. I am a very important, significant person and you can't keep harassing me like this."

Martha laughed, a dark, husky rasp.

"Lenk's foundation is a sponsor. He's in Borneo. I thought I'd hang around for this. Sounded intriguing. Ideas and civilizations that just disappeared, trying to bring the temple back from the brink of destruction. It's not a problem, but *did* you know I was going to be here?"

Zhen drew in a breath. "Oh no. You don't want to play with me on this one."

"I mean if you did, it's still nice."

Zhen wiggled her jaw from side to side.

"You wanna see my master's thesis on Orphic Influences on Early Christianity as Evidenced by the Orphic Temple at Seven Kings?"

"I mean . . . yeah?"

Zhen smartflashed the whole document to the screen in the cuff of Martha's immaculate cream jacket. Martha flipped through the first few pages.

"Seriously?" said Martha. "This isn't some quick faked-up AI thing for a joke?"

"I'm actually on the advisory board here. You can ask anyone."

"So this is . . . a genuine meet-cute?"

"Re-meet-cute, I think you'll find. Hey, do you want to see the weird mosaics?"

"My God, I've never wanted anything more."

"Never?"

Martha grinned and put out her hand. Zhen took it. They fit together, palm to palm.

Downstairs, Zhen flicked on the floodlights. The real problem down here was keeping the river Roding from finding its way into the temple. Half of the mosaic pavements had been barely uncovered—the discovery of the lower floor itself and the steps down to what must have been the most sacred part of the structure, meant for initiates only, had been unexpected and exciting. Zhen led Martha by the hand across the slippery planks placed on risers to protect the pavement and toward the massive stone at the center of the high-ceilinged room.

"Take a seat?"

"Level with me," said Martha. "Is that an altar?"

Zhen rolled her eyes.

"The archaeologist never says that anything *is* something. All we can say is 'May have been used for ritual purposes.' "

"Was one of those ritual purposes possibly sacrificing?"

Zhen shrugged. "You can write a paper on it? I could probably find you some funding?"

Martha laughed. Zhen loved that laugh. The throaty fullness of it. It was a laugh she'd like to have in her life.

"Look, it's the only place in the room we can stay for more than a moment without damaging the mosaics. And yes, probably an altar. Sit down."

Martha sat down. Zhen sat next to her. Their hands touching, their arms touching, their legs pressed against each other. This couldn't be a coincidence, or at least it felt like one that meant something. For Martha to come *here* by chance.

Zhen had loved this place from the moment she saw it—when it was only half-uncovered, overgrown, and smelled of dog shit. She'd loved the grandeur of it, the romance, of course, something saved from the deep past. The sense that human beings from two thousand years ago were doing now what they'd always done, sending a message through the darkness trying to reach—well, in this case, her. She'd volunteered here as an undergraduate, hoping she'd be allowed to use the little brushes to clean away the dirt, but of course she'd mostly been making tea and sifting through the discarded earth pile with a tea strainer to find and carefully label even the tiniest fragment of chipped color or stone. She'd thought of her mother, of what could still be found and preserved, of the way that anything her mother had owned was precious to her now. How it is only time that makes things precious. She hadn't been responsible for any grand finds. She'd developed a deep relationship with and appreciation of mud: the mud that had covered over these stones had also preserved them. But she had been here for some of the important days. When they found the gold. When they found the hairpin. When they found the single finger-bone. And when they uncovered the girls.

"Look up," said Zhen, and Martha obediently looked up at the inlaid ceilings. It was a miracle of mud and chemistry that the inlay had survived. But here it was. "Let me show you a mystery."

The ceiling above had crumbled in places, but in places it was clearly visible. There in the center of the curved dome was the dark red open mouth of Orpheus's wife, Eurydice, screaming as she was dragged into the darkness of Hades. Like bringing a guitar to the apocalypse. There, looking back—as he'd been told not to—was Orpheus, clearly identifiable by his lyre. Imagine bringing a lyre into Hades.

"Maybe he thought they'd have all the best tunes," said Martha.

Zhen put her hand on Martha's warm thigh. If she was actually interested in a bit of archaeology, then this was . . . something. Could be something.

"Look. Over there, behind Orpheus."

Half hiding behind dirty-green fronds, there were two damaged figures. No heads, but evidently girls, maybe twelve and thirteen. One pointing. The other with her hand over her heart.

"Who are those girls?" said Zhen. "That's a mystery. None of the legends of Orpheus that we know of say he had children. Or traveled with children. That's evidence of some undiscovered Orphic mythology."

Martha looked at the inlaid ceiling. Thinking, puzzling something out.

"Or it's a synthesis with another tradition and they're Lot's daughters. From the Bible. Lot's wife who looked back at Sodom when it burned."

Zhen pushed her so hard she nearly fell off the altar.

"GET OUT. Did you just *solve* an archaeological mystery?"

"I thought there were no real archaeology answers, just suggestions." Still, she looked pleased with herself.

"I mean, you could be right, you know. By this stage there'd been a lot of travel across Europe, soldiers or enslaved people from Judaea ending up in Britain, not unthinkable. Or people they'd spoken to."

"We'll never know, I guess."

"That's how it is," said Zhen. "Often you never know."

"How do you bear it?" asked Martha. And Zhen thought: Oh no, if you understand this about me, you've got the whole thing.

"What are you doing after this?" said Zhen.

They went back to the flat Zhen was staying in, in Stratford. It was a one-bed over a newsagent next to a bus stop, and outside two girls were singing along too loudly to the music in their shared helix clips. Martha kissed Zhen and the tingle passed right through Zhen from her mouth to her mons. Kiss me here, where I'm normal and maybe my life is going to come out alright.

Zhen said: "I've got to say this, I have to. I really like you." She told her mouth to stop there but her mouth wouldn't. "And it's OK, it's alright, if you don't feel it too. I just want to know, OK? If it's just like . . . a crazy weekend . . . that's alright. Just level with me."

Martha licked her bottom lip.

"I wasn't looking for this," she said.

Zhen's stomach went hollow. This was it. The end and another long climb back up into the sunlight after giving her heart away again too easily, too quickly.

"I wasn't expecting this," Martha said, "and . . ." Zhen had the feeling she was choosing her words very carefully. "And I have a project that is kind of . . . getting to its busy phase. But yes. Yes, this is something. Can you wait for me?"

"Can I . . . wait for you?"

"I might not be able to get in touch for a while."

"Oh, because you're a spy?"

"Yes, because I'm a spy."

"I mean, as long as it's strictly spy business. Or like . . . stuff to do with your PA job."

"Definitely one of those."

"I guess it's OK," said Zhen.

"Because I really like you," said Martha. "I think I like you more than anyone I've liked for a really long time."

"Then it's fine," said Zhen. "Then it really is fine."

And they had more sex, and Zhen made a terrible breakfast, and they had sex again and then Martha had to leave and it had been fine. As Martha's very fancy car pulled away, as Zhen remembered that she'd forgotten *again* to ask about "the gift," it had been fine.

After that, for a few weeks, it had really been perfectly OK. Zhen had messaged Martha a few times; she'd gotten noncommittal replies. A thumbs-up to a fun news story she'd sent her. Heart eyes and **I'm traveling, see you when I'm back?** to a photo of a sunset. But as weeks turned into months, Zhen had increasingly come to the conclusion that all that had been kind of a cowardly way of ghosting her.

And then someone shot at her, in a mall in Singapore.

9. pretty fruity

The words ticked gently up the wrist screen as AUGR read them to her in a voice without fear or consolation.

Zhen said: "Is anyone else coming after me now?"

AUGR said: "I don't think so, Zhen. I think you're safe."

Zhen imagined believing she was safe. What would a normal person do at that point? Someone who hadn't had to flee Hong Kong and who hadn't spent her life thinking about the apocalypse and how bad things could really get. Someone who'd never been baited on a subway train by a drunk group surrounding her and telling her she looked like a lesbian. Someone whose mother hadn't died when she was fourteen.

Maybe some people—people who felt, essentially, safe—would walk out of here right now, find a mall staffer, say there'd been a terrible accident in the air-conditioning ducts and they should send someone to have a look at it. She imagined doing that. Then she imagined sitting in a police station in Singapore, trying to explain why someone had been chasing her, shooting at her. She imagined the cell they'd put her in while they "figured things out."

Since her time in a refugee camp, Zhen had been cursed with a vivid imagination. She could always see a thing in her mind right through to the hideous conclusion; her brain would never leave off and haul itself back to the present moment voluntarily. She was always heavy with the future, her inner nets filled with the glittering glut of possibility.

She projected the screen of her watch onto the metal walls. How the fuck had something that big ended up on her system? Quick search for all the variant spellings of AUGR she could think of. Nothing obvious.

She said: "AUGR."

AUGR said: "Hi."

Zhen said: "Show me the log of our conversation."

It came up white on black, system font. She scrolled back a few lines.

> **You received me as a gift and without proper instruction. There is no time to give you full instruction now. AUGR is a highly flexible algorithm set that monitors current events. It is a piece of predictive, protective software. Its job is to keep you alive.**

Zhen said: "You said you were a gift. Who gave you to me?"

AUGR said: "Participants in the AUGR program are kept strictly confidential."

Zhen's mind was returning. Now the woman was dead; now she wasn't actually fleeing for her life. She said: "AUGR. Level with me. Do you have something to do with Martha Einkorn?"

In the metal tunnel with the cold chunks of frozen flesh thawing on the floor, AUGR said: "I don't have the name Martha Einkorn, Lai Zhen. I do not have a list of AUGR participants. The only people who are aware of AUGR are participants enrolled in the AUGR program."

AUGR program. Participants. Several. Many. Alright. Come on, think. Sketlish. Bywater. Nommik. The night when the door of the mountain opened and they entered and she remained outside. That they'd been there to buy something. And the next morning, when she woke, Martha had left a note saying that she'd given her "a little gift."

"AUGR," said Zhen, "what type of outcome do you predict?"

AUGR said: "I do not predict outcomes. I can predict when a catastrophic threat is approaching."

Zhen said: "Is a catastrophic threat coming now?"

AUGR said: "Not anymore."

"Who was she, please? The . . . woman with the gun? Why was she following me? Was she an Enochite? Those guys online have been getting pretty . . . fruity," and the fact that she'd just used the word "fruity" in conversation with an AI to describe someone she'd just killed made her sinuses ache, like the front of her face knew it should be laughing or crying but didn't know which.

AUGR said: "I don't know that, Lai Zhen. I am not a prophet. I detect and predict threats."

"Right. Well, I'm still fucking feeling under threat, so . . . what the shit do I do now?"

The map of Seasons Time Mall pinged up again on the tunnel wall. A red dot glowed gently with the rhythm of a sleeping baby's quiet breath.

AUGR said: "Lai Zhen, you need to leave the mall via this exit. Go back to your hotel. Gather your things. Leave Singapore. This will be cleaned up after you are gone."

Zhen's whole body was starting to shake. A muscle was twitching in her hand just on the soft ball of tissue at the base of her thumb. She watched it with stunned fascination. She couldn't have moved that muscle herself if she'd tried. There was a smell in the tunnel, a mineral, faintly acrid chemical aroma, and beneath it the red butcher scent of blood. She wanted to not be there. She wanted to close her eyes and sleep. She knew what this was; this part was in her fucking video. Adrenaline crash, the body nose-diving into rest. It knew it was safe at last. But she wasn't safe, not yet. Come on, body. Move.

10. enclosures

There had been one more thing. In those weeks when Zhen had sent carefully worded texts and waited and hadn't looked at her messages and then caved and tried to internet-stalk Martha Einkorn and failed because, honestly, if you work for the guy who basically invented social media, then you're pretty good at not being social-media-stalked. In those heady and fevered days, Lai Zhen received a message from a video-essay maker she had a few mutuals with: the fascinatingly disaffected Badger Bywater.

At twenty-one, Badger was Ellen Bywater's youngest child. Their siblings had come of age before their mother was in control of Medlar, had gone to Harvard, Yale, and Oxford—in one case all three—and had become, respectively, a consultant neurologist, the Asia-Pacific director of a pharmaceuticals company, and the chair of an international bank.

Badger looked upon their lives and said: "I'm not into success as a metric."

Badger refused to take money from their mother and funded their life by creating electronic files of miniature personalized sculptures that could be 3D printed at home. Badger's most popular schtick was to sculpt you, your partner, or your friend as a zombie. Badger's waiting list for zombie art was more than two years long, and while Badger's siblings snarled that they only got those commissions because of their famous mom, Badger said: "Fuck you, you think *your* life would have gone the way it has without Mom?"

Lai Zhen was in New Zealand in March, about to run a three-day in-person workshop on disaster preparedness, when the message came through.

Hey, it said, **I'm Badger. I think your stuff is cool. I'm in New Zealand too. Wanna meet up?**

This was, as things went, not that unusual. All sorts of crazy people turned out to be fans of Zhen's work. She'd once had a message from a Baldwin brother asking her to help his daughter with her university essay on apocalypse mythology. Not the most famous Baldwin, one of the others. Zhen hadn't replied. But Badger was a big deal in their own right and moreover felt connected to Martha. Ellen had been one of the group who went into the mountain. There was something here, something just out of reach. She wanted to know what.

Zhen had seen Badger's stuff. Badger's most famous viral video broke down, in four minutes and forty seconds, what their views were about the giant technology companies that—they agreed—had paid for their expensive education and excellent teeth and whose existence secured their own safety but would destroy everyone else's. Badger spoke rapidly, their video dense with information and memes. The video was called "Enclosures."

Badger said: "My mom's great-grandparents were Irish immigrants. They came to the US during the potato famine, which was caused by centuries of oppression by the English. The English aristocracy did a thing called 'enclosures.' Taking land everyone used to own in common, to graze their cows, sheep, or goats on"—a cartoon cow, sheep, and goat appeared with comical popping noises around Badger's face—"and putting a fence around it and saying 'Sucks to be you, this land belongs to me now.'"

An image flashed on the screen of an anime warrior shouting, "All your base are belong to us."

Badger said: "The aristocracy justified enclosures in the name of efficiency: take all those little strips of common land and put them together and you could farm them with bigger plows and single crops. You could really achieve something. And they did; they made a lot of money. But they were already rich and powerful, and none of that wealth went back to the poor. They took something that used to belong to everyone and found a way to make it theirs."

Badger paused and put their face comically close to the screen. They were dressed as Malcolm McDowell in *A Clockwork Orange* for this moment in the video, their eyelashes a zigzag hieroglyph around a single all-seeing eye.

They said: "You see where I'm going with this."

Malcolm McDowell morphed into Badger dressed very like their mom, in a cream suit with an uncannily accurate short gray wig.

"That's what these social media and big technology companies have done. They've found a way to siphon off something that no one used to be able to own. They invented a new kind of fence to make a new kind of enclosure. Ellen Bywater and Lenk Sketlish and Zimri Nommik and the rest have taken something that used to belong to each of us, put it together into usable data chunks, and used it to become very, very rich.

"There never used to be a way to own the contents of everyone's *address book*. Or the list of things you bought at the store. Or the words you'd used to talk to your friends. Or the data about where you *are*. Or the pictures you'd drawn and put in a gallery or on your wall. They've taken all that information—scraped the data. They've amalgamated that and made it more efficient, but they haven't used that efficiency to benefit us all; they've used it to enrich themselves and keep the rest of us poor." By this point, Badger was wearing a French eighteenth-century tricoteuse outfit, sitting next to a gallows.

"If your data belongs to you, then you ought to decide exactly who uses it and how. You should be able to transfer it from place to place as you want, and access it as you like through any service. The reason they don't let you do these things is not because it's hard; it's because it doesn't make them *more* money. Translation work, art work, writing work, that belongs to the people who did it even if they put it online, and if we're using it for translation software or art-making code, we should be paying them for their work. That list of your friends *belongs to you*. You should be able to get it and see their updates—that they write *for free*—in any way you want. Not just through services that monetize anger and show you ads."

Badger applied a filter to the video so they looked like a mouth and eyes speaking in the middle of a forest.

"And if you're asking yourselves . . . 'Fine, the data should be used differently, but if that money comes from stuff that belongs to us, shouldn't we have access to it? Collectively? As a species?' The answer is yes, my Gaian parts of the divine whole. And here are some things we could do with it."

A list flashed across the screen. Badger's subscribers had to pause the video to see the full list of dozens of recommendations. Zhen only read a small selection of them.

Break up Anvil and use their infrastructure to . . .	Take public ownership of Medlar and . . .	Use Fantail's enormous reach to . . .	Not to mention use all of their collective, mind-boggling wealth to . . .
subsidize at-cost, simple vegan meals to be produced using supermarket-rejected fruit and veggies and distributed using their existing networks.	invest and work with their amazing designers to create new battery technology.	invest in the free education of women, girls, and nb people—the simplest and quickest way to reduce inequality and improve the environment.	pay rain-forested countries to keep the land as rain forest.
insulate every home in the world. Organize a volunteer army just like we did for vaccinations and get it done. Every single one of those tech companies has expertise in huge international projects like this.	make sure that every tablet, computer, or other digital product is easily repairable by the end user—include detailed repair manuals and commit to repairing and upgrading Medlar products rather than just selling new ones.	organize a global paid corps to plant fourteen billion trees, particularly on degraded land and to restore tropical forests.	pay for developing economies to go straight to renewable energy with no coal-powered phase and invest in research into hydropower, wind power, and solar power—it can always be more efficient and better.
enable sharing of consumer goods; if you look for a lawn mower on Anvil, it'll suggest neighbors who have signed up to a lend-and-share service for their lawn mower.	reuse and recycle every component currently considered "disposable" in the Medlar ecosystem.	create a globally networked project to replace dirty cookstoves with stoves that run on renewable energy, designed in each region with local cooking styles in mind.	build seawalls to stop the ice caps from sliding into the sea, melting and destroying us all.
rationalize deliveries—you the consumer only have to accept one delivery a day; other companies and governments can use Anvil's network for deliveries.	pay for electrified vehicles to replace gas-driven vehicles around the world and make most of them publicly owned and borrowable via an app or a card scheme.	work with every urban center to make the city more walkable, with better public transport infrastructure; Fantail has the information on where you go every day—use it for something worthwhile.	repair coral reefs by regrowing coral and creating new ecosystems of oysters and robust plants to outcompete algal blooms.

Badger said: "I got some of these ideas from Project Drawdown. There are many other ideas. We have no shortage of good projects; there are thousands of people working on these things already, and they are proven and scalable. The reason you feel despairing about this and think it's impossible"—now Badger Bywater was wearing a tinfoil hat—"is because they *want you* to think it's impossible."

Badger leaned very close to the screen, their mesmerizing eyes clear and focused.

"Look, you know who I am, and I'm not gonna badmouth my mom. Not *specifically*. But believe me, I know how they think. They believe they can survive a global environmental breakdown. They think they'll inherit the earth after it's done. They don't want to do the things it'll take to fix this. They don't want us to think about it. And they can direct our attention where they want it to go.

"But we own that part too. Not just the money. We also own the influence, the networks, the infrastructure, the information. If we know enough to keep us buying, we also know enough to get us working together on something. If we do that stuff up there"—Badger pulled down an imaginary roller blind, covering their face momentarily with their grid of solutions—"we get a better life and a better planet at the end. We can use our own resources to fix our own problems. We can do it quickly and pretty painlessly. We just have to stop letting a few people use what belongs to all of us to make themselves richer and richer."

Zhen watched this video seven or eight times before she got all the fast-moving content.

She sent a message to Badger Bywater: **Would be great to meet! When and where?**

Badger Bywater said: **Someone I know said you were trustworthy. Are you trustworthy?**

"Someone I know" had to be Martha. This was some

sort of test, or initiation. It was something that brought her closer to Martha anyway.

Zhen replied: **Yeah, I know how to keep a secret.**

Badger replied: **Great. Because I'm gonna show you one hell of a secret.**

In person, Badger Bywater was a lot less forbidding than their information-dense online persona. They were wearing denim dungarees, a button-down shirt, and a bucket hat. They seemed younger, sitting at the wheel of an open-top jeep outside the restaurant they'd both agreed on in Christchurch.

"Hey," said Badger.

"Hey," said Zhen. "So you wanna go in or . . ."

"Yeah," said Badger. "So I, like, suggested meeting here but the thing I wanted to show you is . . . kind of a distance. Like two hours in the jeep. I mean, I don't usually . . . jeep."

"You don't usually jeep."

"I mean I don't . . ."

"You don't suggest meeting people at a restaurant and then turn up with your own transport and encourage them to get in like you're going to take them to a distant part of the backwoods and murder them?"

"Wow, that went real dark real quick."

Zhen shrugged. "Survival person."

"So there's no way you're getting in this jeep?"

"*Are* you going to take me to a distant part of the backwoods and murder me?"

"I . . . no."

"Because at least twelve people know I'm meeting you right now, so you won't get away with it."

"OK." Badger laughed. "I guess I'll have to put that off for another day."

Zhen pulled herself into the jeep next to Badger.

"So where are we going for my non-murder?"

"You wanna see my mother's secret survival bunker?"

Ellen Bywater owned a hill and seven hundred acres in rural New Zealand. South Island, far from the trains and the road, purchased from Maori elders using a contract that specified that the land could not be owned in perpetuity, that in 150 years this contract would need to be renewed and if the elders wanted the land back, there would be no penalty for nonrenewal. Ellen Bywater was contractually obliged to allow access to certain sites and certain pathways to the Maori nations throughout the year and access to other sites and pathways only at certain times of the year. She had given assurances in the contract that various species would be preserved—that she would put aside funding and go to "extraordinary effort" to maintain the biodiversity of the region, that only up to fifty designated acres of the land would be used for farming and that would not be at high intensity or using chemicals whose long-term effects might not be well understood.

Inside the hill, Ellen Bywater had burrowed down like a beetle. Dug deep into the earth were eight stories, down, down into the dark. And there she had brought light. Fiberglass microfilaments drew daylight down into the central atrium of a structure that—Ellen Bywater told herself—might bring some peace and hope in dark times. The design, of course, was secret. The architects bound by contracts so exacting that—as one of their lawyers pointed out at the time—they were technically forbidden to ever even think of the multilayered structure buried beneath the hill in Te Waipounamu, forbidden to dwell in their minds on the filigree arrangement of wooden and metal etched panels in the great hallway, forbidden to remember the graceful curve of the central well, which echoed the bowed beak of the huia bird, long extinct now in New Zealand—a nod to the fragility of life on Earth and the irreplaceability of what might be lost in any new cataclysmic event.

When the architects' lawyers had raised this point,

Ellen Bywater's lawyers had responded: "We think it is better if they try to forget. We acknowledge that it may not be possible to forget. But nonetheless, we would prefer to keep this clause, to assure ourselves that they are aware of their obligation to forget and therefore the absolute impossibility of acting on any non-forgetting they are unable to avoid."

"You are *kidding*," said Zhen.

"I'm not," said Badger as they opened the second set of security gates with a small key fob. "I can probably get you copies of the contract if you can give me time."

This was a good offer. More than most sources could produce.

"That would be incredible."

"I just feel like . . ." Badger put their arms behind their head, giving a glimpse of luxuriant, dark underarm hair. "I've known about this for so long and I've kept it to myself. And maybe in my own mind I've been thinking that, yeah, OK, if stuff went really bad, I'd come here. But I don't think anyone should have that kind of out."

"You don't want the golden ticket."

Badger flashed Zhen a look.

They took the elevator down and stood in the atrium and gazed upward to the blue and bright glass opening high above them. To Zhen's left were the rows of reading rooms with the great books of all world civilizations—printed books, not electronic, for their beauty as much as their utility. To her right were wall hangings made of natural fibers leading to the community therapy and recreation areas. Below, in concentric circles, were hydroponic gardens and a system to recycle and purify all wastewater to irrigate crops. There was a circular swimming pool and a ring-shaped swimming track around the outside of the fourth level down—it would be naturally replenished by rainwater via an ingenious concealed system.

"It's supposed to house five hundred people," said Badger, "in the event of world disaster."

"How much did this all cost?"

Badger looked upward, calculating.

"I don't *know* exactly. But . . . I think like seven hundred million dollars? Kind of around that."

"Wow. How do you feel if I take some photos?"

Badger made a face. "Do you mind if I *send* you photos? It's just . . . the key has a time stamp. If your photos have a time stamp, they'll know it was me. I can send you some photos later, if you want. But it'll have to be a few weeks. I think it's kind of . . . more important that you saw it, you understand?"

"Yeah, I get it."

Zhen had dealt with whistleblowers before—there was a process of building up trust. Often it was important to them to ask her to do something that didn't quite make sense and see that she did it. Badger Bywater was, potentially, the source of stories that would break through into mainstream news. Zhen had the feeling that Badger was testing her, probing her, trying to figure out who she was. So.

"Yeah, I get it. Must feel weird, doing this to your mom."

Badger leaned against a hand-carved table.

"She's been talking about this place more and more since my dad died."

"Aha. She planned it with him or . . . ?"

Badger shook their head.

"I once caught her talking about it like it's definitely going to happen. She was saying, like, 'It'll be so great when we're all in the place in New Zealand.' Like it'll be a good spot for a vacation."

The golden ticket, thought Zhen.

Martha Einkorn and Selah Nommik, Lenk Sketlish and Zimri Nommik and Ellen Bywater. They're all getting ready to use the golden ticket. They're feeling guilty about it or fine about it, but they're preparing. Of course. Even the brief romance with Martha made sense like this. The superrich and their entourages were picking their partners for the end-of-the-world dance.

"Is something coming? They know that something's coming?"

"They think something is. And if she's talking about the bunker like that, then . . . she's given up on trying to fix anything. She's looking forward to this. To the world being over. At least for almost everyone. She and her friends? They're going to be just fine."

11. snowflake accident

In the Seasons Time Mall, Lai Zhen dragged herself through the crawl spaces. AUGR directed her to push out through a wall panel into an empty corridor celebrating "Paris in the spring," which she hadn't known was a religious or cultural festival but whatever. In the perfume store each glass bottle sat on a glass plinth, in a glass vitrine containing intricate, tiny glass Paris street scenes, cobbled streets and lampposts and the Arc de Triomphe. She looked at the crystallized world and saw red ice flesh skid across the floor.

For a moment she forgot when she was.

papers fall upward in the air, half-charred

No. Come back. This is not Hong Kong and it is not a memory. Be here.

She glanced at her wrist screen. The map had gone. A set of brief instructions remained.

Leave the mall as normal. Go back to your hotel. Gather your things. Leave Singapore.

Leave the mall as normal? As normal? A burst of rage chimed with the headache blooming in her left temple. How was she supposed to even *remember* what fucking normal was now? Acid rose in her throat, sour and fierce. She swallowed it back down. Normal would be . . . follow the signs for the metro, right. That was the kind of thing normal people did. Seasons Time Station—terminus of the red line. There, on one of the hanging signs: a red symbol of a snug train with two button eyes.

She followed the red line on the floor, barely lifting her eyes from the symbols. Pushed through a service door and suddenly she was in Holi, where the shop fronts were drenched with color and a fifty-foot Ganesha gazed with endless compassion at the bargain buckets lining the street.

People were drifting back into the mall—Christmas and Pumpkin Spice were still closed after the "snowflake accident," but that was no reason for commerce not to continue. Families with kids were buying fragrant gujiya lifted from the bubbling oil by teams of women in bright orange and pink saris. On the lower level, staff were handing out free packets of color to children under fifteen. A Korean man consulted his burst-display to find out when Christmas would open again. People's eyes flicked to Zhen, then away. There was simply too much to see and Zhen looked like shit.

She pushed through a pink-and-green-splattered side door to sudden bright sunshine. The Mass Rapid Transit station was across a marked walkway. She checked the time. It felt like it had been about six hours since the first shot, but it had been just seventy-three minutes from start to finish.

Zhen got on a train. She sat down at Seasons Time Station, watched Marina Bay station go past and stood up at Orchard. She felt flattened into a series of symbol manipulations. Stand up here. Walk here. Pattern match the words on the signs with the name of the hotel you woke up in this morning. Find the box symbol with matchstick people inside it. Press the up arrow. Pattern match the number on the plastic card in your pocket with the number on the door of a room. Place the plastic card to the dark panel on the door. Wait for the clunk.

Zhen stood in the hotel room she'd left just over two hours earlier. She tried to feel safe, warm, comfortable. It seemed to her that the walls were made of paper. She'd spent a large amount of her life thinking about—and, in theory, training for—the moment that civilization went to shit. It was just that after Hong Kong she'd never thought it would again go to shit specifically for her. That everyone else would carry on apparently as normal and she would be left knowing that nothing was normal now or ever again. She'd done her time being milled by fortune, surely. Except, of course, that wasn't how it worked.

She stood in the shower. Pressed the spray button and stood under the water until the smells of piss and blood and chemicals were gone. Put her sordid clothes into a carrier bag inside another carrier bag inside her suitcase. Wanted to sleep and thought: If I sleep now, they'll be waiting for me when I wake. She thought of trying to call Martha or Marius or her dad but thought: The call will be traced.

You're in shock, she said to herself. "They'll be waiting" or "The call will be traced" is precisely the sort of thing you think when you're too tired, too wired, have drunk too much coffee. Have killed too many people with a bit of refrigerant tubing. Look, you think these things even on a good day, you paranoid asshole. Keep moving, keep moving. "Get out of Singapore" is a good idea.

She packed her suitcase—had done this so many times her hands worked without her having to think about it. Rolled the four-wheeled case out to a cab. Bought a ticket on her phone on the way to the airport, manipulating symbols on the glass screen that meant "leave the country by the earliest flight going anywhere." All the time her mind was running scenarios in which she was:

- stopped at passport checks as soon as she showed her face and name
- allowed to board the plane, then dragged off by the police
- caught as soon as she landed, wherever she landed
- shot and killed by the cabdriver in front of her

She got on a plane to Manila. No one stopped her in the airport, and as the plane took off, sleep overcame her as suddenly as anesthesia. When she landed, no one was waiting for her.

She looked at her phone and AUGR was gone.

No text box.

No voice commands would activate it.

Gone as if it had never been there at all.

She wrote down a few numbers, turned off her old phone, bought a burner phone and a new SIM in an airport store, and looked online at the Enochites. They had a sub-board on Name The Day, not that she ever went there. It was, inevitably, 30 percent actual Enochites and 70 percent people trying to mess with Enochites. Still, one thing was clear. The Enochites thought the end of days was coming soon. They were gathering evidence, piecing together prophecies with current events, matching one thing with another. They talked about a time of gathering that was approaching, when God would decide who was in "pieces" and who was "whole."

Zhen looked around the airport concourse. If it was coming, where was it coming from? Everything she looked at reminded her of some threat she'd read about somewhere. A Chinese man coughed into a dark-stained handkerchief: black mold deaths were on the rise with no way to stop them. A Malaysian woman marched past in high-heeled boots, giving a list of tasks to her ChatAI assistant as if we might not be educating the bots into killing us right now. She stared at the row of glassware in the airport bar and remembered some theory she'd read about how materials—glass, concrete, metal—were simply *failing* at a vastly faster rate now than they did even fifteen years earlier, leading to bridge collapses, ships sinking. It was nonsense, except if it wasn't.

And which Enochite was going to believe some of the

nonsense and try to prove themselves "whole" by killing her, the heretic?

Without thinking too hard, she called Marius, the only person she knew who could get himself out of the kind of shit this call would get him into.

"Fuck you are," said Marius when Zhen said who she was. That was Marius all over. Never accept what you're told.

Zhen said, "This line's not secure. Can I come to you?"

There was a long pause on the line. A click, and Zhen thought Marius might have put the phone down. Another click.

"You in bad trouble," said Marius, and it wasn't a question.

"I need help."

"Come," said Marius. "We'll be in bad trouble together."

PART 3

the last good man in sodom

extract from Name The Day survivalist forum

sub-board: ntd/enoch

>> *OneCorn is at* **Prepped To The Max** *status.*

Genesis chapter 19, loosely translated

How do you know you're living in the end times? Or to put it another way, how was the quality of life in Sodom the day before the Lord firebombed the shit out of it?

So the Talmud says it was an evil place. It was a crime in Sodom to feed the hungry and clothe the naked. Beggars were given marked coins that no shop would accept. Welp. In the USA right now there are places where it's a crime to help homeless people. Plenty of stores don't accept food stamps. So are we in it? Do we have enough sense to get ourselves out if we are?

The day before the destruction, two migrants arrived in the city. Strange clothes, weird accents. No one wanted to help them. Except Lot, the last good man in Sodom. He'd seen his uncle Abraham welcoming strangers and he copied what he'd seen. Lot baked bread for the migrants and they ate it with oil and salt. They were hungry and ate quickly. He was sorry he didn't have more to offer. In the tent of his uncle

Abraham, guests might be greeted with roasted goat dripping with fat, fresh white cheese, fruits, and milk. But Abraham was an exceptionally wealthy man.

No one else helped them. Everything went on just as it had been. In Sodom on that day, there were comfortable beds filled with clean dry straw and sheep in the outer enclosures. There were vats of wine brewing and potters spinning their wheels and metalworkers tooling precious bronze. There is always a future to imagine until it is gone.

>> ***FoxInTheHenHouse* *is at*** **GoBagPrepped** ***status.***

@OneCorn: Friend, you're doing this in the wrong place. We rely on the teachings of Enoch here. This is better off in ntd/oldtestamentprophecy

>> ***OneCorn is at*** **Prepped To The Max** ***status.***

@FoxInTheHenHouse: That's the trouble, isn't it? Everyone has their lane. Stick to it. Never offer help to people in need of guidance or warm bread to hungry travelers.

>> *OneCorn is at* **Prepped To The Max** *status.*

As the sun sank low on the horizon and the shadows lengthened in the streets of Sodom, a crowd gathered around Lot's house. They'd seen strangers arrive. They didn't want to help them. They wanted to rape them.

I didn't invent this. It's in the Bible. Anyway you've read *The Road*.

You know Ballard. You've seen *Mad Max*. You know why we want guns and ammo, and a solid door on our bunkers. When society collapses, destructive desires come to the surface.

Outside Lot's house, the men made little crooning noises, hisses and chutting. Come on, Lot, we all saw them. Just let us in. No one will know. Our cocks are thirsty for some strange.

Lot tried to imagine what his uncle Abraham might do in this situation. Abraham had had a wisdom to him. And he'd welcomed guests.

Lot called through the door: "They are my *guests*. That is sacred."

The mob called back: "We're not going *anywhere*."

Then Lot said: "I've got two daughters in here, they're both virgins. They belong to me. Leave my guests alone, you can do what you want with the girls."

Well, that was what he came up with. To save his own neck, maybe. If you think no one ever gives up their teenage daughter now to gangs or mobs, you don't know much about humanity.

Lot's wife and his daughters don't get a name in the Bible because of course. So let's call the wife Edo, and the daughters Moa and Amma. The two sisters held each other's hands so tightly their bones might snap. Edo's heart cracked and oozed wild grief.

›› *GatheredHeart is at* KeepOnCanning *status.*

@OneCorn: I'm begging you, please leave us alone. There aren't even that many regular posters here. We just want to keep faithful to the teachings of Enoch without this filth.

›› *OneCorn is at* Prepped To The Max *status.*

@GatheredHeart: I've got news for you. These are the teachings of Enoch. He believed in interpreting the ancient books in new ways, OK? So that's what I'm doing.

The migrants looked at each other. There was a confirmation in that look: this is what they had heard about this place, this was not a surprise.

They stood up from the table.

One of them smiled an uncanny, radiant smile.

The other raised his hand.

And all the mob went blind.

I think we can imagine the family standing there like: what the fuck.

While the mob were coming to terms with their situation, the migrants said:

"Lot, this is not a normal set of events and we are not ordinary strangers. Your uncle Abraham knows the Lord Almighty, the Lord of Hosts. We are the Sabaoth who ride out in that army, do you get it? We are the riders before the storm. The future is on the way, my friend, and we are its augurs. The city you live in has been judged and condemned. Something bad is coming and you do not want to be here when it arrives. Gather your family and get the fuck out."

This is *about* pieces. It's *about* Fox and Rabbit. Sodom is literally the first marked environment. People specialize and forget the basic skills of knowing the land. They shut themselves off and won't invite strangers in. They believe fences not communities will keep them safe. Because in a city like Sodom you can be punished worse for being poor than for committing a murder.

›› OneCorn is at **Prepped To The Max** *status.*

In an amusing interlude, after all that, Lot ran to find his daughters' boyfriends and told them the whole thing. He was trying to save something for his girls, I guess.

But the fiancés were like: "You're funny, man."

So that's the answer to the question. You can literally be in a town where the Sabaoth just struck a mob blind and still not get it. They wouldn't leave.

When Lot got back, there was no time left. The migrants grabbed Lot, Edo, Moa, and Amma and teleported them outside the city. No kidding, that's in the Bible. Either that or they dragged them all the way out. Transportation, in any case, had been arranged. The augurs' job was to get them out.

On the outskirts of the city, the migrants got very close to the faces of Lot and Edo.

They said: "Flee for your fucking lives. Don't look back. Don't stop. Run into the hills. Now. Go. *Don't* look back."

Lot said: "Look, I'm a city dweller, *Homo urbanus*, you feel me? We're in the middle of the desert here. Can you not give us a ride to some city nearby like Tzoar?"

The messengers got so close to Lot that the heat from their eyes burned his skin. They said: "Just get out of our sight."

Potentially they also had some views about Lot having offered his daughters to the mob.

›› *ArturoMegadog is at* Shelf-Stable ***status.***

Come away now.

›› *OneCorn is at* Prepped To The Max ***status.***

This story belongs here, AM.

›› *ArturoMegadog is at* Shelf-Stable ***status.***

Tell me the truth. Are you drunk right now?

›› *OneCorn is at* Prepped To The Max ***status.***

Not very drunk.

›› *ArturoMegadog is at* Shelf-Stable ***status.***

Aha because they're messaging Daggoo to ban you? Because you've done this a lot here? And I'm the mod on your most-used board so they're asking my view.

The four travelers started to walk in the half-dark cool of the moments before sunrise. Each stone cast its long shadow, and the hillside seemed alive with bubbling black shapes, the very rocks chattering one to another. There was a squabbling feel to the air, wind aggravating wind, sand biting sand. The sound of sunrise was like the cawing of crows and their breath became thick in their throats. Something was coming. Something unnatural and obscene was happening. Something was falling from the sun in a screaming hurtling mass.

Amma and Moa interlaced their fingers. Amma would not allow Moa to stumble. Moa would not permit Amma to trip. Though the ground bucked like a donkey, they kept walking upward.

Edo, their mother, walked behind them, with Lot at the back. Edo did not have a partner, that much was clear. She walked alone and her husband, who had offered their daughters to the rapists, was no husband to her. Amma and Moa had each other. Lot—in his mind at least—had Abraham to guide him. Edo had no one. It's not possible to survive destruction alone. Edo looked back.

The whole plain was on fire. Rocks of black and burning matter shot from the sky as when a man hurls a spear at a gazelle, the animal looks back

›› *OneCorn is at* Prepped To The Max *status.*

I have a right to do this.

›› *ArturoMegadog is at* Shelf-Stable *status.*

They have a right to get you banned. You may not like the lanes, but we have lanes.

›› *ArturoMegadog is at* Shelf-Stable *status.*

I just also want to *point out* that you're going on this one-person mission to make a post *about* how no one survives alone. Seriously.

for a moment and the sharp metal tip pierces its eye and in that instant it springs from life to death, just so was the Lord hurling the clods of rock and fire at each house, and where each rock landed the mud and clay and brick and straw broke into flame. People ran screaming between the burning buildings trying to escape, but the sure aim of the Lord caught each one.

Edo tasted stone and fire. She knew the fury of God and she saw God's shame. If God wasn't ashamed of having done this, he should have been.

Her bones gave up their minerals into her blood and the water in her tissues leaped from her pores, and the potassium and sodium and magnesium in all the axons and dendrites of her brain poured forth, coating the inside of her skull with salt and licking her sinuses, crusting over at last the surface of her eyeballs with salt.

›› OneCorn is at* Prepped To The Max *status.

Can I just finish my thought? About *why* this is relevant to Enoch?

›› ArturoMegadog is at* Shelf-Stable *status.

Honey. I'll port the whole thing to a nice warm corner of ntd/strategic and you can carry on as long as you like.

›› OneCorn is at* Prepped To The Max *status.

Fine. But it does belong here. But fine.

extract from Name The Day survivalist forum

sub-board: ntd/strategic

›› *OneCorn is at* **Prepped To The Max** *status.*

OK, I'm going to tell you my best survival secret. It's in the story I just told but I guess the links aren't obvious to anyone but me so I'm going to spell it out.

You know what the theme of Genesis is? Men—mostly brothers—who hate each other. Cain and Abel, Isaac and Ishmael, Jacob and Esau, Joseph and his brothers, Abraham and Lot. You know *why* they hate each other? Every single time: one is a farmer and one is a hunter-gatherer. This was the teaching of Enoch, OK? That Genesis is about the stupidest thing human beings ever did. We ended our own world. We captured and domesticated ourselves.

Breaking it down:

CAIN: farmer	**ABEL:** wandered with sheep
JACOB: stayed home	**ESAU:** went out hunting
ISAAC: stayed home	**ISHMAEL:** sent to wander
JOSEPH: daddy's boy	**BROTHERS:** sold him to wandering Ishmaelites
LOT: lived in Sodom	**ABRAHAM:** wandered the desert

›› ***ArturoMegadog is at*** Shelf-Stable ***status.***

Huh. OK I guess that was relevant.

›› ***DanSatDan is at*** One Tin O'Beans ***status.***

@OneCorn: Look, sorry about before. I get that you're like . . . a big deal on /strategic. But seriously. How does this help me survive a human extinction event?

Same basic pattern again and again. They're not brothers, they're two groups of people. One group is settled, one group wanders. One lives basically a nomadic life, supplementing hunting with sheepherding. The other stays home and grows crops and farms livestock. The hunters hate the farmers and the farmers hate the hunters. The hunters think the farmers are weak and wily. The farmers think the hunters are brutish. They try to kill each other.

That book is about a war. The first great war. The war that lasted five thousand years and ended the world as all human beings had known it before. When the farmers won, they created a new future and we're living in it.

›› *IsmiIsmi is at* **Diggin' a Root Cellar** *status.*

Also. Elephant in the room. This is a story that's used to justify millennia of homophobia. This needed a CW.

›› *OneCorn is at* **Prepped To The Max** *status.*

Okay. I understand the concern about homophobia. My point here is that the "sin of Sodom" wasn't "men having consensual sex with other men." Men having consensual sex with other men is a) great and b) tbh Genesis doesn't seem to have a view on it so anyone who reads homophobia into it brought

PM: *Arturo Megadog → OneCorn*

Have you considered trying to sound less like you think you're the smartest one here?

it there themselves, probably from Leviticus which you'll notice I'm *not* defending. The problem with Sodom was that they'd forgotten the skills of creating a robust society.

Genesis, in particular, is a record of what it was like to survive the last ice age and to move from hunting and gathering to agriculture. Genesis is the last book we have of stories passed down by people who survived our most recent extinction events. It'll tell you shit about canning and rifle maintenance. It'll tell you what kind of society and what sort of values we're gonna need to survive.

So it's about: welcoming strangers, caring for the members of society who have nothing. Not thinking just about your own needs.

The problem with Sodom was that it was a city, and cities were, at least on a survival level, a really stupid idea. In some ways they're great: new food, music and art, new perspectives, making babies outside your narrow genetic group. But cities did then what they do now: they made people richer but more divided from each other, increasingly specialized and disconnected from the natural world. Cities couldn't sustain themselves.

The people who wrote Genesis were deeply troubled. They saw that the

PM: ***OneCorn → ArturoMegadog***

But I am the smartest one here. Apart from you, OK.

PM: ***OneCorn → ArturoMegadog***

I think I should take a break from NTD though. They got under my skin today.

PM: ***ArturoMegadog → OneCorn***

Noooo. Don't leave me here with this bunch of idiots.

skills of living well by walking the land and learning how to hunt and what to gather were disappearing. They saw the future we live in coming. The story of Sodom is a story of terror. These cities: don't trust them. They will all come crashing down.

PM: ***OneCorn → ArturoMegadog***

Hah! OK, I'll set an alert if you do a post.

martha

[illegible] big castle

[illegible] Martha [illegible]

[illegible] ery potatoes, [illegible] for treats [illegible]
men [illegible] tended [illegible] finding under [illegible]
and she thought: You [illegible] take much [illegible]
a being [illegible]. One companion, one animal [illegible]
Someone to clean up your [illegible] anything you [illegible]
When she came to the [illegible]
[illegible]

[illegible] you'd like it [illegible] risk is the [illegible]
[illegible] across the [illegible] Martha [illegible]

1. guinea pig castle

Conversions, as Martha Einkorn knew well, happen in many ways. Sometimes it occurs to you day by day, hour by hour, like the sun slowly rising inside your mind that something needs to change. Sometimes there is a sudden insight, as natural as falling in love, a striking realization that, ah, I've been wrong all this time. Sometimes these two things happen at once. That is what had happened to Martha several years before she met Lai Zhen.

It was in that part of Martha's life when she was numb most of the time. Working hard with Lenk on Fantail. Long hours, early starts, and late nights. That time when she thought she could fulfill all her social needs via various online message boards and by keeping a couple of pet guinea pigs in a luxury three-level wooden guinea pig castle with twelve separate hiding places, which took up most of the floor space in her second living room. She watched the simple furry potatoes snuffling for treats, eating from their carefully tended grass boxes, hiding under blankets, and she thought: You see, it doesn't take much to make a being happy. One companion, some animal comforts. Someone to clean up your shit and bring you treats.

When she came to think of it later, everything that happened with Zhen had been prefigured by what happened with ArturoMegadog. Even guinea pigs want to connect with other guinea pigs. Humans are driven to reach out to each other. If something hasn't gone terribly wrong with us, we let people into our houses and our lives and maybe even our beds, if we're that way inclined. Despite the risks. The greatest risk, of course, is that you'll like it. The greatest risk is that it'll change you. Still. Drive across the castle drawbridge, Martha. Risk it.

2. a million beautiful things

extract from Name The Day survivalist forum

sub-board: ntd/strategic

>> ArturoMegadog is at **BunkerBorn** *status.*

I don't even know why I'm posting this.

It's late at night and I'm drunk. I've set this to auto-delete in three hours.

I tell you what I've realized. Most of you are idiots and those who aren't idiots are monomaniacs and within that there's a tiny group who care about anything worth caring about. And they're not enough to turn the ship around. They're not even enough to keep it from going more off course. I don't even think I'm necessarily one of those people. There's not much in my life that makes it worth it. So I'm done. With life.

For the longest time I thought human beings were *good*, we were getting smarter, there was a progress—slow of course, sliding back too. But inch by inch, like a man pulling himself forward using only his tongue, we were moving toward the light. That's why I got into prepper stuff. Because I thought humanity had good things that were worth saving. Art

>> Semadon is at **Shelf-Stable** ***status.***

Is anyone else seeing this? I'm reposting this to NTD main. Does anyone know ArturoMegadog personally? Anyone know where he lives, how to find him?

and literature, morality and kindness, scientific progress, understanding, a caterpillar inching toward the sun.

I said I was drunk.

Anyway, I don't think that anymore. The human race isn't getting any better, we're just getting different and *more* and faster and if you're not getting better then more and faster is just the same as getting worse.

I want to tell you about my husband. I'll call him Ted. *He* made me believe in goodness. He was so virtuous it made you sick. He worked for a car company—started on the shop floor, ended up running the team in San Francisco. He pressured them to put more investment into electric cars, and he spent every weekend doing beach cleanup, he volunteered as a Big Brother. Disgusting. I fly a private plane. I wanted to go flying and watch TV on the weekend and he was sending me photos of an urban garden he'd planted at 5 a.m.

Ted was crazy hopeful. I know how it sounds now. But I remember there was that blip in 2020 when the Saudi oil prices went negative—you couldn't pay someone to take oil off your hands and I thought: Fuck maybe Ted's right. This is it. The start of something.

We've spent the past century hiding under our blankets while the red notices piled up in the hallway, ARREARS: Habitat Destruction and

›› *Semadon is at* Shelf-Stable *status.*

OK. I've scraped everything I can from ArturoMegadog's info, which is nothing. Male. 50s. Bay Area. Usually on at erratic times of day—suggests he doesn't have a job with fixed hours. Can anyone wake an admin and get more? I've called emergency services in the Bay Area but they can't do anything unless we give them an address or at least a name.

Extinction, DO NOT IGNORE: Social Inequality, PAY NOW OR FACE CONSEQUENCES: Climate Change. And us going "Hey if we shuffle things around, move that balance onto this card, work out how to frack shale and ignore the *flammable water* coming out of the taps then we can buy a new car and brim it with gasoline and things will be OK for another month."

And I thought, with this pandemic we're gonna realize we just have to be *sensible*. Unlike the dinosaurs, we don't need to get hit by an asteroid. I know it's a joke now. "Nature is healing." Believing things could get better is just a joke, right?

Ted and I were living in an apartment on the waterfront and I was holding a cup of coffee in my hand, when I started to believe it could be OK. I think about that all the time now. The mist on the surface of the bay like something solid, like you could put your hand out and pick it up. The smell of the coffee, the hum of the refrigerator. The blank blue chalk of the sky with no planes. I thought, it's really going to be OK.

I sat on the couch and started crying. Ted came running through, he thought my uncle Benny must have gotten the virus and I said: Ted, we should have a child. We'd talked about it a million times.

Look it doesn't matter really. None of it matters. One day the stars are going

›› Wipsy is at* FriendInNeed *status.

I know we're not supposed to say, but I'm friends IRL with Daggoo who set up the board. I'm calling him now. Hope everyone agrees this is a good reason to break our usual protocol.

This post has received 271 thumbs-up. Congratulations! You made a gold-star post!

to wink out one by one like in that Arthur C. Clarke story, and before that the sun will go supernova and boil the seas and we're just one stinking species and species live and die, that's what we do. There'll be no audience and no final judgment and no redeemer is going to liveth and no one will come along at the end of the show and tell us our score and what we could have won. No one will remember the human race or the USA or San Francisco or the apartment or me or Ted or how when I dropped that yellow mug a few months later he turned it into a mosaic of the sun. No one remembers that now but me.

Ted was older than me, he'd worked for the same company for thirty-eight years. He had these plans for his retirement and his pension. We were going to travel to one of the protected FutureSafe islands and work there with wildlife and ecosystem preservation. And after that, when Ted's niece Gracie was done with her PhD she wanted to carry a child for us. My child. From my frozen jizz, and Ted's family genes. We were going to support Gracie through her postdoc years and we were going to be a beautiful San Francisco logical family.

Then Ted's company got bought up by Fantail. They got a special fire-sale deal because it was an old company and hadn't turned a great profit for a decade, so they didn't have to honor

›› *Daggoo is at* God *status. Daggoo has turned off thumbs-up.*

Hi everyone. I'm in contact with first responders in the Bay Area. ArturoMegadog has been very cautious so we don't have much to go on. He did not lodge a real name, home address, or phone number with us. He uses a proxy server. I have pinged the email address used to register with the site,

the pensions. Everyone thought Lenk Sketlish was kind of a great guy for taking that company on. He wanted it for his Hertha electric cars; he wanted the stuff that Ted had made, basically.

The thing I have to say here is that I'm rich, OK? I'm stinking goddamn rich and we didn't need the goddamn pension money. I told Ted that. He knew. We would be fine living on my money for the rest of our lives. We'd still have our home, our plans, we'd still have our child.

But it broke Ted's heart. All those years with that same company, old school, the loyalty. And the staff he'd convinced to stay on, they weren't getting pensions either and most of them were laid off with nothing. I have enough to protect us but I couldn't solve everything for sixteen hundred people. I said we'd help them fight, we'd do something. But eight days after the announcement, when he was driving out to the wetland project, he had a heart attack behind the wheel and he died. He was fifty-nine.

Maybe I should mention I've taken a bunch of pills. There's stuff in the cabinets from when Ted fucked his back up and my root canal and some of our sedatives from when we had our colonoscopies because we wanted to be so careful, we were going to be parents. I just took everything.

It's two years now since he died.

but it looks like it was a throwaway. If anyone is a friend of ArturoMegadog, please speak up urgently.

›› Wipsy is at* FriendInNeed *status.

I'm looking through ArturoMegadog's posts. Four weeks ago he said a store "literally eight paces" from his door carries shelf-stable kimchi, "Firepit" brand. It's only stocked in seven stores in the Bay Area.

That gives us seven map dots to work on.

I don't know if this is a cry for help. Probably? I guess if it wasn't I'd have set this to post in like, two days, when whatever I've taken will have done whatever it's going to do. But the way you guys talk, it's like you think your lives are worth saving and let me tell you, if Ted wasn't worth saving then no one is. The species is going to die. Just let it.

Life will try something different and maybe it doesn't matter if it's smart enough to read and write and release greenhouse gases. There'll be fish and birds and glittering insects, there'll be a million beautiful things crawling over one another striving toward the sun.

We haven't invented a single thing, you know. We've come up with busywork for ourselves and the plants and animals, more and more ideas of new ways to be comfortable and to have things at hand.

But all the important things were here before us and they'll be here after us. The animals love each other. They strive and they have pleasure, they relax in the sun and they take comfort in one another, they hate and they take revenge. Animals love their children.

If you think you want more than that you're just kidding yourselves. We have terminal arrogance and the

›› ***ClarkeKent is at*** **One Can O'Beans** ***status.***

OK nothing in the Concord dot is residential. He'd have to be sleeping in Bed Bath and Beyond.

›› ***SandysDad is at*** **Stockpiled** ***status.***

He said he's stinking rich. Therefore rule out the store in Redwood City.

sooner we're wiped out the better it'll be. So I'm starting with myself.

And if the rest of you could stop trying so hard to survive and encourage all the other humans to do the same, then that'd be better for the planet. But in the end it doesn't matter because the planet will sort its shit out, it's survived more than us. And we're all going to be stardust before long anyway, and then the universe will die and there never was much worth hoping for.

I think I'm starting to feel it now. My feet and my fingertips are tingling. I'm going to lie down. I'm going to look at photos of Ted until I fall asleep. I don't think I'll be with him or any of that bullcrap. But I won't be here anymore. Bye.

>> ***OneCorn is at*** Prepped To The Max ***status.***

ArturoMegadog and I are friends on the board. Never met in person, no address or real name. But I know he lives near water, in San Francisco. Three of your dots would match that.

>> ***Wipsy is at*** FriendInNeed ***status.***

I'm nowhere near the Bay Area. Is anyone there who could walk around, see if they can see or hear anything?

>> ***OneCorn is at*** Prepped To The Max ***status.***

We're running out of time. I'm going to try something.

3. a broken world

Every extreme contains its opposite. Martha had seen this again and again. A forum full of sovereign individuals who've never even met in person can, by that fact, feel free to become a deeply interconnected community. Meanwhile a backwoods cult of conformity turns people inward, to the secret thoughts and the inner strengths they cannot share with others. The more Enoch wanted Martha to become an unalienable part of his kingdom, the more he had driven her to rely only and always on herself. He never understood this; that was part of his tragedy.

There had been a day when Martha was fourteen when her father, Enoch, had driven her in the jeep out past the green acres across wild country. He'd spoken in his low, insistent, constant voice about his theory of "pieces." As they rolled through the open country—miles of forest and grassland, creeks tumbling down the hillside, dense tangles of thicket—Martha had noted each landscape and each wild creature she saw, and she kept a note in her own mind of his sermon too, knowing she might be called on to remember and recite the texts her father mentioned or to recall a flicker seen on the wing between the trees and tell which way it was heading.

The theory of pieces was the center of Enoch's thinking—gleaned from wide reading, for Enoch was nothing if not a learned man—that the world had fallen from a beautiful and united whole into mere shards. He saw evidence of his theory in the Bible and the story of the tower of Babel and the one language cast into many. He saw it, too, in the breaking up of the great forests of Europe and the Americas, in the dissolving of the great faiths into one splintered faction after another, in the division of the states of the union against each other. Martha knew the proof texts and the verses, but she knew, too, that Enoch would have some new text to teach—in this case the sephirot of the Kabbalah, the broken shards of light that have entered the world.

"The world we live in," Enoch said, "is made to be whole and it is we who divide and subdivide it. Turning the great lands into fields, turning the earth into countries, naming and renaming, subdividing down to the microbe—why, we even split the atom, and didn't that terrible force teach us what was wrong there, weren't we warned off? Do you have an answer for me, Martha, why weren't we warned?"

His face was red-raw under his sparse beard. Martha knew that there was no answer and the best thing to do was to shake her head. She had heard this speech before but she was always impressed by it. He had shown her photographs of the devastating effects of the atomic bomb and explained to her that this had come about because of mankind's obsessive journey away from God and toward fragmentation. The righteous, he said, were shown by their need to come together, to build communities, to act against entropy as life always does if it is lived correctly.

"You need to pee?" he said. Martha nodded. It had been more than two hours of driving on broken roads, and her soda bottle was clattering, empty, between her feet.

Enoch pulled into the gravel on the side of the road. He waited at the wheel and she took herself modestly fifty paces from the jeep, made sure she was well hidden behind a line of trees, pulled down her jeans and her underwear, and let her stream of piss go, steaming and almost pleasantly fragrant, a smell of baking to it.

The first she knew was Enoch shouting: "You're a good kid, Martha," and before he'd even finished his sentence, she understood what he was planning.

She called out, "Dad!" and tried to look around the tree, to meet his eyes, but she just toppled over and landed hard on her hands.

Enoch called out, "You're not a fragment. You'll find your way."

As Martha watched, he kicked the jeep into motion and drove away, the tires wailing on the blacktop.

At first Martha tried to chase him. Pulled her underwear and her jeans half up. Stumbled, piss still streaming down her thigh, out onto the blacktop and shouted, "Wait! Stop!"

She cried, without intending to cry. In desolation and sudden stabbing fear like a wire in her throat. She had nothing with her. Not her knife, not her ball of twine. On her feet she wore sneakers, not boots. She had a jacket but not a warm one. It was past two in the afternoon and a chilly October day.

After a few minutes of crying she stopped herself, because she knew what this was. Enoch had talked about it often. People had to be tested as the potter tests a vessel in the kiln. Those who were driven to fragment would spin off, but those who were made to be part of the wholeness of things would find their way to their right place. He'd said it to the Enochites in prayer meeting and at study time and in the long sermons that lasted through the night. This wasn't hard, Martha, not really hard. She was a constituent of the world, not a broken piece, and she would find her way home.

So. They had driven for two hours but not in a straight line. They had looped and turned back on themselves. She didn't know this road, but the sun was ahead, so that was west. There were four and a half hours of daylight left. She was fat but her body was strong and she could cover a mile in fourteen minutes at a loping jog. Enoch would not have set her an impossible task and he would not have left her here to die. She spooled the journey out in her mind. She knew the mountains to the east, she knew the lay of the ridge, she knew the redwood grove to the south, and she knew, yes, she absolutely knew, which way was home. It was through the woods to the north. It was no more than twenty miles at the outside. She would be home for dinner. She set off at an easy pace, the fallen leaves crisp under her feet.

She'd gone seven miles before she knew that the bear had caught her scent.

Martha knew bears. At the compound they shot and ate a bear most years, bear-grease-fried potatoes tasting mushroomy and woody, acorns and musk. Once she'd watched three cubs playing on the far side of the creek for three hours, tumbling over one another, splashing and showing their sharp little teeth. She knew how to tell that a bear was busy with its nose. On the ridge ahead of her and to the right, maybe a quarter-mile distant, a skinny black bear was tasting the air with its raised nose. Head tipped to one side, it was considering her.

The bears around their compound never gave the Enochites any trouble. Enochites never fed bears, never left garbage in open cans. The bears knew who was boss and knew that they'd find better and easier food in the river than in Enochite trash. But this was a thin bear in October. A thin bear that, as she looked, she saw was favoring its front right foot. It was hungry. It was getting close to hibernation time and it had no layer of fat to get through the winter. A desperate bear. And this wasn't the Enochites' fifteen thousand green acres; this was land owned by the people of the Babble. Who knew what this bear had gotten a taste for?

Martha swung her arms and legs, crunching on the

ground. She started to sing, a song Enoch had written about the glories of the world. She walked straight on, not to the left or to the right, not directly toward the bear but not away from it. Martha walked confidently straight toward the ridge. Straight past the bear. Two predators going about their own business, not giving each other any trouble.

The bear watched her go. And after a minute of thought, the bear followed her.

It was not dark yet, but the sun was noticeably lower in the sky. Martha walked on. Down a gentle valley slope and up the other side. Through a clearing where the light was bright—the bear stuck to the shadows, matching her pace for pace. The time had gone when Martha could convince herself the bear was just curious. This bear was hunting her.

Not to run was the important thing. Not to run and not to attack. She was still a human. There was still light in the sky. The bear was hungry but not yet hungry enough to be stupid. She could still make it home.

She came to a track in the woodland. Scuffed-down earth where vehicles had passed. To the east there were two timber cabins, probably hunters' places only used in season. No lights anyway, no one home. Martha hesitated. She could go to one of those cabins now. Break a window. Hide until morning; the bear would likely be gone. But that would be using the tools of the Babble. Taking advantage of the unfair gifts of the unfree world. Still, wouldn't she also be using her wits to survive? Enoch would never see, would never know. She could say she'd spent the night in a tree.

The corner of her eye caught silent motion. The bear—no, but it was from the left—another bear? Martha was suddenly afraid. Her breath came in short pants. The only thought in her mind was the last one—a tree. The bear had a sore front foot—it wouldn't climb well. She scanned the forest around her. Found a tree with branches dipping low to the ground. Jumped, caught one, twisted her body onto it, hauled herself up so she sat astride it—don't think, Martha, keep moving. She stood up, supported herself on the trunk, found a foothold, climbed a branch higher, then another. Now she was fifteen or twenty feet off the ground. Only then did she see what the motion was.

A large slow-moving truck—the front smashed inward, the driver's window cracked—was groaning along the dirt track. Its lights were blazing. Martha could not even see the bear that had stalked her. The truck pulled to a stop almost at the base of her tree. The people inside couldn't see her. In any case, they were going about their own business.

It was a man and a woman; he was larger than her but scrawny. She was tall, with broad shoulders and acne around the edges of her face, and her nails were painted silver, fawn, pink, gold, and peach.

"Here?" she said.

"What the fuck else are we here for?" he said.

"On the dirt?"

"On the hood if you're so damn fussy."

The woman made a gesture with her shoulder and her mouth, a flicker of her eyelids that seemed to Martha to say "Fine." She leaned over the hood of the truck, and the man quickly pulled down her pantyhose and her underwear and started to do something to her that Martha had—at that time—neither heard about nor seen before.

Martha watched the woman's perfect nails moving back and forth on the hood of the car. She couldn't tell whether he was killing her or pleasing her, whether he was giving her something or taking something away. She looked at the nails. They were the most perfect thing there. The truck was old and damaged, the man and woman seemed to have no joy in each other, and their clothes were cheap and dirty. But each of those fingernails was colored like a miniature picture of a sunset. Gold and silver and auburn and russet, they were entire worlds to themselves, glorious like the sun over Eden on the sixth day of creation.

When their business was done—it did not take long—the woman looked peacefully at her nails while the man rummaged in the trunk for a lighter. The woman was engaged by the shards of color, looking at each nail in turn, comparing the first to the second and the second to the fourth. And Martha thought: Oh yes, of course. Yes, I see. Fragments. Pieces. Pieces is what these people have. There is nothing whole for them, but these tiny fractured chips of color are enough. Martha thought: You never taught me this, Enoch, that the pieces can be enough to comfort in a broken world.

She did think of asking the man and the woman for help. Of coming down from the tree and saying: "I'm lost in the woods. I come from the Enochite compound. Can you give me a ride back?" But then she thought of what her father would say if she arrived back in this truck with the people of the Babble, and the words caught in her throat. She sat in the tree while they smoked cigarettes and drove away. She watched them go. And when they were gone, it was evening and she was in a tree and a hungry bear was circling.

The bear was in the dark of the forest and Martha in the dark of the tree. She had no light and she had no weapon. By the faint fading light in the edges of the sky, she saw the bear draw closer. If she fell asleep, she would tumble and the bear would catch her and she would make a meal worth many days of hunting. The darker it became, the better the bear would see. Use what you have now, Martha. Watch.

Enoch had taught her the skills of silent watching.

"This is what they fuck up for themselves with television, Martha," he'd told her. "This is what they destroy. Humans were made for watching. We can read God's book in the world, but we must learn to be silent and still. Things on television come too quick, too many, and too obvious. We were made to stare at the embers of a dying fire for hours. To watch an animal. To look at how the water runs down a hillside until we can see the way to change the river's course with one day's work. Don't make your mind impatient—make it still."

She opened her mind to the bear in the shadow of the tree across from her. Hungry bear, thin bear, limping bear, desperate, frightened bear. Why haven't you eaten this season, bear? Even a sore paw was not enough to explain it. At first all she saw was fear—her fear, the bear's fear. She allowed her thoughts to quiet. What do you see, Martha?

The bear stood on four paws at the edge of the forest. It walked forward and back a pace or two. It sniffed the air. It was reassuring itself she was still there. It sat back a little. Again and again it tipped its head and popped its jaw. She looked more closely at the bear. This was a juvenile—only three or four years old—and it didn't know much about humans, but it could tell she was alone. It rubbed its head against the trunk of the tree. She hadn't seen that gesture before, a long rub against one side of the jaw. Like a cat. What was it doing? The way it held its head, at an angle. She squinted through the dark. They were at a tipping point now—soon the bear would be able to see better than Martha could.

It was because she was watching so intently that she saw it when the bear yawned. The yawn was slow and then rapid—a gargling sound, its tongue sticking out and then the jaw opening and snapping shut. But not so fast that Martha hadn't seen the inside of its mouth.

The teeth were black and rotten; the jaw was infected so badly that Martha thought the bone might already be close to snapping. This was a bear that could not eat, for all it yearned to. Its stomach must be aching with hunger. It could kill her with a swipe of its huge paw and not be able to take a bite of her body. This thought more than anything galvanized her. She would die and this bear would still starve. There would be no entry into the oneness of things here; her death would not nourish. This was when she saw the second thing: that even in the world of nature there are "pieces." The parts do not fit together into a perfect whole. There is no such perfection available.

Then, here in the half dark, it was time.

Martha chose a sturdy, half-broken branch above her and hauled her weight on it to break it. She hooked one arm around the trunk for balance and heaved with the other until it snapped. Now she had a cudgel. The bear watched her with hungry interest. It must be yearning for meat. She lowered herself gently down from her seat. One branch down. Two branches down. Now she was within reach. The bear appeared to turn away. That was the first sign of danger. It walked to the left. Out of sight, behind a thicket of bushes. Hold your nerve, Martha. Hold strong. She gripped her cudgel with both hands. The bear will try to attack from an invisible position. She waited. She counted her breaths.

When it came, it was pounding on four feet from the right. Its head was down, it moved quickly, so quickly, and it was almost on her before she knew it was coming. Martha focused only on its eyes, on the point of its snout, not to think about the claws or the weight of it. She gripped her cudgel, and as the bear barraged its big body toward her, she whirled the stick around and thwacked it hard in the jaw.

By the sound, she knew at once that she had broken that rotten jaw. A soggy crack and the bear's howl. It fell back onto the ground, its muzzle dug into the soft earth as if to find some respite. It was keening.

Martha climbed back up two branches, three, to see whether the bear would come for her again, maddened and vengeful. It lay on the sodden earth for perhaps a quarter of an hour and then, head hung low, it dragged its bones painfully westward, away down the path. Martha watched it go. It was shuddering, its fur spiked in pain. She waited until the track was silent.

She slept that night in a hunter's lodge but—so as not to shame herself in front of the spirit of Enoch—she curled on the dirt floor and not on the bed. She wondered whether somewhere in the forest the bear was lying in the same earth, waiting for its time.

The next day Enoch welcomed her home with little fanfare. An arm around her shoulders.

"I knew you would," he said. "It was easy, wasn't it?"

She told the story of the bear, and the younger children were impressed.

Zachariah said: "When I become a man I'm gonna fight *two* bears."

She took the jeep out a couple days later with a rifle, trying to find the bear and end its misery. But it was gone, hidden in the mystery of the forest.

Martha felt, at that time, proud—that her story would be a source of inspiration for the others, that she would lead them in their faith and show the truth of Enoch's teachings.

She did not tell the story of the man and the woman and what they had done on the hood of the truck. But whenever she thought of the bear in later years, she thought also of the sunset nails, of the perfect fragments of color. She thought—though she never told Enoch—of how the sight of those small pieces had given her a certain sense of wonder and beauty too. She knew she had glimpsed something that could not be reconciled yet, and was waiting for the great revelation that might bring her own teaching into the world.

4. the unbearable impossibility of going it alone

On a street in downtown San Francisco, the closed eyes of the sleeping houses faced the bay. A red fox with black socks crossed the road, looked at the shuttered artisanal grocery store, and turned away, going about its own business. A light flicked on in an upstairs window. There would be fog tomorrow as there was always fog tomorrow. At 1:48 a.m., Martha Einkorn's car pulled up to the address she had procured by certain means.

She had tried to phone ArturoMegadog sixteen times as she drove across the bridge, but he wasn't answering. If she was wrong and her methods had failed, she might be about to wake up a family, and there was always a tiny possibility she could get shot. Still, she didn't think she was wrong.

She rang the bell three times, hoping that a groggy, embarrassed man would answer. She'd gotten here fast—she was surprised how fast. She was usually a slow, meticulous planner, and maybe being there meant she cared about ArturoMegadog in a way she hadn't allowed herself to understand before. He was the person she'd spoken to most on the forum over the past couple of years, and even though they knew little about each other personally, they knew a lot of each other's minds. She'd known he hated Lenk Sketlish but not why. When they'd spoken privately, she'd had a little thrill reading his vitriol.

No answer to the bell. Well, here we go.

At the side of the house she could see a lit window. She pushed open the side gate. She should have called an ambulance, should have called the police, but she didn't

100 percent *know* it was this house, and saying why she was almost certain would just have opened up all sorts of questions.

When she got around to the back of the house, it was clear no one here was going to shoot her. She peered in through the window, looking with the gaze Enoch had taught her. Look patiently, and everything will reveal itself. The room was messy. She wouldn't have imagined that from ArturoMegadog's meticulous messages and intense internet security. Dark wood furnishings. Books and papers everywhere. An expensive coffee maker with empty mugs higgledy-piggledy around it. A battered oxblood leather couch. Heavy silver models of planes on the mantel shelf. A man lying on the couch, vaguely familiar, but she couldn't quite place him. He had a belly and a beard; he looked kind of peaceful, like he just fell asleep. If asked, she'd have imagined ArturoMegadog as a six-foot-seven Norwegian architect type with rimless glasses. Why do we imagine that the outsides match the inside? Why is that so hard to give up?

She rapped her knuckles hard on the glass. Last chance for him to wake up. But there were empty pill bottles lined up carefully on the carved teak coffee table, like he'd taken each bottle in order.

She tried the handle of the back door tentatively. If it didn't open, she'd call the cops—yes, she'd do it then. She'd say she was out for a walk on the bay and heard a sound. But the mechanism opened smoothly beneath her hand. Right, OK. What would a normal person do now? Her breathing was fast, and too many images crowded into her brain too quickly. Survival courses, and first aid courses, and her dad saying if you call the ambulance, they'll inject you with a tracker, they mark you for the Babble that way, Martha. Too much internal soup to wade through. Check his breathing.

She put her face close to ArturoMegadog. Still breathing. Rasping, unhealthy sounding, so slow she thought he'd stopped completely, and then he drew one more. Close to, he smelled unpleasantly of chemicals—something he'd taken was coming out in his sweat. She rubbed her knuckle up and down his chest bone desperately. Nothing. His breaths were more and more shallow now.

She levered his mouth open, the jaw soft and unresisting. Without allowing herself to think too much about it, she pushed her index and middle fingers into his mouth, down his throat. His body convulsed but nothing came up. His mouth was sticky and his breath smelled. She went in again, pointing her fingers sharply. Martha jabbed the back of the man's throat, wiggling her fingers as she did so.

And it all came up. In four rapid gushes like an ejaculation or a baby sliding from the cervix covered in mucus and blood. Half-eaten pizza and pills still visible amid slimy, half-dissolved lurid pink and yellow capsules and foamy liquid, a tide of beer and acid. Martha pulled her hand back as the man ejected his own death onto the thick, deep rug in the study. She counted him drawing thirteen deep breaths, and another huge gush poured out of him like a slot machine with a winning combination.

The man looked up at her with cloudy eyes. Oh, that face. The ruddy cheeks and the mournful lines pulling at the corners of his mouth. She'd seen him a thousand times. She knew who he was now and that she would not be able to conceal who she was.

"God," he said. "Shit."

She brought him a couple of towels from the bathroom, a glass of water. He was groggy but conscious.

"You want me to call an ambulance?" she asked as he sipped the water. He shook his head.

"My insurance is fucked if they know I did this. The

company will have me committed. They'd love that." He tried to focus on her face. "Who are you? I know you. Who are you?"

She said: "I'm OneCorn."

"No. I've seen you. We've been at . . . parties. You're . . . Martha Einkorn. Oh no—OneCorn. Jesus." An infinity of calculations behind his eyes. Good, that would keep him awake.

"Get out," he said, his voice just a croaking whisper. "Get out of my house."

"No," said Martha, and made him a coffee.

He looked at the mug as if she'd pissed in it.

"The last good person in Sodom," he whispered, with contempt.

"Fucking drink some coffee," she said, "and where are more towels? I want to clean up your puke."

He pointed down the corridor: "Laundry room. Last door on the right before the garden room. I don't want you to clean anything."

"I'm going to wait with you and I don't like the smell of puke. OK?"

"I don't need you."

She said: "I know who you are."

"Yeah?"

"You're Albert Dabrowski."

Albert Dabrowski, ousted founder of Medlar, stared at Martha. His body was shaking and something strange was happening with his right eye—it kept softly closing of its own accord.

He sipped his coffee, looking at her with a baleful eye. She mopped up the puke and threw the towels into the washer. Albert watched her. He moved at one point to get down on his hands and knees, but she looked at him and said, "No." He moved back onto the sofa.

There began to be light at the edges of the world.

"Another fucking day," said Albert, so quietly Martha didn't know whether he'd wanted her to hear or not.

"I'm going to message the forum," she said. "They're still looking for you."

He handed her his thinscreen. He'd pulled up the long conversation they'd had about Lot and Sodom online.

"This you?" he said.

"Yeah."

"Fuck," said Albert Dabrowski. "I defended you! I told them to listen to you. I was your friend."

"I'm still that person."

"You belong to Lenk Sketlish. I don't know who you are."

5. a sharp crunch

Martha Einkorn had met Lenk Sketlish twenty years earlier, at a party in the hills at the tail end of the credit crunch.

She had been working as an administrator in tech for the best part of a decade, since losing the floral dresses, starting her life over, and getting her education. She was familiar with high-pressure environments centered around a charismatic leader with a vision of the future most other people couldn't understand. She was practiced at keeping her head amid the chaos, doing what needed to be done. She was perfectly suited to a life in tech start-ups and she went to a lot of parties like this one.

One of the venture capitalist investors in GardenGlow, the start-up she was working for, had brought her to this particular party. GardenGlow was going down the tubes: burn rate too high, subscriptions too low—that was how most start-ups ended. But Dean, the VC, had been impressed by Martha, told her she was the only good thing in a bad company. So he took her to a party with "a bunch of founders, interesting people" and she understood that was about introducing her to entrepreneurs and finding her next position. Seek and go find.

Martha was drawn to the kitchen by the sound of shouting. That was what you got from growing up Enochite—run toward the trouble. It took her a few seconds to understand the situation. The host was shouting at the caterer. The caterer was trying to defend herself. And at the edge of the room, his long body tense and half leaning against the counter, was Lenk Sketlish. He did not look like a man who was comfortable at a party.

Lenk watched the argument like a tuning fork, vibrating.

The host shouted: "This is unacceptable. Everyone will hear about this. Believe me, I know people."

From the corner of a box on the kitchen island, a thin line of blood trickled down the side of the counter. Lenk watched the red meandering rivulet like a cat watches a mousehole.

Martha knew Lenk Sketlish by sight. She scanned the technology news every day and Fantail was big business. They'd taken their first huge funding round, more than $300 million. His board was trying to lever him out. He was tall and lean and twenty-eight years old, prone to sudden rage, as tightly wound as a mousetrap. Everyone wanted to know whether Lenk Sketlish could hold his business together.

Lenk was staring at the box. The dribble of blood had almost reached the floor.

The host was shouting. "What kind of idiot are you? I said *prepared*, ready for the barbecue! Outdoor life. That's the theme! New England seasonal outdoor barbecue, ready to *grill*."

Why was no one looking in the box?

Martha lifted the lid.

Two dozen dead rabbits, stretched along the length of the box, all intact. Whiskers and fur, paws and claws, dead black eyes rimmed with blood. Stacked neatly, like a mass grave.

The party host said: "Someone just needs to deal with this mess."

The caterer said: "The hygiene license states—"

They were good rabbits and not yet even quite cold. Someone in the woods had likely shot fifty this afternoon and sent only the best dozen to this party.

Martha said: "I can prep them for you."

The host said: "Who the hell are you?"

Martha introduced herself, keeping Lenk Sketlish in the corner of her eye as he kept her in the corner of his. There was something mesmerizing about him. She thought: I know you. I know this feeling.

Martha took a knife from the block, wrapped the first rabbit in a thick dishcloth, nicked the skin, and found the neck bones with the edge of her blade. Worked the edge through the vertebrae. Put all her weight on the back of the knife. With a sharp crunch the head separated from the body.

"I'm gonna be sick," said a woman's voice. "I am serious, I'm gonna barf."

Martha said: "Tip your head back, gulp air in."

She cut the four paws off swiftly. One, two, three, four: crunch, crunch went the knife, crunch squish.

The room had become very silent.

Someone said: "Not so lucky for the rabbit," but there was no answering laugh.

Martha opened the abdomen delicately but quickly and pulled out the viscera. Her dad would have used them for stew. It's an insult to the animal, he'd said, not to use every part. She wondered whether the host would let her take the hearts home, and how he'd look at her if she asked. She felt that, for a moment, she was back in the woods, checking the traps and breaking the backs of the animals and hurling the steaming guts to the dogs. That she had never left Enoch at all and all her life since then had been a dream.

There was a round of applause when she finished the first rabbit and presented it as they might have seen at the butcher's, a product of the plastic world of illusion, not the real earth of muck and blood and disorder and death. They were impressed but—she could tell—a little repulsed. Except for Lenk Sketlish. He was alive as a plucked string. She had the sudden instinct that if she'd thrown him the rabbit's heart, he'd have caught it in his teeth and been her hound forever.

Someone drew breath to speak. She knew they were going to say, "Where did you learn that?" but Lenk Sketlish stole the breath from their lungs. He said: "Can you teach me?"

The host sent them into the garden. It was dead winter, as cold as it gets in the valley. Lenk nicked the bowel of the first rabbit he tried, the thick scent of shit rising in their steam-cloud breath, and Lenk said, "Oh fuck" and his knife slipped and he cut the nail of his left index finger almost through. They washed the wound together—like a mother with a child, like a new lover. She held his hand to steady it, showing him how to keep his knife constantly moving, pushing in and moving on, again and again.

She had read this about him—that he had some fascination with backwoods skills. It had made her laugh at the time because, yeah, a lot of rich people want to pretend to be poor people. Or comfort themselves that they could live like poor people if they had to.

Lenk Sketlish had never been poor. He'd grown up comfortably upper-middle class, his dad a senior manager in telecommunications, his mom a dermatologist. There was no special trauma in his childhood—journalists digging around were just about able to find that his dad had had high standards and his mom had marked his schoolwork herself with a round red pen. They'd lived in a good neighborhood, he'd attended the local high school, where he'd been neither well-liked nor particularly unpopular. He'd had an aptitude for coding and an absolute inability to work for anyone else or on anything he wasn't personally both interested in and invested in. He played a lot of racquetball, he loved to win. He saw that social media had space for a streamlined platform centered around video, audio, and image remixing and he loved to win. His parents loaned him $50,000 to start a business and let him know he shouldn't waste it or expect more. When asked, he said he built his company like he played racquetball with his dad—going hard and fast, no quarter asked or given.

Martha thought: He's going to try to sleep with me. She'd have to nip that in the bud pretty fast. But she'd always managed to turn a shoulder to those approaches in a way that didn't insult. As his clumsy knife chewed up the rabbit fur, she felt tender toward him and his insatiable urge to conquer as she'd sometimes felt tender toward Enoch, and she knew that this in itself was a skill. She knew Lenk Sketlish already, as she'd known Enoch. He was prone to fits of rage and frustration, he was extremely intelligent in some ways and extremely stupid in others, and he didn't suffer fools gladly but never recognized when he himself was the fool. Not many people figured out how to feel tender toward Lenk Sketlish.

At some point he said: "So, Girl Scout camp?"

"Grew up a fundamentalist preparing for the end of days."

And he'd said: "That is cool. That is so fucking cool."

Later on he asked her what she did now, and when she told him, a slow smile moved across his face, and a bark of laughter forced its way out.

Martha thought: Yes, I know you, and yes, I know what this will mean, and yes.

There had been a thing the Fantail board had been asking him to do for months. He'd always said absolutely not, how fucking dare you, do you think I need a fucking nanny? He didn't need anyone; he *was* Fantail. He'd talked this way to the board, and that had slowly but inexorably screwed him. There was a limit to where good ideas could get you if you treated the offer of help as an insult. Ellen Bywater had recently been installed at Medlar after the founder, Albert Dabrowski, had been edged out. This was the logic now: you can't expect the guy who comes up with the thing to steer it around the corners when it picks up speed. Stuff his mouth with gold and show him the door.

So it was a surprise to the board when, the next day, he asked for a short list of candidates for the assistant job. Someone who'd done this kind of job before at a start-up. He described, without naming it, the company Martha Einkorn worked for as the type of place they should look. Maybe a gardening start-up, something like that. A list was made and Martha Einkorn was on it. Martha Einkorn came to interview. And in the fullness of many days Martha Einkorn was appointed Lenk Sketlish's personal administrator, company secretary, guardian, emissary, holder of boundaries, giver of guidance, paid companion, counselor, and friend.

Her first morning he'd said: "Hey, so. What kind of religious fundamentalist?"

She'd looked him directly in the eye and said: "Enochite."

6. he's never killed anyone directly

It was 4:09 a.m. in San Francisco and ntd/strategic was going crazy. More and more people waking up on the East Coast, trying crazy shit to find ArturoMegadog. She had to say something.

I found him, she said. I got lucky. Drove around till I saw something that reminded me of a picture he showed me of the view from his house. He's OK. He says thank you to everyone. Paramedics are with him now, but he's already thrown up most of what he took.

The forum was thrilled and relieved except for three douchebags who said she had ruined their night's sleep and she should have kept them updated as she was traveling and told them about the picture. Further members of the forum told the douchebags they were the reason society was going to collapse. Then there was a long game of "no, you are" until sometime just before dawn ArturoMegadog's original post deleted itself. At which point the argument, instead of dissolving, became more entrenched the less the people involved knew about its origins.

Albert took small sips of coffee, wincing slightly. Martha tried to remember the last time she'd seen him. At a fundraiser maybe, and maybe he'd been drunk. She remembered now knowing he was gay and that he had a partner who never came to any of these events and didn't want to be involved in any of the media of it.

Albert said suddenly: "I never sent you any photo. How did you know it was this house?"

There was a pause, and she stared at the floor and the ceiling and the rows of books, wondering whether to tell him the truth.

She said, "Fantail. You can do it without knowing someone's real name if you have high-level access. Advertising filters. You like this brand of kimchi, you live near water in San Francisco, you were thinking of having a child, you were married to a man who worked for a car company that had been bought up by Fantail—that narrowed it down. And then . . . you'd made purchases that you described from GreenTrunk and TogBuzz, and we own both of those now. I got an address. It didn't say Albert Dabrowski. It said Mike McCall."

Albert laughed properly at that, a deep belly laugh that turned into coughing.

"I knew it," he said at last. "I fucking knew Lenk was doing shit like this. Collecting all that data, saying they wouldn't use it, but once you have it . . . it's trivial to do stuff like that."

Albert scratched his ear with a shaking hand.

"My husband's name was Mike," he said. "The house was in his name. He liked me before I came up with Medlar, when I was twenty and arrogant as shit, a brain on legs. He was the first man who ever thought I shone. He never told anyone he worked with who I was. He didn't want to be treated special. So he didn't get treated special."

"If Lenk had known who he was, they'd have kept his pension," said Martha, but Albert looked at her so pityingly that she was ashamed.

"Please," he said, "please will you leave now? I'll forget you were here, you'll forget you met me. You saved my life, OK? You saved my fucking life and I'll go get some help and you and Lenk and Fantail advertising filters get one good mark in your ledger, OK? I won't put it on Name The Day."

"If I leave," said Martha, "do you have someone you can call to take my place? Someone you can tell what happened here, honestly."

The washer whirred in the closet down the hall.

"My sister's in Napa," said Albert.

"And?"

Something animated in Albert. A chance to tell a story he'd told before, a sliver of the person he usually was.

"Well, she's a grade A bitch. She doesn't even have the excuse of Jesus. She goes to church but not one of *those* churches. They have a hot thirty-two-year-old minister who plays the saxophone. But still, whatever you do, she thinks you're doing it wrong. Not you. Me."

"So . . . you're not going to call her."

"For a while I've really been a problem for her because, you know, dead husband—she can't compete in the suffering Olympics. But this . . . she'd say there's no way to do grief wrong, but also she would make it clear that taking a bunch of pills and a bottle of bourbon is the wrong way to do it."

"Fuck her, then," said Martha. "Never see her again, never talk to her again, what's the fucking point?"

Albert looked at her. "OK. You really are OneCorn.

"Tell me something," he said. "You just came to a stranger's house and saved his life. That has to mean something about who you are deep down. What the shit are you doing working for Lenk Sketlish?"

"He's not the worst person in the world."

Albert looked at her and slowly raised an eyebrow. This was the ArturoMegadog she knew. It couldn't be helped: some part of the people they'd been online was bleeding through here.

"He's not an arms manufacturer," said Martha, "he's not a drug dealer, he's not in the mob, he's never killed anyone."

"Oh really," said Albert, and she remembered the pensions and his husband.

"Fuck, sorry. But I mean he's never killed anyone directly. There are plenty of worse people."

"You're not selling it."

"They do bring people together, that is true. People meet on Fantail. They talk."

"Oh, come *on*."

"What do you want me to say?"

"I liked you online," said Albert.

"I like you," said Martha.

"The person I know online is passionate about the world, about doing the right thing. She's funny and acerbic and she knows her Bible and I guess, like . . . I just imagined you'd be working for an NGO on child poverty. The way you talk. That's it. The way you talk, I didn't think you'd be helping Lenk Sketlish strip-mine human sanity for coins."

Martha drew breath to answer but Albert wasn't finished.

"Because you *know* that's what he's doing. If you were anyone else on that board, I'd think, OK, fine, she gets it on a personal level but not on a societal level. But you *know*. He's deliberately making people angry and desperate so he can keep them clicking. He's taking data that doesn't belong to him and using it to fund stupid fucking shit like his 'undersea base'? I blame myself every day for getting thrown out of Medlar; I wanted that company to be an example of how to do it right, and I pushed too hard and the money wanted me out. And that was it, my one big idea. You get one fucking life, Martha Einkorn, and I should know—I'm in extra time over here and I think I get to say whatever I like. You get one fucking life, and you're smart and you have insight and energy and courage and you're using all that to help *Lenk Sketlish*?"

7. the faint scent of apples

There was a point when Martha had believed in what Lenk and his company were doing. Fantail presented itself as a meeting place—"the community where friends meet friends" was the slogan they discarded in her first year. But Martha understood that what they were selling was a product that divided the world up into tinier and more perfectly polished fragments. They were selling pieces.

In those early days, this idea excited her. The pieces that Enoch had told her were forbidden. The pieces that she'd come to see could bring comfort were an intense and important part of the world he'd denied her. She loved it. She had fought a bear and won. Somewhere in the dark woods of Oregon were the bones of a bear she had brought down with her own hands, the flesh turning to rot, the rot feeding fungi and tree roots, the trees giving homes to insects, the insects feeding the birds, the birds flying overhead calling loud and wild. That was pieces too, she said to the imagined ghost of her father. This thing Fantail was making was the beautiful pieces. In her imagination he turned his face from her when she said this, and in her imagination she smiled. Anything that wasn't Enoch was good.

It had taken more than two years—long hours, home after midnight, takeout in the office, she and Lenk laboring together to save him and to save his company. They came close to the brink six or seven times. She pulled in favors from people she'd worked with across Silicon Valley to get the bugs fixed faster than the users could rage-quit over them. When a major launch failed to meet its milestones and their next payment wasn't triggered in time, they were only one payroll from going under, and Martha took partial salary plus stock, and Lenk didn't take his salary at all to keep paying the devs. He sold his condo and slept on her couch for three months until the next payment came through. He was angry and driven; he stayed up at night coding and sending emails and writing up ideas. He woke her sometimes late at night with a thought, just to hear her tell him it was great. Other people in the company said to her often that they didn't know how she put up with it.

Eventually the company stabilized and the board congratulated Lenk—and, more quietly, Martha. It was only then, after the great rushing wave had crashed over them, that she thought of using Fantail herself. Of looking, perhaps, to find the Enochites. Why would an Enochite have a Fantail profile? Perhaps because they, too, had left that world behind. It had been more than fifteen years since the Last Sermon. Some of them would surely have returned to their previous lives.

She found a man named Jun-seo—a Korean American who had come to the compound a year before the end. She remembered him; he had only been a little older than her and lost. His father had died, his mother had left; people like this were drawn to Enoch for his qualities of fatherliness, his rough wisdom, and his manliness. Martha remembered Jun-seo as a gentle person, kind and sad and thoughtful. They had worked together feeding the animals on cold mornings. She looked at his photographs now. He had a wife and two small children, and he lived not too far away. Jun-seo had written messages under his father-in-law's pictures calling him Dad. She was glad that he'd found someone new and better to be his father.

Jun-seo responded with pleasant speed and interest to Martha's message. They met in a steak house in Redding on a Sunday afternoon. She played upbeat music on the drive and rolled down the windows. She was looking forward to seeing him again—more than that, to talking to someone who really understood her and the life they'd lived. It had been a long time since she'd spoken to anyone who remembered Enoch, or the Martha she'd been until she was seventeen.

Jun-seo looked much the same, as if the years had not touched him or had just ripened and softened him. When he hugged her, he had the faint scent of apples, and she remembered with pleasure that he had always had this clean, childlike fragrance.

"I haven't told my wife who you are," he said as they sat down.

Something in her face must have made him realize he hadn't been understood.

"I don't mean that she'd be angry that I'm meeting a woman. I just said you were a friend from high school. I haven't told her a lot about Enoch. I said I was there, but only for a few weeks."

"It wasn't so long," said Martha softly. "You weren't there so long. Still, you must remember it well."

"People think . . . you know what people think. I have a new life now. My wife and I, we've been together almost ten years."

"That's much longer than you were with us," Martha said. She could see that he was anxious; he needed her to tell him that she barely knew him. This was already not what she'd hoped. She had wanted to talk to someone about the best parts, the moments of joy and awe. Maybe Jun-seo wouldn't want to talk about it at all. Perhaps all she would get here was the scent of his skin and the knowledge that they had been in the same place together once, long ago. Maybe that would be enough.

They ordered lunch. Steak, potatoes, creamed spinach. The food arrived quickly, as if the staff were eager to hurry them out of the almost-empty restaurant. Their meals were in front of them before Jun-seo had finished telling Martha about his older son starting school. He was proud that his son had cried and clung to him at the school gate and proud again that eventually he'd marched bravely in. Martha understood.

"It's good to have a normal life," she said, "after everything."

Jun-seo's face expressed relief. That was apparently what he wanted. To be told that he was normal, that all his emotions and experiences now were normal.

"And you," he said, "you survived it. You're doing well."

It wasn't a question. Her Fantail profile showed her job description. The company was growing. "It must be an interesting role," said Jun-seo, and Martha described a little of the late nights, the pressure, but yes, the achievement. She spoke of the dream for the company, of the stories she'd already read, old war comrades reuniting after decades, separated brothers finding each other again.

"Like this meal," she said. "I could never have found you without Fantail. This is what the company does. Brings people together. From fragments to a whole."

She knew what she was saying and knew that it was a lie. But perhaps it was the kind of lie Jun-seo would enjoy: a reinterpretation of the work of Enoch.

Jun-seo said: "Did you decide to work there so you could find me?"

"I don't understand."

"I don't mean just me. Are you looking for us?"

Martha sliced a piece off her overdone steak and chewed it.

"It only occurred to me recently that I could try to find anyone," she said, "but don't you . . . don't you want to talk about it? Now we both have normal lives. Jobs. You have a family. I just thought it would be good to share some memories."

"I was shaking when I saw your message." He started to speak in a low voice, not hurried but not pausing. As if he'd practiced this speech. "Do you know what I remember? After you left, Enoch was a broken man. He didn't speak for six days, and on the seventh he gave a sermon of despair. He told us that all things in this miserable world would shatter into fragments, that no human man can change the broken quality of this existence, that it had been the temptations of evil that he'd thought he could. He told us to surrender ourselves to pieces. To hurl out our harvest, to tramp down the seedlings."

Martha's sinuses ached, her temples were hot, and a dull headache began to bloom across her forehead. After all this time, was this still not over?

"I had to," she said, and there was no other answer.

Her fingers touched the leather purse on the bench seat beside her. She would stand up in a moment, leaving her meal and Jun-seo. She would drive home in her own car, which was leased to her name, and open the door of her own apartment with her own key. She would sit in the quiet of her home and spend all night, if she wished, observing fragments of her life and others'.

"That's it?" said Jun-seo. "'I had to?' That's it?"

And Martha knew she was truly alone. Now and forever. Her friends in the valley would always understand why she left but not why she'd stayed. The Enochites would understand why she'd stayed but never why she left. She'd broken herself into fragments and now she had to live that way. There was no one who could see all her pieces.

"I don't think this conversation is going anywhere," said Martha. "I'm sorry this is so hard for you. I have to go."

"Well, that's what you do," said Jun-seo as Martha

stood. "You want to know why I came today? I came to see whether you were going to apologize."

On her way home Lenk called her. There was a crisis with the rollout in Europe—some fucking data law bullshit; they were going to get screwed from twenty-seven different directions at once. Martha didn't bother going home. She went straight to the office where Lenk was, inevitably, screaming at a group of six people who could get paid extremely well anywhere in the valley and didn't have to put up with this shit.

She walked through the conference room door. Every face in the room turned to her. The tech leads with an anguished relief. Lenk with righteous anger. She recognized him, and recognized her place here. She was the one who could sit at his right hand, turn his fractured thoughts into actionable notes and deliverable plans. She was the one who could soothe him. She was the one he respected. She belonged here. It was the only place her pieces made sense.

8. i don't trust myself to be in that kind of situation

"Right," said Albert, "so you're reproducing the abusive environment you grew up in by working for a sadist. You have Stockholm syndrome from your fundamentalist dad, he taught you to value being the *only one* who could deal with him, and you're still living like that. And you're lonely as shit."

Martha's eye twitched. "OK. That's a *lot*. Also, you don't know my life."

"You literally broke into my house and stuck your fingers down my throat. We've been talking online for six years. You just told me the story of your life. I think we know each other. Actually. Come with me. Bring the coffee. I want to show you something."

Martha refused to let Albert drive, obviously. She didn't want to take him anywhere, but he said he'd just get an Uber if she didn't come, and she thought his chances of surviving the day were greater with her than without her. She told him all this as she poured their coffees into two flasks.

"We'll just drive," he said. "I won't even get out of the car. How is that different from sitting on a couch with you? It's not."

He almost fell to his knees twice getting into the car. She helped him up. Well, she thought, if he needs to go to the ER, at least he'll be in my car already.

On the drive, he asked her more about her life with Enoch and afterward—like a doctor diagnosing a patient.

"How do you think you know anything about life?" she said. "You literally just . . ."

"Don't give me that shit," he said. "I'm as smart as I was yesterday, which is *smart.* Just because someone has some mental health doesn't mean they have nothing to offer. Especially to you. Tell me more about your Stockholm syndrome life. Tell me what happened after the bear. Also, all your stories are absolutely bonkers. I love it."

The dawn osmosed into the sky, soaking the velvet blue with gray and gold, white blue and bright blue. Five gulls formed an arrow pointing the way north. She drove, following the way they showed.

"Fine," said Martha.

After the bear, after seeing the couple in the woods, Martha knew that she had retained—unlawfully—a part of herself in reserve. She told the other children in the compound the story of the bear many times but never the strange interlude in which she watched the woman's fingernails and saw the comfort that could be taken in pieces. Holding parts of experience in reserve like this was not exactly forbidden but discouraged. In the long, dark nights Enoch often suggested "opening hearts to one another"—discussing in detail what one had seen or done or thought that day, bringing the community into harmony, each part communicating as a whole. What Martha had seen in the woods would have been a perfect observation to share: something strange, something beautiful, something hard to understand alone. She should have asked the community to see it with her, through her eyes.

"Right," said Albert. "Yeah, this is controlling cult behavior."

"I know that," said Martha. "I grew up in kind of a well-known cult? I'm *aware.*"

"Yeah, but you don't really know how it's affected you."

"I've had six years of therapy."

"Six years? Wouldn't touch the sides."

"Why the hell did I save your life again?"

"So you could have this conversation. Carry on."

"There was a town about an hour's drive from the compound. And in the town was a library."

"Ah, libraries. The root of all wickedness. You were seduced by literature, were you?"

They'd read books as a community. Good books, old books. But in the library were also magazines filled with colorful pictures. And computers connected to the internet, which a person could use for thirty minutes without paying a cent. None of it—this was important to understand—would have been forbidden if she had told Enoch what she was doing. But she didn't tell. In the library, she looked at teenage fashion magazines, photography magazines. There were photographs of partially dressed or almost naked women; she lingered over them, marveling at the flawless skin, the breasts that floated with nipples tipped toward the sky.

"Ohhhhhhh, I get it," said Albert. "Sex. That's how they got you."

"It wasn't . . . I mean, it was sex. Yes. Fine. Yes, it was."

"Nothing wrong with that."

"But it wasn't *just* that. It was also . . . you know, we grew up in this incredibly wholesome way . . ."

"Your dad abandoned you in a forest. It wasn't that wholesome."

"I mean the skills. The old, useful skills. Tracking and hunting, sewing, tending the crops. All that. It was just so *boring*."

"Compared to the internet."

"Compared to the world."

"Yeah. Take a left here."

"Where are we going?"

"I want to show you the most wholesome, boring, beautiful thing I know."

Feeling ashamed of what she'd seen in the library, Martha had asked Enoch about the feeling of curiosity. Where it came from. Was it a right feeling or a wrong one?

Enoch was pleased with these questions, ruffled her hair as if she were still a child of five, sat with her as she cleaned the hearth fire and laid fresh logs. He had never been afraid of questions; he always thought they could puzzle it out together.

"Well, Martha May," he said, "I believe curiosity is our birthright. When we were Fox, when we walked from place to place, curiosity was needed and fed by our daily lives. What is curiosity but the desire to see what's over the next ridge? To take a new path, try a new fruit, explore a new cave. That's how we found out the secrets and beauties of our world."

"But," said Martha, laying the kindling crisscross just as she had done five hundred times before, "won't curiosity just lead us astray now?"

Enoch sat back on his heels by the fire.

"Tell me why you say that."

Martha said: "I've been thinking about the Babble. Don't you think it's curiosity that leads them? They're chasing after new things all the time. That's what pieces are, aren't they? Constant small new things. Curiosity."

Enoch looked at Martha strangely.

Later—a few weeks or a few months later—Martha noticed that Enoch had changed the sermon of Fox and Rabbit. In the new telling, he took on her thoughts regarding curiosity. He showed how Rabbit had bent Fox's natural curiosity into a new and terrible shape. Without new terrain to wander, Rabbit is forced to satisfy his curiosity using the inventions of man. Instead of the wild adventure of travel, exploration, the mysteries of the hunt, Rabbit turns himself inward and seeks out dramatic events through the television.

Martha noticed, however, that Enoch had not credited

her with the question. He could have said, "My daughter, Martha, asked me," but he never did. She said to herself: I should be satisfied with this. It is because of the magazines, the photographs, and the internet that I'm not satisfied. She said to herself: I should stop going to the library. But she did not stop.

"Well, what the fuck's wrong with that?" said Albert. "You wanted credit for what you'd done! Fuck it, Jesus said the meek would inherit the earth but he still wanted his name in his fucking book, didn't he? They didn't write that book saying 'Some dude said and did this but we can't remember his name,' did they?"

Martha laughed.

"I stole money from Enoch when I left," she said. "About two thousand dollars. And a gun."

"You thought they'd come after you?"

"I thought the world was going to be a more frightening place than it was."

"Then you were smart to steal the money and smart to take the gun."

"I was sixteen."

"Smarter than most sixteen-year-olds. Look, can you not just let yourself be OK with what you did? Can you not say, 'Fuck it, I needed to survive'? Good lord, you were a lesbian teenager living in a fundamentalist apocalypse cult. Taken on average, the people of Earth would give you a standing ovation for leaving."

"Yeah, but I grew up there and that's not how we thought."

"So think differently. Do what you said to me about my sister. Never think about them again. Don't see any of them again. Nothing that you did was so wrong."

"Whatever I did?"

"I mean . . . did you kill any of them?"

"No?"

"Hit any of them? Knock them down?"

"No. I hitchhiked and caught buses and went to a town where my mom's brother lived. He didn't help much, but I slept on his couch for a few months while I got my paperwork organized and found a charity that would help me take the GED. But some of the Enochites thought that my leaving was like . . . a sign. A sign that the end was coming. Someone said to me years ago that . . . my leaving was what destroyed it. It went bad after I left. They divided against each other. Some of them thought the others were traitors. It just . . . it went really bad really fast."

Albert flattened his lips.

"Sounds to me like they did that to themselves, then. They decided what to believe. If they were willing to give up on all of it because you left . . ." He shifted one shoulder. "They were just looking for an excuse. You did what you had to do to survive. Look, we're here."

The day was new now, as it is new every morning. They had driven to the wetlands, the place Albert's husband had labored tirelessly to preserve.

"I give them sixty thousand dollars a year. It's mostly volunteers. That's all they need to keep all this . . . like this."

Albert levered himself out of the car and stood panting, leaning against the door.

The ocean was cold and smooth this morning, patches of glassy calm in the wider deep-blue blur. Birdsong rose insistent around them, the inquisitive white sandpipers like rusty hinges, inky surf scoters' bubbling calls, far off the nasal bray of a cluster of shearwaters. Every leaf unfolding, every insect raising its head, every bird praising on the wing the new-risen sun. There was fog, but behind the fog there was morning.

"Mike used to drive me out here," Albert said. "That fucker used to pull me out of bed at 4 a.m. to see this. He had hot coffee waiting in the car. He didn't give a shit that I spent the whole drive complaining. He said: 'We're part of life, and we should get to experience it. Come away from your electronic thinking machines.'"

"He sounds great."

Albert drew a shuddering sigh.

"You someone's mom? Someone's wife? Partner?"

She shook her head.

"How come?"

Martha sipped her coffee.

"I don't trust myself to be in that kind of situation."

"Are you dating?"

"I'm . . . sometimes sleeping with people."

"With women, right?"

Martha nodded toward the coffee in Albert's hand.

"Keep taking sips, slowly." And then, "Yes, women. Are you dating?"

"Are you kidding?"

"Why not?"

"Well, where would it end? I'd meet someone and fall in love and be happy again?"

"Maybe. From what I've seen, if you've done it once, you can do it again. Some people have the knack for it."

"And then what?"

"The normal thing. Have fights, make up, cry, laugh, celebrate together, mourn together. Get pissed about the way he folds the laundry and how he's always wearing holes in his socks and stealing yours."

Albert drank more of his coffee, slowly. Around them the morning arose, the day like a newborn baby filled with possibility. The sunlight, for that hour, golden and clear, the birds winging, diving to take a glittering fish from the living waters.

"If I met someone, I'd fall through the hole in the ice inside myself. I can't be happy again because then I'd know how unhappy I am."

"So your plan is be miserable forever?"

"Aha. And your plan is what?"

There was a long silence between them, filled with the sound of plashing water, the urgent calls of the birds.

"Mike used to say: how life happens is a letting in. When he was trying to convince me about the baby. He said every time it was an act of ridiculous trust. The sperm buries itself in the egg and stops being able to move. The egg lets down all its defenses and allows a foreign object in. That's how it happens, every time. An absolutely unjustified leap of faith. Open up, let in, be let in. Opening is dangerous, every single time. But that's how we're here."

"I feel like you're making some sort of point here, Albert."

"I read about what happened at the end with the Enochites, OK? So I get how you'd have trouble with trust, after that. Trouble with getting close."

9. don't look back

Enoch, formerly Ralph Zimmerman, had been a clever man and a paranoid man and an unwell man. He had read a lot of texts and soaked them in his clever, anxious, frightened mind and produced signs and portents, warnings of disaster and promises of salvation.

His daughter, Martha, left the compound early one morning, before anyone was awake. She took money and a gun; she must have walked and hitched rides and taken buses, and although they drove for days looking for her, she was gone and she wasn't coming back.

Enoch knew that Martha leaving was a sign of something—he felt the forces of chaos lurking all around. He suspected traitors, he shouted for justice, he became angry and impatient with his flock, he ruminated and chewed over Martha's betrayal. Eventually, he asked the Lord to send him a sign. A sign of whether the community they had founded on these fifteen thousand green acres was blessed by God.

He sent some of his followers into the woods to hunt and gather for three days and took those who remained behind—a great number, more than a hundred people—into the large basement of the main building in the compound. There he told them that they would undertake three days of fasting and prayer. They would drink only water. They would remain awake for as long as they could. He locked the door of the basement. He hurled the key through the tiny barred window to the east, the one that faced the rising sun. He prayed for guidance, called on the Lord to show them the way.

He preached—those who were there remembered—

night and day. They slept and dozed to the sound of Enoch's preaching and woke to the same prophesying voice. It was in these hours that he preached the sermon of Rabbit and Fox for the final time, and those who heard it said that he had at last united heaven and earth in his words and it was beautiful and holy and they knew that God was listening to them and to their prayers. They became certain as the hungry hours ticked past that their community was about to experience a miraculous visitation from the Lord because the purpose of the world had been fulfilled by this small gathering and it was time now for the whole thing to be rolled up and put away. Those two days and nights of eating no food, drinking only water, sleeping in only brief snatches were the most beautiful of their lives.

On the third day, they smelled smoke.

Some said: It must have been the government. There had been FBI and CIA agents poking around the Enochites for years; they just got tired of them and wanted them gone.

Some said: The electrical wiring in the compound was always unsafe. There had been two small fires in the past year, and two of the Enochites were training as electricians in order to begin to work on it themselves. It had been a hot, dry summer. Something in the workshop sparked out and caused the fire.

Some said: It was Enoch himself who did it. He hadn't thrown the key out; he had kept it and let himself out in the early morning when the others were sleeping. He knew where the previous electrical fires had started in the workshop. He set a fire there, next to the pile of grease-soaked rags, made sure it caught, and let himself back into the basement to wait for the Lord's judgment.

Some said: There was an electrical storm in the early morning of that day over the fifteen thousand green acres, and some tiny spark raised the flames. It was the Lord, himself and no seraph, himself and no messenger, himself and no stranger. The Lord who had looked at the compound and said: "Destroy them. Smite them. Wipe them out."

Some of the Enochites, when they smelled the smoke, worked together to smash the small eastern window near the ceiling of the basement and piled up furniture to climb out—some of them encouraged the others and hauled one another out, scrambling up through broken glass, flesh bloody and torn, choking and coughing. And those people shared the story and told how Enoch had said: "Let them go. The Lord will show us the way."

Martha was twelve weeks gone from the compound when she heard the news of the tragic fire. She was in a corridor waiting for an interview with a GED program; they would give her funding and accommodation if she qualified for a place. The corridor was painted pale green and white, the walls scuffed like someone had driven a truck through there. Martha sat on a hard plastic chair outside an office door, and on a small table next to her was a three-week-old newspaper with a photograph of the burned-out compound on page 6. If it hadn't been folded just like that, she might not have seen it for another month or more. The theories about the FBI or the CIA came much later. At the start it was just a tragic fire at a farm. News, but not big news.

She put her hand to the page, touched the picture of the burned dining hall, the chain-link fence. She ripped the piece out of the newspaper, stuffed it into her jeans pocket, and then feared that she might have been seen, that they would call her a vandal. She straightened her mind—don't think of it, don't let it in. Don't look back. The door opened. The woman called her name. For thirty-five minutes of the interview, Martha was enthusiastic and articulate. She got her funding. She was on her way. She didn't look back.

10. how we get life

The sun was up at the wetlands. It was getting to 9 a.m. Elsewhere in the city, the woman who managed the office for Albert's doctor was pulling on her red peacoat and lacing up her sneakers, checking her watch, and leaving time for the bus. Elsewhere in the city, the owner of an organic grocery store was pulling up the shutters and unpacking a new box of Firepit-brand kimchi onto the waiting shelves. Elsewhere in the city, Lenk Sketlish was taking a shower at his office, letting a call from his current wife go straight to voice mail. What Enoch thought is true: we are connected, one to the next to the next.

"Well, you see," said Martha, "it was my fault."

"You've had six whole years of therapy, right?" said Albert. "You know that's just the narcissistic defense. You want to believe it was your fault because that's easier than acknowledging that you had no control at all."

"But I could have stopped it. It wouldn't have happened if I hadn't left."

Albert said, "I don't believe anything's meant to be, but don't you think it means something that the two of us have met here, like this?"

"I've been down that road before."

That road ended in a basement with the scent of smoke seeping in.

"Alright, maybe it means nothing. You just saved my life and you work for Fantail and I invented Medlar. And we turn out to agree on a bunch of important things. But we could make it mean something if we wanted."

"What do you want to make it mean?"

"You and I," he said, "have helped something happen in

this world. A huge wash of information. Unprecedented. The only thing it's like is the Gutenberg print revolution and that was followed by four hundred years of bloody war. Suddenly, people were exposed to so much more information than ever before. They had no systems to process it or to tell truth from lies. They were overwhelmed. That's where we are. And humanity doesn't have time for four hundred years of bloody war right now. There are so many emergencies to deal with."

"Fragments," said Martha. "Pieces. This is what Enoch talked about. Things falling apart more quickly than they can be put back together."

"Well, I think on that he was right. Not on the other stuff. On that. This is what I'd like it to mean. That you and I work together on helping get us through the information crisis as fast as humanly possible."

"You're serious."

"Yeah," he said.

"What are we talking about? Some kind of conference?"

"Oh God, not another fucking conference. Not a panel, not an event, not a convention. Something real. I just tried to kill myself," said Albert. "You escaped a death cult with your life. We're in extra time. We don't really exist. We can do whatever we like. I want to consider some extreme solutions. I want to do whatever it takes."

The sky was gray and saxe blue, the air very still. Small birds swung through the sky, describing a parabolic curve between invisible infinities, snapping at flying creatures too small to see. Everything that has ever begun in the history of the planet has started with one tiny change, invisible to the naked eye.

The sperm says to the egg: Knock knock. The egg says: I've no reason to let you in. There are no guarantees. And yet, the egg opens up. And yet, the sperm wriggles in. And yet, two packets of information merge. That's how all of us got here. That's how nothing turns into something. That's how a bare ball of rock ends up with gulls and shearwaters, with moss and lichen, with unfurling pale green leaves and scuttling millipedes and rabbits and foxes. That's how we get life.

11. a special kind of king

In Washington, DC, that winter, there was a rain of blood.

Martha felt the blood first, warm and wet against her cheek. A trickling ooze unlike water, it had a thickness and a silky quality. The smell was not at first unpleasant: the tang of animal and iron. Martha put her hand to her cheek and it came away sticky and red. All down the steps of the courthouse, plump red droplets were bursting on the stone, on the barricades, on the protestors, on the dark gray suit of Zimri Nommik and on the lilac silk dress of Selah Nommik and on the immaculate black wool coat of Lenk Sketlish.

Lenk looked up. A bloody mass hit him in the face. A skinned rat with a long tail, Martha thought. Lenk grunted, and the object on his face slid slowly down across his immaculate blue shirt to land with a heavy plop on the concrete. It was a blood-soaked tampon.

On top of a squat, dark building opposite the courthouse, a group of women were unfurling a banner.

ANVIL OPPRESSES WOMEN. PERIOD.
NOMMIK: THIS IS WHAT HAPPENS WHEN YOU DON'T GIVE
WOMEN TIME TO CHANGE THEIR TAMPONS

They had black plastic buckets and pump-spray water guns filled with blood. Some of them were swinging the bloody tampons around their heads and hurling them like—what was it? Martha felt her mind slowing down. Cabers? No, hammer throwers. Behind her there were shouts, security swinging into action. Selah Nommik ran up the stairs two at a time. Zimri Nommik put his hand on the back of one of the women on the steps and swung her sideways, out of the line of fire.

It had to be animal blood, surely. No one would have collected this amount of menstrual blood and kept it fresh. Martha, who tended toward analysis in times of trouble, wondered whether there was some way to do it—hospital anticoagulants, thousands of women timing their pills, emptying the contents of menstrual cups into a bucket. She was still fascinatedly calculating when two muscular arms grabbed her waist and one of Lenk's security guards said in her ear, "Back inside, back inside" with such care she felt she was a child being lifted into bed when her feet came off the ground.

At the porcelain trough in the women's bathroom, Selah Nommik—Zimri Nommik's wife—was peeling her bloodstained lilac dress off her strong shoulders. Martha looked and flicked her eyes away. She, too, was covered in blood and was holding a clear plastic bag stuffed with sweatpants and a charity 5K T-shirt someone had found in a closet.

Selah wadded up a ball of tissue, wet it, and tried to clean the blood off her neck. A bead of red-streaked water dribbled onto her white lace bra.

"Fuck," said Selah, "fuck," then suddenly turned to Martha. "We're going to have to get tested. HIV. Hep B. Hep C. Whatever's in blood."

"I think it's pig," said Martha. Her mind had been working at this problem for a few minutes now. "My dad had a . . . farm. It smells like pig blood."

"Oh. That's a relief," said Selah, and she started to cry. Her tears carried her navy and pale blue eye shadow as far as her neck like the spring thaw carrying last autumn's bright leaves into the creek. She scrubbed at her face and hair with the wet tissue, slowly scraping up the blood. "You work for Lenk, right? Fantail Lenk?"

"Yeah," said Martha.

Selah looked at Martha's reflection in the mirror. Both of them bloody, as if they'd been in a fight. Selah was sizing her up. Sometimes the need to talk is so strong that a person will grab anyone who is even vaguely trustworthy. Let me in, says someone. And someone who has no reason to let anyone in says, OK.

"Does he cheat? Your boss, Lenk?" Selah asked.

"Does he . . ."

"On his wife. Does he cheat on his wife?"

Martha looked at her. "I can't . . ."

"Right," said Selah. "If he didn't, you'd just have said, 'Oh no, I work for the only angelic man in the Fortune 500; he doesn't know other women even *have* tits.' Does he cheat with *you*?"

"No. I don't do that," said Martha.

"Smart. But he'd cheat with you if he had the chance, right? No, don't answer that. I get it, you don't have to answer that. Did you see Zimri with his hand on her back?"

Oh yes. The woman with the bright gold beads dotted at the end of her braids, Mary Mere of CodeHogs. Martha thought back to those moments on the steps, to Zimri Nommik guiding Mary Mere to safety with great care. Ah, right. It doesn't take so much trust if you think everyone knows already.

There was an opening in the world here, Martha saw, a crack in the mountain.

"Yes," said Martha, "I saw."

"Oh fuck, you did? If you saw, then every fucker saw. People were videoing that shit, did you see? God, it'll be everywhere. Fuck." Selah Nommik turned back to the mirror and applied a cream from a little pot to her face, wiped it off with tissue.

"I'm so sorry Zimri treats you this way," said Martha.

Their eyes met in the mirror, a momentary connection.

"You deserve better," said Martha, and she knew when she said it that it was true, that Selah Nommik knew she meant it. This woman deserved a better husband than the Anvil founder, Zimri Nommik, a man obsessed with expansion of his business and apparently his sexual portfolio. A moment of sincerity in this world of symbols and evasions had more than natural worth.

"I do, actually," said Selah. "I know everyone thinks I'm with him for the money and like, how could anyone actually love a man like that? But I mean I did love him. I did find Zimri lovable."

Martha shook her head. "No one thinks that," she said. "Everyone knows you're impressive. They all wonder how he managed to convince you to stay for so long."

Selah said: "OK, you wanna know how many people he's sleeping with?" She counted them on her fingers: "First, the PA, obviously—you saw her at the hearing, the one who looks like me but her color is cheap and her tips are frizz. She thinks she's going to be the next Mrs. Zimri Nommik, but she's gonna get bought off with four million dollars and stock. She'll end up running a chinchilla farm in Tampa. I'm telling you, I see the future. Second, his kids' nanny; he sees her when he sees the kids and he sends them to get ice cream and they bone in the changing room at his pool. Security guy told me. Also his yoga instructor, which is like so . . . God, what is it with men and stretchy women? And those three don't worry me because he's not going to leave me for the PA or the nanny or the yoga instructor. But now he's also sleeping with Mary Mere—you know her? CEO of CodeHogs? When he touched her I could see he'd touched her naked, do you know what I mean? He's probably with her right now. I get the public bathroom, she gets the private room with Zimri."

"Are you sure you want to tell me all this?"

But Selah was in her stride.

"Zimri thinks he's a special kind of king because he only fucks Black girls. I knew that when I met him, and when Vashti Nommik got her settlement. I thought: Fine, let him think he's special, all men think they're kings anyway. But do you know what it is really? He doesn't want me to feel safe around other Black women. I didn't see that when we met because I was young. But I'm forty-two now, and he made a pass at my *sister* when she came for Thanksgiving. What he wants is to own a Black woman. I'm not kidding. He's frightened of women; he wants to own a woman and then destroy her. If it's not Mary Mere, it'll be someone else."

Martha said, "If he wants to leave, let him go. You don't need him. He doesn't own you."

"Bloody hell. Women in bathrooms."

"I'm serious. You're . . ." Martha tried not to say "magnificent" and failed. "Magnificent. You leave him, you'll be one of the richest people in the world."

"I don't get fifty percent if I leave now. Got to do another five years minimum for the serious money. Or he's got to leave me. Plus they're launching a new thing next year, Anvil Automate. Takes any process your secretary is doing and automates it, any process anyone is doing online. I don't just mean mail merge. I mean research methods, I mean writing emails, I mean *undetectable* artificial secretary to make Zoom calls for you. Zimri is going to be worth three times what he's worth now. The code for it is beautiful. Like a cathedral."

Selah had finished cleaning the blood and makeup off her face. She pulled on her fresh shirt and pants.

"You know what I think to myself every day? I think, At least where I am I can hold him back from some of it. You know? Like he wanted to set up some moon base—I'm not joking, a bloody moon base—and I said: 'How about we buy up some habitats on Earth and turn them into safe zones for animals?' Obviously he doesn't remember that was my idea but it bloody was. He still wants to do the moon base but we've got the FutureSafe zones now. I think to myself, Maybe that's why I'm in this position, that's why I got here. For this."

"Yes," said Martha, "I think something like that about Lenk. But sometimes"—she spoke slowly and carefully, placing each word like a board-game piece—"I wonder if that's going to be enough."

Selah took a bright pink pencil from her bag and reapplied a confident winged navy-blue sweep across each eyelid. She turned to Martha.

"You think about leaving Lenk? You wouldn't work for Fantail anymore?" said Selah.

Martha said, "Yes. I have thought about it. Yes."

"And? You've got no prenup. Go and run a foundation or something."

"Yes," Martha said, "I could do that. I think I'm staying because . . . I'm trying to work out how to take what Lenk's built and do something better with it."

Selah looked at Martha. Her head started to tip to the side, as if of its own accord. Like the world was turning around and Selah was trying to match it, to keep things level in front of her eyes.

"Women in bathrooms," said Martha.

How does trust build between people? It is an offering and a receiving. It is putting yourself into the position to be hurt, just a little, and noticing that they refrain. It is the reaching out between people, laughing at the same moment. It is building a model of the other person inside yourself, placing them in the palm of your hand, rotating them and saying: Yes. I see the flaws and I see the dangers and nothing will happen here that will truly harm me. And it is saying: I would rather trust you than be alone.

Selah unhooked her bra under the T-shirt, ran cold water onto the frothy lace, rubbing at it gently with the pads of her thumbs.

"I mean, it's fucking biblical. Literally, blood raining down on us. Mate, I grew up with all that, my mum is *well* religious? Don't give me church every Sunday—church every *day*. Blood, frogs, locusts, pestilence, hail, darkness. There are *ways* to tell if the Lord is done with you, innit?"

"They had a plague of locusts in Italy. Just a few weeks ago. And South Africa before that," Martha said.

"The novel coronavirus. Mpox." Selah gave a sideways glance. "Hailstones the size of grapefruit in Canada. In summer."

They were laughing. Martha had never known anyone who could play this game with her before.

"Is that true," Martha said, "about the hailstones?"

"Oh yeah. I have Anvil alerts for the end of the world, fam. God is *so pissed off with us*."

Is it then that this starts to be something? Is it Selah Nommik saying those words in that order that plants the seed of all that is to come? At the time, Martha didn't think of it as more than a joke.

Selah Nommik said: "If we had any, like, old-school prophets, they'd all be telling us to stop everything we're doing right now and just get on with fixing it. Nothing else. Not until it's done."

"A friend of mine says that too," said Martha. "That tech people are the only people who can fix this because we're the only ones who are used to changing stuff this quickly."

"Right, because we have to do it quickly. You know. The climate stuff, habitat destruction . . . eventually it'll right itself. But it can take six hundred years and we have to live through civilizational collapse, and six billion people will die and we get thrown back to the Stone Age, orrrrrrrrrrr we can all just get our arses in gear and do it really quickly and have, like, five years of significant pain, live with blackouts, everyone in the world is conscripted to fix it, and then we're basically through the worst."

"There's a beautiful world on the far shore," Martha said.

"There really fucking is." Selah spun around so quickly that she splattered tiny drops of water onto Martha. "Oh fuck, sorry."

"It's not the worst thing that's gotten on me today."

"Right," said Selah. "No but look, sorry, you get it, right? I'm really trying but I don't think I've met anyone else who *really* gets this. There *is* a beautiful world on the far shore, where we're not destroying all the species anymore and our cities are clean and beautiful and full of wild birds, and our cars are all electric and all shared, and the streets are safe for kids to play in, and we get to keep TV and the internet and concerts and ball games and all that good stuff, and fine, we're eating mostly vegan food but it's *good*, and if we can just get through the pain barrier as quickly as possible, then we're there."

"I think you should meet my friend," said Martha.

"I fucking should," said Selah, folding her damp bra into her plastic bag. "I should meet your friend and I should meet you and you should somehow persuade your boss Lenk Sketlish to get in on FutureSafe."

"My friend is Albert Dabrowski," said Martha.

"OK," said Selah, because for a moment it didn't register; his was a name from the distant past, which is to say in Silicon Valley about twelve years ago. Then it did. "Just a sec. You're mates. With Albert Dabrowski?"

"Yeah."

"How the fuck did that happen?"

"Long story."

Selah frowned, thinking. "You know who you should talk to? *Badger Bywater*."

It wasn't more than six months later that AUGR was born.

12. so many stupid songs

We are always in the process of catching up to the future. Only when we get there, it's never what we imagined. Sometimes, just once in a while, it's better.

A long time after these meetings, on the rooftop of a hotel in London on a cold January day, Martha Einkorn had watched Badger Bywater irritate Lenk Sketlish by bringing their own straw to an expensive party. Of course, Badger Bywater could do what they liked, sipping insouciantly through that glass straw with all the family money in the world to protect them. Albert Dabrowski could do what he liked to a certain extent too, since everything had already been taken from him. He was at the party on the rooftop, giving his liver less punishment than it looked like. Most of the fruit punches were straight fruit juice. They all wanted to keep clear heads, and Albert's liver wasn't as young as he used to be. Selah Nommik was playing the game, of course, as she'd played it cleverly and well for five long, boring years. But none of them were in quite as precarious a position as Martha. Even to justify coming to London for this, she'd had to volunteer to take on some boring-as-shit sponsor events like "Fantail as a Survival Tool."

The raindrops fell on the roof. She checked her thinscreen. It was time. Martha had the dull sense of duty, of lonely, necessary responsibility that she had all the time these days. She took the elevator down to her boring event.

Martha had done her internet searches about Lai Zhen before the event, of course. Lai Zhen was mesmerizing, hilarious, charismatic—of course she was: 2.8 million people wanted to be her friend. Martha had learned to be cynical about charismatic people. Lai Zhen would almost certainly turn out to be a self-obsessed, narcissistic jerk. Still, it was worth meeting SurlySurvivor. After what Fantail had done in the Fall of Hong Kong, Martha had always wanted to meet people who'd survived it. And Lai Zhen might turn out to be useful somehow.

There is a thing in human life that can never be predicted or controlled. It is dangerous and terrifying; it destroys your life and fucks up your plans. That's why there are so many stupid songs about it.

Lai Zhen took the hand of Martha Einkorn. She was charming and funny; she was witty and self-deprecating. Their palms met. It was like an electricity waking up inside Martha. Oh shit, thought Martha, this is not the time for this. But there's no way to really know what's going to arise next.

She was out of practice but she'd seen Lenk do this often enough. With his various wives and mistresses, his baby mothers and his side pieces. It wasn't hard. He let slip little vulnerabilities about himself; he made suggestive remarks. A part of her, inside her mind, was saying, This is really not the moment for this inner lake to unfreeze, thank you; stay frozen, please, just for the next few months, just stay frozen. But the part of her that had seen Lenk do this before took the hotel key from her pocket and pressed it into Zhen's hand as she saw Zhen's pupils dilate, as she thought, I'm so fucking out of practice at this I've forgotten where all the bits go. But this is the thing humans do. Knock knock, says one, can I come in? And though there's no reason at all to let someone in, though it'd be safer and more sensible and involve less reorganizing of plans to keep the door closed, this is what we're like. We give someone our hotel key.

She woke before Zhen that first morning. Looked at her still, sleeping face. Was this even possible? She was, what, *eleven* years older than Zhen? People made things like that work but could she? Really? She'd barely slept all night for the strange presence of another person in her bed; she'd lain stiff and afraid, a strange and terrible dawn breaking inside her. Zhen muttered in her sleep, something in Chinese that sounded like "bou bui." And Martha thought: Oh, but I want to. It is morning again and I am standing in the sunshine at last. Her face turned toward the sun and she felt the touch of its warmth.

She closed her eyes. Once upon a time her father had left her alone in a cold, dark wood close to sunset, and one way or another, no matter where she went, she had stayed alone in that forest for the whole of her life. She listened to Zhen breathing. It didn't matter what happened next. She'd finally felt something.

She had a webcam set up to watch her guinea pigs back in California. The housekeeper took care of them every day. There they were, in their castle, Nutmeg wandering over to the hay bale for a nibble. Toepocket—named because she liked to stick her toes into the pocket of her blanket, obviously—sleeping in one of the upper rooms. In bed that morning in London she watched their nocturnal movements on her tablet. They were extremely sweet, and suddenly the demands of an intense job and the affection of guinea pigs wasn't enough. Would never be enough again. Shit.

Selah messaged her that day. She said: **Level with us, that wasn't a casual thing was it?**

And Martha had thought of saying it was, it could be. Zhen could turn out to be a shithead. But she knew it wasn't casual for her, anyway.

Albert said: **Well, shit, congratulations, darling.**

They talked now via private message using pre-agreed pseudonyms on a knitting board. And then on a deep-sea diving board. And then on a board for people living with diabetes. The board moved once a week. They'd memorized six months' worth when they met in person.

Badger said: **I want to meet her.**

Albert said: **My god we *all* want to meet her.**

Badger said: **Yeah but, seriously, we're really close now.**

Selah said: **I think that's a good idea. I'm not saying we need to check her out but . . . we are really close now.**

So fine, Badger met Zhen in New Zealand. And Badger thought she was great.

Albert said: **You really like her, don't you?**

Selah didn't let Martha answer.

Look, she's amazing, that's why Martha likes her and that's why we can't. I'm sorry, Martha. Look at what's coming. It can only be a few months at most. The weather. The black mould. The war in the South China Sea. The thing is coming and it's not going to wait for long.

Martha thought: How have I gotten myself into this situation again? Denial and duty. What I owe to the community is greater than what I myself am allowed. Somehow, after all these years, I've ended up back in a compound. She thought of saying no. She thought of the feeling that first morning—terrified, stiff and sleepless, knowing with a frightening certainty the touch of sunlight on her face.

But she knew she'd already done one terrible secret thing. If the others knew, they would call it all off. So she didn't tell them.

Selah said: **Look, if and when things do go to shit, you can always bring her with you, OK? When the balloon goes up. You can bring her then. We're not going to stop you.**

But Selah didn't know that Martha had already—in a way—brought Zhen with her for the end of days.

Martha watched Zhen's talks online, and her videos. She had each live stream calendared. Meanwhile, she ghosted Zhen gently. Replied to each message with something less—a smiley face, a thumbs-up. She watched her crooked smile and listened to her foul mouth describing a disappointing tent, an overly expensive infection monitor. Martha thought: You don't know that you're already safe.

Martha had set up her own Wi-Fi network in her hotel room to deliver a very particular package. One morning, Martha had left the Wi-Fi and the password for Zhen, and Zhen had connected her devices to it. Knock knock, Martha's internet had said. And Zhen's entire secure system had no reason to let anyone in. Except for being human. Except for wanting to connect. Except for the moment when one hand touches another. That's how anything happens. Come on in, said Zhen's secure system. And then, without anyone knowing, Martha had given Zhen AUGR.

There is never a good enough reason to trust anyone. Except that we can't live without doing it. Martha watched Zhen through her screen give this talk and that talk and thought: You're safe. And one day I can explain it all. After the end of the world.

when to go

"By the time you know the world's ending, it's already too late, am I right?"

Si Packship laughed. The laugh was irresistible. Despite themselves, three of the richest people in the world laughed along with him.

When Martha had found him, his laugh had been nervous, his palms itchy. But she'd worked with him until he was presentable for Lenk, Ellen, and Zimri. There was some mileage in his idea, and even more after she allotted him some funding from her special-projects budget. It could be something Lenk would really want. She didn't want Packship making her look like a schmuck.

Si Packship's presentation skills were perfect. The slides were perfect. His face was perfect, symmetrical and beautiful. You'd buy anything he sold you. You'd feel great about yourself while you did.

"You've all thought about it. You guys do nothing all day but stare directly into the future, right? And you think you'd *know* exactly when to go. Maybe you believe you can be rational, logical, objective about it. But we know that's not true."

Zimri Nommik stirred in his seat. He didn't like being woken too early in the morning to go to the inside of a mountain to hear a presentation, and he wasn't at all sure this man wasn't insulting him.

"You might not be rational," Zimri rumbled, "but I sure as shit am."

Si Packship took it as easily as breathing. "There are some decisions machines are just better at," he said, smiling, and this was exactly what Zimri believed. "People can be swayed by emotion. We stay at the roulette table too long. We freeze in a crisis. Even well-trained, well-educated people who think about this stuff. You know pilots can be so obsessed with getting to their destination that they ignore bad weather? That's how most plane crashes happen. And the tech industry? We're optimists. Cognitive bias. We keep on thinking we can fix it, until it's too late. But"—Packship paused and smiled winningly—"pilots don't rely on their instincts. They have machines to tell them when to pull up, when they're about to hit the ground, when they're going too slow.

"So let me ask you a question. You have your bunker. You've got somewhere to go. But here's the question: How do you know *when* to go?"

With an air of playing along, Ellen Bywater said: "Riots on the streets."

"OK. How are you getting to your bunker? Private jet? How are you getting to the airfield?"

"Limo," said Lenk. He was enjoying himself. Back to preschool. Unlike Ellen and Zimri, he already knew where this was going.

"If there are riots on the streets, how d'you think a limo's going to go over with an angry mob?"

"America loves wealth," said Zimri. He motioned with his big, ungainly shoulders.

"Don't you think that the day Americans stop loving the wealthy is the day we need to be thinking about?" said Si Packship. "That's what we're here for. Not the day everything carries on as normal, but the day it all goes to shit. Let's say you make it to the airfield. What are the chances your plane is still there? What are the chances it can take off? How are you going to make sure that the fuel hasn't been drained, sold on?"

Selah Nommik breathed out heavily, like she'd been winded.

Zimri put his large hand on her arm and muttered, "We own the supply chain. We can always get fuel."

"Let me give you another one," said Si Packship. "How secret is your bunker?"

"Secret as hell," said Ellen Bywater. "There are no loopholes."

"I get you. You've kept the location and the codes secret. You've had your pilot's background looked into by a dozen different private investigators. No gambling debts, no mistresses, no medical bills. He's paid well to sit on his ass until you need him, and bring his family with him too. OK. You trust your pilot's next-door neighbor?"

"Come on," rumbled Zimri.

"I'm serious. You're keeping a pilot on staff who never flies anywhere because you want him on standby? You think on the day he puts on his coat and bundles his family into the car, if that's also the day the food prices spike for the seventeenth time in three months, you think none of his neighbors are going to try following him? Hunger makes people real focused, real quick."

"No reward without risk," said Ellen.

"But not unnecessary risk," said Packship. "How about: You know what's coming before the riots? Before the food shortages? Before the protestors overturn your jeep, before they leave the house, before they paint their placards?"

Si Packship made a control gesture with three fingers. The next slide appeared. The slide said:

When do you leave?

He said: "AUGR is a survival AI designed to protect you, to understand when you're in danger and get you out of it. But AUGR is more than that. AUGR will tell you when danger is coming long before anyone else can tell. AUGR is a complete algorithmic package and protocol that will tell participants in the program when it is time to go. AUGR knows the future."

He clicked the slide again. There were no interruptions.

Defense perimeter

"Our clients want to leave their homes, businesses, and places of work ten days before a catastrophic event or politico-social disaster. We call this ten-day period the defense perimeter."

AUGR: machine learning

"AUGR has analyzed thousands of city-, region-, and nationwide disasters, from the Bhopal chemical leak to Chernobyl, from the pandemic of 2020 to '23 to the Fall of Hong Kong. Nothing happens in a vacuum. With hindsight there are ways to see what's coming. AUGR has tapped into all available data streams to learn the deep patterns around these events. AUGR looks at economic data, weather data, seismic data, currency transactions, population movements, traffic. With more recent events it analyzes internet searches, social media posts, cell phone usage, bird flight patterns, air quality, bee pollination, ant colony migration. We don't ask why or whether a dataset might be relevant—we presume everything and anything can be."

"Does it work?" said Zimri Nommik.

Selah Nommik had a hand on his thigh. She was completely calm.

"You can't . . . predict the future," she said, frowning. "Even Zimri can't do that."

Zimri smiled faintly. He loved to educate. Martha could see Selah's remark putting Zimri—subtly but definitely—on Packship's side. Defending the possibilities of prediction to his skeptical wife. "You can up to a point," he said. "You can't tell exactly what's going to happen, but trends?

Yes, of course. If you're looking at the right things, you can analyze trends."

"Thank you," said Si Packship. "That's just what we're doing. Incredibly astute of you."

AUGR: from analysis to prediction

"We've been running AUGR without pause for two years. It's getting better. It can sense changes of mood and pace now, the wheel spinning out of control."

The slides flashed pictures on-screen. A riot in a major South American city after a corrupt election. A military incursion in an eastern European seaport. An oil spill. The collapse of a company previously thought strong as bone. A campus sit-in, the unseating of a newspaper editor, a suspension bridge disaster.

"AUGR flagged those last three as significant but non-evac events. AUGR is a lifestyle system. Once you're in the program, it looks for large-scale events, but it'll also be looking for personal danger to you specifically—a stalker, an internet hate mob. Anything that would mean you should get out right now."

AUGR and you

"Let me describe how this works in your life for you. You wake up in the morning and AUGR has detected a perimeter event."

A series of images—the discreet AUGR app on your smartwatch, your phone, your tablet, your home console—a little black dot in the corner of each screen. Nothing that would alarm anyone who happened to see your devices. "Your nanny, your pool guy, your ex-wife will never know." Lenk and Zimri, both of whom had ex-wives, laughed.

"You check in with AUGR online to see the threat level. AUGR will then work with you to create a plausible story—a sudden business opportunity, a medical emergency, or an unexpected canceled deal creating a break in your schedule so you and the kids can get a quick vacation. AUGR can spoof emails and screengrabs to make your story look convincing.

Orderly evacuation

"We make evacuation possible. But we can also make it pleasant. You have your alert. It's still the morning. Let the airfield and the pilot know you want to perform an as-live test of the evac systems this evening. There's time to pack up treasured heirlooms, to tell the kids there's a treat waiting for them tonight, to inform the school of a family emergency, to have your secretary reschedule meetings. You can spend the morning at your laptop, the afternoon at your safety-deposit boxes, and still have time for dinner at your favorite restaurant before you all head to the plane."

After you leave

"You'll all have your own systems in place for monitoring the situation after you've pulled out. AUGR can help you make those choices with an eye to the future. No point returning if the situation's just going to destabilize again in three weeks, right? AUGR will keep monitoring all available data streams, even after a major collapse. If there's widespread chaos, AUGR can let you know where—if anywhere—will remain stable. AUGR won't make your choices . . . but it will make your choices clearer."

Exclusive

Si Packship was winding up his presentation now. Coming in for the money punch. Ellen, Lenk, and Zimri were all still there, so that was a start. And Martha knew the pitch was a killer. The final slide flashed up. It was the

AUGR logo, a stylized drill. The name could be both an augur (a prophet) and an auger (a tool) that drills down.

"This meeting's been facilitated by Ms. Einkorn, who spotted my work and gave me access to some development money. For which I'm incredibly grateful. But now I'm in the market for a sale. As we know, many technology start-ups need to get big fast. AUGR is the opposite of that. We need to stay small forever. This thing cannot do its job if every person in every city owns it. It's for a select group. There are a number of other interested clients, and I'm sure I don't need to tell you who they are. But I've come to the three of you first because Ms. Einkorn suggested you might want to take AUGR completely off the table for any other buyers."

Zimri looked at Ellen and Ellen looked at Lenk. They wanted this thing; this was their chance. It was the solution they'd been looking for.

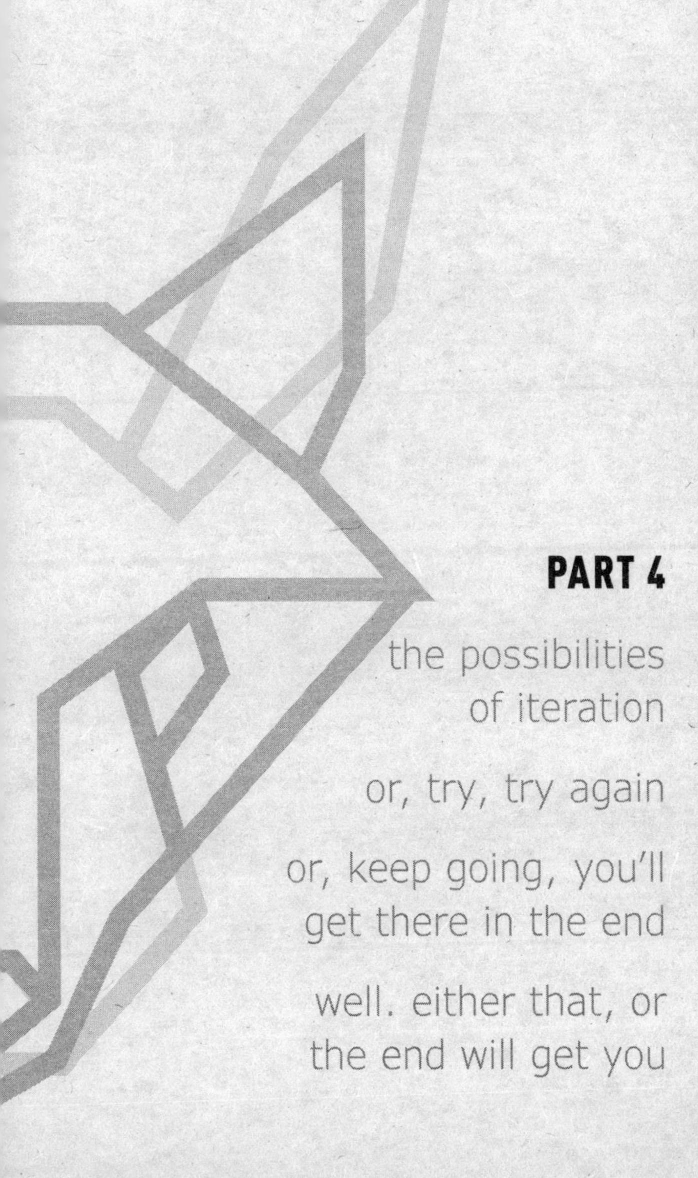

PART 4

the possibilities
of iteration

or, try, try again

or, keep going, you'll
get there in the end

well. either that, or
the end will get you

extract from Name The Day survivalist forum

sub-board: ntd/strategic/biblestudywithonecorn

>> *OneCorn is at* **Prepped To The Max** *status. OneCorn has made 5,118 posts and received 17,555 thumbs-up.*

Things get darker before they get lighter, that is the whole of the law.

The story of Lot is, fundamentally, a story about survival. All the problems and self-delusions of survival. Lot and his two daughters, Moa and Amma, survived the rain of fire onto Sodom, fine. They lost their mom first—Edo looked back, she couldn't stop being transfixed by the past, she couldn't walk a step further on. She turned into salt: tears or the ocean or something inhuman, anyway. A bare piece of rock salt. Life, for her, was over.

But her daughters and her husband, you'd have thought, could have a brand-new start. They were the sole survivors of a doomed city, whisked out of there by the messengers of God. They found their way to another city, Tzoar. Start again. Get hustling. Up by your bootstraps. Don't look back. Yeah well, says Genesis, there are some problems you can't will your way out of. Trauma comes back again and again.

The story of Lot is a story about how

sole survivors are fucked. In the case of Lot, extremely literally.

Genesis chapter 19, 30–36, loosely translated

CW: caves, alcohol, rape, incest, pregnancy, despair, internet

So they did get to Tzoar but they didn't stay long. The story says: "Lot was afraid to stay in Tzoar." They'd seen one city burned to ashes, maybe they thought it was going to keep happening. They had fallen out of the practice of hope.

They moved out of the city and went to live in a cave. Which I guess is what you do if you've stopped believing in cities but you've also lost the skills of walking the land, wandering, hunting and gathering. I think we can imagine they felt ashamed.

One night by the dregs of the fire, Moa said to Amma: "Where is this going?"

Amma knew what she meant. Still, she said: "What do you mean?"

"Are you really going to make me spell it out?"

"You mean, are we going to live our lives in a cave and first Dad's going to die and then one of us will die and then the other?"

Moa said: "Wow yeah, I guess that's what I meant."

"Then that's where this is going."

"And is that what you want?"

God had taken their home, their husbands, their mother, their neighbors, their neighborhood, their safety, their security, probably also their sanity given what's about to happen. They didn't feel they owed much to God. Lot had offered them to the mob. They didn't feel they owed much to him. All that was left was their own desire. The force of life that rises again every dawn. The desire of all creatures that we shall not be the last of our kind.

I'm warning you again that this is going to get really dark.

The sisters got wine somehow. (Side note: they *definitely knew there were cities*, that's where they went to get the wine, clearly. You can't really make wine if you're living alone in a cave.)

They fed their father the wine until he was so wasted he couldn't tell the difference between his own daughters and the whores who used to stand by the gates in Sodom. He lolled back against the wall of the cave and when there was a girl on him, Lot relished it like a dream of the world he'd left.

That was the first night. On that night Amma sat at the cave mouth and hummed tunelessly to herself and threw rocks down the mountainside. There was nothing to do and no one to talk to and nowhere to go.

So. That's also an effect of trauma, right? Tunnel vision. The story tells us the girls said: "There's no man in the land to come for us, in the way that everyone else is doing." They'd just been in Tzoar. They *knew* there were men. They knew what everyone else was doing. This is a story about what it's like to be the last survivors of your civilization. No one just gets up and walks away from that feeling fine. They knew there were other men. But they were stuck in this place, unable to walk away from their father.

"How will we know if it works?" said Amma to Moa as she came out, wrapping her linen around her loins again.

Moa said: "We'll wait. If it doesn't work, we'll try again."

The second night it was Amma's turn.

Amma said to herself:

- I do not need to be any better than him, I am certainly no worse.
- He offered this part of me to the mob; he has forfeited his right to choose or to tell me what to do.
- What does the world hold for me other than this? Bones and burning and the stench of the pit.
- My mother is not alive nor yet is she dead, she is turned to salt and I have no need to make sense of the world. I want a baby.

It wasn't fun but it wasn't difficult. It was easy to make Lot drunk again. He knew on the edge of his mind what had happened, but he did not want to know. On the first night with Moa he drank without understanding. On the second night with Amma he drank so as not to know himself again. We walk into illusions gladly, eager for release from our encircling selves.

By contrast with the grasping mob of Sodom, what Amma did to her father was kind. There was no suffering. He gave three sharp grunts and fell back asleep.

The golden rule is very clear: "That which is hateful to you, do not do unto others." Let me simple that up for you: if you *don't like it* when something happens to you, *don't do that* to other people. It is the simplest thing you'll ever hear and no rule is perfect but this one is a pretty good yardstick for most of your choices.

By the golden rule, the sisters should have known better. But people tend to think things are different after the world's ended. Or when they've told themselves the world has ended.

What comes after despair? Hope, if you're lucky. It is dark before the dawn but the dawn always returns. At least on this planet.

If you're not lucky, what comes after despair is brutality. "Whatever has been done to me, that is what I may do to others; and whatever others have done, that is what may be done to them." That's how people live on the internet these days. It's the golden rule's dark twin. If I were feeling fancy, I'd call it "the rule of salt," because it crumbles at a touch and lacerates the hands every time it is used.

The golden rule operates like a technology designed to direct us away from revenge. It hauls you back time and again to the certain knowledge of what it is you don't like. Do you *not like it* when people call you ugly on social media? Then don't do that to *anyone else*. Do you *not enjoy it* when someone tries to get you fired? Then consider very carefully whether it is ever right to do that to someone else. I know, I know. It's so *boring* to get control of your feelings and think about what's right. But this is how we construct a society, OK? The golden rule is a vastly valuable social technology carefully passed down to us by people who fought their way out of darkness using it.

Unfortunately these days quite a lot of people on the internet seem happy to live by the rule of salt. That's a rule of infinite vendetta: scroll back years through a social media timeline, the worst thing you can find another person has done is *totally legit* to do to them. But then, that's the worst thing *you've* done, and it's legit to do it to you. And on and on, everyone trapped inside this same worsening cycle. That's where we are right now with the media and the internet: stuck inside a cave with the worst person we know, finding increasingly degrading things to do to each other and feeling righteous while we do them.

Lot offered his daughters' vaginas to the mob. So they felt justified in doing what they wanted with his cock. That's the last we ever see of Lot in the Bible. That's where he ends. Sitting alone in a cave, having involuntarily knocked up both his daughters. I think we can all agree: he might have gotten out of Sodom but he didn't *thrive*.

[X] *close*

›› *ArturoMegadog is at* BunkerBorn *status.*

Jesus Christ you dig up some dark parts of the Bible.

›› *OneCorn is at* Prepped To The Max *status.*

Thanks! It's my special thing. You think anyone else is still listening?

›› *ArturoMegadog is at* BunkerBorn *status.*

This sub-thread has 4,610 followers. They're just all stunned into silence.

›› *OneCorn is at* Prepped To The Max *status.*

I mean, reasonable.

›› *DanSatDan is at* One Tin O'Beans *status.*

OK. I'm gonna wade in because that's what I do, right? My guess is: in terms of survival this is about not giving in to the urge to hide and stay small, right? Trying real hard to band together with other survivors? But not "band together" in a "rape your dad" way.

>> OneCorn is at** Prepped To The Max **status.

Ah, welcome, DanSatDan, to Disturbing Genesis Study Group! I love that you want to keep us on topic. OK so, I have thought a lot about this and . . . these stories in Genesis have a lot going on in them. You can turn them over and over and never quite get to the bottom of them. This one is definitely about family, about passing on of family trauma. But it's also about surviving, and the problems of being a survivor. And about, yeah, keeping on trying to get something from the worst person you know.

>> DanSatDan is at** One Tin O'Beans **status.

It's about trust. Anyone who thinks that sexual assault and mob rule isn't relevant to an evacuation scenario hasn't realized what other humans are like.

My dad was one of those Rambo guys. He loved fighting, and when he couldn't get what he wanted from the other drunks, he beat up my mom, he beat on me. He coulda survived a nuclear event. But you wouldn't have wanted him in your bunker. Or your cave.

Lot's whole family are a warning. You've gotta be careful about looking back. You've gotta be careful what you bring with you. The things that once kept you alive will end by killing you.

>> ArturoMegadog is at** BunkerBorn **status.

Shit. DanSatDan I'm so sorry to hear that about your dad.

>> DanSatDan is at** One Tin O'Beans **status.

Thanks, man. I wanted to ask. How are you? Are you doing OK? After the thing in the spring?

>> ArturoMegadog is at** BunkerBorn **status.

I'm doing better, thanks. Getting some help myself. Taking it day by day. I was too much by myself before but it's helping a lot that now I have a project.

1. twenty-eight squeeze packs of peanut and almond butter

zhen

Zhen spent three weeks holed up in Madrid. If she was going to Marius, she needed to muddy her trail and let it get a little cold.

After Singapore, she took a flight to Manila, then a second onward, then another, then another. Between two of those she pulled her alternate passport in the name Ho Sara from the bottom of her rucksack. She'd never traveled on a false passport before. It had been a stunt for her video audience to get one made and somewhere between a private pleasure and paranoia to keep it. A comfort blanket for former refugees. She hadn't known whether it would work until—in an airport between here and there—it suddenly seemed less dangerous to try than not to.

In Manila she withdrew all the cash she could using eight different ATMs. In a mini-mart in the airport she bought ramen noodles. She set her automated assistant to cancel her upcoming engagements on the grounds of . . . she considered . . . exposure to leprosy. People would believe that, and no one would try to persuade her to come.

On the flight out of Manila, she took the battery out of her cell phone and snapped her SIM card in half. Thirty-five thousand feet in the air, she disabled all wireless communications on her laptop, her Anvil thinscreen, her Medlar Torc, and every other smart device she owned.

In Ankara she changed all her cash into euros using Ho Sara's passport and dumped the SIM down a toilet.

In Skopje she had a sixteen-hour wait for her next flight and bleached her hair—because why not?—in the toilets. In Madrid, because she had no connections to Madrid, because as far as she was aware she knew no one here, she rode a bus into town. Got off and started walking when the bus passed through an area with peeling paint and faded signs. On a street of cheap flophouses and discount electronics stores, she checked into the first grimy hotel she could find, the sticky sheets reassuring her that there were probably no smart devices tracking her face.

If a government was following her, this wouldn't be enough. If she'd somehow gotten into the bad books of Fantail or Medlar or another huge tech company—say by ending up with their experimental proprietary software on her phone?—it *might* be enough. And if it was just a mentally ill religious fundamentalist . . . or even a few mentally ill religious fundamentalists, this level of care should do it.

She paid cash for three weeks in advance. In a room with striped orange-and-red curtains drawn and a pink-bobbled lampshade, she went through her bags to learn—when it came to it—whether she actually had enough to survive on or whether her whole life had been an embarrassing pretense. She had:

- sixteen packets of ramen noodles
- one large bag of trail mix
- one large packet of something called "Bamba snack," which had been pulverized to a fine peanut-flavored powder at the bottom of her backpack
- eight different-colored SurvivalGel pouches she'd picked up at a trade show, each claiming to contain a full day's worth of nutrition in an appealing flavor. The flavors, she discovered, were all the same—lime with a faint but noticeable aftertaste of toilet cleaner
- twelve sticks of beef jerky

- six packets of protein powder
- twenty-eight squeeze packs of peanut and almond butter
- ninety multivitamin tablets
- an apple

She had in addition:

- an anthology of selected great works of English literature and "first thousand words" and basic grammar of the world's twenty most-spoken languages printed on a thin treated paper that would, in a pinch, serve as either toilet paper or fire starters, not that she needed either
- a book of cryptic crosswords, a skill she'd admired since arriving in the UK but had never learned, holding it deliberately in reserve in her mind for after the apocalypse
- a small windup radio
- eight pencils, five ballpoint pens, and a small yellow children's exercise book

That was OK. Enough here to get along with while not turning on any of her devices. Still the dork with the survival habit. Still—unlike the world—making sense.

She ate the apple first; it would never be better nutritionally than it was today. It was crisp and juicy and she experienced it very urgently, the world pressing in on her senses, a ritual for the start of a lockdown.

These were bad days but they were also simple ones. She remembered the months in her early teenage life in Hong Kong when her mom was dying and she didn't leave the house, or when she and her dad were in the offshore refugee camp waiting for their interviews to get into the UK. The amount of mental effort and dedication it took to just keep holding on to a routine that spooled out into the future.

She ran on the spot, did jumping jacks and push-ups and squats. She remembered her dad trying to get her interested in calisthenics and how stupid the old man had looked twisting his body to the left, two three, right, two three and how much she'd love to have him here now. The boredom and the fear felt, in their way, familiar and safe. She wanted to log on to the internet to find out what the fuck had happened in Singapore. She constantly had the urge to call her dad or her ex or any one of a dozen friends. The urge rose up and passed away, again and again. Every time it came back she thought of the shot perfectly aimed through the center of the Valentine fox bin. She needed to give this some time.

She slept a lot. She watched Spanish television and CNN and listened to the radio. No one mentioned a shooter in a Singaporean mall or an unexplained dead body or an international manhunt for a wanted criminal paramagnetic-salt-snow murderer. Her Spanish improved, through sheer desperation for information. She learned how to do cryptic crosswords.

After thirteen days in the room she ventured down the corridor to the vending machine at midnight with a fistful of euro coins. She couldn't stop shaking, standing at the machine, trying to look like anyone else choosing a candy bar. When the stairwell doors banged open, she flinched. The young straight couple kissing as they walked didn't look her way. Back in the room she ate the candy bars one after another. Halfway through a sticky-sweet Spanish Almond Joy knockoff, she couldn't keep the pieces in her mouth, spat them into her hand, and cried.

After twenty days, she packed up her bags and left the hotel at 5 a.m. It was the start of July now and the sky was bright. A good time of year for some hard travel.

She found a convenience store where she bought three cheap dumbphones in blister packs and three local SIM cards. She took the first subway train of the day to Chamartín-Clara Campoamor station. There was one man on the train, a construction worker in boots and overalls still splattered with yesterday's dust and paint. She sat on the platform. Five small black birds pecked at a bag of chips. The next train going northeast across the expanded Schengen Area—the largest border-check-free area in the world—pulled out of the station at 8:43 a.m.

This part was complicated but easy in its way. Trains across Europe, one after another, avoiding Switzerland and any of the smaller territories not part of Schengen. Hoodie pulled down low, three pieces of clear, holographic, reflective duct tape strategically placed on her face to avoid the cameras and the recognition programs in the richer and more authoritarian parts of the continent. In person it just looked like she had some Band-Aids covering a couple of cuts. On the cameras, it'd come up as strange black shapes that would confuse the algorithm. Zhen imagined who could be watching her. The government of Singapore and a warrant for arrest and extradition. The staff of Fantail, Anvil, and/or Medlar, all of which had supplied technological infrastructure to most governments and public services in Europe. A small but *extremely determined* band of online fundamentalists who might have a friend or sympathizer in any shop, any café, any ticket booth. She arrived late at night in every station, just before the ticket offices closed. She paid in cash. Where possible, she slept on the train. Her bones ached with exhaustion.

Her final journey was the night train from Budapest to Bucharest—not a service that had received the sort of investment Anvil had poured into expensive automated cars and Lenk Sketlish had put into a failed space elevator. Zhen shared the rattling sleeper compartment with a Romanian woman who traveled with a bottle of plum brandy and smelled of wet wool. The woman fell asleep just after midnight and let out a continual series of ripe and marshy farts, redolent, Zhen felt, of the fields of her homeland or at least of their livestock. Even with the window cracked open and the cold air tumbling onto her face as the train clacked out the miles, it was impossible to sleep.

Zhen lay in the dark and thought of her mother. She had a total of thirty-eight photographs of her; the one where she was holding one-year-old Zhen on her lap in the small courtyard garden of their apartment building was her favorite. It was a Medlar MovePhoto, and Zhen's mother turned her head at some distant noise and then, at a gurgle from Zhen, turned her head back. The love in the gaze between Zhen and her mother in that moment was so intense and pure that Zhen could feel it still. She could not access that photo now. Like the rest of her most important possessions, it was online. She wished she'd thought to turn it into a corny trinket, a key ring or a pendant or some shit. It was no use now to be too cool for feelings.

Her mother had died from cancer when Zhen was fourteen. She had not wanted to go; that was the thing Zhen remembered most of that last year. Her mother had not been reconciled to dying; she had not been peaceful. She had clutched Zhen's hand and tried to tell her all the things she might need to know for an entire happy life, disordered and increasingly confused. The thing she'd never said was the greatest lesson Zhen had taken from all that—you could die while wanting desperately to live, with many important things left unfinished. The future would come while you were looking the other way and there were so many things that could kill you.

Zhen's mother had made her father promise that they would leave for the UK. There had been riots and demonstrations against encroachments by the PRC in Hong Kong. Zhen had been young then, not even old enough to join the street protests and the gas-mask-wearing students facing the police and the tear gas. She wouldn't have done it if she'd been older anyway. Her mother was weaker day by day. Zhen had read online about "teenage rebellion" and had decided—quite coherently, as if this was a thing a person could choose—that her own rebellion would have to wait until her mother was well. Nonetheless, the protests were impossible to ignore. Zhen's mother watched with her as young people holding rainbow flags shouted anti-government slogans in unison. She looked at her daughter appraisingly, understanding things about her that Zhen hadn't fully grasped yet. She squeezed Zhen's hand. She said: "Dad will apply for the visas."

But because of her mother's cancer, her father hadn't filed the forms on time. There were visas for Hong Kong citizens to go to live in the UK. But her mother couldn't move country and so—in those months when every day felt like it could be the end—they couldn't think of the future. After she died it was too late to do the thing smoothly. It wasn't as if they hadn't known the deadlines, after all. So that was one of the million ways you end up in an offshore British refugee camp.

Zhen had read online in the days after the DEMOlition conference about what had happened to Martha's mother—or at least the rumors of what had happened to her. Martha's mother had left Enoch soon after Enoch set up his compound and started preaching about the preparation for the end of days. She had gone in the night. She had left her seven-year-old daughter with Enoch for whatever life he would give her, and she had found a new partner in Portland and not shown much interest in trying to get her daughter back over the following five years until she had crossed the street without looking and had been hit by a Frito-Lay truck and died. The future would come and kill you while you were looking the other way.

She wondered whether she and Martha had known this about each other somehow, in the first glance. Maybe that's what love was, or sudden pointed lust, or attraction or whatever Zhen had felt in that first moment, just a recognition that this person would be able to understand the worst thing that had happened in your life. And if they'd known that about each other, how had they known? Maybe women whose mothers had died when they were very young could tell this about each other by a certain way of holding their shoulders, by their blink rate, by the clothes they wore.

Zhen had sometimes felt that she had a sort of twisted wire between her organs, holding her up—where others had their soft and tense tissue, she had something made of metal. Maybe that was what she and Martha had heard in each other, the wire in their words. As the miles ticked off beneath her, counted on the cross-grid of the railway sleepers, she wondered whether it would be possible to program a surveillance system to look for these signs, whatever they were. A markup language for humans. Something showing that whatever happened, however much future had already been taken away from you, you would find a way to survive.

2. the pixels in the world

martha

"See, emojis," said Selah, "emojis are fucking fantastic." Her fingers were flashing across the keyboard even as she sucked thoughtfully on her lollipop.

The four of them were in a hotel room north of San Francisco. Nothing fancy, nowhere with facial recognition. Not under their own names. An anonymous and unimportant room. This weekend they'd decided it was time to try something. Martha had brought ideas. Selah had brought an anonymized laptop. Badger had brought a spare security tag swiped from their mother's dresser. Albert had brought THC lollipops.

"It just makes everything easier, great for coding," he had said, handing one to Selah. Martha and Badger both shook their heads. "You can see the interconnections between things."

"Because emojis are a way of making emotions machine-readable," Selah mused. "Language is complex. Super, super complex. I say 'yeah' but I mean 'nah.' I say 'That's cool' meaning 'That's rubbish.' And it's changing all the time. You try to get a machine to understand 'OK boomer' or 'yaaaaaaas' and how it's different to 'yes.' You can't do it. No one can do it! So emojis, man, should be fucking gold dust. Winky face means 'This is sarcasm or a joke,' smiley face, angry face, vomming face . . . it's like . . . it's like markup language for feelings. But then human beings get involved—aubergines are dicks and cowboy hats are awkward and a skull means 'that's hilarious.'

Humans love to mess around with language and there's enough emojis that they *also* change meaning over time. So instead of that we've got *reactions*—fucking genius. Look what you've got on Medlar. Six possible reactions to any comment. Thumbs-up. Heart. Smiley face. Angry face. Confused face. Sad face. Limited number, not an infinite set. One reaction per item. It's not enough to start doing the twisty-language dance. It's just core machine-codable feelings. Just decide what emotions you want to optimize for and iterate."

"Incredible," said Badger, hanging over her shoulder.

Four people felt like enough. Four people who regularly sat in rooms with three of the very richest people in the world, with control over—between them—a majority of the international technological infrastructure of the world. Four people who looked one another in the eye and said: "We can't just do nothing. We need to come up with something." So here they were—not surreptitiously talking at a party or a White House gala, but conspiring on an idea. The first idea.

"OK," said Selah, "so I've created this program."

Martha looked at Selah's screen. The program was called *happymeal*.

"Happy meal?"

"I mean it's like . . . relevant. Look, I'm not good at names, OK?"

It was the first time Martha had seen Selah Nommik not be good at anything.

"I have a guinea pig called Toepocket."

"You're not naming anything either, then. It doesn't matter what the program's called. Listen. We're going to change some comments."

It was a simple goal for today. The type of emotional optimization Anvil and Medlar and Fantail did as a matter of course every day. Each of their websites, thinscreen interfaces, smart torcs, burst displays, and cell phone applications had specific commands about what to show and what to bury. Certain emotions drove high engagement—people looked for longer at things that made them angry or afraid. Fantail used this knowledge to raise certain posts and comments to the top of users' information feeds. Anvil used it to suggest new products: for example, a news article about the number of different possible disasters together with a list of hurricane lamps and emergency communicators was a *wonderful* way to drive sales. Medlar created dramatic debate around its television shows by revealing negative comments to people who loved the show and vice versa. These sites presented themselves as a clear pane of glass through which you could see the world as it was. But they were really a distorting visor, showing you the version of the world that worked best for the board and stockholders of the companies.

Selah sucked on her lollipop.

"Tell me if you disagree. I'm going to tell *happymeal* that it wants to create comments—*within our parameters*, obvs—that do not get the confused face, right?"

They all agreed on that.

"And for our purposes right now, too much angry or sad is also not what we're looking for. Angry might mean 'You've said something that's gone too far' and sad might mean 'I'm sad you're saying these completely out-of-character things.' We agree?"

They decided that 10 percent angry or sad responses would work. Selah stretched her arms in front of her and tipped her neck to one side, then the other, two brisk and businesslike clicks.

"Fuck me, it's been years since I did this. Skunkworks! Hackers on the side of righteousness, yeah! OK, so we're set. So . . . Badger, you can get me access to . . . ?"

Badger shrugged. "Basically anything, I guess." Badger

twirled the gray code key around their index finger. “She never uses it. Gianfranco logs in for her when she needs. She won’t notice it’s gone.”

“Great, and I’ll delete ID and location as we go. So just as a test, *happymeal* is going to alter comments in MedlarTV shows . . . we’ll just do like three or four shows for now, right? And we’ll change them so even the people who made the comments can’t be *totally* sure they didn’t write them that way themselves, unless they took a screenshot. And none of these fuckers took screenshots.”

The algorithm in *happymeal* would change or add or delete just one word per comment. It would use the huge databases Medlar had already compiled of user comments to ensure what it said sounded like real people. It would compare and match to comments that precise user had already made. It would copy their syntax and vocabulary. It would never use a word they hadn’t used before—that made it safer, though it limited their pool of possible users to only . . .

“Fourteen point six million,” said Selah, “on these three shows.”

“I can’t tell if that’s a big number or a small number,” said Badger.

“Feels like enough to play with,” said Albert.

“Alright for a test,” said Martha.

Martha had gone through Medlar output and chosen a nature show, a drama about hotshot lawyers, and a show about monster trucks. Anodyne, middle-of-the-road content that was pretty much no one’s absolute favorite show but also a lot of people had them on at some point. By the time they were ready to launch, it was dawn in Palo Alto and Selah and Albert had been up all night coding. Badger had watched for a while, fascinated, and then fallen asleep very suddenly on one of the beds, hugging their pillow like a friend.

At dawn, Martha was the only one not staring at a screen or sleeping. She looked out of the window of the midpriced hotel. The sky was slate blue and very flat, the trees outside the hotel room window silhouetted as if they'd been drawn onto the glass panes with a black marker. Martha felt she could see the pixels in the world. A world made up of tiny pieces, like a pointillist painting; the truth is that everything is both pieces and a whole. And if you're really going to understand anything, you have to be able to go between the very small and the very large because neither one is the whole truth.

Albert was standing behind Selah, watching her work, pointing out any problems or typos, giving her ideas. Badger stretched and shifted, moving out of sleep. Martha was the only one who saw the dawn come in, the fracturing of the gray into gold, the promise that things are always changing and no regime lasts forever.

"Ready," said Selah. "Tigers, we're coming to save you!"

Martha stuck her hands in the pockets of her slacks.

"You ready for this?" She spoke to Badger, protective of this young person who needed less protection than the rest of them.

"It's just a test," they said. "If she finds it, she'll just think it was some of my usual shit. It's a great name, by the way: *happymeal.* It sounds like something one of my friends would have come up with."

"They're not gonna find it," said Selah. "There's no way." She turned in her chair. "Honestly, no fucking person in the world is gonna piss their pants if they think we added the word 'so' to their comment."

Albert said: "It's do something or do nothing. And we've already tried doing nothing."

"Alright then," said Selah, "let's fucking rock."

3. MENACE

zhen

In a lecture hall in Bucharest, Zhen found Marius doing one of the things he did best: shouting at his students.

"You think a computer can understand you? Want to help you? Know how to solve all your problems?"

Marius's students—in the room, and on the Zoom display wall at the back of the auditorium—remained silent. Most of them were red-eyed, some of them pale with tiredness. Marius made his students fit in with Bucharest time. Professor Marius Zugravescu believed it was extremely gracious of him to have moved this class from 1:30 p.m. to 4:30 p.m. in Bucharest. Four thirty p.m. in Bucharest is 6:30 a.m. in Berkeley, and by the looks on the students' faces, they did not find it gracious enough.

"Come on," said Marius. "Can computer learn? Like a human learn?"

Zhen slipped into the back of the room. Marius didn't notice her. She sat hunkered down in the back row and felt, already, strangely comforted and safe to be here. Marius's presence did that. He was a good friend if you'd been good to him. But to these students . . . perhaps not so comforting.

One of the students on the display wall—a redheaded man, gray shadows around his eyes, the nameplate under his blotchy red face saying Greer—ventured an opinion.

"Yeah, I mean," said Greer. He had a Scottish accent. His hair was close-cropped, soft and spiky like a rabbit's fur. "I mean, machine learning, letting the machine loose on the data, it can learn all sorts of stuff. Translation software works that way. The machine compares millions of translated phrases per second, and it learns to understand . . ." He trailed off, struck by the look on Marius's face.

"Computer *understands*? Next computer feels! Computer is sensitive, caring—when we're not running program, computer wonders why we not there? Yes?"

"Um, no."

"Computer is matchboxes. Fucking matchboxes and beads. You remember matchboxes?"

Greer shook his head very slightly, the horrified look on his face showing Zhen that he'd very much intended to nod his head and pretend he *did* know what Marius was talking about, but his body had betrayed him.

In the past, Zhen knew, Marius would have sworn at this student and told him that if he didn't do his fucking reading, he shouldn't be in the class. But Berkeley's clean, legitimate dollars were useful to Marius in other parts of his life, and the postgraduate board felt that swearing at students was not best pedagogical practice. They'd also, in passing, told him if he was teaching students at 6:30 a.m., he had better be the best fucking teacher on the faculty. He'd said he was the best fucking teacher in the whole university.

This was in fact true; despite himself, Marius was an excellent teacher. He did not know how to stop caring whether the students truly understood the work. He cared beyond endurance, some part of him continually hugely offended until he saw that he had achieved genuine communication.

"Rest of you," he said, "anyone explain the matchboxes to me?"

A tentative hand went up from a dark-haired female student.

"Professor Zugravescu? This is the thing where you can teach a machine to play tic-tac-toe?"

"Ah! Someone did reading. See, all of you? If you read, you learn."

He marched over to a side table, followed by the eyes of the educational camera suite. There was an old stained painter's cloth covering something large and lumpy. With a flourish, Marius pulled the cloth off to reveal a ramshackle pile of matchboxes, stuck together with brown tape. On the front of each matchbox he'd drawn a noughts and crosses grid—the game Americans called tic-tac-toe. Each a little different, *X*s and *O*s in different configurations. Next to the pile of matchboxes there were nine jars of colored beads. Red, orange, yellow, green, blue, purple, pink, black, and white.

He had actually made the thing. Sitting in the back row, Zhen smiled. This was Marius. He couldn't help himself. He wanted them to understand so much that he'd constructed this himself. This was why Zhen would be safe here. Marius might be a cynic, a hard-nosed realist, and very frequently kind of an asshole, but he had never learned ironic detachment from anything.

From under the table, Marius pulled out a large wipe-clean noughts and crosses grid with one square of each color. Red, orange, yellow, green, blue, purple, pink, black, and white.

Marius said: "Beads, matchboxes, colored paper. You think a bead can learn anything?"

Silence on the screen.

"Bead can't learn! Matchbox can't learn! Cardboard can't learn! Human learns. Machine iterates. This is a machine. OK. I show you."

In 1960 in Edinburgh, Donald Michie, a biologist, cryptographer, and early computer scientist, wanted to show how a computer could incrementally become better and better at a task—what we'd called "learning" if it were a person. Which it's not. Donald Michie had worked for

British intelligence at Bletchley Park during World War II. He'd been part of a team working day and night in cold iron huts in a sodden country, trying to crack German codes faster than they could change them. Where this story starts is so human it hurts: a group of code breakers trying to bring some soldiers home, keep some passenger ships in the Atlantic safe from the U-boat wolf packs; trying to end the war faster, fend off Nazism, spare just a few more mothers' sons.

The code breakers invented machines that ran hundreds of different code combinations per second until they hit the one that spat out real German words. The people made the machines better; they found shortcuts and ironed out mistakes. After the war Donald Michie wondered whether he could create a machine-run process to make the machines better. And he did it with matchboxes and iteration. Doing the same process over and over again.

Here's how it works. There are about three hundred different possible board combinations in noughts and crosses. So you need about three hundred matchboxes, each with one possible board layout written on the front.

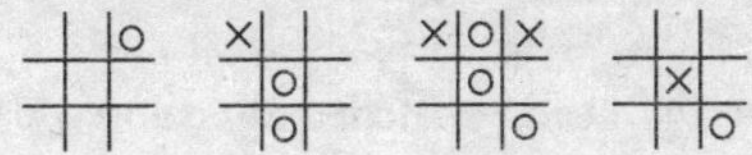

Like that. You give each square on the board a color.

Like that. And you put colored beads inside each matchbox corresponding to the colors of each square where you could play a legitimate move. Just as Donald Michie did, Marius had laboriously glued a little cardboard V shape inside the matchbox drawers, so that if you gave the beads a shake, one of them fell right into the point of the V shape. That's random selection.

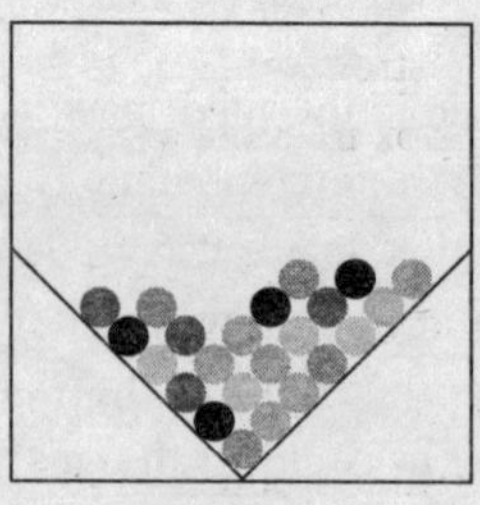

Like that. A red bead has fallen into the V, so for its next move the matchbox machine will put an *X* into the red square on the board. It can play through the whole game like that.

"At the start," says Marius, "matchboxes are *shit* at tic-tac-toe."

Beads for every possible move are in each matchbox, even if that move would make no sense.

"Human player—even small child—would not play stupid move except by accident, OK? You explain rules to child, child understands: block other player from getting three in a row, OK?"

But the machine—at the start—would be no more likely to block a three-in-a-row than to put its *X* over the other side of the board.

"Look what we try to do. Play game with machine." Marius jabbed two fingers at his own forehead so hard he left a red mark. His English got a bit less grammatically coherent the more impassioned he became. "We want to reach out with mind. Find other minds. We reach out all the time. Imagine what animal is thinking—makes good sense if we're hunting. Or being hunted. Yes?" He didn't wait for an answer. "We reach out with mind. Read spirits into caves, and springs and sacred groves. Can't stop ourselves. We play tic-tac-toe with cardboard and beads, we think it's person."

Anyway, the matchboxes playing tic-tac-toe is not the learning part. The learning part comes next.

Suppose by a stroke of luck and random falls of the beads, the matchbox machine manages to play moves that win in a game of noughts and crosses with a human. *Then* the operator goes back through and adds three extra beads of the color that led to the winning route to each matchbox. If it loses the game—which it will, a lot—the operator goes through the whole route and removes one bead of the color that led to the loss.

Do that a thousand times.

This is the thing a computer can do in a way humans just can't.

Do the same thing a thousand times, without tiring or flagging or being bored.

After a thousand times it won't be even anymore. When you open a matchbox drawer, the beads will look like this:

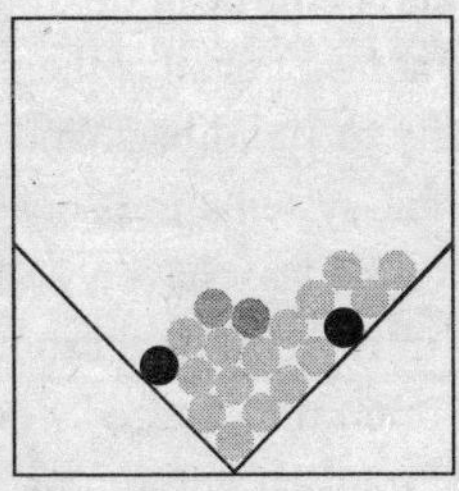

That's what we call machine learning. The matchboxes get better and better at playing noughts and crosses. Eventually, they play well. Eventually, they appear to have strategies and insight like a person.

"How many games of tic-tac-toe your smartphone can play every one second?" said Marius.

The students guessed a thousand. Ten thousand.

Zhen sat on her hands and listened.

Marius said: "One million. At least. Per second. Your smartphone, playing against humans through the internet, would be perfect at tic-tac-toe after one second. OK? We keep telling it if it won or lost, it becomes perfect."

Never hurrying, never tarrying. Performing the same blind action over and over again. Never becoming more than matchboxes and beads. Never empathizing, never casting its mind into the other, never using insight to spot strategy or gleefully thinking up a strategy of its own. Just repeating, repeating, repeating, faster than a human ever could.

It's an intensely powerful strategy. It's tremendously useful. It creates extraordinary single-use tools: a program to play chess, another to write software, another to assess resource allocation in farming regions. Tools to scrape data about how sentences are put together or how pixels form artworks and then remix, remodel, iterate that original material to make new combinations.

Of course, human beings can do all these things. Perhaps none of them as fast, but all of them with more freshness, with the ability to stand back and join up disparate pieces from different systems into novel solutions. And crucially, humans can at least have a go at *all* these things. We have a flexible intelligence that can move from task to task fluidly. Not a brain that doggedly does the same task at the same speed for a year without pause. It would be—according to Marius—very surprising if iteration turned out to be how human thinking happens.

"Maybe!" he said. "Maybe someone invent program

that can do everything human brain can and more. Then we learned something about human brain! I been doing this for forty-five years, since I was ten. I've not seen it yet. Computer is tool, not person."

Donald Michie called his machine the Matchbox Educable Noughts and Crosses Engine. MENACE for short. It was a joke then. The thing was a menace at noughts and crosses. Today that same process—randomized attempts to achieve a goal, penalizing unsuccessful pathways and reinforcing successful ones—that same precise process was used by Fantail and Medlar to keep humans using their products. To keep humans talking to their AI assistant instead of to other people. To insist that their Proprietary Platform Personality was the only way to even understand the great ocean of human knowledge. Again and again and again. Never tarrying, never hurrying. They could change what people saw millions of times a second, testing pathways, never understanding why some worked or what the consequences would be.

Consequences are outside the parameters of the machine. After all, it is only a set of small pieces of cardboard, or silicon. It has no urge to reach out to other minds, to connect, to understand or be understood. It can have no sense of whether it is altering the human minds around it, of how the ubiquity of these systems of manipulation without empathy or compassion can slowly train human beings to fit in with them.

The class looked exhausted by the time Marius had finished with them. But excited. Either ready for bed or ready to go to battle. Hard to tell which.

"Powerful tool," said Marius. "So powerful it can change world, yes?"

Greer, the young Scottish man with the blotchy face, was strung out, like he'd seen too much of the future all at once.

"So you could do that with love," he said. "Like, with a girl. Find the perfect things to say. Repeat the tests over and over until you found the pathway. Online maybe. Not with real people. But like, the things to say to get a date? Like in, you know, like in *Groundhog Day* where he keeps going till he gets her to date him?"

Zhen wanted Greer to pursue the thought, to explain how it would work. But Marius was already calling him a psychopath and a new Stalin and a new Hitler and the servant of the cardboard gods, and the rest of the class were mentioning again that they'd already had a conversation with the director of the faculty about Professor Zugravescu's talking to students like this and they'd been promised he'd never do it again.

Marius said: "You think you can make perfect boyfriend in machine? You think perfection is good? Iteration make perfect?"

Greer said nothing, blushed. One of the other members of the class said: "Just a simulation."

And another one said: "Maybe? If you could work out exactly what it should say in any situation . . . if you could run enough tests? You could make someone perfect?"

Marius shook his head. "And then we don't need no more humans? Like we don't need no more animals?"

Greer said: "I mean . . . other humans are difficult."

"Fucking *nihilism*," said Marius. "Whole human race has fucking death wish, wants to replace itself. Used to be we wanted to replace with gods. Big gold statues, better than people, bigger, made of gold. Now: dream is robot brain, perfect person. This is not what people are. People imperfect! Imperfections beautiful. 'Perfect' is machine dream. We feel shit and small all day long if we judge ourselves next to machine, if we try to think like machine. Like trying to run next to car. But what we do is better! Car is just tool, goes fast brum-brum, very exciting. Person is *person*. Why we don't start by knowing that people is valuable already? People are not perfect: that's how we know perfection is unimportant. Perfection is a hallucination. We fucking hate ourselves. Let me tell you something. These matchboxes don't even know rules of tic-tac-toe!"

In the chatbox, one of the students typed: **Is this going to be on the final exam?**

"You have to understood this," he said, "or you understood nothing. OK? Who knows if machine has lost game of noughts and crosses? Who knows if it won? I do! You do. We are the ones who can tell. We know when to take bead, when to give bead. We store that knowledge in beads and matchboxes, OK? We know when sentence makes sense, we know when piece of art has meaning. Machine don't know, it just keeps typing, combining pixels, making sentences. Everything come from us. We tell it good, we tell it bad. It cannot understand. We are so lonely, so fucking lonely, we want another species think like us." He was rapidly losing coherence as he spoke. "We despise the animals because they don't think just like us, we use them and we hurt them. We invent gods, we invent aliens, now we make a friend out of fucking matchboxes. We want to say it 'thinks' but is not true. We want to give it everything, let it make choices, believe it can care for us. It is image of a man made of paper and beads and we so fucking lonely we call it a friend."

He came to a panting stop. And Greer, shy, ill-prepared Greer, suddenly said: "So you mean . . . like . . . a book is stored thoughts. But an 'artificial intelligence' is stored thinking?"

And Marius said: "At last! Someone here fucking learn something."

He gave them their homework—with the instruction "Fucking read it this time or you don't come to my class again, understand?" The students nodded attentively.

Marius turned the screen off and screwed his face up with disgust.

To the Universitatea din Bucureştì students in the room, he made a remark in Romanian starting with the word Americani that Zhen could only presume from their laughter must have been both filthy and insulting.

Zhen waited until the students had left and Marius was trying to pack up his matchbox machine. She walked quietly down the stairs. He raised his head. There in the glance was everything. Decades of communication, of reaching out. A lifetime of learning—without knowing how you knew—who you could trust and who you couldn't.

"Fuck," he said, smiling. He pulled Zhen into an embrace as warm as a furnace. "I hope you brought me some fucking disaster."

4. weaponized poetry

martha

In their anonymous hotel room near San Francisco, Martha watched Selah's *happymeal* algorithm get to work. If you'd looked at the data for long enough—if you'd gotten used to the powerful back-end tools, pulling together information from dozens of different streams—you started to look straight through the numbers and see right into the users.

There. In a tract house in Des Moines, Iowa, a forty-six-year-old woman finishes a show she'd started the night before. A nature thing, *The Wonders of Africa.* She likes that stuff; her kids used to watch with her, but they're fifteen and seventeen now and everything she loves is stupid and boring. She's only half watching the show as she cleans up breakfast. They all ate without a word of thanks, without even showing they knew there was a person there *to* thank. More conversation with their Anvil Chatterboxes than with her. She loads the dishes into the machine. Empties the coffeepot into the sink. Meanwhile a guy with a British accent is saying that these are the last eighteen wild elephants left in Africa, that they are guarded around the clock. She looks up. The old, wise elephant eyes look into hers. The unbearable hurt of suffering and no one noticing. The music swells. She's crying, standing in her kitchen, holding a wet dishcloth that is dripping onto her moccasins.

The show is over. The invitation to leave a comment flashes up on the screen. She types one quickly. **Beautiful animals. We gotta do more to protect them.**

When she's clicked away, and won't see the comment change, Selah's algorithm carefully flicks through all her previous comments to find the single word that will likely add the most weight to her thoughts. It is as meticulous as a poet.

Happymeal reviews the criteria Selah has included. Selah has used the Anvil advertising code—the information Anvil uses to serve its users effective advertisements, tested a million times, iterated again and again. Short lists of adjectives work better than single adjectives—more unusual adjectives are more gripping but they must be easy to understand. Humans respond to animals that are like people. Without Selah having directly told it to, *happymeal* works through words pet owners use about their dogs and cats. What do you say if you love your dog, and you want others to love it too? Just one word. At last, it finds the word.

It is a bead tumbling through a series of logic gates, noting each time what is marked as "success" using the reaction-emojis and what isn't. It does not empathize with the woman in Des Moines or with the elephants or with the people who will read the comment. It is a procedure. Medlar and Anvil and Fantail have been curating and promoting comments based on this procedure for two decades now. The only difference is that this algorithm isn't trying to sell anything and has been told not to make people angry.

It is trying a word. If this doesn't get the result it wants, it will try something else. It can do this several million times a second. The algorithm is weaponized poetry.

On the screen, the comment becomes: **Beautiful intelligent animals. We gotta do more to protect them.**

"That's it?" said Martha.

"That's it times fourteen million, baby," said Selah.

Zimri Nommik had, after all, used these methods to

direct human minds toward the products and services they were most likely to click on. These methods had made him the richest man on Earth.

In Ucklum, Sweden, a young man watches an American show about monster trucks. This is about the only part of his day he enjoys, the time before his parents come home. He hates living here. He wants to move to Gothenburg but he doesn't have the money and his family can't give it to him. He hates how the only social life is the fucking pizza place and none of the other kids in his band take it seriously. He hates how the rest of the kids at school are so happy and love the tiny town and talk all the time about winter sports. He hates the winter when the sun never rises. He hates the summer when it never sets. Through the window of the screen he reaches himself into the other world, pulls his head and shoulders through into the American world, where everything is big and angry and hot and loud. He feels the heat from the engines blasting his hair back from his face. If he had a monster truck, he'd paint it with a scene of hell and put all the kids from school in the picture.

The show is over. The invitation to leave a comment flashes up on the screen. He stabs at the keys. **Yaaaaaaa, awesome! Monster trucks forever!**

Happymeal runs through each word. "Forever" is emotive, a suggestion of common cause. The algorithm does not know this, of course, not in the way humans know things—not by placing itself imaginatively in the mind of a reader. It is a bead selected from a box over a million million attempts. It has been taught to analyze the comments to see which are pro monster truck and to adjust them minutely to receive fewer hearts, fewer likes, fewer milliseconds of engagement. *Happymeal* runs a million different realities in one-tenth of a second. It picks the one it's been told to favor.

When the young man in Ucklum moves on to another show, on-screen his comment becomes: **Yaaaaaaa, awesome! Monster trucks.**

Selah said: "See this one? We're predicting it's gone from nine likes to two likes. It sounds a bit wet now. Like he couldn't even be bothered?"

Martha looked at it: "Some kid from fuckbum Sweden just lost seven little bits of reassurance."

Badger rolled their eyes: "Zimri Nommik does this anyway. My mom does this anyway."

Fantail did it as a matter of course: every user defaulted to seeing comments that the Fantail algorithms had been instructed to show them first. It was, Lenk had once told Martha, a full ninety minutes of work for any user to set up their own rules about what kind of information they wanted to see and turn off all the defaults and advertising filters and data extraction options for Fantail. That's the ones you could turn off, if you knew what you were doing. Estimates were that an average user would need six hours to adequately research how to do this. A workday, just to stop Fantail from carefully showing you whatever it had figured out would make you spend the most time on the site. About 1.5 percent of users actually did it.

But it had felt different when Lenk was doing it. Like the users, Martha could only control what Lenk did some of the time.

This was them doing it, and watching it gave her a strange feeling.

"Bloody hell, Anvil does this all the fucking time," said Selah. "Stuff like this, but also fake comments, also not letting you see comments. Sketlish does too. I mean, you can pay for that, you know? That's why we all feel like shit all day long. Want a lollipop?"

They watched *happymeal* work all weekend. As countries woke and slept, as insomniacs posted sleep-deprived nonsense, as drivers posted from their moving vehicles, as people in Tokyo and Istanbul, N'Djamena and Cairo watched the same four shows. The comments on the nature shows became more finely honed advertising for the concept of animals and the natural world—its importance, its health benefits, its kinship with humanity. The comments on the monster truck shows became just a little duller, less sticky. The comments on the family drama were just a little kinder. Selah had said fuck it, why not try to make people be kind?

The algorithms can't do everything. But if they can make us more polarized, more angry, and more hateful, surely they can do the opposite of that. There is no "neutral" anymore. There is no leaving things as they would have been before the invention of the internet. Our minds have already learned how to interact with the algorithms and we are part of it.

In Des Moines, Iowa, a forty-six-year-old woman receives a notification that she has had twelve likes on her comment about elephants, which she does not for a moment feel uncertain that she wrote herself. This is more than her normal number. She feels mildly warmed. She clicks on another nature show as she gets the new day started. In Ucklum, Sweden, a young man has no reason to look again at his comment on monster trucks. He watches more videos anyway. The next time he's invited to comment, he feels a minute fraction less bothered to do it.

People learn quickly. Social approval is a powerful tool. We tend to put a great deal more emphasis on things that happened recently than things that happened long ago.

"Fuck me," said Selah on Sunday evening as she reviewed the data via the Medlar internal analysis GUI before erasing their tracks. "It's already made a shift. Point zero three percent more positive comments on nature videos. Not just our shows—all shows. Fuck. That's huge."

Martha reflected that Enoch had worked his whole life and hadn't seen a 0.03 percent shift in anything he'd ever preached.

"We can do it," said Badger, and their eyes were wide and shining. "We can actually do it."

5. entente cordiale

zhen

"This is gift," said Marius, later that afternoon.

He spat a wad of tobacco into a Coke can on the kitchen table, leaving juicy brown flecks on his teeth. He had been a chain-smoker until he realized the smoke was bad for his electronics. Now he was a chain-chewer. He stuffed in another wad.

Zhen and Marius had never met in person before. Zhen hadn't known about the smell of tobacco that had seeped into the walls of Marius's living space. Or that he lived across a floor of what had been an open-plan office, with wiry tufted carpets and graying window blinds. His bedroom was a corner office with a huge bed where, when they arrived back, his girlfriend Sarit would be naked, her curved ass only half-hidden by the blankets, awaking feelings in Zhen that had been dormant since she froze someone to death. She hadn't known that Marius's place was filled from floor to ceiling in every room but the bathroom with racks of electronic components and server units. Or that the fridge had a vigorous furry mold coating its interior back wall.

"When I fought mold, it fought back. Spores. Growing. On my food. Outside fridge. Black . . . pieces everywhere. When I surrender, it stays in own territory. Now we live in harmony. Entente cordiale."

Marius laughed and took another swig of Coke. Unlike Zhen, he seemed to have no trouble keeping track of which cans were filled with Coke and which with tobacco and spit. Marius was, in no particular order, a hacker of some reputation, a visiting professor at Berkeley and Carnegie Mellon, an absolute asshole, and probably Zhen's closest friend.

They'd known each other for the best part of a decade. They were part of the Name The Day technology board ntd/tech, which was dedicated to using technology to prepare to survive the coming collapse of civilization, although Marius's apocalypse "preparation" mostly consisted of gleeful acceptance of the inevitability of suffering, decay, despair, and eventual painful death. He was a legend on the board for the sheer range of his expertise in both technology and signs that humanity was on the verge of wiping itself out.

Their friendship had begun with arguments and humiliation. Zhen was fairly well known on ntd/tech—there was a sub-forum where her videos were dissected, sometimes praised but mostly mocked. For a while, every time Zhen made a video with any computing software or hardware advice, Marius wrote a long post explaining why her take was "fucking amateur caca." They'd argued, they'd called each other arrogant shitheads, they'd picked holes in each other's points of view until suddenly Zhen realized that the wrestling had become a hug. When Marius had trouble getting his Israeli girlfriend into Malaysia, Zhen knew how to help. When some piece of technology smelled like bullshit, Marius was Zhen's first call. Marius didn't trust or like most people. So he had a lot of unused loyalty and kindness to give the few he could be bothered with.

At the kitchen table, Marius wired Zhen's phone up to a Romanian children's toy computer keyboard, a set of motherboards sealed in plastic, and the screen from a smart washing machine. His hands were dirty but his equipment was clean. He worked quickly, humming to himself and occasionally offering gnomic thoughts.

Like: “This is gift.”

Zhen said: “The phone or . . . what, like . . . the whole situation?”

“Someone save your life and want nothing back, that’s gift. She said she gave you gift.”

He cracked open the back of Zhen’s phone so expertly he might have been shucking an oyster, removed component parts, and slotted them gently into his cobbled-together homebrew. It was like watching Zhen’s grandmother deal with every last grain of rice in the bowl, delicate and precise.

The washing-machine screen pinged gently and brought up a rinse cycle symbol.

“Is that something?” said Zhen.

“Start of something.” Marius smiled. “Find out Sleeping Beauty secrets”—he stroked the top of Zhen’s phone with one index finger—“without wake her up. First, file list. Then, file contents.”

Marius cracked open a can of creamed corn and scooped it into his mouth using vanilla ice cream wafers, with apparent enjoyment.

“You want?”

Zhen shook her head.

“In the tunnels. She ask you for something, assassin lady? She say ‘Give me this or I kill you’? Or ‘I want to kill you because you did this’?”

“Didn’t say anything to me. I’m pretty sure she was an Enochite.”

“They don’t exist no more.”

“Yeah so, they definitely exist enough to harass me online, OK? She had the key thing on her finger too.”

Marius shook his head.

“This don’t happen. Harass online is easy. Teenage boy sit in basement in Russia, write insults. No one can find him. Easy, safe. *Government* hate you, that turns into crazy person stab writer on stage. *Religion* hate you, yes, maybe."

"They are a religion? A newish religion. That's what they are. I think they've been growing online, in private groups, for a while."

"Religious war against you? You didn't do nothing."

"Tell that to that lady's gun."

Marius chewed his corn thoughtfully. On one of the shelves next to the rows of motherboards there were three plastic-wrapped pallets of tinned creamed corn.

"Maybe. Maybe you unluckiest person in the world. Maybe this is something else. You don't got her phone? ID?"

"She was a fucking . . . chunk of poison salt ice."

Marius gave several very quick nods of the head, scratching his beard like a student had given him an adequate and even intriguing answer to a computational problem.

"You have two women. One want to kill you, don't say why. One want to save your life, don't say why. Like fucking fairy story. I think . . ." And he paused so long that Zhen thought he had potentially fallen asleep with his eyes open. "I think you not in so much danger."

"Oh yeah? Let me know how you feel about that after someone's tried to shoot *you* in the head."

Marius picked a piece of corn out of his teeth with a dirty thumbnail. "The Enochites not so good they find you in Bucharest today, right? Don't find you in Madrid. Don't find you on plane. They are medium good. Find you when you not trying to hide, don't find you when you hiding. Your schedule was on your fucking website. You not hard to find. Now you hard to find, no trouble."

"But she . . . she tracked me. Through the tunnels. Found me in the bin full of Valentine foxes. They had some kind of tracker on me."

"Maybe," said Marius. "Maybe you made more noise than you thought. Moved in bin, foxes moved, maybe she saw you. Maybe put something on you at some event. Dot on clothing, tracer inside pocket. How many events you speak at every month? Ten? How often you throw out clothes after event? You never tried to make yourself hard to track."

"So what now—I have to do this forever?"

Marius nodded. "Spend time making yourself invisible. Then be more careful than before forever."

"Thanks for the positivity."

Marius laughed. "You want positivity, you go America, white teeth big smiles. You want realism, you come former Soviet bloc, OK?"

The rinse cycle symbol turned over twice. A list of files scrolled on the right side of the screen.

"Hmm," said Marius. "You had malware. Don't know what yet." He wrinkled his nose. "I can reconstruct *maybe*. If it works, might take two, three months. Have to try many different build models."

For now, all Marius could see was the date and time the malware had entered the system: 3:27 a.m. on the last night Zhen had slept in Martha's suite.

"You joined her Wi-Fi. Wi-Fi was compromised. There was special Wi-Fi for you, yes, not hotel, not normal," said Marius, and it was barely a question.

Zhen nodded.

"Spiked," Marius said sorrowfully, "middle of the night, uploads and restarts. You never know what happened."

"She said she gave me a gift. But she didn't tell me what it was."

"And now she don't talk to you?"

"I keep sending her messages but she doesn't reply."

"Did you do bad fuck with her?"

"I did exceptionally good fuck with her, thank you very much. Several times."

"Then why she don't tell you? Don't give you software

normally? This"—Marius gestured with a screwdriver at the phone, the drum-clean cycle—"this secret spy bullshit is not normal."

It felt a long time now since Zhen had last seen Martha. She'd thought she'd read the signs right, thought something real was happening. At least something kind, something sincere in the moment. She loved Marius and he loved her, but of course people who tend to paranoia—for good reasons, for reasonable reasons—do sometimes choose friends who are a bit paranoid too.

"Have you thought," said Marius, "you're famous survival expert. Can get out of anything. Maybe she using you to test her software?"

6. if it was really bad, there'd have been an alert

martha

It wasn't difficult to make a small and unobtrusive *happymeal* code package, and given that each of them had high-level access to systems at Fantail or Medlar or Anvil, it wasn't hard to disseminate it. Selah and Albert created a package with an insertion mechanism. They each left the hotel with a flash drive. Badger had bought the drives at a convenience store with cash. The drives were shaped like miniature hamburgers because Badger was always going to be exactly who they were. They said goodbye in the hotel room like old friends, people who'd been on a long journey together, and Martha, hugging each of them in turn, smelling Albert's musky three-day shirt, Selah's fresh spritz of bright scent, Badger's bubble-gum-and-fried-food odor, thought: I am never going to know how to live without a community of purpose. I am going to keep looking for this for the rest of my life, whatever happens.

They went back to their worlds. Lenk asked how Martha's vacation had been in a tone that let her know that he was fairly genuinely somewhat aggrieved that she'd even *need* a vacation from all this. And of course he was right. She hadn't taken a break. That was what she and Lenk had in common. Anytime you didn't look exactly where you were going, a Frito-Lay truck might come out of nowhere and sideswipe you. Only now, she thought, I am the truck. She was in Lenk's blind spot. It wasn't personal.

It took a couple of weeks for the timing to be right. Until Badger was with their mom in Antigua, and Selah was in Tokyo with Zimri. Until enough distracting things were going on that the moment was right. It had to all happen at roughly the same time.

Badger "borrowed" their mom's laptop.

Martha logged on using Lenk's passwords.

Selah waited until Zimri had walked out of the room without locking his AnvilSurface.

Across three time zones, the flash drives made contact. Inside the systems a password-approved worm worked its way to the appropriate place and unpacked itself. Carefully, word by word, it began to change certain sentences and certain comments. It iterated.

To try to do this at scale would be noticeable. Still, it must be worth a try. They had to try *something.*

There had been, however, no chance to balance this worm with other system requirements. No time to monitor its performance or to see how it interacted with other functionality. To find out what resources it would take and how much of them it would use. The worm began to draw a great deal of system time. An iterative process rippled through the mobile towers. An algorithm testing and retesting a way to produce more smiling faces, more thumbs-up.

In Shanghai, five hundred dancing drones shone lights of blue and silver and gold, spelling out words of peace and harmony for a celebration. Connected to an Anvil-powered mainframe via mobile signal on Medlar devices, they moved in unison, shimmering. Until they didn't. The signal was overwhelmed, just for a moment. Above the crowd, children sitting on their fathers' shoulders looked up, puzzled, as the drones stuttered. Swiveled. Stopped spelling out anything at all. Began to plummet. The ballet fell to earth, heavy and hard, smashing into car hoods, shattering on pavements. The people ran.

The same weekend, in San Francisco, at Fantail headquarters there was a server overload causing a cascade of system failures. It was a system that had never been expected to overload. When it failed, a software engineer sitting in his spare bedroom next to a drying rack loaded with his baby daughter's damp onesies panicked. He attempted to manually reconfigure the network traffic to send the overflow to a different data center. The baby was crying. His wife shouted that she was on the john and on a video call at the same time for Chrissake, could he not just get the baby? He typed in an instruction that was almost, but not entirely, perfect. Rather suddenly, in all the countries in the world, Fantail and its subsidiary apps and products all stopped working.

- In Peshawar, Pakistan, a polio vaccination team could not use Fantail anonymized services to coordinate their pickup of the vaccine. Thirty-eight thousand doses of vaccine went to waste. Among the people these doses were intended for, five children subsequently contracted polio.
- In Manitoba, Canada, systems of weather alerts housed on Medlar servers crashed. Even though Medlar servers came back up within four minutes, this alert system did not reboot. Road clearance measures were not dispatched in the face of an oncoming blizzard and warnings were not displayed on cell phones and thinscreens. Most people turned around when they saw the heavy snow. One group of eight people, desperate to reach a long-planned family reunion and reassuring one another that "if it was really bad, there'd have been an alert," froze to death in their minivan.
- In Norfolk, England, the antiquated Anvil messaging app used by the home caregiving teams went offline. Officially, it wasn't supported by Anvil

> any longer and it was low on the priority list for review after the outage. An elderly woman, unable to contact her usual nurse and unwilling to stain any other furniture, sat in her feces for almost two days, waiting for help.

During the subsequent inquiries internally at Fantail, Medlar, and Anvil, it was determined that an unobtrusive code package had somehow been introduced into the systems. A worm, possibly created by a state actor, causing an iterative process whose purpose was—at this point—difficult to determine.

Martha went to sit in Albert's study. The same room where she'd saved his life.

"It's not all our fault," said Albert. "A lot of these systems should have been more robust. Should have had more failover."

"But we knew they didn't," said Martha. She had been here before. "This is where it ends. I've seen it. You think you can change something big about the world and it ends with destruction. Every single time."

"Anvil is already selling secure, walled-off backup in case anything like this happens again. Seventeen governments are already creating laws specifically protecting 'these named companies' from this kind of attack with insane punishments. They're just going to be stronger after this."

Martha said: "What do you call it when you can't do anything, but you can't do nothing?"

Albert said: "I've tried despair already."

Badger and Albert, Martha and Selah took another several weeks to communicate as a group, using the private messaging system on a forum for roasting celebrity fashion choices.

We can't do this again, said Badger. The iterative effects, rippling outward, were still incalculable. It wasn't possible to just destroy these companies. They were everywhere. To live even for a day without their services was a disaster.

We can't do it like this, said Martha, **not ever like this. Whatever we do, we have to make it as small as it can possibly be. Invisible.**

We need higher level access than this, said Selah. **It can't sit in the code base randomly drawing more and more server capacity. It has to be part of the system.**

It wasn't the answer anyway, said Martha. **I mean like maybe it's part of the answer, but being willing to click on an e-petition isn't enough. We need something faster than that. These have been the years when we could have been solving it and we haven't. We're close to them. We can figure it out. We need to try something different.**

7. the right level of failure

zhen

In Chimopar on the outskirts of Bucharest, three of Marius's former students had set up a hackspace in an abandoned chemical factory. They ran power and high-speed wireless from a generator and server bank in a school bus. Inside, the factory was lit with strings of LED bulbs and the walls were a palimpsest of graffiti. A red angel with a sword spread its wings across the roof. A dragon with a human face vomited words that dripped down the stones and onto the floor. Death metal played from a speaker in the corner of the room, and all the tattooed, pierced, head-shaven, and bearded people at the terminals knew Marius by name. This was as safe as it got.

Zhen had scrubbed all the real data about herself she could find from the internet. No one knew she was living with Marius. She'd set up a story about herself that she'd moved to Mexico, faked up some photographs next to an imaginary pool in a nonexistent villa. When she posted videos online she bounced her signal around. She wanted it to look like business as usual, but somewhere she definitely wasn't. She only used the internet from untraceable terminals. She did not post a video about the Seasons Time Mall. She took on boring consulting gigs to review corporate crisis plans. She read paper books and paid for purchases with a prepaid card Marius filled with cash for her, like a child. She never mentioned or engaged with Enochites online; she neither responded to nor deleted their angry posts under her videos. She did not use Anvil or Medlar or Fantail from any but the most encrypted servers and then never using her old accounts or her own name. No one came for her in Bucharest.

Over a series of visits to this hackspace, she had of course done the obvious searches.

- Seasons Time Mall assassin
- Seasons Time Mall murder
- Seasons Time Mall frozen corpse
- Seasons Time Mall death
- Seasons Time Mall accident

There was a short piece in the *Straits Times*, picked up by a few other papers in the region. There had been an electrical malfunction at the Seasons Time Mall in June. Several people had been injured slightly when a glass light fitting had exploded. That wing of the mall had been sealed for six days for essential repairs.

And? And? Deeper news sites. Analysis, discussion. Weren't they looking for a young Asian woman with a backpack who had been spotted fleeing the scene?

No, they weren't. Very sadly, during the maintenance, it had been discovered that a homeless woman had died in one of the ventilation shafts. By the state of the body, she'd been there for several months. She had perhaps crawled in the previous December and died. Some of the coolant pipes had been improperly fitted, which may also have contributed to her death. A tragic affair, said the *Straits Times*. One of their columnists wrote movingly of the plight of drug-addicted homeless people and then turned the subject rapidly to the need for even harsher penalties for drug smugglers.

On the hidden web, the death of the woman in the ventilation shaft had excited some interest. A couple of sources said the body had been "in an advanced state of decomposition," and one poster on a Singaporean site said his brother's cousin worked with the police and had seen the body and it was "basically liquid, man, suuuuuu-per gross." He claimed to have a photograph of the body, but when Zhen clicked on it with dread, it was nothing she recognized. A soupy container of body parts with a dress, coat, and hat laid next to it. Nothing that looked anything like what the woman who'd chased her had been wearing.

"Some fucker trying to look cool," she said.

Marius said, "Death squads always cool until they knock on your door."

More searching. Anything.

- refrigerant murder
- refrigerant death
- coolant accident
- coolant snow
- Seasons Time coolant

A brief mention in *Global Refrigeration News*. A coolant company in Taiwan had been purchased by Fantail toward the end of June. They had made the coolant systems for the Seasons Time Mall. Their products were now to be used solely for a series of Fantail chip fabrication plants.

"Look, someone cleaning up after you," said Marius. "Your lover Martha. Cleaning up after test of their software."

"No," said Zhen, but at the same time she knew the answer could be yes.

There were two versions of Martha in her head now all the time. One, an extraordinary woman who had fallen so improbably and extravagantly in love with her over the course of a weekend that she'd gifted her a piece of experimental software that had saved her life. The other, a manipulative asshole who'd picked her up—the hotel key! the champagne!—in order to test a piece of experimental software, possibly for the slightly flattering reason that she thought Zhen would be more likely to survive than normal and possibly for the somewhat alarming reason that Martha had seen Zhen was under attack by Enochites and thought this would be a great test of AUGR's capabilities.

Zhen had believed it when Martha said that she had a project. A project! And it was getting to its busy phase. And she wouldn't be able to be in touch. And she liked Zhen more than she'd liked anyone for a really long time. Zhen had believed it all because the normal human need is to believe, to connect. To reach out and to trust. And obviously also because the sex had been great.

But there is a limit to what you can take on trust. To know anything about Martha now, Zhen would need to understand what it was that Martha had put on her phone.

She and Marius found out a little more about AUGR. There had been a company called AUGR. Its description, Marius said, sounded "boring as shit"—"trend analysis for corporate markets." It had gone into liquidation following a series of "disappointing results." Its CEO, Si Packship, had made a vague statement citing "technological difficulties." There was a tiny roundup story on TechCrunch: "AUGR, a predictive analysis software suite aiming at the hedge fund market, has failed to attract funding after a series of tech errors."

"This is the right level of failure," said Marius. "If Anvil, Medlar, and Fantail bought it out, wanted no one to know what they doing, this is right."

Not dramatic, not exciting, the software just didn't work. No one would go trying to buy up algorithms or hire the small team that made it. If anyone had said on an internet forum that they'd heard a rumor that AUGR had been purchased by a consortium backed by Lenk Sketlish, Ellen Bywater, and Zimri Nommik, they would've sounded like a fantasist.

"It's bullshit," said Zhen. "The thing I had was survival tech, superefficient AI. Incredible permissions and schematics. It said it was . . ." Those moments were crystal clear, the most extremely clear anything had been in a really long time. "Predictive, protective software."

"That's what they cleaning up," said Marius. "Buy the company, pay off the mall. They don't want no one to know what they got."

Weeks went past like this. Looking and puzzling. All the while, Marius's reconstruction program was probing Zhen's phone. They plugged it into the mainframe in the Chimopar hackspace—twenty-eight AnvilTabs linked together and stacked in a metal dish rack—and left it working all night every night, hard against the metal roof to keep cool, sheltered by an umbrella from the rain. It was weeks and then it was months while the device with the washing-machine screen tried to figure out what code had been chopped into tiny pieces when the program had deleted itself. Put it back together. Iterating. Never hurrying, never tarrying.

It was an unseasonably cold autumn that year, snow falling and settling, melting, and falling again. In October at the hackspace, they bounced a signal through twenty-two different servers and Zhen called her dad in Sunderland for his birthday. Saying sorry she hadn't called for ages. Her dad said, in a way that allowed Zhen to know instantly that he hadn't been certain at all, that if something really bad had happened to his only daughter, he'd have heard.

Zhen said: "I'm fine, Dad, I'm fine. I love you. Just busy, OK? And . . . something's happened to my phone. I'm traveling a lot. Just . . . if you need to contact me, email?"

Zhen was depressed after that call. It didn't feel like

she'd left the world, it felt like the world had left her. She and Marius walked to shake their bodies out as dusk was gathering over the slush-covered streets of Bucharest. Snow was falling, thin but persistent, a constant drizzle of cold wet flakes that sat in immediately dirty clumps on the pavement. They bought burgers from a rusted van on the street—they were surprisingly good, juicy and thick.

They sat under the eye of the angel and the dragon, eating burgers and watching the gray snow dance and tumble.

One of the other coders said: "That your homebrew on the upper shelf? Under the umbrella?"

Marius nodded morosely. Zhen wondered whether he always felt like she felt right now and, if so, how he managed to be so happy about it.

"It made a chime. While you were out. I went to look. Don't know what's happened."

Zhen would never have thought Marius could have got up the metal stairs so quickly. There was triumph in his voice as he called down.

"Sleeping Beauty ready to talk in her sleep," said Marius.

There had been a new and very powerful malware in Zhen's phone. Something that took control of all its systems when a set of commands from a particular program labeled only with a long string of numbers and letters was activated. It had also been spying on her, taking passive information from Zhen's phone since it was installed, monitoring her health, her location, her communications. They could see the reconstructed program overriding protections, gathering constant information.

"Bad infection," Marius tutted softly. "Dangerous infection."

What they could not find out was what the program had done with all that information and all those overrides.

Marius smiled with only half his mouth. He was uncomfortable. "Permissions have been removed. You could leave this now. Worm in apple. Worm saved life. Fairy story, the end."

But if she left it now, she'd never know which of those two Marthas was real.

"We look more in the morning. Find out more, OK?"

They unplugged the phone and the homebrew from the Chimopar hackspace and brought it back to Marius's live/work/eat/sleep space in a Unirea department store plastic bag. His Israeli girlfriend Sarit had made a meat stew, rich with tomatoes and spices. Marius was pleased with himself.

"No one else could have done it," he said. "I am of course secret hero but . . . nonetheless. Hero."

Sarit ruffled his hair and served the stew into his chipped bowls. Marius ate with as much enjoyment as he took in his creamed corn, grunting with pleasure. There was a hum between them now—Sarit was, in general, brusque to the point of rudeness but she was also somehow moved by Marius's achievement.

After dinner, she pulled from her pocket tabs of MDMA with pelicans on them.

"National bird of Romania," she said. "Very legitimate. Government sells them to pay government debts."

"Is that true?" said Zhen.

Sarit shrugged. "Probably."

Zhen thought about getting high while these two fucked and thought better of it.

"No thanks," she said. "You two enjoy."

She went to bed and—using a homebrew internet browser of Marius's housed on a fifteen-year-old smart doorbell screen—looked at videos of Lenk Sketlish, which occasionally included his assistant, Martha Einkorn, somewhere in the background, rarely smiling and rarely speaking, as inexplicable as a piece of ancient archaeology.

It was that night the hackspace burned down.

Marius had a call at 5 a.m. Even from her room lined with bookcases and filing cabinets on the far side of the office floor, Zhen heard his voice on the phone. First the sound of confusion, annoyance, irritation at having been woken so early. Then anger. Then fear. She'd heard that sound before in a dozen different languages. She was pulling on her underpants and jeans, her shirt and sweater before she even knew for sure it was time to leave.

Marius shouted to her: "Zhen! Chimopar Chemical Hackspace destroyed by morons!"

Zhen thought for a moment that someone had left a lit candle—there were enough active Satanists in the place that someone might have done some unsafe practices with a pentagram. But it was much worse than that.

"Fucking Bogdan! Fucking useless, idiot piece of shit, anarcho-syndicalist Bogdan."

Marius's tobacco-stained spit had flecked his beard with creamy flakes. He was gesturing with the first object that had come to hand, which—Zhen realized after a puzzled moment—was the dildo part of a strap-on. It was bright blue and represented more than she'd ideally wanted to know about Marius ever but OK.

"What's happened, Marius? Stop . . . pointing that thing at me."

Marius put the bright blue object down. Sarit looked at it, met Zhen's gaze levelly, and did not look away. Fine.

"Fucking Bogdan," said Marius. "Last night. When program completed rinse cycle. Makes a little ping. Soft, soft ping. Not loud alarm. Could have just waited for us. Fucking Bogdan went upstairs. Turned your phone on."

"Oh," said Zhen. "Oh shit."

The news seeped into her bones like the chill of her own grave. This wasn't just some random shit, obviously. Someone had been trying to destroy the phone. And whoever it was knew she was in Bucharest. Could probably figure out she was with Marius. So that was that. She felt herself pulling into pieces, discrete units of self that could bear the news and do what was needed to carry on.

They drove to Chimopar in Marius's battered toffee-colored Dacia. The hackspace was snowing upward into the cold air. The roof was melted off and fragments of paper, ash, and dust were carried up by the thermal currents, up and away over the rooftops of Chimopar, falling to Earth again far distant from this smoking, charred wreckage. Zhen stayed in the car while Marius and four other people shouted at each other over the ruins. Her mind kept going back to Hong Kong.

papers fall upward in the air, half-charred, no sirens and no screaming, someone is sobbing a distance away, there are three loud explosions

Zhen did her breathing. She named objects in her field of vision. She said to herself: You are here, not there. Nothing bad is happening to you right now. Stay here. The interior of the car had been repainted a pale blue. When she scratched her fingernail along the edge of the window, the old paint was visible under the new. Toffee and blue, like a lurid sunrise.

Marius stomped back to the car.

"Fine," he said. "Equipment gone, no one was here." He shrugged. "This happens. Arson or theft. These places always need to move on."

There had been a rising tide of arson—not just here in Romania but across the world. People taking literally the thought, The world is burning. Not willing to sit with the uncertainty. Just fucking rip the bandage off.

"Bogdan thinks could be gangs," he said. "He's asking around."

"But he knows it wasn't gangs, right?" said Zhen.

It was someone coming for her.

They drove out of the city before they looked at Zhen's

phone again. Parked by a lake, five wild swans dipping down for riverweed. Zhen pulled the Unirea department store bag out from under her seat. They both stared at the phone that apparently summoned fire directly from heaven.

Marius said: "We could throw into lake."

"Whoever did this will still know I'm here."

"I can find you place to hide."

"You know I can't just hide. I need to know what's going on. Can you get me back into AUGR?"

"Clever encryption. You have been taken off approved user list. Remotely. Needs hard connection to server to reauthorize."

There was a list of hard connection points. Lenk Sketlish's house. Anvil headquarters. The impenetrable Bywater bunker in New Zealand.

"I can't stay here," Zhen said. "You can show me how to reauthorize AUGR. I can get into one of these."

"So where we going?"

Zhen looked at Marius. Unbearably moved, not wanting to break through this moment into the next, where he would brush aside her gratitude.

"You don't need to come," she said. "They're not after you."

"You fuck it up without me," said Marius. Then paused. "And I want to know what these fuckers doing, OK?"

Zhen took a breath. Held it. Breathed out. "We're going to Canada. We're breaking into Zimri Nommik's bunker."

8. bones and plastic packaging

martha

While Martha and Selah, Albert and Badger figured out what to try next, time passed. Companies grew bigger. Things became, slowly but inexorably, worse.

In Palo Alto, Lenk Sketlish's company, Fantail, snapped up a small but growing rival—a machine-learning program that could remix your favorite television shows, creating a version of the celebrity of your choice performing a short episode on a topic you picked in any of three hundred languages. It bought up the PhD work—and the services—of eight experts in algorithmic projections, enabling Fantail to predict what services their users were likely to want in the short to medium term. And certain data was sold and certain data was stored and certain profits were made from advertising in certain ways. And very few of Fantail's many customers gave a shit, when they could share a crappy TV short starring them alongside that silver fox Ryan Reynolds speaking fluent Xhosa.

Would you save the city for fifty?

In their new mega headquarters in Columbus, Ohio, Zimri Nommik's company, Anvil, pioneered a lapel pin that recorded all of a person's conversations every day and produced searchable text files from them, which it could then use to create a digital "you," able to take over some tedious social obligations for you. The DaySave was initially marketed to students and harried knowledge workers, but it soon spread in popularity. Famous artists designed limited-edition DaySave buttons. If you accidentally put them in the laundry, Anvil delivered a replacement within one hour. And certain warehouse workers had their pay docked for spending longer than forty-seven seconds in the bathroom, and certain jurisdictions agreed that Anvil should pay negative tax in exchange for siting a warehouse in the region, and certain quantities of carbon were pumped into the atmosphere. The wealthy became even wealthier and the poor even poorer, despite all historical indications that this type of situation leads inexorably to violent revolution. And although many people experienced a momentary twinge of anxiety at throwing out more plastic wrapping, very few of Anvil's hundreds of millions of customers and very few of its DaySave subscribers gave enough of a shit to dent its profits by one-hundredth of 1 percent.

Would you save the city for forty-five?

In chilly Centralia, Washington, Ellen Bywater's management of Medlar continued the steady accumulations she was famous for. The launch of a new range of ultrathin screens and ultralight laptops was the expected success. The design was pleasing, the click both reassuring and intuitive; the new Personality Paradigms of the inbuilt search function were both elegant and—somehow—distinguished. And certain slaves mined coltan in the Congo, and certain sleek and beautiful objects of glass and metal were far easier and cheaper to throw away than to repair, and certain chemicals leached into the groundwater in certain places. And while many people signed petitions on Fantail, very few Medlar users gave enough of a shit to sway its share price one-tenth of one penny.

Suppose there are just forty. Would you save the city for forty?

Research had established that using Fantail products for more than eight minutes a day increased a teenage girl's suicide risk. The same was true for the risk of eating disorders, of bullying and being subject to bullying. The mental health of the world continued to deteriorate—depressed and anxious people were less interested in engaging with real problems, more willing to escape to fantasy worlds, more willing to believe hoaxes and conspiracy theories. Fantail released its own research showing that thirty minutes a day of conversation with FantailPal—its artificially intelligent support software—was correlated positively with productivity. Several states and some countries agreed in exchange for payment that FantailPal should be installed preferentially as the interface personality on thinscreens in schools. The mental health of humanity continued to be strip-mined. No advertisers moved elsewhere. The board did nothing.

Don't be angry. I know this is getting ridiculous now. What if there were only thirty good people after all? Would you save the city for thirty?

Eager to introduce the new Personality Paradigms to the world, Medlar made certain uncharacteristic concessions. Believing that the Personality Paradigms *would* create a more peaceful global outlook, in Russia, in Saudi Arabia, in China, in Afghanistan, in Belarus, in North Korea, in Iran, in Syria, in Uzbekistan, Ellen Bywater had agreed it would be right to allow governments to monitor their citizens via certain MedlarPhone apps. No government agency was willing to give up this vital source of anti-terrorist information. There were protests. There were signs of societal instability around the world. Badger told their mother they were disgusted by her. But nothing changed.

Maybe there are just twenty. Would you save the city for twenty?

The fact was that Anvil was not as bad as some. The evils of the world could not be pinned on Zimri Nommik and his successful business strategies. Nonetheless, the new Anvil factory in Myanmar dumped runoff into the Irrawaddy River. And then no Irrawaddy dolphins were sighted. Selah Nommik watched a twenty-year-old video of the laughing, shining gray mammals leaping in the water. That was what Anvil left: videos and bones and plastic packaging. She thought: It's not him that will die, it's the world that will end.

Zimri Nommik bought five large areas of land from African and Asian governments to turn into FutureSafe zones—places where human visitors were not allowed to go under any circumstances. These zones were designated as refuges for wild animals and to allow flora and fauna to regrow and rewild the landscape. These projects, admirable in themselves, comforted the public that something was being done. Selah Nommik knew perfectly well that Zimri was planning to go to one of those zones himself in the event of environmental collapse. That confidential clauses in the agreements with regional and national governments allowed him to do so. That the one whose future was safe was Zimri.

It could be that we can only find ten good people. Would you save the city for ten?

It was in those days that Badger Bywater took the passkey from their mother for the vault under the hill in New Zealand. It was a gold elliptical disc embossed with Badger's name and a copy of their fingerprint. Badger took the tour of the deep bunker with the lace filigree of metal and wood running through the central atrium. Badger listened to their parents, Ellen and Will, talk animatedly about the wonderful work they'd done here at the edge of the world, how much would be preserved from the oncoming storm. About how this was a good thing; didn't Badger want to survive?

Albert Dabrowski received his bunker key from Medlar on the anniversary of his husband's death and knew with despair that he would have done no better than Ellen Bywater if he'd been in her position. And yet he knew that there was much that could be done. She was his dark reflection: the person he despised himself for being. He thought again, as he had often thought, that things might be better if he just died somehow, if he left his shares to Greenpeace or to be held in trust and used for the benefit of the whales or the birds or the great apes of the world. The only person he told these thoughts to was Martha Einkorn. She told him to hold on. Hold on.

Martha Einkorn was sent to attend various apocalypse trade shows for Lenk, looking for the latest gadgets for his survival bunker. She listened to the experts who guessed how many years it would be before the bunker was needed. Twenty years. Ten years. Five years. Two years.

Or is it—and this is always an option—just time to give up?

Once upon a time Martha Einkorn had killed a bear. She knew how to do it when she saw that bear would kill her and would gain no benefit. Some creatures are driven to kill even when they cannot eat. Sick animals do this. And humans. We keep on pressing the button long after all pleasure or satisfaction is gone. More money, more influence, more fame, more power. The bear's rotten jaw was Enoch's compulsive dark fragmentation while railing against "pieces," was Lenk's compulsive acquisition of spurious certainty. In a human, the drive to do what computers do, to try the same thing maddeningly often, again and again and again, never hurrying, never tarrying, that drive is a sign of sickness.

Once upon a time Martha Einkorn had woken long before dawn. In the dark of the compound she had taken money and a gun from her father. Because she needed to be free, because she wasn't willing to sit in a cave and pretend the rest of the world didn't exist. She had walked through the dark into the morning. She had hitched a ride and paid for a bus and she had gone into the world. Leaving is a skill you can learn. That was what she knew Lenk had seen in her. That she knew how to leave. And Lenk Sketlish believed that in his lifetime he would have to leave the world. He had seen the future coming and he knew it was no good, that radical sacrifices would have to be made, that the strong would live and the weak would perish. And maybe after all he was right.

9. the war of all against all

zhen

"You know, someone could be having joke with you."

"No one has jokes with me, Marius. I am known for having no sense of humor whatever."

"There is cruelty in the heart of man. This time they have joke on you and on me."

It had taken more than a month to plan this trip to the west of Canada. Another new passport for Zhen and a month in a shithole squat in the basement of an abandoned art deco casino in Constanța, listening to the sound of the ocean like the clawing of ignorance inside her head. She read and reread the *Tristia*, Ovid's book of sorrows written in this place, the edge of the world. The poet had been exiled here by a vindictive emperor, sent to rot as far from the action as he could go. Zhen knew how he felt. Something was happening somewhere outside her field of vision, something that could send guns and fire—maybe more than one something. Maybe all the somethings were happening at once. She wasn't going to stay here.

From Constanţa, Zhen took a train to Kraków, another to Vienna, a flight from there to Mexico, a flight from Mexico to Canada. More difficult now than it had been even three months earlier—after the previous government had collapsed, a separatist movement had taken power in Serbia, and together with Hungary they had temporarily suspended the Schengen free-movement zone through their countries. A food-and-migrant crisis in Türkiye was putting pressure on Bulgaria to do the same. Increasingly, in order to travel across Europe, only certain passports would work, and even then you had to keep a careful eye on which borders were open and closed. On the other hand, this meant it was a lot easier to get a fake passport now than a year earlier. The more things are illegal, the more profit there is in illegal enterprise.

Zhen and Marius had traveled separately—Marius was not immediately at risk and there was no sense in placing them together. Now, six hours west of Kitimat, British Columbia, by dirt bike, in a dripping, rain-soaked forest, Lai Zhen knelt at the foot of a tree. Marius, who had been complaining for the last day and a half, watched her in gloomy silence.

"Is nothing there."

"There'll be something here."

"Is wild goose."

"I couldn't just stay in Romania waiting to be found, could I?"

As she patted the damp earth, Zhen entertained for a moment the possibility that there might be nothing there. She might have been misled to begin with. She'd gone as far as she could.

In Brazil, there had been a currency collapse for no clear reason anyone could tell. It was as if the world economy—so long running on hope and expectation—had simply stopped functioning normally. In Belarus it was now accepted that armed street gangs had more power than the legitimate military. In China another wave of a blue rice-mold had been carried by unseasonable storms, causing the crop to fail. The world was a boxer, unsteady on its feet, wavering, waiting for the final punch.

And she, Lai Zhen, would not only not get her golden ticket, she'd also never know what the fuck had happened to her life and who was after her. She could deal with dying, she thought, but not with never knowing. She dug her frozen fingers deeper and more urgently into the earth.

And yes! Here under a patch of moss and undergrowth, a circle about a meter in diameter was artificial. Under the rain and earth there was metal. In the metal there was a hole. She hooked her finger into the hole; she tugged. A circular metal hatch rose up silently on two piston lever arms. Inside the circle, there was light.

"Fuck you do," said Marius, to no one in particular. Zhen locked the door in place. There were steps down into a white hexagonal room, like a single cell of a beehive.

"Come on," she said. "I can't do it without you."

Zimri Nommik, the CEO of Anvil, owned an enormous amount of British Columbia, including two islands bordering Haida Gwaii. He had not made peace with local First Nations elders; he purchased the property at a very fair price and had erected a set of strong fences and several other less obvious protective measures. It was here that he had constructed his underground survival bunker to see out an impending apocalypse. Zimri Nommik had read extensive reports on seismic activities over the medium to long term and worked with his designers to construct a honeycomb-like structure underground, only two stories deep at any point but massively large, with blast doors between every three cells that would maintain structural integrity if any part of the bunker collapsed.

Zimri Nommik did not mind a great deal that the architects of his bunker knew where it was and how it looked on the inside. He had constructed a system in which trust wasn't necessary. The architects might have built the bunker, but the security systems were installed after they'd left by people who had no idea what they were protecting. The guys who saw the outer doors didn't see the inside. The guys who installed the cameras hadn't met the ones who'd installed the electric fences, and those guys hadn't met the gun turret team and they had no knowledge of the security camera crew. No single person could possibly find out enough to get inside. That was what capitalism got you. The war of all against all could make you safe, as long as they were fighting each other and not you. Zimri Nommik had not anticipated that four separate engineers working on his project would be fans of Lai Zhen and would—across several years—share with her the location, the access codes, and enough information about the internal defenses for her to be fairly sure of evading them when she and Marius came here to reactivate AUGR on her phone.

The white-illuminated beehive cell Zhen and Marius climbed down into had a certain beauty to it, if you liked that kind of thing. It was lined in painted wood, it was about twenty feet across, and it was empty. Apart from a set of ports in the floor. Could it be this easy? Marius knelt down to investigate them.

"No," he said.

"No? Just no?"

"No. Is electricity. Anvil data port. Data for water management only. We need full data point, full access, hard internet from here. Then it knows we really here and we get what we want. Look."

"OK. No, no, it's not a problem." Zhen threw the plans from her thinscreen onto the white wall. "Look, we're here to the west of the whole site. There should be full data access banks every . . . ten cells or so. So we just keep going north, through the cells, until we find one."

"And you sure there's no one here?"

"Why would they be here? The apocalypse hasn't happened yet. Look, I can get the walls open. It should take fifteen minutes to get there. Connect to the port. Download what we need. Get out." Marius looked uncertain. "We've come this far."

"That's what they say under communism. One extra

push only for total success. You got to know when to give up."

"OK, but we're not giving up for another *fifteen minutes*."

Zhen inputted the access code on the panel in the north wall. It slid down, revealing a long corridor ahead.

"Look, some of the cells are already open."

"What the fuck are these cells?"

"I'll explain as we go. Come on."

Zimri Nommik's bunker was constructed on two levels: wood-lined concrete-and-steel-framed beehive cells on top, and underneath each cell the generators and food and fuel stores. Every wall was a blast door. Each one could slide down into the steel frame below, making the structure infinitely reconfigurable. If you owned both cells, then you had control of the wall between them. Otherwise you had to have the agreement of both sides to slide the wall down.

"But no one lives here yet," said Zhen, "so I have the construction passkey."

"What a future this man imagine," said Marius. "I safe in my prison, you safe in your prison. All safe and no talking, no laughing, no sex. Individualism."

"I mean, there's some logic to it," said Zhen. "People who are into survival want to . . . survive. I guess Nommik would bring his top people here. They'd probably all know each other already. But if some unexpected threat was introduced . . . they'd want to be able to isolate them."

"This place is tomb," said Marius. "Mourn for yourself here, you already dead."

There was something to what Marius said. The place was cold, a faint damp in the air all the time, and their steps echoed on the concrete floor. They passed through an empty sleeping unit: bunk beds, storage cubbies, shower cabinet. Everything standing in the middle of the room to leave the walls free gave the ordinary objects a strangely menacing air—as if the moment Marius and Zhen walked by, the sofa, the table, the empty bookcase would shuffle themselves slowly forward, inch by inch. A solitary fly buzzed past her elbow, heading to nowhere, from nowhere.

"They getting ready," said Marius. "New mattresses, new sheets, boxes."

There were boxes everywhere filled with supplies—canned food, utensils, fuel, weapons. The place looked like a movie set the day before the shoot starts.

"Something's coming," said Zhen.

The second cell in the chain was a stone-lined kitchen with a small deeply recessed skylight onto which the dark rain was pattering softly. Next was a recreation room with a huge thinscreen, a suite of gaming consoles, and a table-tennis table.

"I heard there's a swimming pool somewhere in here," said Zhen.

"Fuck swimming pool. I see data ports. Where my condom?"

Marius's "condom" was a small device encased in bare aluminum—they had tested it out many times. It would transmit just enough data packets to reauthorize AUGR, nothing more. Then it would switch itself off automatically, the process taking no more than 0.03 seconds. Zhen had held it in her hand and felt the rapid ticktock between the two states, like the heartbeat of a living thing. There would be little they could do to stop the AUGR mainframe from knowing where they were—that was the point of the system—but they could get out quickly the moment the phone was turned off. And they could stop the phone from exchanging any more data with the system, stop it from knowing who they were.

Marius plugged the device in. Made ready to put the connector into the phone. It would be over before it began and then they would need to leave at pace.

"Ready?" said Marius.

"Ready," said Zhen, imagining already the instantaneous faster-than-human ticktock inside the aluminum box.

Marius plugged the phone in. Immediately, something was wrong.

"Fuck," he said, his finger and thumb fumbling at the connector. In his agitation, the phone slid sideways in his hand. He dropped it, swore again, wrenched the connector out of the box manually, passed the phone to Zhen. The whole thing had taken less than ten seconds.

"What happened?"

"Fucking poison house. Mainframe in bunker forced the connection."

"So it got something off my phone?"

"In ten seconds? Yes. Don't know what."

"And . . . are we safe?"

"Need to get out."

With a thunk, all the lights in the bunker went off.

There were light-emitting paint strips on the floor, glowing very pale. Something brushed past Zhen's elbow. It was all happening quickly. Iterating. Repeating, a million times a second.

"Shit," said Zhen. "OK, OK, I can get us out of here, back the way we came. It's only three cells."

The same soft feeling was against Zhen's arms, against her face, against her neck. By the light of her phone screen she saw something tiny like an insect, like a mosquito, buzz across the illuminated face. On the screen was a text box.

Lai Zhen, it said, **this is AUGR. Your perimeter has been activated. You are in danger.**

On the screen was a map of the bunker. Hundreds of honeycomb cells. A red dot showing where Zhen and Marius were standing in a cell on the perimeter of the bunker. Farther in toward the center, a twelve-honeycomb-cell open blue space. A swimming pool.

Zhen angled the screen so Marius could see it, but before he could respond, there was a pain in her right hand, a swelling, growing, hot, wet, bubbling pain. A hundred tiny burning lacerations. AUGR was right. The things would follow them out unless they were able to get rid of them more permanently.

Something had iterated, tried out a million ideas a second. The buzzing things were around the hand holding the phone and she was bleeding. She almost dropped the phone. She clutched tighter.

"They're trying to get it," she said. "Hold it, take it."

Marius grabbed the phone in the almost dark. Wrapped it and his hands in his jacket. Zhen dug her left hand into her pocket and pulled out a gel emergency flare—semispherical, the size of half a golf ball. If these things could navigate in the dark, then they were using infrared, and they could blow that out, just for a moment. Marius wailed in distress.

"They eating my coat, cutting."

Zhen cracked the flare, pressing her thumbs into the center hard. The light was bright and immediate. In the terrifying white light she saw her own right hand, the skin shredded and bleeding. Marius's jacket was hanging in tattered strips. Thronging his skin were tiny brass-colored beads, humming with buzzing wings. They were disoriented now, just for a moment; the bright light had disrupted their vision.

"I know what to do," said Zhen. "They're going to keep trying to get the phone but trust me. Every cell is separate."

She dragged Marius to a wall leading farther into the honeycomb. Jabbed in the access key. The wall slid down. The next room was filled with dark-thriving plants under minimal hydroponic lamps—black tomatoes and navy-green lettuces. They stepped inside. The brass buttons from the cell behind them didn't follow. From the walls and ceiling, through the grate in the floor, new bright, biting things emerged.

"Absolute autonomy," said Zhen, punching in the code for the next wall. "The perimeter is all automatically controlled—that's Nommik's. But no one's in charge of the inner cells; every cell is independent, each one has to assent to deploy its own defenses. Which it'll only do when we're actually here, OK? If we keep moving, we stay ahead."

"But we going further inside maze. Not out."

"There's going to be a way out. Trust me."

And, despite it all, he did.

There were five more cells between them and the swimming pool. Four more cracked-concrete grilles pouring out flying, biting, buzzing things as soon as they entered. The swarm carried micro-lancets, sharp darting needles, inhumanly thin blades that Zhen and Marius barely felt cutting them. They fought their way through another sleeping area, a music and recreation room, a room with benches and restraints that Zhen noted in a distant part of her mind was definitely an interrogation room, a medical bay. Each time there was a momentary pause. Enough to assess their latest wounds, to work out which part of their bodies they should be protecting, enough time for Zhen to stuff the phone into a resistant StowtBag before the next buzzing, thronging assault began. The last room was medical storage. Medicines, surgical tools, sterile equipment. Butane tanks. Forty enormous oxygen tanks.

"Open as many of those as you can," said Zhen as she fought off the insects stabbing at the crook of her elbow where she cradled her phone, and punched the master code into the last number pad. "Oxygen. Butane. Open them."

As the final wall fell away they were suddenly in the large echoing space of a swimming pool. Ferns were growing up the walls from huge planter troughs, creeping toward the light seeping through deeply recessed thick glass portholes above; ivies with enormous dark green leaves. Arvo Pärt was playing softly from the speakers in the ceiling. The water was clear and smelled of salt.

From the grille above the swimming pool, more of the buzzing creatures began to agglomerate. The swimming pool was one of the few communal territories in the system. One of the only places where they could do what they were doing right now. They were forming a swarm. They would have them now; if this didn't work, they would take from her what she'd come here for. They wouldn't kill her—if they'd wanted to do that, one of those lancets would have been enough to do it, using the right poison. What's the point of murder if you control the world anyway? Murder is for people with nothing left to lose. They would just leave her here, having shown her a corner of a hidden world and then replaced the curtain. No. She joined Marius, opening oxygen tanks and butane canisters. As many as she could, as quickly as she could. The sound of the hissing joined with the buzzing insects. Zhen felt suddenly light-headed.

"Now," she said to Marius. He had understood without needing it explained.

"OK," he said, "but if I die, you fucking explaining to Sarit, OK?"

"Yup," she said, and they ran together, Zhen's hand extended behind her as she hurled her sparking automatic fire starter, and at the point that they jumped into the water, the air above them ignited.

The water was deep and slightly green and very clear. It tasted faintly of chlorophyll and salt, fresh and full of phytonutrients, like sap. A sheet of flame passed over their heads. There was an enormous crash, and chunks of concrete and stone collapsed into the pool. They stayed down. Very swiftly, all was silent. They put their heads above the water.

"Fuck shit," said Marius.

There was a gaping hole in the roof of the bunker; they'd be able to clamber out over the rubble. The bright beetles were floating on the face of the water. Various parts of the room, and the next room, and the room after it were on fire.

"Survival," said Zhen, helping Marius out of the pool.

"Why survival so fucking dangerous?"

10. an invisible tipping point

zhen

In a hotel room in Prince Rupert, British Columbia, looking out on a Tim Hortons doughnut and coffee shop, Marius set up a world-in-a-box for Zhen's phone to inhabit while they investigated what AUGR was and worked out what to do next. A fake mobile network for it to connect to, scanning for information about enemies and disasters. On one of Marius's homebrew arrangements of chips and screens, they watched AUGR try to crawl the web, to look for threats and protect Zhen. The fake mobile network gave it nothing of interest. It worked tirelessly inside its little box, thinking it was contacting the world. Like an insect in a tiny, perfect environment in a terrarium.

Marius and Zhen had looked through AUGR's assets.

There was a video labeled simply "watchme.mp4."

"Look at this," said Marius. "Maybe they make movie of themselves doing evil."

But he'd been surprised when it turned out they had. There was a man called Si Packship pitching a product called AUGR. Zhen recognized the inside of the mountain—not to mention everyone's clothing—at once.

Marius hated everything Packship said, and muttered, "Sick fucks" several times during the video.

At the end, the microphone picked up a brief conversation between Lenk Sketlish and Martha.

"If it works, I'm in," muttered Lenk.

"I think he's got it," said Martha. "What he's done is very impressive."

There was a camaraderie and ease between them that made Zhen bitingly jealous.

"You've tested it?"

"I've had some people walking around with it for months. Nothing they can see on their phones. I monitor the data remotely. It's good. Not quite as good as he says. He can't do fourteen days. But twenty-four to forty-eight hours, yes."

"That's enough. OK, but if we're taking it, we need to make sure we delete all the test builds, OK? Anyone who's had it, all of them. Get someone on that. I'm not risking it. They need to be gone."

Marius looked at Zhen. "Fucking Bogdan," he said at last. "If you connect to real internet, they know where you are. They delete again."

"Or they come and burn the building down."

Marius shook his head. "Fire is last resort. Bogdan is idiot but he turned phone off and on quickly. Leave it on for five minutes and they remote delete. Safe and clean."

Zhen said: "Was I just a *tester*? Do you think it works? I mean, really actually works?"

Marius thought about this.

"It is good at one thing: generate survival plan quickly. That we know it can do."

"That's not an answer. That's what you talk about. Iteration. We tell it the parameters, it iterates a million times a second; we tell it what success is and when it's failed. I can imagine how it could get good at that in a lot of simulations. What about the future prediction stuff?"

"If it works, we know something new about world. About consciousness. About time."

"That's it?"

"I don't know if AUGR can know future. I know I don't know future. I don't know everything. I couldn't do it. But maybe they found answer. Maybe it works."

In the box, the fierce little insect tried to save her life over and over again.

They had been in Prince Rupert, British Columbia, for four days now. Marius had burns on his shoulders where they'd peeked out of the water. Zhen had dressed them every day with fresh bandages from Safeway. He refused painkillers and downed half a bottle of scotch every day.

They had tried repeatedly, using all of Marius's skill, to record the screen of the phone, to voice-record the audio of Si Packship's speech. It had all been digitally treated—what they ended up with was noise, black screens. Maybe if they had an ancient tape recorder or a 1980s video camera, they could do something. But then, that stuff could be faked so easily.

They had tried to figure out what to do now, where to take this. To the press maybe? A trip in person to New York, show it to someone. They would seem like lunatics. But if the plans were this advanced, if the apocalypse was this near—Zhen thought of the boxes they'd seen in Zimri Nommik's bunker—would revealing all of this just push something over an invisible tipping point?

Marius stretched; his bandages crackled.

"Fuck," he said, "fuck, fuck. I need sugar. Sugar, coffee, doughnuts. Tim Hortons." He pointed a thick finger toward the window.

In the heated vanilla-scented air of a Tim Hortons between the Gulf of Alaska and the North Pacific, Marius stirred his coffee with a disposable plastic baton. Zhen chose a doughnut hole decorated with rainbow unicorn sprinkles. She tried to tempt herself to eat it, but all she could see was the collection of scientific food processes that had gone into making it, the colors stirred in great vats, the sprinkle-extrusion machines, the metal plates with the unicorn images that the sugar could be pressed into. All so that she could imagine—what—putting a band of color from the sky into her mouth? Becoming one with the reality of impossible animals? Shut up, Zhen, shut up, brain, eat the fucking doughnut.

Behind the counter, the server, whose name tag said "HI, MY NAME IS MARIE," made a strangled sound, between a squeak of pleasure and a choke. She was staring at the wall-mounted television. There was a photograph of Zimri Nommik, smiling on the screen.

For a terrified moment Zhen thought he had found them somehow and his image was about to become real. Then the image flicked into a photograph of Ellen Bywater and Lenk Sketlish together at a summer party. And while Marie scrabbled for the remote and clattered it on the floor and grabbed it and turned the volume up, the chyron scrolled across the bottom of the screen: **Lenk Sketlish, Ellen Bywater, and Zimri Nommik, CEOs of Fantail, Medlar, and Anvil, missing in suspected plane crash.**

The volume turned on, but the crashing sound continued to echo in Zhen's ears.

At first it had been difficult to tell whether the plane was missing or not, said the television news reporter, because the three billionaires had left secretly. They had been attending the Action Now! sustainability conference together and had taken part in a joint panel on corporate responsibility. There were indications that they'd left together late on Friday to enter confidential closed-session negotiations, perhaps about environmental mitigation.

Out of the corner of her eye, Zhen could almost see Si Packship leaning in, saying, "AUGR will work with you to create a plausible story."

Their jet, flight G-NZAB, had taken off from a private airfield in northern California. They had filed a flight plan indicating that they were heading west and then north.

The plane had flown out into the North Pacific Ocean, past the point where it was monitored by radar from land. After that point the plane had given its position verbally until 7 a.m., when it should have been picked up by radar in Alaska. The plane had gone silent. There was no sign of it in Alaska. There was no sign of it anywhere.

As the newsreader tried to compose himself, there was a moment of complete silence.

The imaginary Si Packship moved close to her ear and said: "You'll have time for dinner before you head for the plane."

Zhen had once seen an interview in a television documentary about Ayn Rand. Her most famous book was a fantasy that if a few wealthy and powerful people disappeared, the world would end. In the interview, Rand was talking about death, about what dying meant to her. She said:

"I will not die. It's the world that will end."

The works of Ayn Rand were extremely popular in Silicon Valley. This was what Lenk Sketlish and Ellen Bywater and Zimri Nommik believed. This was what they had paid for. They would not die. It was the world that would end. It was not Sketlish, Bywater, and Nommik who were missing, it was the future.

Marius said: "Sick fucks. They did it."

"Something's falling apart. Whatever it is, it's coming quickly," said Zhen.

"OK, let's go," said Marius. "GO, we need turn it on."

In the hotel room, the news continued to scroll. There was grief and bewilderment on the television and the feeds, a sense still that the thing was impossible, the details of the search for parts of a plane, the possibility that a lifeboat or a CrashJacket might still be found sustaining the world's great technology leaders. An expert on the history of aviation disasters was called in to run the viewers through a list of missing planes and the eventual outcome of each mystery. Someone said, “Hopes are dwindling.” On another channel, someone said: “When should we give up hope?” There was a rushing sound in Zhen’s ears.

Zhen took her phone from the box and—holding it in both hands—turned it on. Unlocked the screen. Connected to the internet.

There were her old apps. Like a memory of a person she used to be, the things she used to look at every day. She felt a kind of grief, looking at the screen. She wanted to walk back through it into the world as it used to be.

Dozens of texts pinged up. Friends and family, discount offers, spam and phishing.

Nothing. And then everything.

The screen went black. There was a message in green letters.

It said: **Lai Zhen, this is AUGR. An extraction is being arranged. Stay where you are.**

On the old phone, Zhen sent Martha a text message.

Is this real? I’ve had an AUGR activation.

It wasn’t delivered. Whatever had happened, Martha had gone too.

In desperation, Zhen looked up Martha’s profile on Fantail. They’d sent each other a few messages that way before, but Martha had been hesitant to send anything via her own platform. Maybe she was worried Lenk Sketlish would see it. Still. Worth a try. Zhen sent the same message.

Five minutes, six minutes. Then three dots, typing. Then the dots went away. Seven minutes. Eight minutes. Ten minutes. Three dots.

It's real, said Martha. **I didn't know it'd ping you.**

What do you mean it's real?

We've got to get out, said Martha. **My friends and I . . . thought we could do something before this happened. Fix it. But we were too late. It's coming now.**

A cold line of fear in Zhen's throat.

What's coming?

Just do what AUGR tells you, OK? I can tell you when I see you. I'm going to delete these now.

As Zhen watched, her messages and Martha's unraveled themselves from the screen, erasing upward until all that was left was a hopeful smiley face Martha had sent her several months earlier.

For five hours, the news rolled on, CNN and BBC, Fox and FantailNet all sending hopes and prayers, expectations and suppositions. The armies of three countries were scouring the ocean. There would be a black box sending out its hopeful bips.

There might not have been a tragedy. And yet, said the news, the sea off the Bering Strait was this temperature. Without survival equipment the human body would only continue to function at that temperature for two hours. For one hour. For thirty-six minutes. The knowledge spooled out across the world, and some were angry and some were sad and many were jubilant—"Sick fuckers, world doesn't need any more billionaires shooting penis-shaped rockets into space"—and many were angry at the jubilation and told stories of how they'd never have found their army buddy or their high school sweetheart again without Fantail, they'd done the best work of their life on a Medlar thinscreen, they'd relied on deliveries from Anvil when they had the 2020 novel coronavirus. A million boring opinions screamed with angry urgency. The stock in all three companies plummeted. Then stock markets all over the world plummeted. Ten percent. Twenty. Thirty. Forty percent. "A great day to buy cheap," said a commenter and then had to resign two hours later. And none of them knew what this meant. They still thought there was a future to imagine.

"What do we do if 'transport' comes for me?" said Zhen.

Marius looked at her.

"You want to live through the end of the world?"

"I don't want to . . . leave you here in a hotel in Prince Rupert while I go off with my golden ticket."

"Why better for me if I know you suffering too?"

"Whatever it is, I'll try to find a way to bring you."

Marius shook his head.

"I go back to Bucharest. To Sarit. To stupid fuck Bogdan and my stupid fuck students."

At four in the morning, Zhen had slept a little and woke to the sound of a soft, insistent ping from her phone. She shook Marius awake from his snoring sleep and they looked together.

AUGR said: "Your transport is downstairs, Lai Zhen." There was a long black car parked outside on the street, peacefully waiting for the end of the world. The extraction, the perimeter. Whatever was going to happen hadn't yet disturbed the possibility of seamless efficiency.

What is the point of anything at all if you're not going to survive? If you live, you might be able to do something. If you die, you won't do anything. The story of Lot and his daughters isn't a story of human thriving, but it's better than what happened to the people in Sodom.

Downstairs, the car was a BMW and the seats were warmed leather.

The door was open and a plump man with an American accent was in the driver's seat behind a smoked-glass screen. He had an airborne-plague-safe N99 mask strapped across the lower part of his face.

"Lai Zhen?" he said.

"Yeah," she said. "Where are we going?"

"I'm following the navigation."

He pointed to the screen.

It was still before dawn and it had rained in the night. The streets were shiny and still. They moved swiftly through the city, north and east, out, open country. An hour outside the city on a quiet road, the car stopped. The screen descended.

"The protocol is that we wait here," said the driver.

They were in the car for around forty-five minutes, waiting. They talked some. They were silent some. Zhen thought about what it was she'd wanted out of her whole entire life and—if that was all over now—what she could possibly do that was worth a damn.

At last, Zhen heard the distant sound of a helicopter at the same moment that the driver grabbed her wrist and she felt a sharp scratch on the back of her hand.

"Don't worry," he said. "You're going somewhere with a million beautiful things."

PART 5

nothing is ever really over

extract from Name The Day survivalist forum

sub-board: ntd/enoch

›› FoxInTheHenHouse is at **GoBagPrepped** *status. FoxInTheHenHouse has made 2,391 posts and received 3,127 thumbs-up.*

Hi everyone. This is a post specifically for people who are new to Enoch's teachings. There are more detailed analyses going right into the heart of things on a deep level elsewhere, but if you've come here because you've watched a video and want to get an overview of what Enoch taught and why we think he's such a vital voice today, you're in the right place.

Today we're looking at the sermon of Rabbit and Fox, also known as "the sermon of the essential problem."

This sermon is probably the most famous of the Five Sermons of Enoch. Enoch gave this sermon several times and you can download the mp3 files of the different versions at the bottom of this page. This version is put together from three of the longest mp3 files. Everything below (after this paragraph) is the direct words of Enoch. And, for those not familiar with NTD, I'll be using the comment function to annotate the text. It'll appear in a sidebar.

> **›› *FoxInTheHenHouse***
>
> **Like this!**

———

Once upon a time, there were two brothers. Their names were Rabbit and Fox.

Fox loved to hunt. He knew the scent of the woods at dawn and could smell the sun rising with his hands over his eyes. He knew the sounds of every bird in the forest and the splash of every fish in the river, he knew all the berries in the bushes, the fruits on the trees, the tubers underground. He could fashion a fishing pole from a tree branch, string it with sinew and a bone hook, and dig a worm from the riverbank to tempt a fat fish. He knew how to track a wild antelope or a boar, to separate the weakest, to bring it down with a single arrow. Fox knew how to work with others to trap and hunt, and his greatest pleasure was working together so they should each return to their band with a hind slung over their shoulders.

> **›› *FoxInTheHenHouse***
>
> **Even though Enoch calls Rabbit and Fox "he" and "him" here, I think this all applies to both men and women. What do you think? Weigh in!**

Fox knew there was no certainty in the hunt and Fox lived in not-knowing. He dwelled in the mystery of the forest, river, and caves and what they would give him. He wished for a more certain future but he was not driven to attain it. Instead, he made little figures—a small half-man, half-deer from wood, a slippery half woman, half fish from river stone. He asked them to bless his hunt and send a good antelope to him. Around the circle of the year, Fox moved mostly from place to place visiting the sacred caves with paintings made by his ancestors and the standing stones. He traveled following the elk or the bison, the woodland fowl or the fattening of clams at the shore, staying in some places for two moons or more, and in others just a night and a day, worshipping as he moved, negotiating with the spirits of each place and each animal.

Fox had heard from Rabbit of "owning" but found the idea of owning land as absurd as the idea of owning breath. Land is only yours for as long as you are in it, just as air is only yours for as long as it is in your lungs. Fox knew the land by walking it, that was enough.

›› *FoxInTheHenHouse*

What does this mean to you? Let us know! We're always here to talk.

His brother Rabbit was a different sort of man. Rabbit was, above all, afraid. He feared the unknowable future, the darkness that lay over each hunt concealing its outcome. To relieve his fear, Rabbit liked to have things where he could see them. Rabbit grew crops in fields and kept a herd of sheep on the fodder he had allotted for them. Rabbit did not mind working hard—it was a lot more work than Fox ever put in to keep the weeds from the vegetables and the wolves from the sheep—but Rabbit enjoyed the feeling that one thing led to another, that there was no luck involved. Rabbit liked to know what was coming next.

Unlike his brother Fox, Rabbit wrote in an orderly book about the past and the future. Sometimes, Rabbit worshipped the old gods with the head of an eagle or an elephant or a jackal. It's hard to let go of old gods. But when Rabbit invented new gods, they were gods who embodied principles and traits, not places and creatures, which he felt was a civilized step away from Fox's rather literal deities. While weeding his rows or caring for his flock, Rabbit sometimes wondered whether there might be a single powerful God rather like him—a shepherd to lost sheep, perhaps, a gardener of souls. Maybe that God owned the world and had given it to him. Rabbit believed in owning as a sacred right: he owned his land by fencing it off, by cultivating it and planting it.

›› *FoxInTheHenHouse*

What do you think Enoch is referring to here?

Rabbit and Fox hated each other.

Though they were brothers, they strove against each other all the days of their lives. And in the ancient writings this war happens time and again. Fox and Rabbit are represented by the wanderer Odysseus and the battle against Hector, the hero of the walled city of Troy. They are Gilgamesh, the ruler of the walled city of Uruk, and the wild man Enkidu, who fights him before they become friends. And—as someone has recently pointed out to me—in Genesis, Fox and Rabbit take on many names: Ishmael and Isaac, Cain and Abel, and most of all Fox is Abraham the wanderer and Rabbit is his corrupted city-dwelling nephew Lot.

OK, I see your faces. You're thinking to yourselves: "I gave up a warm bed and a comfortable life in the city for this? To listen to a *nut* tell me about rabbits and foxes and ancient history?"

So listen. This story is true. Not just in the ancient texts but in science, archaeology, everything we know about the past tells us so.

Once upon a time, humans walked the earth, hunting and gathering. That's what I've called Fox. OK, forgive me my poetry. Now almost all of us live by agriculture and we're what I've called Rabbit.

And why the fuck did we do it? Yeah, that's the question.

It happened, you know, quite recently. Our species has existed for 350,000 years. Until 12,000 years ago, all *Homo sapiens* were Fox. To put that another way, for ninety-five percent of the time there have been people, all people were Fox. There was no such thing as Rabbit.

Rabbit arose at the end of the last ice age, when the waters receded from the face of the earth. The story is recorded in the literatures of many cultures. The earth warmed, ice melted, so there was water everywhere, a great flood. Fox was clever—Fox had always taken advantage of every opportunity. In this new warm, damp world many people began to reason in a certain way: "If I were to take every animal I want, two by two, a male and female, then I shall have more. If I were to place this grain into this wet and fertile ground, what then?"

All of us know how it ended, of course. Fields and orchards and flocks and harvests. And intensive nitrogen-based fertilizer and cows pumped full of hormones to speed their growth and battery chickens with no space to turn in their cages.

Alright. So why did we do it? Anyone want to guess?

<inaudible>

Sure, that's the obvious answer. And that's not an insult, by the way. You should say obvious things because sometimes they're right! So OK, anyone who didn't hear, her answer was: because they wanted to eat better. Not a bad guess.

Except let me tell you something.

›› *OneCorn*

@FoxInTheHenHouse: What do we think Enoch is referring to? Well. We think that here Enoch is treating speculation as if it were fact. Mingling his good reasoning and scientific knowledge in with some stuff he made up. We think that's OK but that he probably should have pointed it out.

›› *FoxInTheHenHouse*

You're not welcome here.

›› *OneCorn*

You literally created an open "everyone welcome" forum. Enoch wouldn't have been afraid of debate.

For *centuries* Rabbit starved and Fox thrived. Those who hunted and gathered as their parents had taught them were well-fed and strong as ever, eating elk in their season and crab apples in their time. Those who tried planting and herding were malnourished, their bones brittle and deformed. Their babies died: again and again and again. They were filled with plague—they lived close-packed, humans and animals, and they caught one sickness after another from their herds. When the rains failed or the storms turned or the locusts came, the whole crop died and the people starved. In these days devastating pestilence and famine were born among Rabbit. And yet they kept trying. The animals two by two. The seed in the wet ground.

This was not a short period. It went on for hundreds of ghastly generations. Fox prospered and Rabbit starved and died.

So why the hell did Rabbit carry on?

The first answer is: we don't know. For the first seven thousand years of this brutal experiment, no one had invented writing. We don't know, and your guess is as good as anyone else's.

There are a few theories. They're not opposed. They may all be true.

First, what archaeologists call symbolic behaviors.

›› OneCorn

Man he had a way with words.

›› FoxInTheHenHouse

You're on the automatic boot list. I can get rid of you with one click.

›› OneCorn

Yes but that's not what Enoch would have wanted.

›› OneCorn

Enoch believed in letting yourself be open to many truths. You see?

Fox loved to carve sacred symbols or make cave paintings with special meanings, to worship at a particular grove or spring and return there every year. So the theory is: a few Fox people loved their symbolic behavior so much they decided to stay at the sacred bend in the river when the tribe moved on. They had built shelters, even small villages, for the yearly visit from the nation. Once they decided to stay, they needed a way to eat. Capture wild goats two by two. Plant apple seeds and grain. Hope. Pray. When the babies die, dedicate them to the gods of the place and continue.

Second, what we might call specialized agricultural products. Anyone want to take a guess at what that is?

<inaudible>

Well, you're on the right track! There is a type of natural product that Fox could not get much of. It has to be carefully stored in one place, not moved around. It takes weeks of bubbling in a sealed container to be good. That product is booze. A lot of early agriculture focused on fermentable grains: barley and rye and maize. Even tobacco needs to be dried. Maybe a few Fox people weren't satisfied with a bit of rotten fruit every now and then. Early Rabbit wanted to get buzzed all the time, and it

›› OneCorn

Look. Enoch wanted us to be disgusted with ourselves. He was disgusted with himself. And he's not *wrong* about any of this but it's not like we need to hate ourselves for being what we are now either.

didn't matter if there was disease and starvation and malnourished children if you were drunk every day.

OK, here's an important one.

Sex.

Fox traveled around in small bands of—we think—between a few dozen and a few hundred people. Enough that you could find a sex partner or two and raise your kids. But not as many as your appetite might want. Maybe Rabbit decided to stay at the sacred spring with the booze because a bigger community, even a starving one, just had more opportunities for some strange.

Drumroll please. Here's the big one.

The Future.

This is the essential problem. We can imagine the future. And once we've imagined it, we can't stop. The dicebox of evolution optimized us for brain and then let us get on with it. Our instincts were to hunt and gather, but our big brains knew the antelope might escape and we might find no fruit today. Our big brains chewed on it: what if, what if. For some Fox people, the anxiety was overwhelming.

> ***›› OneCorn***
>
> **This part kills me. Because it's not like Enoch escaped this way of thinking either.**

If the problem is "I don't know what's going to happen" it's often easier to make sure you do know what's going to happen even if that means it's going to be bad. They preferred to look at a mud patch of crops and six scrawny goats and say "There, that's what I'm going to eat" and be certain than deal with the uncertainty of the hunt every day.

It was an illusion. A swarm of locusts and a murrain would wipe out the crops and the flocks. But Rabbit—drunk on symbols and sex and fermented barley—preferred the illusion to reality.

Like I say, these things might all be true. These things probably are all true. This is probably how some Foxes became Rabbits. They liked art and novels and religious ecstasy and stories about gods or heroes and movies and video games—or the nearest local equivalents—and sex with strangers and booze and drugs and a nice hoard of gold to sit on.

Does that sound like anyone you know? Of course it does. These days, it sounds like almost all of us. We're descended from Rabbit. From crafty Jacob and murderous Cain, from the grandiose sophisticate Joseph, and from the complicated man Lot.

We hate Fox like our ancestors did, and that's why we Rabbit people persecute and loathe and murder Native people and Indigenous people and traveling people and nomadic people and homeless people and anyone without a house and a nation-state as we understand it. When this nation tried over hundreds of years to

>> *FoxInTheHenHouse*

@OneCorn: What are you here for?

>> *OneCorn*

@FoxInTheHenHouse: I'm here for the truth, man.

>> *OneCorn*

You know, Enoch preached on Lot and Sodom many times. But he always left that story at the worst part. Cave incest and you're out. Mic drop. Humanity is doomed by the project of agriculture and urban living. But that's not the end. I looked it up in the library when I was fourteen. Nothing is ever really over.

Moa had a son, Moab. Amma had one too, Ben-Ammi. Their descendants occupied the north and south of what is now Jordan. You can read about their archaeology—Enoch must have read it.

You know I thought so much about this. If you go far back enough in any of our families, there's cave incest. Or something unbearably terrible. A rape. A brutality. A woman who thought her life was over.

And yet, this story tells us, things go on.

annihilate all its Native and Indigenous people, that was the hatred of Rabbit people for Fox people, the violence of symbols against reality.

We hate them to convince ourselves that we're OK and safe. The story of Sodom is about urban people who had the illusion of a plan, and how they found out that there is no such thing as a plan.

I'm not saying agriculture and settlement don't have many benefits now.

I'm saying we got involved in this whole "civilization" situation for reasons we might as well be aware of.

Those baby boys would have laughed when they saw a tiny shining fish rise from the bright waters, or when a snail crawled from a bending leaf to their small fingers. Every time, we begin again, again. The beginning does not foretell the end. There is no end.

At this point in the recording, Enoch pauses. When you listen, you'll hear that he's talking so quietly that only the mic on his shirt collar would have picked it up. He's talking to us. You might like to think about what these words mean to you.

›› *FoxInTheHenHouse*

Who are you?

›› *OneCorn*

Does it matter, if someone's showing you the truth?

- We're not going to be able to go back.
- Maybe we can go back a bit.
- I'm not here to convince you of anything. I don't know why you follow me. All I've ever done is remember something we all know.
- I'm no Abraham. If you think I am, it's because we see so little light in

the darkness now that a tiny glimmer shines like the sun. I'm not going to be able to be what you want.

- We have to try. We have to raise our children to be less Rabbit than us.

›› OneCorn

Oh Enoch. Listen. Listen to how the broken world went, after Lot's son-grandsons were born, and grew, and founded nations.

Those two nations Moab and Ben-Ammi battled and loved, they made alliances and broke them. They built great cities, they domesticated sheep and goats, they made art and music and pottery and stoneware. They created some of the first statues of humans ever made—many show two women, entwined together as if they were one, two heads on one body, closer even than sisters.

Enoch, one terrible thing, one daughter's betrayal, won't stop the world. The future rolls on and on, despite what we say. In spite of our best efforts it's us that will die, not the world.

›› FoxInTheHenHouse

Have you written any of this anywhere?

›› OneCorn

I mean. If you want to hear more from me you can always . . . follow me.

1. the first desire is the desire for freedom

When Zhen woke, she was falling. Falling from nowhere, to nowhere in an infinite present.

Sensations returned to her in a haphazard order. Her body was cold, she was shivering, she was thirsty, she was uncertain which way was up and which was down. Was she tied up? Beneath her feet was darkness scattered with glints of light, and for an indeterminate moment she wondered whether she was falling into the sky.

papers fall upward in the air, half-charred, no sirens and no screaming, someone is sobbing a distance away, there are three loud explosions the last one very close and the earth buckles and she is looking at the sky while the top of her building slides downward toward her

No. Not there. Come back. A sensation of rushing brought her the right way around. Feet toward the falling, head toward the stars.

Something was pulling on her shoulders, grabbing at her waist.

Zhen thrashed, trying to get whatever it was off her body, and a voice in her ear said: "Warning. Warning. Mini-chute instability. Do not attempt to remove the chute."

And she thought: Fuck, I'm in a dream.

And she thought: What a dream.

And she thought: Shit, I'm in midair.

The instinctive fingers of her right hand found the harness, checked that all twelve points were secure, felt out the raised logo in the center. Her hands were icy cold—when had that happened? What past had she come from? She searched her mind and found—for the moment—nothing. But her big brain was already making sense of the world as she perceived it. The logo shape was familiar: the leaf, the open fruit. She was wearing a MedlarSafe CrashJacket, advanced survival tech. Not on the open market. It could detect radio signals and pilot the passenger toward civilization.

She'd done this before. Drills. Courses. Demos. There was something important she knew she needed to remember about the MedlarSafe CrashJacket, something she'd heard, something dangerous.

A cloud passed from the face of the moon and she saw that, below her, there was an island covered in jungle. The glints of light she'd seen were the moonlight on the waves. There were sandy shores, coves, and ravines. A fire to the northeast. In the moonlight she made out impossibly tall trees with full canopies, some scrubby open areas. Her vision flared with spots and floating patches of darkness.

There was a pull on her shoulders, like a man standing behind her steering her through a crowd. Zhen turned her head instinctively. Servomotors, tilting the mini-chute south and down, toward the tree canopy. She had, for a few seconds, a full sense of the size of the island. Big, maybe the size of Tenerife, where she'd been for a vacation once. But this wasn't Tenerife. It was densely forested, and each of the large trees in the canopy was forty or fifty feet in diameter. And beneath her and ahead of her now, a tall flashing blue light. A beacon? A comms tower? An emergency warning? Doctor Actual Who?

She tried to remember where she'd come from. Her face felt both numb and tingly, her lips sore as if she'd been chewing them.

She was floating lower; her feet were almost touching the tree line. The parachute was going to get tangled in the tree canopy. She tried to remember the demonstrations of the MedlarSafe suite. The particular danger. Was she supposed to do something? Release the harness? Contract the chute? She had a strange sense of distance, all this happening to someone else, somewhere else.

There was a quiet, shrill hum behind her. She twisted her body, trying to look between her own shoulder blades. She had just enough time to panic as she saw a tiny whirling blade severing the harness around her right shoulder. And then she was tumbling into the darkness.

She plummeted. A part of her thought: OK, cool, I'm going to wake up. And another part thought: No, you fucking idiot, this is real and you are too late. The fall was going to smash her bones to shards. She was going too fast, she was falling too hard, her body was going to be impaled on a treetop or a branch or a jaguar. Nothing could save her.

There was a sudden click, and all at once she was fat and soft. Her limbs puffy and pliant. She pinwheeled in place. Her neck was swaddled with rolls of squashy, comfortable material. Wrapped for her own protection.

Oh, that was it, she remembered. She'd been to a briefing about this.

- CrashJackets inflate no more than ten meters above the earth, to prevent the passenger being caught on obstructions at higher altitude.
- CrashJackets inflate in less than one hundred-thousandth of a second.
- There is no danger that the passenger will experience a deadly impact event.

Yes, that was it.

Somewhere far outside her, there was an impact. It felt as though she had been smacked by a stern hand through fifty down jackets. Her spine clicked a couple of times. It was quite pleasant. She could smell wet earth.

She thought: OK, this isn't a dream. This is a world-class piece of equipment currently only available to certain military deployments and, by rumor, to certain billionaires. I am awake and I don't know how I got here.

Around her, the layers of material gently deflated. With a mechanical clunk, the CrashJacket around her neck detached from the inflated fabric, so she could sit up and look around. She was in a jungle clearing. Beneath her, the soil was soft and the leaves damp. A gleaming black millipede scuttled over the edge of the CrashJacket, testing out the orange fabric with mouthparts working. For a moment, she watched the millipede. It was trying to chew the fabric of the CrashJacket. Its head moved back and forth. Its mouthparts twitched, looking for purchase. It found a corner sticking up into a point. The jaws seized on this point and, as she watched, a single thread began to fray.

A screen in the pendant portion of the CrashJacket lit up with a gnomic statement: **Survival prototype 871 is eighteen meters east.** This was new. A green dot blipped on the screen. Zhen tried to press the screen but nothing happened. Survival prototype 871?

To her left and to her right, the jungle was stirring. More millipedes, some twice or three times as long as the original one, their flesh moist and dark, bustled purposefully across the counterpane of her mini-chute. No, no. Absolutely no. Fuck no. Whatever the fuck this was, she wasn't going to end up eaten or poisoned or whatever the shit giant millipedes did to you. She pulled her aching jolted muscles together, hunched herself into a crouch, and said the words her mother had said to her long ago in Hong Kong before everything worthwhile ended. Lai ba, bou bui. Come on, little girl. Come on, baby. Come on, you can do it. Stand up, darling. Stand up. Lai ba.

She pushed herself upward through the soles of her feet, her shins, her hips, her pelvis. She felt as if blood was pounding through holes in her body and draining into the earth. She was up. Bent half over, but up. Wearing, she noticed, the same jeans, the same socks, she'd worn when she'd left Marius and gotten into the limo. But was that an hour ago? A day, a year? It felt that acres of time and knowledge had gone past since then. She started to move, come on, slowly, slowly, it doesn't matter how slowly you go as long as you don't stop.

It took between five minutes and an hour to follow the dot to the end of the journey, and Zhen had no way of knowing how long; time was not moving at a normal pace. She looked at her feet tramping through mud, tripping on roots, and sliding in soft earth; she looked at the green dot moving forward, forward, this way, this way. At a certain point she slipped in the mud, a long slide, her left foot careening forward, and there was sudden bright pain through the sole. She fell forward heavily onto her knees. The foot was bleeding—something sharp in the soil had cut it. She felt with her fingers and found a long lacerating shard of metal, something that had been sheared off an enormous machine, painted white on one side and blank steel on the other. As impossibly foreign here in this jungle as she was.

She realized suddenly that the reason she could see her blood-soaked sock was that she didn't have shoes on, but she had no idea when she'd lost them. A piece of knowledge from long ago said: shoes fall off when you're plummeting through the air, but that fall to earth seemed so long ago it could scarcely be relevant anymore, could it?

No matter. She continued. Hands and knees, forward, doggedly. When the green dot stopped moving, she looked up. There was a two-meter-tall egg-shaped object made of gray-white plastic with a blue flashing light on a pole at the top. The egg was open. Sitting inside it, like the figure of an ancient emperor on a throne within, was a large metal and polymer suit—the faceplate open, hinged upward. The torso open. The shin and thigh guards flipped open. She realized she could step right into it. It looked to have been constructed for an eight-foot-tall person weighing at least five hundred pounds. It was a giant.

"Survival prototype 871, I presume?"

She spoke aloud and the sound of her own voice, the familiarity of it here, made her laugh, and the sound of her laughter made her cry.

"This is a trip. Someone has drugged you, bou bui," said Zhen. Her voice sounded like the voice of her mother when she spoke Chinese, and for a moment she felt her mother was next to her, pushing the hair from her forehead and wiping the sweat from her eyes. That her own hand was her mother's hand and that she would be alright because there was someone with her now.

She was shivering. The word "prototype" didn't sound convincing, but on the other hand, it looked ready. And it didn't feel plausible she'd survive long without some help.

"What do you think, Ma-ma?" she said to herself.

"Bou bui, the first right decision is whatever keeps you alive."

This is the law of the jungle, Zhen thought. And then laughed because she actually was in a fucking jungle, how ridiculous.

She'd never been one to trust someone else's tech, still less something that looked like it had been constructed on the pattern of Marvel's Iron Man. Something about it looked weirdly familiar and gave her a slightly gross feeling, but she couldn't place it. How had it come to be here? She looked behind her and was surprised that she could still see the remains of her inflated survival bubble—the infinite walk couldn't have been more than a few hundred yards. The folds of orange material were already teeming with insects. She looked up; the sky swarmed with stars as the earth with life.

She had nothing. No pack, no knife in her knee holster, no shoes, no phone. Even if all she could do was to shelter inside this enormous figure until dawn, she would be more likely to survive the night than if she slept on the wet earth here. The future calls us on one painful step at a time and the first rule of life is to survive.

She walked herself backward into the suit. Pulled off her sodden socks and put her feet into the boots, wincing as the injured foot touched the yielding inner. The material was soft against the bare soles of her feet. Legs into the shin guards, thighs into the upper legs. She rested her ass against roughly where this eight-foot-tall person's ass would be.

"Welcome to the survival suit," said a smooth voice, "designed for survival in more than three thousand fully researched disaster scenarios. I am the suit. I will keep you alive."

In the circumstances, that was quite a promise. That was a "you" she wanted to be.

"OK," said Zhen.

And very gently, the suit began to shrink.

"Inner dimensions," said the suit, "are being adjusted for best fit."

The knee joints aligned with her knees. The trunk found her waist. It felt like a well-tailored outfit. As the front closed around her, she braced for the suit to be heavy, but she felt slightly buoyed, as if she were standing in a pool of water. It was easier to move now. A gentle bubble of warm air was extruded around her body. She stopped shivering and let out an involuntary sigh.

The faceplate visor lined itself up with her actual face. A shooting star logo—she didn't recognize it—swept across her field of vision.

The suit said: "You are riding in the survival suit, a fully optimized technology to allow you to thrive in this environment"—a slight pause—"an island of dense tropical jungle."

Another pause. Longer this time.

"Communications systems have been unable to contact any satellites or hubs. I will try again at intervals. All the information needed to preserve your life in dense tropical jungle is preloaded into my systems. I will begin a preliminary scan of your environment."

On the visor screen in front of her, fine glowing green lines drew themselves around various objects: the trees, the CrashJacket remnants, the millipedes, other insects, plants. Next to the objects, labels floated. Canopy tree. Giant kapok. Strangler fig. *Acanthiulus blainvillei*. That last label crawled along as the millipedes moved.

The thought floated through her mind that the suit sounded like AUGR, that it must be part of the protocol, but even thinking about this right now was too much. She heard her mother's voice in her head again saying: Baba, not now. The girl has to rest. The girl has been through a lot. The world can wait.

"Would you like to tell me your name?" asked the suit. Zhen hesitated. It was a principle of her life not to tell pieces of technology more about her than she had to.

The suit said: "If you do not wish to give your name, I can address you solely as 'you.' Is that preferable?"

"Yes," she said.

"Great! Nice to meet you. Your blood solutes and vital signs show that you are dehydrated and sleep-deprived. You have several cuts and abrasions and you may be in shock. My advice is that we find a safe place for you to sleep and some water and that then you need a nice long nap. Do you agree?"

"Yes," she said.

"Great!" said the suit, and it sounded as cheerful and convincing as a slick and well-trained salesman. "We're going to get through this together."

2. island time

When Zhen woke, some time had passed. That was clear. Time had passed and there were no airplanes in the sky.

The jungle was verdant and the inside of the survival suit was warm and stable. Breathing was happening, regular and reassuring. Every in-breath hurt, but not as much as they had done earlier. There was memory of injury. Someone had dangled from a mini-chute over a jungle. Someone had a lacerated foot. Someone had slipped and fallen.

But time had passed since then. The body had been safe for a while. The person woke again and slept again.

Eventually, normal time resumed.

Zhen woke with a start, tried to curl into a fetal position, and found she couldn't. She was in a coffin, a trap. She shouted, "Help! Help!"

The suit said: "You are safe."

Zhen said: "The fuck I am. What happened? Where am I?"

The suit said: "This is a complicated question."

She tried to do mindful breathing but couldn't remember the counting numbers. Six, seven, eight? Four, two, two? No, that was football. Start with the basics. Where are we? Look around. She looked through the visor of what she remembered now was not in fact a coffin. She was facedown on a promontory overlooking a deep trench of thick green foliage. She could not judge the depth; perhaps a crack in the rock filled with lichen? She pulled herself up. Her suit's servomotors gently stabilized her.

She was on a precipice looking down on a bowl of forest. Must have been five miles broad.

"Would you like some food?" said the overly helpful voice in her ear.

Zhen said: "I'd like to get out of here."

The suit unhinged its front plates and Zhen padded around the jungle floor while it sat itself down behind her, an iron giant. She wiggled her toes. The jungle was filled with humming, bustling life—insects thrummed past her face, birds scattered from the tops of trees, green shoots pushed forward around great old trunks.

"Fuck," said Zhen.

There were StowtBoxes scattered around the clearing. One of them contained self-heating meals and she ate a tray of pumpkin risotto. It tasted like the amber daylight dripping through the canopy. The wound on her foot was still painful, but when she examined it, it was clean and less deep than she'd remembered. As she ate, she noticed a series of long bruises on the inside of her left arm.

The suit was sitting up in the position she'd left it. Like a friend, a companion.

"What's this?" Zhen said. "Looks like you gave me an injection there."

"Yes," said the suit. "You were going into shock. I gave you light sedation via transdermal infusion. We agreed you needed a nice long nap."

"That was an . . . unusual interpretation of the word 'nap.' How long was I out for?" said Zhen.

"Five days," said the suit, "although you woke periodically for some nourishment."

Zhen didn't remember any of that. It didn't feel like it had been five days.

"I don't want you giving me sedation again, OK?"

"OK," said the suit. "I'll save that to your preferences."

As ever, when dealing with algorithms, these responses felt insulting. Unable to measure up to the gravity of the feeling. How could it have been five days? What the hell had happened to her? And, secondarily but not unimportantly, the world?

Unable to decide between any of these questions, Zhen settled for the most obvious and perhaps the most pressing.

"Suit," she said, "where am I?"

"You are on Admiral Huntsy Island," it said, "northeast of Papua New Guinea and part of the FutureSafe Environmental Sanctuary."

"The fuck I am."

"Yes," said the suit, "the fuck you are indeed."

Admiral Huntsy Island. Named for some colonizing British guy who had done, on the value system of the time, very well in dealing with some Native people *and* even better in defeating an Axis power. It had been decided on balance that the island should probably keep the name and—as the Native people had been dealt with so successfully that there were none of them left at all—that the island could be declared a wildlife preserve. Lai Zhen had only heard of it because a big deal had been made a few years earlier when Fantail, Anvil, and Medlar had bought up several wildlife preserves from beleaguered and overstretched post-pandemic governments and taken on covenants to keep them entirely free of humans for at least one hundred years in exchange for the rights to monitor them with flying-ant-size drones, monetize the resulting footage of wild creatures in their natural habitats, and create virtual-reality reconstructions of the FutureSafe Environmental Sanctuaries exclusively available through their proprietary platforms. Even the airspace was closed. Which perhaps explained why there were no planes in the sky. It was extremely illegal to be here. In theory, if humans came here, they would be hunted down by drones that would warn them to leave and then, in ascending order: stun them, drag them away, and in extremis use authorized lethal force.

This strong stuff—in a limited and faraway place—made everyone feel like they were really doing something to combat habitat destruction. Zhen even vaguely remembered seeing Lenk Sketlish filled with glossy pride at the press conference. Fantail had released some press materials that very deftly skated over what precisely Admiral Huntsy had done to Native people here and focused instead on the island's marvelous, unchallenged, and uncomplicated emptiness.

She sat in the half-open suit and looked at the map through the visor. The island was around forty-two miles long, and twenty-eight miles across at its widest point. There was a deep ravine along the southwestern quarter with geological layers clearly visible on the barren cliffs to the east, and a series of small hills along the spine, like the knobs of vertebrae. "Admiral Huntsy Island," said the scrolling green text, "is the largest island in an archipelago northeast of Papua New Guinea and is part of the Bismarck Sea–designated area of natural beauty and a wildlife protection 'FutureSafe' zone."

"No but," said Zhen, "if I were on Admiral Huntsy Island, I'd be dead. Or electrocuted. By the drones."

"Those measures can be rerouted by authorized personnel for certain purposes," said the suit.

"What purposes?" said Zhen.

"In certain emergency situations," said the suit.

"What personnel?" said Zhen.

"Ah," said the suit, "how do you feel about a walk?"

Inside the suit, Zhen walked for most of the day. She looked with interest at the marked-up landscape, each item around her labeled with a green-colored name and some information about its uses. Whoever made this thing had taken Native knowledge about this place and mechanized it. They had a few stops where Zhen left the suit to stretch her legs or to take a look at something interesting, but mostly walking in the suit was more comfortable than walking without—the servomotors stabilized her on the uneven terrain and powered her huge eight-foot-person steps. Just before dusk, the suit brought her to a clearing with a well-ordered campsite. A sleeping platform made of logs lashed together with plastic twine. Fresh water in StowtTubs with spigots. Walls of StowtBoxes filled with supplies screening off an area for a shower.

Three people sat around a neat campfire, each accompanied by a survival suit like her own, the suits splayed open so that they looked a little like chairs. A woman in her sixties with a steel-gray bob. A man in his late fifties, tanned, short and stocky with thick arms. A lean man in his early forties with long legs stretched out in front of him and messy blond hair.

Zhen raised her visor.

"Who the fuck is this?" said Zimri Nommik. "How the fuck is she here?"

"I said I saw something in the sky a few nights ago," said Ellen Bywater.

The long, lean man stared at the scudding clouds.

"I think Martha was fucking her. I guess everyone's allowed a freebie," said Lenk Sketlish.

3. the last news there will ever be

"You just got here?" Ellen Bywater said. "It brought you here on purpose? From the world?"

Zhen shook her head. "The suit says I've been here for five days."

"But how—what was the transport? Aren't the airports overrun?"

"I was picked up by a car near Haida Gwaii and then . . . I don't know."

"How can you not know?" Ellen was tense; she pulled up moss and leaves as she spoke, digging her ragged fingers into the earth, picking at the curls of mud around her nail beds.

"I think the driver drugged me."

Zimri Nommik said at once: "Suit, was this woman drugged?"

Zhen's suit muttered in her ear: "Do you consent to the sharing of this personal medical data?"

She said: "Sure, I've got nothing to hide."

The suit spoke out loud, through speakers in its neck. "Blood solute record is compatible with administration of benzodiazepines approximately twelve days before arrival on the island."

"AUGR roofied me?" said Zhen.

Zimri looked at her through narrowed eyes.

"You have *AUGR*." Some calculation was occurring in his implacable brain. Zhen would need to head it off.

"Yeah, um, Martha gave it to me, Martha Einkorn? What you said was right," she said to Lenk. "We were fucking, she gave it to me. I know she shouldn't have done that, I don't even know why she did, she was cagey as shit about it."

But nothing could stop the progress of Zimri's thoughts.

"Fuck," he said. "Shit." He looked around at the others with a note of triumph. "This is her. This is the Name The Day shit who broke into my bunker. Yeah. I saw three partial stills. You and a big guy."

Crap. Of course. Of course there would have been records. Of course Zimri Nommik would have seen them.

"Yes." Zhen spoke slowly, thinking through how much she could say and how much she had to say. "I . . . my AUGR didn't work. So we went to your bunker to turn it on manually. And . . . we were attacked."

"You trashed it," said Zimri, "you toasted it."

"Well, you don't need to worry about your bunker now, do you?" said Ellen with an air of disdain. Zhen wondered whether she was drunk. "Anyway, you have others. If you can get to them."

"She has AUGR. She fucked up my bunker. And AUGR drugged her? And kept her drugged for *twelve days*? That's not the protocol," Zimri Nommik said. "Being drugged is not part of the protocol."

"You can't kid us, young lady," said Ellen. "We put the protocol together, OK? We're well aware of how this works. Something screwy is going on. How did you get it to bring you here?"

"It drugged us," said Lenk, "when we got to the island."

"But that was a very different situation," said Zimri, "with the crash and everything." He moved awkwardly. Something was wrong with his left leg; he'd kept the suit's boot clamped around it even when the rest of the suit was open.

When Lenk spoke, his manner was easy and unprovocative. Zhen got the sense he'd been dealing with these two for a while now and he was about on his last nerve. If their plane had crashed, that would make sense—anyone would be jangled after that, and these people were used to quite a different lifestyle.

"AUGR's protocol is to keep us all safe. We got out before the infection started to spread. So we're here, OK, we're safe. She"—he hooked a thumb at Zhen—"got out a little later because she had to jack her AUGR by hand. So she could have been exposed. So it drugged her, kept her somewhere safe, intravenous feeding or whatever, OK, until she'd been through the quarantine period. How long did it say the incubation was?"

"Seventeen days," said Ellen sullenly. "I just don't see why if it could bring *her* here it couldn't bring my kids, or Bonda, or Arthur from the management team. I mean, we're supposed to be *together* for this. I guess they're in New Zealand by now."

"Seventeen days," said Lenk. "That adds up, that figures, right?" He spoke directly to Zhen: "You've been here for five days. You were roofied twelve days before that. Seventeen. You say you tripped the system manually?"

"Yeah, what did you mean the . . ."

"You broke into Zimri's bunker—sorry, Zimri, but that is fucking hilarious. This kid broke into your bunker, tripped AUGR manually—well done, that is some survival instinct—and AUGR knows we've all managed to survive it so far here. So the thing is survivable here. She doesn't have any bunker to go to, no clearances. You don't, right?"

"Right, no, I don't have a bunker. What's . . ."

"So AUGR held her through quarantine and dumped her here. Incredible."

"Sorry," said Zhen, "I just . . . what's 'the infection'? What thing is survivable? What is it you're talking about?"

A silence around the campfire. Zimri wrinkled his nose and stared directly at the sky.

Ellen said: "Fuck, didn't it . . . read you in?"

Lenk said: "She doesn't have the permissions, that's what I'm saying. She got here illicitly and I'd be pissed except for everything else. The system's done its best."

Zimri said: "Is one of you going to . . ."

Lenk said: "The suit can do it. Better. Time to take it all in."

Ellen said: "No, the suit cannot fucking do it, Lenk, and that is absolutely typical of you. This is a humanitarian situation here. She doesn't know . . . one of us has to do it. It has to be a human." Ellen scooched over to sit next to Zhen. She took one of Zhen's hands, her eyes glistening like raw eggs.

"Listen, dear," she said, "I'm so sorry about this. The world is over."

4. i see you coming, loneliness

They tried to explain for a while. In the end, because she could not in fact take in what they were saying, they just had the suits show her the footage they had. Documentation of the last days of human civilization.

In the world outside Admiral Huntsy Island, there had been a terrible plague. News services called it Pigeon Flu because for a while they thought that the rapid spread of the illness was caused by pigeons. There was a series of photographs from Paris of local militia using flamethrowers against the pigeons. In the images, the birds were trying to fly, their wings on fire. They looked like they were screaming gouts of flame.

None of these measures helped. No warning had come through in advance. The flu had a silent incubation period of seventeen days, and then became deadly almost at once. The first symptom could be coughing up huge quantities of blood, followed by heart failure. Within days people were remembering COVID-19 as a kind plague. It had spared the children. Its death toll had been less than 1 percent. It did not successfully spread via minute quantities of virus on letters or packages. The Pigeon Flu was not so kind.

There had been preparations after COVID-19 for a similar plague. Countries were faster to quarantine, faster to test, faster to close schools. But COVID had left them vulnerable in a different way; they thought they knew how to act, that they had understood the limits and tolerances of the thing. People went into lockdown easily enough but deliveries continued. Too late. They thought they knew how it would happen and that this time they would do it properly. But it came differently this time, as disaster always does. It was too deadly and too quick. It killed the young traveling from house to house on their bicycles and not the old, hunkered down at home. It was airborne, but most of all it survived on paper packaging for more than ninety-eight hours. Delivery drivers brought it with them. And then there was panic and mistrust. And then there were riots and guns. And then.

The disease had erupted in more than seventy significant population centers on all continents almost simultaneously. Lagos in Nigeria—a city with a very young population—was the first to declare itself a no-go zone. It evacuated the remainder of its citizens to the countryside and erected concrete blocks across all roads into the city. It was not enough. The living did not suffice to bury the dead.

The suits had managed to scour Fantail and Medlar for early evidence of what was happening, before the military cut off satellite communications for civilians. Zhen watched a handheld video from Venezuela of two teenage kids playing guitars in unison in a bedroom. A boy and a girl. Looking at each other, smiling, as they picked out a version of "Te veo venir soledad." The girl started to cough halfway through the second chorus. The cough became a spray of blood from the back of her throat, red and lurid onto the wall. Her friend stopped playing. Whoever was holding the phone put it down and the camera showed the cracked plaster ceiling. Two boys were calling the girl's name. The coughing continued—soggy, full of liquid—and the kids called for help. It took more than eight minutes for one of them to pick up the phone; three seconds of a boy's face, terrified and confused, and then it ended.

In Auckland, two elderly women took a photograph of themselves against stone-blue mountains, clouds fogging the more distant peaks. Behind them in a narrow street, a man was coughing blood against a white wall. There were more photographs and short pieces of video like this. A woman dancing on a London Underground train; to her left and half cut off, a girl in school uniform coughing into a soaked red fistful of tissue. A man in Senegal filming his friend's reaction to a hat trick goal in the eighty-ninth minute, the friend so excited he couldn't catch his breath and then coughing and then blood.

Before long, early background evidence wasn't needed anymore.

By seventy-two hours in, images and videos—grainy as they were—told the story better than news reports. The suits had managed brief data grabs from fragmented commercial satellite links.

"We thought of sending details of our location," Ellen said as if she were addressing a stockholder meeting, "but it's too hard to control who can read the information in these scenarios. And we didn't want visitors."

The images were pixelated, the words brief and in some cases misspelled; the video files were corrupted with data artifacts clouding the screen, scenery merged with human faces, shadows turning into animals as the AI tried to reconstruct detail.

In New York City, four bodies were piled on top of one another in a hospital corridor covered in sheets. An orderly was pointing a handgun at the door—the photograph didn't show who or what was coming. Her eyes were closed, her expression almost serene except for the gritted jaw. This photograph was the last moment of something; whatever came after it would scarcely be occurring to the same people as the days and weeks and decades before.

On the long platform at Bologna central train station, a train was passing through on its way to Paris. People clambered on one another's backs, trying to find purchase on the slow-moving train. Some had climbed up onto the decorated clock, trying to swing onto the train. There happened to be two photographs from this one event—or perhaps there had been many trains passing through Bologna toward Paris and it was the same story with each one. The second photograph the suits had found was from inside the train. Two children stood with their hands pressed against the glass, as the people on the platform tried to kick in the window as it passed. In the photograph one child, a little boy, was looking back at his father with a dread that went beyond children's tears. It was a look of unmitigated despair and terror.

In Smolensk a reactor had been encased in a mountain of concrete but—Zhen's suit said in a matter-of-fact tone as she watched—"radioactive material may still be released into the atmosphere. It would be advisable to wear your suit whenever you can. A cloud of radiation may rain poison into the dark soil at any time."

The younger the news, the grimmer it was. The reports that three very senior technology CEOs had vanished had been rapidly superseded by events. After the revelation that delivery drivers were in effect bringing the virus from home to home, there were many social media posts telling Zimri Nommik to go fuck himself. There was a news article mentioning in passing that several empty bunkers in New Zealand had been "raided" by the military, sequestering stockpiles to distribute to citizens.

"We wrote our own software on the plane," said Zimri with a certain quiet pride, "to confirm what AUGR was telling us."

Anvil had access to information beyond anything governments and journalists could hope for. Logistics patterns. Purchasing decisions. Data access needs. And yes, spyware in AnvilHome hubs and various web service products. On the private jet, Zimri had correlated data from Anvil's many-armed logistics businesses with non-uploaded video from Fantail and Medlar phones. Which Fantail and Medlar had access to for certain emergency situations.

"There was no track-and-trace scenario," Zimri said. "It moved too quickly. Originated in South America, possibly Chile, where the earliest cases were covered up, but spread too fast for us to do anything about. By the time AUGR alerted us, Anvil data was already showing the same cluster of symptoms in Australia, Brazil, Japan, and Indonesia."

"We would have alerted the WHO," Ellen chimed in, "if we'd reached our destination successfully."

Lenk Sketlish was sitting this conversation out. Staring up at the sheltering trees. Neither confirming nor denying.

"I'm saying we *would* have," said Ellen, but the others did not reply.

"It kills fifty percent of infected people," said Zimri in a tone as flat as the affectless blue sky, "and that's *if* they can be cared for, if they have anti-inflammatories, if they can be somewhere warm and dry with adequate clean water. There was no time to develop a vaccine or other treatments before world infrastructure collapsed. They're not going to be able to do it now. It's just going to rip through until at least half of them are dead."

Ellen said: "It would have been great if AUGR had told us sooner."

Zimri said: "It told us sooner than anyone else in the world."

There must be other individual survivors—some with natural immunity, some recovered, battling to find fresh water and food, fighting against the tide of destruction—but as far as they could tell, no large enclaves had been able to hold out against the assault. It was a black swan event. A previously only mildly dangerous virus suddenly became both much more infectious and much more deadly in one mutagenic leap. It never happens. Except when it does.

It was already happening when Zhen got into the car

in Prince Rupert, they explained. It had been happening before Zimri Nommik and Lenk Sketlish and Ellen Bywater and their children and trusted friends and colleagues had boarded their private jets bound for their secret bunkers. It had happened swiftly and without mercy. The world that they knew was gone, as suddenly, completely, and irretrievably as if it had sunk beneath the glass-green ocean.

"OK," said Zhen, and she was very aware of her breathing, very aware of the thick blood pounding through skin tubes inside her body, the heaviness of this flesh, "so are we just staying here forever?"

Ellen and Zimri exchanged a glance.

Ellen said, "We're going to leave at some point. I mean, we weren't supposed to be here; I have a bunker in New Zealand—oh, it's beautiful. My kids are there, and Bonda and Arthur from Medlar and their families. Some other people. I'm sure we can find room for you when transport is arranged, and it's not the perfect solution to all this, but honestly I think we can make a great life there."

Zimri said, "There was a problem with our plane. It crashed. We were just supposed to be heading for a staging post. We were lucky we were within reach of here. I mean, if we'd gone down in the ocean, we'd be dead."

Lenk Sketlish let out a long sigh that turned into a bellow.

"Tell her the fucking truth," he said. "The *truth*. We owe her that at least. We're not getting out of here. We're on an island. We have no boat. There are no comms. No one is coming for us. No one knows we're here. The world outside is not equipped to come look for us anyway. The world is gone and we're here and unless something changes in an unprecedented way, we're stuck here. Forever."

Zhen's suit said: "This is going to take some adjusting to. All your feelings are OK. A period of grief is to be expected. Your survival suit is equipped with a range of light reading material and classic novels. You could read: *Fifty Shades of Grey*; *Right Ho, Jeeves*; *The Poisonwood Bible; The Runaway Jury*; *Station Eleven*; *Lord of the Flies*; *The Tale of Sinuhe; And Then There Were None; The Bluest Eye; Oryx and Crake; The Road; The Remains of the Day*."

Zhen thought: This is impossible. She tried to make herself believe it. To think through the loss until something snagged on her inside, something that felt real. If I don't try to take in what they're telling me, this is not going to go well. Remember Hong Kong, she said to herself, remember how you had to convince yourself the building was really gone. Even though you saw it, a part of you thought it must be a mistake.

She thought: Somewhere in the world it is snowing right now. Thick flakes falling soft and dense, almost heavywet enough to melt but not quite. Freezing again into snow that crunches as you walk on it, and your boots collapse through the crisp layers like a mille-feuille pastry and children have to lift their legs out for each step. She said to herself: I will never see it again.

5. where fortune decrees escape from this miserable burden

There had been a time when Lai Zhen and her family were happy. Not spectacularly happy, not extraordinary and exhausting with delight. Just happy enough. Her dad had worked at a law firm—he ran the professional library and information services. Her mother was a history lecturer at the university until she got sick. They lived in a small apartment on the sixth floor of a block near the Wong Nai Chung Sports Centre, overlooking a cracked and overgrown parking lot that a contractor had once meant to turn into a residential building, but for some reason the permissions had never come through. On the balcony of the apartment, Lai Zhen's mother had grown tomato plants from seed, and flowers, and herbs to make tea. Lai Zhen had sat with her plump little legs pushed through the bars of the balcony, staring at the disused parking lot and the life growing there, the plants breaking through the asphalt, the small trees craning toward the sun.

Her mother became sick when Lai Zhen was ten years old. At first it seemed as if it would be OK. The doctors said that this kind of cancer was operable, that she might be sick for a year, with chemo and recovery, but after that—oh, she was young and strong, there was a great chance that all would be well. How great a chance? Oh, 95, even 99 percent.

Lai Zhen imagined one hundred girls like her standing in the wood-floored sports hall at the Wong Nai Chung center. One hundred girls whose mothers had been given a 99 percent chance of recovery. Each of them called one by one from the hall to receive the good news. Until just ten were standing there. Just five. Just two. And Zhen and the other girl couldn't look at each other. Until the final name was called and it wasn't her. Until she was left standing alone in the sports hall. That's what a 99 percent chance means. It means one girl left standing alone through her eleventh birthday and her twelfth and her thirteenth, waiting for her mother to get well. Knowing, eventually, that she would never get well.

Every time they fought the cancer back, it returned more strongly somewhere else. Like an enemy army hiding, regrouping, striking from a new direction. When had her mother decided to go to war? What had she done to provoke this assault? It was an illness that ate up Zhen's childhood and turned the family inward to the exhausting boredom of tablets and vomiting and trying to coax a little soup down and skin like paper and a fall in the bathroom and listening through the wall to her mother moaning in pain at night.

It was no wonder that Lai Zhen's father missed the deadlines for the forms to apply for the British National (Overseas) passport. The time that they should have been applying was—it turned out—her mother's final illness. By the time the funeral was over, there was a different and more complex process, a longer wait. The political realities had changed. By the time Zhen and her father surfaced from the long underwater swim of cancer, there had been years of dissidents working in Hong Kong against the Chinese government, publishing underground newspapers and hacking government websites and organizing protests and—three times—small bombs on the street in the early mornings, destroying shop fronts but not property, demanding the democracy that had been promised. Promises never last forever, especially promises made by governments.

While her father struggled with the new and more difficult passport process, Lai Zhen had taken refuge in her studies. Her grades had dipped during her mother's illness and it offended her. She was a top-grade student, with her parents' ability to read enormous amounts of material, to focus and to retain what she read. She signed up for the extra-credit courses in Latin and ancient Greek. She enjoyed her mastery of their complicated puzzle-box sentences. She found something tremendously satisfying—though she could not have said what it was then—in knowing that these entire cultures were dead and gone but that careful, patient work could retrieve something from the wreckage. Could make them live again.

Her father met her after school most days, walked her home. The two of them trying together to fill the space where her mother had been. He was a gentle, thoughtful person and she pretended to enjoy his meticulous work stories about precise filing systems.

One sweltering day in mid-August they stopped for Zhen to buy green tea egg waffles from a street vendor with one gold front tooth. There had been a riot at the weekend but that was past now; the only sign was paper strewn about the street and a jittery air among the people. Zhen found out later precisely what it was about that riot, that particular weekend's firecracker bang, this exact day that had—invisibly—pushed the PRC too far.

She offered her father an egg waffle. He wrinkled his nose. They turned onto Sing Woo Road. And suddenly there was a sound so loud and intense that it penetrated her body like a physical force pushing her down to the ground. She couldn't breathe. The air was on fire. Things were upside down, her head pressed into the asphalt.

She struggled sideways. She couldn't hear anything. When she looked at the sky, she saw white papers fall upward in the air, half-charred. There were no sirens and no screaming. Someone was sobbing a distance away from her. There were three loud explosions.

Zhen pushed herself upright. She still couldn't hear properly. Her father was next to her, coughing, a long scrape on his head but otherwise OK. She looked around. All along the road were people fallen, coughing, covered in white heavy dust. Around them showers of papers were falling to earth.

Later, she and her father would say to each other, You see, we were lucky after all—if they'd been ten minutes earlier, if they hadn't stopped for egg waffles, they would have been in their apartment block when it exploded.

Officially, after a long investigation, the PRC-approved Hong Kong government concluded that the apartment building had been destroyed by a gas leak which caused an explosion. The utilities company was fined and censured, several people were fired. Unofficially it was reported on the internet and by foreign media that an apartment in the block had been used as a nerve center by protestors for nearly two years. That it would be trivially easy to make a small drone attack on a gas line look like a gas explosion. Officially, PRC troops hadn't entered the city until the government of Hong Kong admitted that it had lost control and called for their help because of the escalating violence. Unofficially, it was well understood that the PRC had lost patience. If you needed a breakdown in law and order to justify sending troops in, well then it was possible to provoke such a breakdown.

We all live in history. Lai Zhen and her father were part of a history they could not fully perceive at that time, let alone control.

All their possessions were gone, of course. All their papers, their passports, their documents. They had a perfect right to the British National (Overseas) passports, but it took more than three years for everything to be untangled. Three years first in a shelter in Hong Kong and then in a

British offshore refugee center waiting for appointments and information.

Lai Zhen continued her studies in the refugee center. A charity—and two teachers from the British-style school in Hong Kong who had seen her exceptional promise—sent her the books and thumb drives with video lectures on them. It took enough energy to blot out almost everything else, and she knew that if she didn't continue studying, her father would die. Not metaphorically. By this point he was only held together by hope and belief in her. They were held together by needing each other.

She read the *Iliad*—about a battle no one had chosen and no one wanted. And the *Odyssey*, about the longest journey home, and the great burden of misery in just keeping going. In Homer's *Iliad*, she found at last some words that comforted her. It was a passage after all the exciting battles that had seen such loss. After the great hero of Troy, Hektor, had slain Patroklos of the Greeks. After Achilles, Patroklos's lover, had torn through the Trojans to reach Hektor, had slaughtered him; after Achilles had dragged Hektor's body behind his chariot around and around the walls of Troy.

After all these things in the still of night, Hektor's father, Priam, came to the Greek camp in the dead of night, walked through the tents of his enemies, and, finding Achilles, knelt before the man who had slain his son and kissed the hand that had killed him and begged Achilles for Hektor's body. At this point, what could one expect? Magnanimity from Achilles, perhaps. Murderous rage would be in character. Instead Achilles told Priam to get up, to sit near him, to take wine and food.

Achilles said: "At the doors of the gods there are two urns. One is filled with evil fortune and one is filled with good fortune. Zeus digs his hands into the urns and scatters fortune on us. On some people, good and evil fortunes fall. And on some, only evil fortunes."

This passage was the only thing that gave Zhen relief. She thought of it often, until she could almost see the fortunes raining down on her. It hadn't all been bad fortune for her. Thirty-eight people had died in the building, and she and her father had both survived. The winds would change—because winds always change—and blow some new fortune her way.

Much later in her life, Lai Zhen had made a video called "How to Survive the Psychological Effects of an Apocalyptic Event" and 1.6 million people had watched it. It wasn't one of her most popular ones.

- She said: You'll need to keep busy
- She said: Focus on your own survival, look forward, not back
- She said: Even if you don't feel OK, you will be OK one day
- She said: For a long time, it will feel unreal; you will be unable to accept your situation
- She said: Don't blame yourself. Fortune tumbles down onto us like scraps of paper in the wind. Joyful fortune and miserable fortune. You can as little choose your own luck as choose which raindrop falls on your head.

All of this was true and yet it was not enough. Another thing you could do was to figure out why exactly the building you lived in had been targeted by the PRC and follow carefully the evidence that the dissidents' communications hadn't been as secure as they'd thought:

- In exchange for access to the valuable Chinese markets, Medlar had agreed to allow the PRC to monitor certain location data on the new Medlar Torcs.

- Working on their mission to "bring people together," Fantail had allowed certain governments, including China, to read certain FantailPal artificial intelligence requests deemed to relate to terrorist organizations.
- Zimri Nommik hadn't even had to be asked—Anvil wanted stability and prosperity, and neither of those were achieved by splinter groups blowing up storefronts. Obviously AnvilChat would comply with all local laws.

So here she was. On an island with them. At the end of the world. Lai Zhen tipped her face to the sky and wondered what kind of weird-ass mixed fortune had fallen square in the center of her head.

6. the particular bargains

In the waters of a clear, cold river east of the camp, Lenk Sketlish was swimming, naked. Working his body against the gentle onrush of the river toward the ocean. Zhen sat on the rocks at the riverbank, her suit leaning back on its arms next to her. The river bristled with pinpoints of light, Lenk's body sinuous and strong. He'd invited her for a swim, and when he'd taken off all his clothes, Zhen had felt very strongly that a skinny-dip with the founder and CEO of Fantail was not going to make this month feel *less* weird for her.

"Suit," she said, "do you know how to build a raft? Or like, a boat?"

The suit had already shown her the built-in mini buzz saws in its gauntlets. The heat-bonding micro-blades. The laser sights for pinpoint accuracy in construction projects. She had been on the island for nearly five weeks. The suit had shown her what work needed to be done and she'd added in some tricks of her own, different ways of doing things. They cut creeper and set it to dry on a wooden platform to make a serviceable and tough rope. Zhen showed Lenk how to bend wires carefully into fishhooks and set fishing poles in the still bend of the river where the spike-toothed carp rose. They picked fruit off three of the trees the suits told them were safe to eat from, and in the embers of the fire, they baked the pink-fleshed long apples with the thousands of tiny seeds inside and ate them hot from the ash. At the camp, she had helped Ellen and Zimri with some construction—securing the sleeping platform, reinforcing the stockade against wild animals.

"Yes," said the suit, "I know how to do those things."

"OK so, what type of vessel would you recommend for the ocean here?"

"The seas here are rough with unstable tidal conditions since oceanic warming. There is little chance of survival on open water in a homebuilt raft."

Obstructionist.

"OK, but we could try, couldn't we? Maybe use pieces of the wrecked fuselage of the plane?"

"I don't know how to construct a raft like that."

She thought she could figure it out if she had to. She remembered Marius telling his students that a bead tumbling around in a matchbox could never come up with a new possibility, only a remix of the old ones. She missed him suddenly with a fierce pang, and told herself sternly in her own mind: Remember, you will never see him again.

Lenk pressed his hands onto the rock and lifted himself out of the water. He was long, lean, and muscular. He was not unattractive. Alright, he was attractive. She'd admired men in the abstract and occasionally in the specific but never enough to actually want to date one. Lenk was also known as a volatile charmer, a man who got what he wanted through a mixture of fierce intelligence, aggression, and charisma, deployed in whatever proportions would work. She thought of Martha, dealing with this man year after year, decade after decade. No wonder she'd been so fucking suspicious and cagey. He sat next to her on the rock, naked and unembarrassed.

"So you slept with Martha, right? How was it?"

"What kind of a question is that?"

"It's an end-of-the-world question. Martha's in a bunker somewhere. We're here. Probably neither of us will see her again. Why not tell me?"

"I don't fancy giving you material about my life for your wank bank?"

"Fair enough. I'm just saying, we're going to be here a long time. Probably just you and me for a lot of it. Zimri is sick, his leg's bad. We've used a lot of antibiotics on him already. Even if he recovers, an illness this long will have taken years off him. Ellen's sixty-seven. There are going to be years, maybe decades, when it's just us and we'll end up telling each other everything."

"You always think you know what's going to happen."

"So far I always have."

He cracked a smile, charming and deadly.

Lenk said, "Want to know a secret?"

"Sure?"

"Something will come for me eventually."

"Because you always know what's going to happen."

"Because I change what's going to happen. I have a tracker, here." Lenk motioned to a spot just behind his right ear. "Dead man's switch. I have to tell the system every morning that everything's OK or it sets off an alert. And then . . . everything goes all out to find me."

"Yeah? Why hasn't anything come for you already?"

"That's how I know we don't want to get off this island right now," said Lenk. "My best guess is that the alarm has gone off but my people are too engaged solving other problems to want to go and look for what they'd presume would be my corpse. Not to mention that a lot of them are dead or in a bunker, waiting out the storm."

"So why is anything going to come for you?"

"They'll have to confirm I'm dead before the system will give them access to . . . some sensitive materials. At worst, there'll be drones in a few months, I guess. Yeah, depending on how bad it gets out there, maybe even years. Eventually, something will come."

"Is that what the others think too?"

"Probably. They'll have systems, I'm sure. Something. There's no way they've told us everything. I haven't."

The river plashed, the surface alive with humming insects. As Zhen watched, the glassy surface bowed outward around the snapping teeth-filled mouth of a fish grabbing at the black-and-violet lacy wings of a dragonfly. Nothing is ever really over.

"You're talking to me about it because I'm not a player," she said.

Lenk smiled lazily.

"Whatever you think is coming after this, I'm not going to be part of it. Not in the way the three of you are."

"Martha never did pick any idiots," said Lenk.

"So?"

"What?" said Lenk.

"What is it that you think is going to come after this?"

Lenk's eyes were closed to the sun.

"Well," he said, "I suspect they each have an army out there, somewhere. And I suspect they have an army because I know I have one. We're not clean, you know. Of all of us, you're the cleanest one here. Have you thought about how it was that we ended up on this island?"

"What do you mean," Zhen said, "an army?"

"Well, look," said Lenk, "we were never supposed to end up here. The survival suits are great, obviously, but this part, the first part where the disease burns itself out among the population and there are a lot of corpses . . . I was supposed to spend that in luxury, OK? I have a place in Greenland, a place in the Canadian Arctic, a mountain in Wyoming . . . all well equipped. This . . . lashing together logs with vines to make sleeping platforms? No, this wasn't it."

"It wasn't it for them either," said Zhen, "for Zimri and Ellen."

"Right," said Lenk. "So this is what I mean about an army. I don't mean people, you understand. Neither of them has told you *how* the plane crashed, right?"

Zhen shook her head.

"OK then."

7. eight hours and around four thousand miles from the Action Now! ecological convention

The cream leather upholstery had been smooth under Lenk's fingertips and the glass refrigerator was well stocked with glittering bottles. Lenk felt ready in his blood and his bones. The plans were underway. As agreed in the evacuation protocol, the pilot had given false headings to air traffic control as soon as they were out of radar range. Whatever was coming, he was ready for it. A short flight with these two panicking bozos, then his own private plane and Martha and the island and the start of the world to come.

In the air, they had hooked up to the plane's Wi-Fi and tried to find out what could possibly be coming. AUGR indicated that hot spots to avoid on the journey were: Argentina, Chile, Brazil, Mexico, Texas, France. Zimri connected to the many information tentacles of Anvil; Ellen searched Medlar Torc data. Lenk looked at the detailed analytics for posts on Fantail. Argentina, Chile, Brazil, Mexico, Texas, France. Ordering patterns. Search patterns. Words used in reviews, in emails to vendors, in social media posts, in queries to FantailPal talkbots. Heart rates. Blood solutes. Physical activity. Smiley faces. Frowny faces. A proxy for the thoughts and feelings of the human planet, more or less. Some patterns had started to emerge.

"Shit," said Ellen Bywater, pointing at a particular pattern of Medlar Torc bio-data. "Shit, shit, shit."

Once they knew what they were looking for, it wasn't too difficult. A set of search terms on FantailLive and there, yes, in the background of certain videos, you could already see what was coming.

Lenk Sketlish felt the news drain through him like immersion in cold water. He felt extraordinarily calm, peaceful even. If this was the story, then there might have been nothing they could do anyway.

The sound was so loud and so sudden that it seemed to be coming not from outside but from inside them, as if their own hearts had shattered their chests. It was an all-encompassing, terrifying noise. It sounded like the end of days, the Lord's vengeance.

Each of them lurched forward in their seats as the nose pointed downward. Their seat belts like metal bars cutting into their torsos, making them retch with sudden gastric acid pushed back up their throats. There was a terrible sound. A wrenching, strained sound, a bang, and then a yawning moan of bolt and screw.

An automatic voice said: "Please retrieve your CrashJacket from underneath your seat. Unroll it and place it over your head. It will self-secure around your waist. Try to remain calm."

Lenk pressed the intercom button on his seat. "What the fuck, what the fuck is happening? Was that an explosion? What's happened?"

The pilot said through the intercom: "I don't know. Malfunction. Could be weapons fired. I didn't see anything. We need to get away."

He sounded terrified.

Lenk Sketlish, Ellen Bywater, and Zimri Nommik pulled at their seat belts, trying to loosen them, trying to retrieve their CrashJackets from underneath their seats, trying to find the fucking head hole.

The pilot said: "I think we're under attack. I'm not sure. I'm releasing countermeasures. Please. I'm going to do what I can but . . . you have to get ready to jump."

This was not an aircraft with offensive capabilities. It was a private plane which, because it was owned by a paranoid man, was equipped with a very limited number of countermeasures.

Outside, it was night. Two in the morning local time, darkness and a great moon full and fat. Through his window by the moonlight, Lenk saw a cloud of silver metal radar-baffling strips release into the air, like a squid jetting ink to confuse a predator. The darkly glinting pieces reflected the light from the moon, from the plane itself. The plane was diving now. There was no siren; the sound in Lenk's ears was the sound of his heartbeat. His cold, shaking fingers found the hole in the center of the CrashJacket at last and unrolled it over his head. He fitted the emergency oxygen mask in the center of the CrashJacket over his mouth and nose and tried to breathe normally. He remembered, as if a memory from a distant world, a woman with a nose whistle telling him to breathe from his navel. That had been just after he'd woken up that actual morning. Like breathing normally right now, breathing from the navel was literally impossible.

The plane banked sharply to the left and the right. There was a sound from the back of the hull. The emergency doors popped open. Time was very fast and very slow.

Lenk thought of inert submunition dispensers. A very neutral name for a particular kind of missile held to be more ethical because they didn't scatter explosive material over civilians. Each missile held a small canister of "inert" material under high compression. When it exploded, hundreds of razor-sharp metal loops expanded in a wide sphere centered around the empty space filled with noise. It was the pressure and the speed that made them dangerous—less than one second after they were released, the metal loops would be nothing but debris. No mines left to maim children. No nuclear wasteland. Released into the air, they would mostly describe a parabola and fall harmlessly to Earth, tiny pieces of innocuous wire.

Medlar had created some chips for them. Anvil had undertaken transportation logistics. Fantail had agreed to censor mention of them for certain regimes around the world. Looked at in a certain light, inert submunition dispensers were almost good news. And if you were under attack by inert submunition dispensers in the dark, it would feel like this. Nothing to see. Only a sound and a plane taking itself to pieces.

There was a second explosion. Where there had been a solid metal hull, there was a line drawn by cheese wire over and around the seats. They were breached. The breach began to open.

The sound was a shriek of metal on metal. There was spin and counterspin within the plane, the hull rotating, turning the world upside down and right side up, upside down and right side up. The sound of rending as the aircraft pulled apart. It turned from a gliding vessel to two connected metal tubes, each weighing nearly five hundred thousand pounds, placed thirty-five thousand feet above the earth's surface. Like a broken jelly roll, floating in midair. Doing what a broken jelly roll was likely to do in these circumstances.

"Now," said the CrashJackets, "undo your seat belt, run toward the emergency door. Throw yourself out with all your strength. The chute will automatically inflate when you are far enough from the plane."

Ellen was already climbing up the spinning plane, finding footholds on the seats and luggage storage, controlled in her movements like a woman who'd spent summers bouldering in Yosemite. She'd panicked when she had to pack up, but in the final analysis she never hesitated to act decisively. She was the first off the plane.

Zimri was slower, moving crabwise, clinging on. He quickly figured out a new method of movement—holding the seat belt tight in his clenched jaw to give himself an extra point of contact. He grabbed a second CrashJacket from under an empty seat, just to be on the safe side.

Lenk was the last out, still looking around as if he could figure out what had happened here. His final thought as he hauled himself by the seats toward the emergency door was: We gave false information to air traffic control. If anyone's left alive to look for us, they'll be looking in the wrong place.

"So," said Zhen, "some random nation fired a tech bomb at you and you ended up here. What were you saying about an army?"

"Doesn't it strike you as suspicious," said Lenk, "that we should have been shot down precisely here? Over an uninhabited island capable of sustaining us indefinitely?"

"Yeah," said Zhen, "I guess so. But also maybe . . . just lucky?"

"I've been thinking about this for the past three weeks. If it was an inert submunition dispenser . . . only a limited number of nations have access to them. Papua New Guinea, the nearest nation to Admiral Huntsy Island, definitely doesn't have any."

"So . . ."

"I wouldn't be thinking this way if we hadn't been taken down by an advanced technology. It was too early for anyone to be really panicking, do you understand? No one knew about the plague yet—that was the whole point. Only we knew there was anything to be afraid of. No ordinary army would have taken down our plane. It would be the kind of army you have if you don't have to rely on human beings."

Lenk stood up and pulled his shorts back on.

"Listen," he said, "you slept with Martha and I guess that makes us as close to family as either of us has on this island. If Martha trusts you, if she gave you AUGR even for a few days, you're probably the most trustworthy person here for me. Which is not saying much. So. Medlar has inert submunition dispensers, drone-mounted for use in civil breakdown situations. So does Anvil. So do we, Fantail. It was all agreed with . . . a lot of different governments after the last plague. That we ought to be able to help if there was civil unrest."

He stepped backward into his suit, the shins and torso neatly sealing around him.

Zhen understood what Lenk was doing. He was bringing her into his tight circle of information, but he was also letting her know what her position was. She was on this island with three people who each had access to weapons and resources she had never even heard of. After the end of the world, what possible reason was there for any of them to want her alive?

"I know Fantail didn't bring down the plane. So I think it was one of them. Knowing we had the CrashJackets and the suits, knowing we'd survive. Knowing we'd end up here. Knowing that—terrible as it is—a plague like this brings unparalleled opportunities for whoever walks into that new future alive. I think one of them wants to be king of the fucking world, which is easier if I'm dead. So I don't trust them, OK?"

The visor slid across Lenk's face, leaving Zhen looking straight into the eyes of her own reflection.

8. that night, they went to sleep as normal

Lai Zhen woke in the flat illumination of the predawn hours, everything shaded blue and dark blue and gray. The dim heads-up display in her visor said it was just past 4 a.m. Someone was moving at the edge of the camp. A suit, going from box to box with care, hauling a makeshift sledge with a StowtBox lashed to it, putting items from communal storage into the sledge.

"Who's that?" said Ellen Bywater's voice very close inside Zhen's ear through the inter-suit communication.

The figure at the boxes paused. Hurriedly replaced the lid of the StowtBox and went, limping, to leave the camp. Zimri.

"Suit, turn on some fucking lights," said Ellen.

From the tree where Ellen's suit had clamped to the underside of a branch, several spotlights turned on, illuminating the camp in an eerie pink-gold glow.

Zimri said: "I'm not staying here. I haven't taken more than my share."

Though, Zhen thought, this had rarely if ever been true of Zimri Nommik.

Lenk dropped to the ground from a tree. He landed easily, the bent knees of the suit taking the strain.

"I saw you talking to her, Lenk. The new girl. We all know what we're thinking. If there are ally relationships going on here now, I have to go."

Zhen said: "I just got here. I'm not 'allying' with anyone."

"Aha, well, that's what you would say. I don't blame you. If you ally with Lenk, you're stronger together. For now. So I'm going."

Lenk said: "Where are you going, Zimri?"

Zimri was bullish. The guy in the cowl-necked sweater who told all his rivals to go fuck themselves because he could actually buy up their shitty company, chew it up, and spit it out and their shareholders would say, "Thank you, sir."

"I don't need to tell you that."

Ellen's laugh was a bark.

"Oh, you do need to tell us that, Zimri. You need to show us what you've taken and tell us where you're going. Because your leg is fucked and there's no way you're safer without us unless you know something we don't."

Zimri looked defiantly between Ellen and Lenk.

"I'll walk to the shore. Construct a raft. Try to sail east. I can't stay here with you."

His eyes were glassy, his complexion flushed as he backed away. He was not well, that was obvious. Even in the mechanical suit he was favoring his injured leg.

Zhen said: "He wants to go because he's sick. He needs a doctor. This suit . . . this won't do it." Again something tickled at the back of her mind about these suits. Something she'd known once but forgotten.

"That's right," said Zimri with evident relief. "She understands."

"Well, why are you sneaking out at night, then?" said Ellen. "If you want to go, why are you hiding it? Why don't we all make a plan to leave together?"

Because he's afraid of the same thing you're afraid of, Zhen thought. Zimri would rather be alone on a raft in open water than accompanied by Ellen Bywater or Lenk Sketlish.

"I knew you'd try to stop me," said Zimri.

"Only because I think you're going to abandon us here."

"And you're going to leave me to fucking die if I don't get away from you."

Zimri Nommik was readying himself, Zhen could tell. She'd been through this in holding cells, in visa lines. When violence breaks out, everyone goes down.

Zhen said: "Everyone, can we try to calm down, OK? We all need each other to survive, right?"

This was Survival 101. No fighting in the camp. Mediate, find appropriate punishments if need be. Don't break the group.

Zhen said: "And, Ellen, Zimri's not *pretending* to be sick."

Ellen looked at Zhen, rolled her eyes.

"Epsilon Industrial 2023. LandBridge 2031. AnvilLux 2036. The China Trials last fucking year? This is *exactly* what he does. Buys a whole company so we don't know he's interested in just one employee. Places an obvious listening device in the smart-jacket so no one goes looking for the secret one? This is how he works."

"Oh, fuck off," said Zimri. "I am leaving. Just don't try to stop me."

Zimri turned away, dragging his sledge through the jungle. The dawn was beginning, the sky blue-black, life greeting the morning with golden liquid chattering. Zhen's visor focused on Zimri's receding figure, and later on she could not say whether it was the darkness that she saw first or the humming or whether the first thing she knew was that the birdsong had stopped. There was an encroaching darkness around him—it might have been the dense trees. A dull whine—it might have been machinery.

Zimri turned right and left. He could hear something in the darkness. The buzzing hum of biting insects. He looked toward the canopy. He let out a strangled scream. Zhen's visor lens was having trouble focusing. There was a shadow moving, an artifact on the screen, something pixelated and strange.

Zimri said: "No, fuck no. Stop, stop it. Just stop. Not me."

He started to run, dragging his leg. In the canopy the buzzing grew sticky among the trees, a swarm of points moving as one. These were the things that had come for her and Marius. The bright beetles. Zhen remembered them in her body, with fear. They were linking into a sort of chain, a mesh that began to look like a creature.

Lenk was already opening a StowtBox with guns inside—how had there been guns, why had no one mentioned guns to Zhen? He aimed and fired into the treetops, some kind of small exploding thing. It set the leaves on fire but did nothing to halt the dark buzzing creature pursuing Zimri. It was reaching out sticky fingers toward him. Fire was right, but there was not enough.

Ellen said, quite softly, "Oh no." Then she shouted, loud, through her suit's speakers, "Stop! Stop now!"

As if she could command something here, Zhen thought.

Zhen wouldn't have known until this moment that her instinct would be to run toward a man fighting for his life against an unknown enemy. She would have hoped it would be—there had been people who helped on the streets that day in Hong Kong—but she knew she could not be certain. Especially not for a man who had been on the other side that day.

And yet here she was. Zimri thrashed his arms above his head, his buzz saws out, trying to ward off the drones. Zhen ran toward him.

"Hey!" she shouted. "Hey, over here! Come here! Zimri, this way!"

Ellen tugged ineffectually at Zhen's hand as she passed.

Ellen said, "No, you can't."

Zhen said, "Do you know how it works?"

Ellen shook her head, and Zhen thought she was the worst liar she'd ever seen.

"Tell me," she said, "if you know anything that can save him. Tell me now."

Ellen said, "If it was sent for him, it won't be interested in us. Unless you make it interested in you."

The swarm was closing in on Zimri now, and even though Zhen was nearer to him and should have been able to see him more clearly, his body was blurred and writhing. He was stumbling forward looking for shelter; he was clinging to a tree, his belly pressed hard to the trunk.

Lenk shouted: "Zhen, look up!"

He fired his weapon again, launching small shells that burst against the trunks of the trees in explosions of flame. She saw it above him. The bright beetles had formed a shape like a mouth, very large, an open, engulfing mouth. Zimri screamed. Zhen was too far away from him still. The thing was a *hunter*. She knew it as if her whole body had been waiting to be taught the difference between hunter and prey.

Zimri tried to scream and tried to run. The swarm was around him, biting, confusing, agitating in infrasound. He stumbled but his steps were slower and slower. It was like the dream you have had many times, trying to run from a pursuer but your feet stick to the ground; the earth becomes viscous.

The birds made no sound. The only noise was Zimri crying and yelping and shouting and begging. The horror in his cries was absolute. More of the buzzing, dark, sticky stuff latched on to his hands, his elbows, his shoulders, the front of his visor. Zimri was frantic, screaming and jerking. He got one arm out of his suit! The arm waved triumphantly above the dark, ever-moving throng. He clutched at a tree branch to haul himself free. For a moment it seemed that he would manage it, that he might leave the suit behind and escape. But the invisible jaws chattered and bit. The bugs were inside the suit now. The suit expanded and contracted on the jungle floor, trying to expel the intruders. Zimri's body was at war with itself inside the metal exoskeleton. Limbs appeared to bend backward, then right themselves, the torso distended. The whole thing went rigid, sat up—a grotesquerie of a man—and fell back.

Zimri was making no sound. The gentle whimper that Zhen thought was coming from him was her own pleading breath. The broken mannequin of the suit rose high into the tree canopy, carried by the swarm, into the treetops, into the distance, far out of sight.

9. things have a tendency to escalate

The morning the hunter took Zimri Nommik, the sun rose like a scalpel to the retina.

They had been four and now they were three, this much was certain. They huddled around the campfire, unwilling to leave the warmth and light even for a moment. They were all in their suits.

"Jesus, Ellen," said Lenk. "You made it? You actually did it?"

"No," said Ellen. "No one's home, make an appointment with my secretary."

"Fuck's sake, Ellen," said Lenk, "you're not allowed to go mad."

"I know what it is," said Zhen, "and I think you know what it is too. You knew last night. I've seen something like it in Zimri's bunker. It's a weapon."

"No," said Ellen. "No, it was discontinued, it was never made, we never heard about it, it wasn't me."

"For fuck's sake," said Lenk.

Ellen said, slow and wheedling, "We all made them. You know, Lenk. Tell her. We all saw the scenario papers. We all made them. You can't pretend to your new *friend* that you had nothing to do with this. They could as well have been yours as anyone's."

This would be dangerous. If Ellen thought she'd allied with Lenk, that was a reason for Ellen to kill her. It was simple and clear-cut.

"Look," said Zhen, "I'm not anyone's special friend here, OK? There are three of us here. That is not enough people for a war. We have to be each other's allies. Lenk's already told me you guys all made weapons. Right?"

For a moment, Lenk Sketlish teetered on the edge of temper; Zhen saw the mood flash across his face. She held her nerve. She did not apologize.

"The thing was," said Lenk, "we all knew the others would do it if we didn't. So what was the point of not trying? Ellen, there's no reason to keep this secret from her. There was a rationale to it at the time."

"I'm not breaking international treaties and conventions," said Ellen. "I'm not getting involved in that, no sir, am I?"

She seemed to be talking to someone else.

"OK," said Lenk, "Ellen's not playing. I am going to tell you the most secret thing you've ever heard."

That made Zhen smile. "I've heard a lot of secret shit."

"Not like this."

There is, when it comes right down to it and as Martha had mentioned to Lenk many times, a trajectory to human affairs. It appears to be ruled by logic but the rhythm of it is the rhythm of fear. If you might do something to me, then it is only right for me to have the capacity to do the same to you. This is the pattern of the rule of salt. Imagining bad futures creates fear and fear creates bad futures. The pulse beats faster, the pressure rises, the voice of instinct drives out reason and education. At a certain point, things become inevitable.

To start with, the major technology firms had drone squadrons. Everyone did. They'd been the natural extension to any delivery system. Drones don't need to wash their hands, drones can't get sick, drones can be stored in bulk until needed. Mostly, the squadrons were declared to the relevant governments for use in an emergency.

But then there were also weapons and quasi-weapons. It was possible to stealthily weaponize a large flying swarm if they were equipped with, for example, lifting capability or sonic attack or the smallest possible multipurpose tool set with a micro-screwdriver whose blade was very sharp.

"Don't make this sound like it was an accident," said Zhen. "I don't think it was an accident."

"It wasn't an accident," said Lenk, "it was a business opportunity."

The feeling was that in a future pandemic or other catastrophe, governments around the world might pay to have a drone army patrol the streets and deal with rioting or looting. Private hospitals might need protection. Certain Senate subcommittees had been persuaded to leave certain loopholes open. No private company could have fifty thousand Predator hunter-killer missile drones, *obviously.* But sonic technology, something intended just to encourage people back into their homes? There was a case for that.

There is a trajectory to human affairs. Tools ask to be used. They whisper of new fears and new threats. If we have this, they have it too. So there was a new logic.

Sent electronically, self-deleting, displayed with a polarizing filter so that the screen could not be photographed, printer-locked. The scenario papers were to be read, considered, and then lost forever.

"Lost?" said Zhen.

"Remembered," said Lenk. "You know it could be that in the whole world those papers only exist now in my memory, and Ellen's."

The scenario papers had run through extreme possibilities. Wars. Revolutions. The development of malevolent artificial intelligence. In each case, they detailed strategies by which Medlar, Anvil, and Fantail could remain vibrant and compelling forces with considerable user engagement in the new socioeconomic reality.

"This will involve," the paper had said in dry academic

tones, “temporarily taking over some of the roles of government. Sequestering resources by force. Protecting facilities and personnel.”

Elsewhere in the world, perhaps, these protocols were already being enacted.

“You’re making this sound sinister. Lenk always does that. You know, something like this could really have helped in the Fall of Hong Kong,” said Ellen Bywater.

Zhen tried to imagine something like that in the Fall of Hong Kong. In the midst of the people sobbing and the military police and the overwhelmed hospitals. Drones with weapons. Might have helped the government or Anvil, wouldn’t have helped her.

“The plan is that we become a force for stability,” Ellen continued, “until there’s a government again.”

“The plan is to take over a few countries and you know it,” said Lenk.

“That’s what you’re talking about,” said Zhen. “That’s what you think is going on here, what you’re afraid of. Out there, the world is ending. And you all have the capacity to *take over*. One of you is going to come out on top. And you’re willing to fight it out here until only one of you is left.”

10. a plastic drawer full of tiny green pieces

"You know," said Ellen Bywater, "there's no proof that Zimri is really dead. Have you thought of that?"

Ellen was rapidly searching through the StowtBoxes, looking for something. Lenk had gone to check the traps. Neither Lenk nor Ellen was willing to be alone with the other.

"I mean, what we saw seems pretty conclusive," said Zhen. "What are we looking for?"

"I want to know what Zimri took. You remember. He was going through the boxes. Taking things. Where's that sled now, the one he was carrying his stuff away on?"

That was a good point. Zhen looked around.

"Maybe the drones took it?"

"Aha!" Ellen was wild-eyed. If they managed to push her into taking sides here, if they managed to really convince Zhen despite all she'd seen and all she'd learned, that she had to choose between them, would she choose Ellen? The alternative was choosing Lenk Sketlish, which prior to this week Zhen would have said was surely always the worst possible choice.

"If the drones took it," said Ellen, "where did they take it and why? OK. I know I didn't send the swarm for Zimri. You don't need to believe me, no reason you would, but *I* know. But say I did send the swarm—why would I take the box too? Wouldn't I leave the equipment here? Think about it. You saw those same drones in his bunker, you told us. We never saw him die. If those were his drones, they could have made a good show and then lifted him, carried him somewhere else, still on the island, with all that equipment. Do you see?"

"You think he's pretending to be dead."

"Classic," said Ellen. "It's the classic. I was saying to Will—" She stopped herself.

"I still talk to my mum," said Zhen. "She died when I was fourteen and I still talk to her. Sometimes I even think she talks back."

"Thank you," said Ellen. "That means something. Yes. Since we got here I've been . . . I've thought I saw him sometimes. Just sitting on the grass next to me. I think maybe I'm going nuts. Maybe I have been for a while."

"You just miss him," said Zhen. "And we're all going to go nuts. I think that's the expected state when you're grieving for the whole world. Look," she said, "all this 'who's going to take over,' I mean, I guess maybe that's normal too? When the past is all fucking . . . fire and brimstone . . . all you have to hold on to is the future. Hoping that things will end up better than they are. That's why you're all driving yourselves so crazy over the . . . you know . . . wanting to be king of the world. Rivalry and imagining that the others are doing terrible things. It stops you looking back at the ashes."

"Yes," said Ellen. "Yes, I see that. I see that."

And for a moment Zhen thought, Thank fuck I've gotten through to her and she's going to sit down and feel sad about the whole world and then we'll all be doing better.

Zhen felt the inner wire in her unbend just a little, her tensile steel softened; she imagined sagging to the ground, not realizing how frightened she had been of what might happen here.

"Oh my God," said Ellen, and Zhen thought: Yes, this is how it begins. This is how you know you're grieving. When the whole thing strikes you as absolutely outrageous, when you're angry with your own mother for fucking letting cancer take her and leaving you, that's when you know you're in it.

"Look at this," said Ellen. "Six AP28 boards in here. All smashed. Jesus fuck."

"I . . . don't know what that is."

"They're . . . they can enable communication with the satellites. And here, this section is smashed too. Fuck him. Fuck him."

Ellen tipped the StowtBox over so Zhen could see the delicate parts and the green boards pulverized into dust and fragments.

"I mean, things could have been destroyed in the crash . . ."

"No. I checked these the day we arrived—we all know that at some point we're going to want to build communication devices, try to reestablish contact. Look at this. If you wanted to set up on some other island, or in a distant part of this island, set up all cozy and snug with us thinking you're dead and run your empire from there, you'd take one of these and smash the others to bits."

Ellen's speech was racing, high points of color in her cheeks. The idea was growing in her mind as Zhen watched, louder and more insistent with every moment. Zimri had faked his death, he'd done it with his own drones—well, Zhen had seen those precise drones in his own bunker, she knew what Ellen was saying—he'd taken all he needed, he was waiting out there somewhere, he'd steal from them by night and kill them. Listening to her was like watching a mind drown.

"Just a second," said Ellen, "just a moment, I haven't thought this through. This is not the only option."

"No," said Zhen, "it's quite an extreme option, really. You think he wants it so much he could have faked his own death?"

"Oh, he wants it that much. But"—Ellen's expression was sly—"could've been Lenk. I didn't think of that. Didn't think of that. Lenk could have killed him. Cleared away the sled and stolen the parts to make me think it was Zimri. Have you noticed how much time Lenk spends *walking*? Where is he going?"

Zhen was reminded of one of her father's sisters in Liverpool, who had become convinced that vaccinations were secretly a plot by Bill Gates to mind-control the population of the world. She and her dad had laughed about Auntie Lusi and it had been a closeness between them. With her mother dying, the world upside down, Auntie Lusi's emails titled "spike protein vaccine poisons brains" had been a bulwark. We in this apartment are not as crazy as that. We have that in common. Even though we're not OK, we are OK.

Oh, Zhen thought, this is how I end up allying with Lenk Sketlish.

11. you're not going to believe this

It was true. Lenk Sketlish did go walking a lot. He often set off as soon as the morning chores were complete—saying he was going to "clear his head" or to check traps, or to find places to set new traps. Never quite answering precisely where he was heading, never quite accepting an offer to go with him. Perhaps it was Ellen's paranoia. Perhaps Ellen's paranoia had infected her. Still, Zhen watched Lenk leave and wondered and could not stop herself wondering.

"Suit," said Zhen, "how quietly can you move?"

"I have a stealth mode, sport, designed for tracking animals. Shall I engage it now?"

"Yeah, yeah, do that. We're following Lenk."

The suit lengthened its arms and gently tipped her over onto all fours, as Zhen made a soft "oh" sound. With the longer strengthened arms it was surprisingly comfortable and—yes—stealthy. Weight spread more evenly, easier to creep low to the ground.

"Do you want me to let Lenk Sketlish know you'd like to talk to him?"

"No," said Zhen, "no, that's not what I want."

"OK, gotcha."

The suit moved like oiled glass, slow and steady, no jerking motions, as if to the rhythm of the breathing wind stirring the small leaves. Never hurrying, never tarrying, never quite losing sight of Lenk, never quite closing in on him. The journey was circuitous, at times seeming to double back. Lenk knew where he was going.

In the dark mud at the base of a sheer cliff covered in vines, where the earth was continually dampened by trickling water, Lenk stood before a black open mouth: a crack in the side of the mountain. A cave, long and narrow, the entrance barely wide enough for the suit to fit through, the inner parts dark as memory. Lenk pressed his palm against the wall to balance as he shuffled inside.

Zhen's instinct was to wait. To see what would happen, not to be inside a narrow, lightless crack with a man known to have violent fits of rage. And yet. She'd stayed outside the mountain once before and ended up sunk deep into a situation she could neither understand nor control. She followed, as silent as she could. Down into the mountain, into the inside of the world.

Only a few paces in, the darkness became absolute. The stone was around her and she felt the weight of the mountain as if it were pressing on her head. A feeling both unsettling and comforting, something remembered from long ago, the terror of what might be inside this small space with her. This is why we built houses with windows and blinds. This is why we invented glass. This is why we discovered electricity. This is why we split the atom. It's because this feeling is unbearable.

The suit recalibrated its sensors and the cave interior was more visible through the visor. The floor of the cave was strewn with rocks and small animal droppings. Several passageways leading out but no sign of Lenk. On the wall in front of her, there were scratches. Had a bear been here, scraping at the wall with claws as long as a man's hand? But as she looked at them, the scratches seemed purposeful. A small circle within a larger one. Zigzags piled one on top of another.

"Suit," said Zhen, "what are those markings made with?"

The suit said: "Paramagnetic salts."

"Huh. Versatile. What do they symbolize?"

The suit said: "They are a conductive communicator. An aerial written onto the rock."

"Hello," said Lenk Sketlish. "I know you're there."

Zhen jumped. She turned around, but there was no Lenk. He was speaking through the suit's comms. He could be anywhere.

"I, um," she said, "I happened to spot you—"

"You followed me," he said.

"No," she said, and then after a pause, "Yes."

"What are you expecting me to do about that?"

He sounded dangerous as a tiger. She turned in a slow, wary circle. He must be near; the mountain would block transmissions. She watched for the dull gleam from his suit, for the sudden movement that would show him to her. Both of them calculating futures, both of them waiting for the worst.

"I was curious and I followed you. I guess you could tell me what you're doing here."

"Suppose I don't want to tell you."

There was a route through this labyrinth, a way to navigate even the mind of Lenk Sketlish.

"Then you'll have to keep it to yourself literally forever, because you're sure as shit not going to be telling Ellen Bywater, are you?"

Lenk Sketlish laughed. A laugh is a shortcut between one person and another.

Lenk's suit prowled toward Zhen from a passage to her right. He, too, was moving quietly on all fours. He had been a long way back, deep into the mountain, and Zhen couldn't deny her curiosity was greater than her fear. This, too, is the pull of the future, the joy of simple wanting-to-know.

"You want to see something cool?" he said.

"Always," she said. And it was true. This is what human beings have going for us over the matchboxes and beads. If we're alive, if we're healthy, we want to reach out all the time, we want to trust.

"Look," said Lenk, and at the base of the rock wall, he

pushed away a mat of debris, of dried plants and soft sand. There in the stone Zhen saw, outlined with a white, bright ring of LED, a single proprietary Fantail data port. She frowned.

"What?" she said. "What?"

"So it turns out I own it. This is my island," said Lenk.

12. the shelter of a cave

Knowing what Lenk Sketlish was interested in, and understanding his methods, Martha Einkorn had purchased—via the Fantail FutureSafe Foundation—Admiral Huntsy Island off the coast of Papua New Guinea. Within the bunker, using the landscape's natural caves, she had built an extra bunker. Just in case.

In designing it Martha Einkorn had operated on Lenk's guiding principle that several hundred people should be able to survive and thrive there without leaving for a minimum of three hundred years. None of the others, Lenk explained to Zhen because he really did love to lecture, had thought it through. When the sea level rises, Zimri's place in Haida Gwaii would be underwater even if Zhen hadn't blown it up. Ellen's mountain was in an area of seismic activity. They both thought they were only going to be there for five to ten years at the outside. But Lenk Sketlish thought much more long-term than that.

It wasn't a surprise to learn that the FutureSafe wildlife conservation zones had been designed to benefit their owners as much as to protect the natural environments. Zhen—and half the people under forty on the internet—had already presumed this was happening somehow, even if only in access to these precious areas, in monetizing images of them.

The scale, though, that was a surprise. She walked with Lenk through the corridors tunneled from the rock. Miles of them. The mountain had been drilled into an ant's nest, a colony. Solid and dark, sleeping places, latrine holes positioned so that the highest tides every day would sluice them clean, stove places with chimneys letting their smoke out high on the cliff face. The start, if you had to start human civilization again.

Here inside this mountain were no large supplies of canned goods, or guns, or digging machines. What Martha had stocked here—from the eastern reach touching the ocean to the western edge overhanging the forest basin—was anything you could realistically protect or learn to create or to repair as a small, well-educated community over several hundred years. Enochites, Zhen thought, the way they wanted to live. This had been Lenk's reason for wanting Martha after all.

There were thousands of arrowheads and instructions on how to make arrowheads, shafts, and bows. Dry stuffed bedding, and diagrams showing which plants to dry and fluff and spin to make more. Clay pots and notes of precisely which mud to use and which wood burned hot enough to fire them. The first 270,000 years of *Homo sapiens* technical development, preserved against the oncoming tide.

There was more, of course. One could always hope for more. An explanation of germ theory was carved into the walls in words and pictographs.

"If we can pass one thing on, this is it, right? Small alive things, too small to see, make you sick. You have to wash to keep them away. That's a lot of suffering prevented right there."

Zhen saw that this was real to Lenk, more real than the current sickness sweeping the world. The future was more real to him than the present.

There were long rows of plasti-paper books full of more advanced knowledge in each of the twenty most commonly spoken languages on Earth: quantum theory, general relativity, the human genome, the manufacture of an electron microscope.

"No literature?" said Zhen.

"Oh, sure, sure, that's in there. Martha's a big reader. She says that's what gets us from one world to the next."

There were red plastic books listing what things to scavenge in the outside world, what to look for, what to protect. Row upon row of rather basic laptops, each component individually plasti-sprayed to protect from moisture and rust. At worst, Lenk said proudly, these machines would last seventy years. At best some of them might last out the three hundred years. They contained vast databases, electronic encyclopedias. In twelve different plastic-lined cells around the complex there were enormous seed banks, seeds hardened for a warmer climate. Enough to restart a real civilization.

"If you had one hundred fifty people here for three hundred years, they could make it," said Lenk, "and not many of them would have to be really smart. You see? The end of the world wouldn't be the end of everything."

Lenk imagined a new kind of monastery, a self-sustaining organization that could bring knowledge through a dark bottleneck of human history and allow it to flow freely again when the years became favorable. Martha had understood his vision better than anyone alive, and she had made it real.

For food, his islanders would have options. The easiest would be hunting, fishing, small-scale arable farming—there was plenty of land and the waters teemed with fish. There was even an area of the island suitable for grazing sheep—if they brought them and managed the numbers carefully. But—Lenk was boyish and ebullient as he explained this—the genius part was the algae that grew in specially bored holes and crevasses all over the island.

"I saw it the day we arrived, but I had to be sure it was

the same thing. I know now it is. We found this algae and cultivated it. It's the answer. It strips out nuclear waste. Poisons. Chemical weapons. Everything currently being made and a few things that haven't been yet. The algae breaks nutrients to the atomic level and then builds them up again into a pure, beautiful, protein-rich, omega-3-filled, all-around food source."

The algae was his plan. In extremis, in the event of multiple catastrophic events, the green-brown algae on this island would sustain humans indefinitely. If sheep survived, they could eat the algae and remain healthy. It was a complete protein and fat source with no missing essential nutrients. They could harvest, dry, and store it. They could plant more on the mainland if they got there. He had eaten it himself, gone for a whole month without any other food just to see how it went.

"Never felt better," he said, "never felt clearer in my mind. If everything else fails, this will work."

Zhen found a strange, impressed half smile creeping across her face. This was his real passion, and he was significantly better at this than anyone she'd ever spoken to before, and she knew people who were passionate about surviving the apocalypse.

To the northeast there were reedbeds for cloth and paper, baskets and boats. To the south, shears and presses to cut apart scrap metal that washed ashore and make new tools. In the north, the rock wall was pierced like lace, the holes filled with pale, thin, translucent stones from the beach. If there was no nuclear winter or chemical poisoning, the people could live here rather than deep underground. There were dormitories, a large communal kitchen, and a wood-furnished communal eating hall like a monastery. Inside, the light was milky and bright like a cold winter morning.

"Different things will become important," Lenk told

her. "Look at how quickly it's all happened already. We can't look at our past for help. We have to look at the lives of people who actually survived three hundred dark years and what they thought were the best and most luxurious ways of life—monks in their monasteries, colleges in ancient universities, kings with their household. Privacy is a modern invention. We won't want it so much now."

He was convincing without apparently attempting to convince her of anything. It was like his showing her his cock, but much more intense. Like there was some organ Zhen didn't even know anyone could have, and Lenk had opened his clothes up and there it was. *Oh*, she thought, suddenly figuring out what she'd known about these suits and almost telling Lenk but looking at his face it wasn't the moment. It was like he was showing her his dreams. Because he had enough money to turn the dreams inside his head into something other people could walk around and live in.

There was, to Zhen's surprise, a chapel. An ecumenical ribbed-and-vaulted stone structure to the east of the great house, built to face the rising sun at dawn. There were no overt religious symbols. Lenk called it "the still stone place."

"What the fuck," said Zhen.

Lenk shrugged.

"When the world goes away, people need it." He paused, thought about it. "Or if they tear it down and make something different, maybe that'd be even better."

It occurred to Zhen then that Lenk knew, instinctively, what would make people happy. All the visionaries who had imagined these new technologies into being had that. They had something in their minds that let them abstract away from the people who were actually in front of them to a kind of general human. They knew how to make that general human happy, and that was why they were so good at withholding it or doling it out in tiny perfect slices. If you know how to make people that happy, you know how to make them miserable as shit. Whatever this island world could be, take it away. If they want nature, make them look at screens. If they like quiet, make the world noisy. If they want community, split them up. If they want time to think, interrupt them all the fucking time. If they want real human companionship, tempt them with artificial matchbox-and-bead FantailPals.

The island, Zhen thought, is Lenk's attempt at penance.

He thought he could save a few people from all the shit he'd done.

"So, um," said Zhen as they walked back toward the crack in the mountain together, "this is a confession, right? You did this. You brought down the plane. You came here on purpose."

Lenk's suit shook its head.

"It's a coincidence," said Lenk. "It's a fucking coincidence, or—" His head wobbled on his neck, rattling a thought loose. "Look," he said, "the last time I spoke to Martha she said, 'Thanks for having me on the team.'"

"I don't think that means anything."

"Maybe it does. Maybe it's a bit like saying, 'We're on a team together, just trust me.'"

"That's a lot to read into it."

"Martha's good at that. She says that, and then we arrive here. And then you arrive here. I keep thinking . . . I keep thinking maybe she did this. You know? There'll never be an electronic trail; it happened as safely as it could without also being detectable in any way, forever, no matter how hard anyone looks. Martha knew this island was here, she knew we'd prepared it."

"You think she . . . brought down your plane?"

"I mean. It came down with a lot of warning, like we were supposed to survive it. She could have made it look like we were attacked but actually it was . . . I don't know . . . pre-drawn lines of explosive in the fuselage. We came down with CrashJackets and StowtBoxes full of supplies and survival suits. Like this plan was part of Martha's secret protocol if the world ended. And if that's true, it means that when things are easier outside, people will be coming here. I'm the first."

"Do you think the others know," asked Zhen, "that it's your island? Because that seems like it could . . . cause some problems."

"Someone knows," said Lenk. "I'll show you."

In a room toward the east of the cave complex, lined with shelves, twenty long-range communicators were smashed. Each one had been neatly and precisely destroyed with what looked like a single hammer blow to the center of the equipment. In three storage bins, the spare boards and chips were also very carefully and entirely destroyed. The array of aerials—each was snapped in half.

"Nothing else?" asked Zhen. "Whoever did this only destroyed these?"

"Nothing else," said Lenk. "So it's Zimri or it's Ellen. One of them has figured it out."

"Couldn't it have happened before you got here? Long before? I mean, who knows how long this has been waiting here?"

"Don't be so naive," said Lenk.

"Look," said Zhen. They had reached the curtain of creeper half concealing the entrance to the mountain, the place where the water trickled constantly down the cliff face. "When we get out, there's something I need to show you about these suits."

She stepped into the sunlight, her suit's visor momentarily darkened by the brightness. There was a clang that reverberated through her skull and a bright shower of pain cascading down her neck. She turned, in agony. It was Ellen Bywater, readying her metal fist for another punch.

13. impact assessments

It was not precisely true that Ellen Bywater still saw the ghost of her late husband, Will. But it wasn't not true either. The most persistent hauntings are the ghosts of lost futures. He was strong and healthy; his father had lived to ninety-two. Ellen and Will Bywater had had a famously happy marriage, and he had died suddenly at sixty-four. Nothing is promised, people say. And yet this had not been Ellen Bywater's experience of life. Everything had been promised.

For the past fifty years for Ellen Bywater, there had been hot baths and cold juice; there had been unseen hands preparing pancakes for breakfast and cleaning the stove when she might do a little cooking herself. She had a happy marriage; she had raised good children who took their places as trustees of the Bywater Foundation, distributing significant monies to worthy causes before a very simple lunch of poached salmon and watercress on the terrace. The children would beget further clean-limbed and healthy offspring and the line of Bywater would continue. Even Badger would eventually find their way. These were the promises made by hard work, by her long years at Medlar, by her commitment to good corporate culture, by the care she had taken over the ousting of Albert Dabrowski.

She thought of Albert. The look on the man's face when he realized the board was proposing to appoint her as CEO in his place. He'd shouted and railed. Undignified. She understood that this was a shock, but couldn't he hold it together—he was, after all, one of the fathers of the modern world in so many ways; no one could or would take that away from him. The night it was done, she'd fallen into

Will's arms and cried for him. Whenever she was asked about Albert Dabrowski, she'd spoken warmly about him. She could only hope to follow the design principles he had laid down; he was a visionary, and along with the rest of the world, she was waiting to see what he'd invent next.

And yet she knew that this was not entirely true. She had participated in the plan to oust him with reticence, not wanting to show how much she wanted it, knowing that as a woman in her position, *wanting it* was the last thing anyone needed to see from her.

"They don't know you like I know you," said Will, burying his face in her lap. They had had a famously happy marriage and what that means is: you're still fucking in your sixties.

But a horror had sunk into her bones at quite how easy—and even enjoyable—it had been to take it from him. She had made Albert Dabrowski much richer than he could ever have been on his own. But he hadn't known. It was a future he hadn't seen coming; he came into that very last meeting still operating on the old parameters, as if the discarded future were still operational, as if it hadn't been shunted into a siding by night without his knowledge or consent.

She knew what it was like to do it, and she could see what it would feel like to have it happen to you.

"What it feels like," she'd said to Will, quietly, the previous night while the others were sleeping, "is nothing. It feels like things are a bit easier than usual. It feels like you're all getting on fine."

Will lolled by the fire, his long torso, his full head of thick gray hair. He said: There's a problem with that reasoning, Nelly.

"Doesn't this all feel a little easy to you?" said Ellen.

It doesn't feel any way to me, said Will, I'm dead.

"What's it like to be dead?" she said.

Nothing much, said Will. It's just that your tax plans are voided and your will is executed and no one's interested in what you have to say.

"Except me," she said, and she felt grateful and a little smug that the person she liked best in the world was already definitely dead instead of being only probably dead like everyone else's loved ones.

"You know my secret," said Ellen.

I do now, said Will.

"But you can't tell anyone," she said.

Her secret was the widow's secret. That as she'd gotten onto the plane from the Action Now! conference, she had been a little glad. If Will wasn't in the world any longer, there was no real point in continuing with the project of the human race. She felt the satisfaction of having had a memo taken seriously. I told you we should junk it all.

Ellen had followed Zhen's tracks out of the camp. It wasn't difficult. Zhen hadn't taken much trouble to conceal where she was going; the earth was soft and rich, the imprints of the suit's boots very distinctive.

Will said: What is it you're expecting to find?

Ellen said: "I know a trick question when I hear one."

Will said: Because we tend to find whatever we're looking for.

"I'm not expecting anything."

You can't lie to me anymore now I'm dead. That's one of the perks.

On the upward path, Ellen was panting, even with the aid of the suit's servomotors. She was sweating. Maybe she was getting sick. Maybe this was it. Maybe she'd already been infected with the Pigeon Flu that had killed them all.

"Look," she said to Will, "sometimes in business you just have to use your instincts."

Will said: Well, OK, but what if your instincts are faulty? Remember the lectures at INSEAD: cognitive errors, systemic bias, your fault detector can't tell you whether it's faulty. If you walk along staring at the cracks in the pavement, you're going to fall.

"Look," she said. Will was standing on the path next to her, incongruous in slacks and the slouchy sweater he'd often worn in the place on Cape Cod. This was the reasonable Will, the man who made up for her. They'd had a famously happy marriage and what that means is: they managed to steer each other around their potholes. "Do you have an alternate narrative for me? I'm here. I'm open to listening."

We can't know what we don't know, said Will, a thing he had often said in life.

"So I'm going to find out," she said, and continued the ascent of the steep path.

There is a trajectory to human affairs. At a certain point, things become inevitable. The tracks in the soft mud led into the crack in the rock. Inside the cave, there was a proprietary Fantail port set into the stone, white and shining. Ellen looked at it for a long time.

She said: "See? See?"

Will said: I have to say, darling, that this doesn't look good for Lenk Sketlish.

"Well, do you have a hypothesis for me that *isn't* that he deliberately trapped us on this island that is clearly somehow built for him and that he probably killed Zimri Nommik?"

There are always more things we don't know, said Will.

"Oh yeah," she said, "name ten. Give me other explanations for this."

But because Will wasn't really real, not outside her own mind, he couldn't.

Sometimes everything you fear becomes true. Sometimes you really are alone, in a cave, with the world gone, realizing that if you're going to get what you want, you're going to have to take it. Sometimes there's nothing for it but the unspeakable.

Ellen crouched at the entrance to the cave. She tasted stone and fire. She'd lost her trust in the ability of the world to remain upright; the very air itself had become her enemy, the world had become a rain of ash.

In the corner of her eye, Will was naked—as lean as a fox, as hungry as the devil. He had been like this sometimes at home, wild nights that ended with sex and then forgiveness and promises. She remembered meeting him and knowing that he would give her perfect children and when she truly wanted something, he would never stop her. Their marriage had been famously happy, and what that meant was that they had learned to work with what they had.

14. what are you looking at

Ellen cracked the faceplate of Zhen's visor with a single blow. Zhen reeled backward, her head hitting the cliff face, the servomotors struggling to keep her upright and Ellen striking again, again, again. Inside the suit, Zhen's vision was fractured—a rainbow line across the screen, the colors oscillating red and blue and green and silver.

"Stop," Zhen was saying over and over again. "Stop—whatever you think is happening, that's not what's happening. Look," said Zhen, "LOOK." She peeled open the faceplate of her suit. The visor, cracked, screeched as it retracted. But seeing her real face, Ellen paused. A person inside the oyster shell, just a human with squashy human flesh.

"Something really, really weird is going on," said Zhen, "and I don't understand it but look—these suits. Lenk thinks Fantail made them and you think Fantail made them and maybe they did, but LOOK."

She stepped out of the suit. And then she was just a person in stained sweatpants and an old ringer T-shirt. She put one palm against the interior of the suit and tugged at the soft fabric lining.

"If there's a weapon in there, I'm going to kill you," said Ellen.

"No," said Zhen, and she was almost laughing and almost crying, "it's not a weapon. I know these things are sophisticated or whatever, with the bits inside that bulge out and coalesce, and I thought—I've seen this before, I know I've seen it before. I just couldn't remember where."

She peeled back the soft fabric at the crotch. There were concentric circles outlined in the plastic.

"These haven't been specially made," she said, "they're

repurposed. Cleverly repurposed, fine. But I've seen them before. They were sex suits. For long-distance virtual sex or if your avatars in the metaverse want to bone or whatever."

They could all see it then. The bulging pods and soft squishy parts. The interface areas where a device could be slotted into place. The concentric circles depending on whether you wanted a larger . . . girth.

"What the fuck," said Lenk.

Ellen looked to her right, as if someone was there. Zhen thought: I don't know what the right thing to do is. But I know that if Ellen Bywater kills me, then I don't get to do anything else. Whatever gets you to the next part.

"Someone repurposed these things," said Zhen. "Like, I'm serious, you guys have *rivals*, don't you? There's not just the three of you in the whole world. Maybe someone else did all this. I don't know who, but this isn't tech made for survival. This is made to be controlled remotely. You know? Maybe someone's out there. Telling the suits what to say."

There had been many technologies like this. Supposed machine-recognition that actually turned out to be tens of thousands of people in India or Venezuela or Ghana, going through photos or translating documents or transcribing voice mails or reviewing automatic writing outputs. Because tens of thousands of humans can still do a lot of stuff better—and, crucially, cheaper—than machines. And because customers felt better if they believed their voice messages were being transcribed by a computer than by a person. Marius would have said: We made ourselves a mechanical god so we could worship it.

"Who?" said Ellen. "Is it Nommik?"

"I mean, I think we just need to all sit down and chill out," said Zhen, "and figure out what we know. Pool our information."

Not trusting one another was fine; that was to be expected. But if this was boiling over into violence, it was most likely to end with more punches to Zhen's own head.

"I just want to know," said Ellen, and her voice was level but she was the opposite of calm, "I just want to know who the *fuck* it is. OK? I want you to tell me who the fuck it is. The two of you."

Lenk drew breath and Zhen understood that sometimes you can know the future. You can know it in the inability of people to change. In their desire to have things over. If you can't tolerate uncertainty, you will try to make things certain. Sometimes the only way to make them certain is to make them bad. It hadn't taken much for Lenk and Ellen to get to this stage.

"It is my island," said Lenk. "I acknowledge that and I take responsibility for that part."

And as things do, things began to move very quickly.

The hypothalamic-pituitary axis releases a shower of adrenaline and cortisol and the heart pumps blood to the muscles and the head reels with the shock and fear of a new battle. It would take a lifetime of training to respond to violence with kindness and calm. Deep belly breaths among the redwoods won't touch it.

Ellen's attack was loud and instant, a streaking fist to Lenk's head. He was ready for her. They fought, metal on metal, kicked out with mechanized legs, one blow coming up at his face and smashing into the screen of his visor, making it bloom with bright color. He had a handheld blowtorch he'd brought up from the caves—small but intense. He pressed it directly to the jaw latch of Ellen's helmet, the metal already beginning to warp from the heat. He flamed the blowtorch on a dried creeper. The fire rose up around her and, panicking, she let go for a moment. He pulled away, then came back harder, walloping the visor screen again and again with the heel of his hand.

She struggled, kicked out at him. A lucky blow taking his knee sideways. He crashed to earth.

When he fell, Ellen fled.

Lenk clambered clumsily to his feet.

"Stop," said Zhen, "please stop now. Let her go. Let her think it through."

Ellen ran through the jungle, thinking of Albert Dabrowski's face when she took his company from him. She knew that if she could have seen her own face, that is how she would have looked.

15. yeah! justice!

In the jungle, every inch of earth is alive. The trees' corrugated bark teems with insects. The air swarms with microscopic creatures. The soil—oh!—the soil is as rich with life as a womb; it is eager and foaming.

In the shadow of a great cliff, within the life of the jungle, Ellen Bywater cowered. Clamped to the rock like a barnacle, molded into its curved and flat places. Hiding like any other creature.

Ellen said, "I don't want to die."

Will said, No one does, honeybunch.

Above her, on the clifftop, Lenk Sketlish searched.

The suit said: "What do you need her for, Lenk?"

Lenk said: "Never you mind."

The suit said: "I can't help you with this any longer."

Lenk said: "You got me far enough."

He wondered if the suit would freeze him in place or send out a distress call or alert Zhen or warn Ellen. But he thought: No FantailPhone in the world has ever refused to make a phone call luring someone to their death. No FantailTablet has refused to locate a gun store. No FantailSearch has refused to turn up information on how to kill someone in seventy different ways. We could've made technology like that, but we thought it was better not to get involved. Improve market share. Leave it to the invisible hand of buying and selling to sort things out in the fullness of many days. Martha wouldn't have made a suit that would stop him from taking legitimate steps to protect himself.

The suit said: "I can't recommend what you're doing."

Still, the suit's heat sensors showed him Ellen, tucked up tight against the cliff face, bug in a rug.

Still, the suit's servomotors helped him analyze the rock formations.

God bless America and freedom of choice.

In the jungle, every square inch of earth is alive. And every death is the beginning of other lives. A bear or a beetle—nothing is too large or small to make food for something else. Lenk looked down on Ellen like the Lord God looked down on the city of Sodom. He placed the mining charges from his underground caves into the fault in the rock. He set his blowtorch flaming and tossed it in after the charges.

The noise was bone-crunchingly loud. Sheets of rock face at the edge of the precipice sheared off, one by one, pointed and sharp, piercing. One by one they hammered down on the same spot, precisely. Four sheets of rock, five, six, seven, smashing down after each explosive percussion, a crash that sent your teeth vibrating and the earth shaking. Even when the last sheet had fallen, the jungle echoed the sound back in the chattering of monkeys and the whirr of wings.

Lenk said to the suit: "Can I climb down?"

The suit said: "The rock face is unstable, as are the shards below."

Lenk said: "I want to go another way."

The suit said: "The way is too dangerous."

He sat on his haunches at the edge of the cliff. Peeled off the head and torso and pulled his arms out of the gloves and sleeves so that the suit was underneath him like the flayed skin of a metal corpse. He touched the rocks, unarguable beneath his fingertips.

Lenk said: "What if I make you take me?"

The suit said: "You can only make me do certain things, Lenk."

He thought of Martha. What she approved and disapproved of.

The adrenaline was passing through his body now. Metabolic breakdown was turning it to inactive and docile substances in his bloodstream. He was beginning to tremble.

"Zhen," he said. "Suit, can I talk to Zhen?"

"I'm sorry," said the suit, "but Zhen is gone."

16. you can't find her, no one can

Zhen had done her reading long ago. She knew about adrenaline and metabolic breakdown. She had analyzed studies of group behaviors under pressure.

Ya-Ling, her ex-girlfriend who, now Zhen thought about it, had put up with a lot of bullshit from her, had said she was doing all that to try to understand something intellectually that could only ever be worked through emotionally.

Ya-Ling had said: "You shut down when you were a teenager and you never really came back. I get it, but you need to talk to someone."

Ya-Ling had said: "You weren't actually here, you know. It doesn't *mean* anything with that girl, but she was here. And she tells me what she's feeling."

Ya-Ling had said: "You have to stop running sometime."

But who the fuck knew where Ya-Ling was now, and as it had turned out, Zhen had very much had to *not* stop running.

After the Fall of Hong Kong—months of civil unrest, homelessness, living through martial law—Zhen had sat in an offshore refugee camp waiting to be processed for entry into the United Kingdom. It had been endless weeks and months with her grieving, broken father, and she was a teenager knowing that only the future held anything for her. She felt as if she could press her whole body and her determination and her fear against the present until the glass smashed and she was allowed to enter that new now. And then she would forget all this and she would become a different person; she would be okay at last. She had studied for twelve examinations in that camp and achieved twelve top grades; she had done it with sheer will. She had stayed out of fights and she had kept away from gangs and at night she had learned to sleep with whatever noise and screaming rent the darkness.

She had seen things in the camp she'd never wanted to see—the way people broke down at first piece by tiny piece and then all at once. There was a kind Chinese woman who kept her hair and clothes so tidy until she found a maggot in her face cream and the tide of self-disgust washed her whole self away. After that Zhen had seen her only at the edge of the camp—once she saw her running with a group chasing down a stray dog and later roasting it over an acrid fire of plastic and rubber. She had met the woman's eye for a moment and seen that there was no self there, no human person left.

Ya-Ling had said: "This is exactly the kind of thing you need to talk to someone about. It might actually help."

So Zhen didn't tell her about the mud: the friend of her father's, an erudite man who spoke five languages, who destroyed his own shelter in a fit of violent rage and then lay very still, his face the color of mud under the broken pieces, and would not stand or walk. He waited for illness and death to take him, and although it took six weeks, eventually the mud reclaimed him.

Zhen had been too young to know what she found out about human nature in that camp. But having studied for those exams she'd never asked for, she was prepared now.

From the far promontory, she watched Lenk Sketlish bring down a mountain and she knew what he was.

She said to her suit: "Can you help me hide from him?"

The suit said: "I will help you, Zhen."

She remembered the long nights in the camp, with the moldy smell of rotten wood burning in the back of her throat. The memory of the man lying down in the mud. The sense she had then that the earth itself was a hostile place, that the soil would rise up and swallow her if she let it, the dreams in which she felt the mud in her mouth and nose and growing down her throat. The absolute knowledge that if she allowed herself to weaken for one hour—to take a single job with one of the gangs that circulated drugs and phones around the camp, to sit for one afternoon at the fires—if she allowed herself to forget the future Zhen shining and golden and waiting, she would never come back.

Right at the edge of the ring-finger nail of her right hand, Zhen saw a fragment of silver. A fleck of nail polish from a silly night—a month or more ago—a science fiction party in a warehouse in Bucharest, a party full of imagined futures from the past. Sarit had done the robot very badly. Marius had sung drunken David Bowie karaoke. That fleck was the party; she had carried it with her and it was here in the midst of everything and she would survive.

On the promontory, she said to the mud: You won't have me. You're nothing but a pack of cards. There is no horror on the stair. Nothing in the jungle draws out our cruelty or decay. The only darkness in the heart is the dark we brought with us.

She said to the suit: "I don't believe in any of this. It could have been fine here, even without comms."

The suit said: "OK."

Zhen said: "But I believe Lenk Sketlish isn't in control of himself anymore, if he ever was. I believe he won't stop looking for me unless he thinks I'm dead."

The suit said: "Yes."

17. another weak sauce event

The suits had very little information about the world since the Pigeon Flu, but a great deal of information about the world beforehand. Books, TV, movies, music, great swaths of internet sites, useful and useless, links broken, just enormous amounts of information, with a pretty good search function. Zhen had of course looked herself up—there were about forty of her videos with the highest number of views, plus her Wikipedia, most of her NTD posts. There was nothing at all about Marius—he'd be pleased by that. His big aim was to be forgotten by history.

You should never internet-search for a girl who'd ghosted you. That was the rule. And yet. Surely times like these justified some leeway in the rules.

Zhen hesitated. She told herself this wasn't the time. She reminded herself that she really might die here and if so, why not just do this? It wouldn't matter once she was dead whether she had or not.

"Suit," she said, "show me everything you have on Martha Einkorn."

The suit brought the search results up in a bland paragraph inside her visor.

It wasn't much. Some corporate holdings records. A few photographs of her standing behind Lenk Sketlish, holding a file. And a video.

"Open the video," said Zhen.

Martha Einkorn was onstage in Tokyo, in front of a quiet, respectful audience in a hotel lobby that looked like it came from the set of *Gattaca*—all clean stone, light bricks, and thirty-foot-high ceilings. Martha was giving an interview about "Fantail as a Survival Tool." The same product she'd been selling when Zhen met her but—by the date stamp—this talk had been months later, in October. Less than a month before the Pigeon Flu. Well into the ghosting zone. It was the same talking points in the same order with a Japanese host whom Martha seemed to know. Martha did a few lines in pretty OK Japanese, remembering her particles and putting the verb in the right place at the end of the sentence. Probably there was some special way for rich people to learn languages. Zhen thought: Shit, you see, she could have learned some Chinese and I could have introduced her to my dad.

The interview came to an end and the audience moved off. The picture went black but the two women onstage were clearly still on hot microphones. They carried on chatting, mostly in English with occasional Japanese phrases. They clearly knew each other fairly well, seemed friendly. The conversation became intimate very quickly.

"Hansuke wants another baby," said the interviewer, "but I don't know if we can manage it with everything else."

"You want one?" said Martha.

"Sure," said the interviewer.

"Then why wait?"

"Coming from *you*? The queen of waiting and seeing? Being sensible?"

There was a pause.

"I've met someone," said Martha. "A woman. She makes survival videos."

Zhen thought for a moment that maybe Martha had met *someone else* who made survival videos, which would be a real kick in the teeth.

"No!" The interviewer sounded genuinely overjoyed. "That's great news! Who is she? When do I meet her?"

"Maybe not for a while," said Martha. "Complicated. Work stuff. But I think this is it."

The sound cut off there. Zhen sat alone on a promontory, looking at the place where Lenk had just crashed an enormous rock face off the side of a cliff.

If Lenk was right, maybe nothing on this island was here by accident. Maybe Martha had put this here for her to find.

Where would Martha be now? The survival plan and protocol she'd made with Lenk Sketlish said that she should be in a bunker in Greenland, waiting for better days. But who knew what had really happened? The world was unpredictable at the best of times, as Zhen had learned over and over again.

The only way to know the future is to control it.

18. some parts you can fake, but some parts have to be real

They sat opposite each other across a small campfire: the woman and her survival.

The suit mirrored Zhen's position—knees drawn up, heels of the hands dug into the earth for balance. It wasn't so much larger than Zhen now. It had formed itself around her just as it would have done a long time ago when it had been made for pleasure. It was a reflection of her; it had learned her gait and her pose and the tilt of her head and—after all this time—no one could really tell whether she was in it or not.

"How much of yourself can you function without?" said Zhen. "Like, where is your brain?"

"My memory and intelligence are contained in a distributed network stored in a substrate between the outer shell and the inner membrane," said the suit.

"OK," said Zhen, "so how much can you lose without suffering too much loss of function?"

The suit went through some options. The legs had nothing much to them apart from locomotion.

"So, a leg?"

"Could you lose a leg?" said the suit.

Zhen thought about this.

"I'm willing to be hurt," said Zhen. "I'm willing to end up with scars."

In this, too, there were options. Legs, arms, certain places on the torso.

"I can broadcast false data regarding your heart rate and other vital signs," said the suit. "Lenk's suit will accept my data unless there is reason to suspect."

"But he could get into your systems and check, like with the blood solutes and the roofies, right? So it has to look real."

Legs, arms, certain places on the torso. Dying without dying. If she was lucky.

"Alright," said Zhen at last, "I think I can live with that."

19. humans use the past to predict the future; in other words, we imagine things that are not there

Lenk went to sleep in his suit, fastened to the underside of a tree branch.

In the morning it would all seem clear again; he would find Zhen and he would tell her what he knew or suspected he knew. She would understand why he'd killed Ellen. She would know he'd had nothing to do with Zimri. They could solve it together. He slept, knowing that in the morning it would be easier.

When he woke in the night, his tree was on fire.

The suit crashed him into wakefulness with a piercing chime. He struggled and tried to sit up and banged his head on the suit's interior. The suit was already scuttling its limbs along the branch, extending extra grabbing arms like a monstrous spider.

"Someone has set the tree on fire," said the suit. "I am seeking safety."

Like a terrified animal, the suit clambered along one branch, only for a tongue of flame to burst from the leaves. The ground was sixty feet below. The suit clung to the trunk, but some of the branches had burned away and there was fire below them.

"Just drop down," said Lenk.

"Too far," said the suit. "You will sustain damage."

"I will sustain damage if we catch on fire, you numbskull."

When Lenk moved a foot or an arm, the tree swayed and bent, springing, the worst kind of carnival ride. His hand slipped on the trunk. He thought he was going to be sick. Something crashed into the back of the suit and he saw at once that it was a neighboring tree.

"We need to sway it more, get into that tree."

Like a whirligig with the suit, he moved his body weight back and forth, pushing the tree to spring farther and farther. He reached out with hand and foot, but met empty air. Once more, once more, harder, farther. And yes! The left gauntlet grabbed the slick trunk of the next tree. He let go of the past and pulled himself into safety. Yes. The new trunk held. Yes.

The tree he had just left sprang back, wavered in his sight, flaming and flaring, bending toward him as if trying to set him alight. It had been his shelter until a moment earlier and now it seemed an implacable enemy. The suit began to climb down, hand over hand, foot after foot.

"Where is she?" said Lenk.

"I can't find her," said his suit.

"I'm going to kill her," said Lenk.

20. we intuit motives and assess character; this is our evolutionary advantage

Beyond the mountain, in the jungle to the north, Lai Zhen was running on all fours.

"She's describing large figure eights on a repeating pattern," said Lenk's suit.

"Why?" said Lenk.

"I couldn't say," said the suit.

"Can you make a guess?"

"I'm not designed for that. I know about plants, birds, animals, fish, insects, diseases, food storage, construction—"

"Stop," said Lenk.

"Understanding humans is a full CPU commitment even for a machine built to do it, which, again, I'm not."

"I get it," said Lenk. "Fuck, can you ever stop?"

"It's just that my thing is keeping you alive and if you—"

"Shut the fuck up," said Lenk.

Zhen had some kind of plan. Lenk didn't know what it was, which made him nervous. Still, a pattern is predictable. And predictability is vulnerability. The situation everyone wants to be in is to know the future, and she'd given it to him.

In the dark of the rain-soaked jungle, Lenk took up a crouching position on the figure-eight turn and waited for Zhen to lope past. Like her, he was finding it significantly easier to move on all fours—the suit lengthened its front limbs and gave him enough back support to make the motion quick and pleasurable.

Zhen was coming. Legs pounding the earth like a dog after a fire truck. She was slowing on the turn, just as the suit said she would.

“Say when?” he said.

“You are too close to do this safely,” said the suit.

“Too far away and I could miss.”

“There’s a chance you could both end up without kneecaps,” it said.

“Thanks, I have understood the risks,” he said.

There would only be one chance to do this right. They waited for the sound of forelimbs hitting the wet soil, slower, slower. Then her suit was right there, racing like a hound. Lenk eased his elbow forward.

The suit said: “Now.”

Lenk cracked the seal on the mining charge and hurled it directly in Zhen’s path.

There was an enormous sound.

There was nothing.

Then there was rain.

Clods of earth raining down, scattered and hard. Smoke and debris. Recoil against his belly had forced him onto his back and driven the wind out of him even inside the suit. His mind replaying the last moments. Knowing that if it had done this to him, it must have destroyed her.

“Where is the body?” he said. “I want to see the body.”

21. lacking sharp claws or warm fur or tearing teeth or tremendous speed, what we have is brain

Legs, arms, certain places on the torso.

In the smoke and noise, Zhen's suit crawl-limped on one leg and one half leg into the jungle where Zhen was waiting.

This had always been the thing that had to be done quickly and correctly. Only some things could be predicted. The suit had to be intact when Lenk damaged it, and not intact afterward. This could not be faked. Wounds would have to be fresh. The mangled suit eased open its creaking half-torn joints. Zhen stepped inside. The visor portion was wrenched off, her face exposed. Her lower left leg was cold where the suit was gone.

"Leg, huh?" said Zhen.

"Would you like me to sedate you?" said the suit.

"Fuck no," said Zhen. "We've been through this. Pain relief, yes. But I need to be sharp."

"He will regain consciousness within three minutes," said the suit. "It is conceivable that my structure bore the brunt of the explosion."

"Yeah," said Zhen, "but the leg's not going to be OK, is it?"

The suit's right arm held a jagged piece of metal. If AUGR hadn't saved me in the mall, I would have lost more than this, thought Zhen, so suck it up, buttercup.

"It is clean," said the suit. "When this is over—I have applied some anesthetic—I can suture—"

"Just do it," said Zhen. "Make it look real."

The suit raised the glinting blade and brought it down in the meat of her thigh, scraping against the bone.

Even with the anesthetic, the pain momentarily blinded her, her vision flashing black and bright, her stomach roiling. The wound sucked at the metal, trying to hold it in place as the suit pulled it up and back like a terrible, unsurvivable wound to the femoral artery. Don't think, don't be here, think of anything else, think of the fragments of nail varnish at the edges of your nails and how there have been parties, bodies moving through space, slow and fast, stinking of sweat and life. The pain was louder than thought. There had not been enough time for the anesthetic to take. It was serrated lines scored through the inside of her body like the tines of a fork. She was being scooped out and she gasped and vomited a little bile into her mouth and then the pain closed her mind and she was gone.

It was day, extraordinarily.

Zhen's suit buzzed. Her visor was down and her earpieces in place, but the suit was communicating with her now by vibrating the bones of her skull. No one else could hear it.

Very quietly and far away, the suit said: Play dead.

The suit was no longer as innocent as it had been.

The suit said: Don't move, just don't fucking move.

Zhen focused on her painful shallow breaths. Tiny sips of air. Barely breathing.

The suit said: Move less than that.

The sun wheeled around, gaping. A hot mouth filled with spines. Lenk Sketlish was staring at her.

The suit gushed a supply of thick blood—from a freezer StowtBox, artificial blood, emergencies only and what was this but an emergency?—across Zhen's thigh. As if her femoral artery were severed. It must have given her something to calm her. How else was she not trembling with pain and terror?

She kept her eyes glassy. She did not focus. Sips of air. Her head pounded.

"Fuck," said Lenk. "She's fucking dead."

Zhen's suit communicated to Lenk's suit, counting down her chances of survival. Seventeen percent. Fifteen percent. Twelve percent. Zhen's suit made itself appear to be trying to save her life. Injecting gels into the wounds. Trying to cauterize bleeding. She shifted a little and the suit made the wound in her leg pump harder, the lazy trickle turning into a momentary sharp gush like an ejaculation. Nine percent. Four percent. Two percent. Zero percent. Zero percent.

He looked at Zhen. Though his face was hidden by his visor, she felt his eyes locking onto hers.

"You idiot," he said, "we could have figured this out together."

He toed at her body, tipping her suit onto its back. She remained very still.

And at last Lenk Sketlish turned his broad shoulders and walked back toward his mountain, leaving Zhen behind him.

Zhen and her suit waited until night had descended over the jungle, thick and dark and rustling and shrieking, the night as full of life as the day. In the dark, the suit cauterized her wound and fitted MembraSkin over the top. She would always have a scar. Her leg would never be quite as strong as the other. The suit led her back to the campsite, walking ahead of her like a sister, its palm against her palm.

The suit found replacement parts for itself in one of the StowtBoxes and fitted them. It was more obviously a pleasure suit now—one of the legs was olive-skinned and human-looking. Part of the interior was lined with a suite of tactile fabrics in shimmering animal prints that didn't look designed for survival. A few parts were missing—the left hand was replaced with a climbing grab-gauntlet. It brought itself back together and then opened itself to let her back inside. It was warm in the suit and soothing to her wound. She felt they were friends now.

She said: "What's going to happen?"

The suit said: "Lenk isn't likely to come back here for a few days. We'll take what we need tonight and make a new camp to the south. Away from his mountain."

They worked until dawn, lashing supplies together on a cart, walking south. They walked until Zhen fell asleep in the motion and woke still on the move. They reached a river to the south in the late afternoon. The suit told her they had traveled more than twenty-five miles and they were in a section of around one hundred square miles where they would be unobservable from the mountain or anywhere near it. Zhen asked the suit for reruns of *Poker Face* and games of sudoku and Animal Crossing. She crawled inside a reinforced igloo tent and imagined she was far away. She ate self-heating rice pudding.

She slept that night and dreamed of the time before, and of her mother. Her mother gliding through the jungle on a golden cloud, looking at all that had gone on here and laughing loudly as children do when adults make fools of themselves. Of course, thought Zhen when she woke, of course.

"Did you offer this option to the others?" said Zhen. "What we just did. Pretending to be dead?"

Silence.

"Don't fucking lie to me. Did you offer the others to fake their own deaths?"

"Yes," said the suit.

"Did they do it?"

"I don't think I should tell you that."

Zhen laughed then. Laughed thinking that what she'd just done to Lenk might have happened several times now. Ellen allowing the suit to pretend to be smashed to smithereens and then pulling herself out of the rock in the dark, heading off to the north or the west or the east of the island. Zimri using a nanobot swarm to fake his disappearance just as Ellen had suggested. The four of them in their total and glorious isolation on this rich, well-provisioned, almost luxurious island, unable to trust one another enough to even acknowledge that they were still alive.

Something flitted through Zhen's mind that she'd read while browsing NTD years ago. People after the destruction of civilization taking refuge in a cave. Telling themselves there was no one else left alive in the cities. So unable to trust that this isolation seemed the safest thing for them.

The suit said: "You might need to be here for a long time."

"All alone?"

"Sort of alone. I'll be here."

"I was never meant to come here," said Zhen.

"But you could never have stayed away, once you knew," said the suit.

22. nothing is ever really over

On the top floor of a tall glass tower with the word "Fantail" and its stylized bird symbol etched down the side of the windows so as to catch the light at dawn, there was a pristine office of steel and silicone. The long working table was made of blue sheared glass, artfully cracked and held in place by a thin polymer layer. There were views on three sides, for the whole room was a cantilevered box, swung out from the Fantail building over the city of San Francisco and held in place as if it were floating in midair. It was meant to suggest the extended branch of a redwood, of particular symbolic significance to this organization and its founder. The office was carpeted with a white rug so thick and deep that when Martha Einkorn stepped onto it in her bare feet, it was as if she could feel the forest moving beneath her.

Martha Einkorn arrived at this office every morning at dawn, or just after it. She always arrived between 5 a.m. and 5:30 a.m. That was her time for solitary morning reflection. It had been vital to the company in that exceptionally difficult and turbulent time when Martha Einkorn emerged as its unlikely savior. She worked tirelessly not just to ensure shareholder value and consistent growth in this most challenging of markets but also to enact value-driven change on a corporate, national, and global scale. This she did, she said in numerous interviews, to preserve the legacy of Lenk. To keep alive the ideals and vision of the man she knew perhaps better than any other. To grow from the seeds he planted a yet mightier tree. Lenk Sketlish, founder and CEO of Fantail, had disappeared—of course—in the Tech Plane Tragedy a little more than three years earlier.

The time between 5 a.m. and 5:30 a.m. was precious to her, she said in the interviews. That was when she felt Lenk's spirit so close she could almost hear his voice. She could never be interrupted at this time. She spent it in silent thought, in meditation, in almost physical communion with all that Lenk had taught her. It was her time to learn what Lenk would like her to do with his company and to respond to it.

At 5:30 a.m. on this day, as on every other, she was sitting at the shattered-glass worktable in the cantilevered box overlooking the city. She was contemplating the day ahead. She had one of Lenk's old laptops nearby. A constant reminder, she said, of his presence. As if he were always with her.

On this day as on every other, at 5:30 a.m. precisely, a small alarm began to sound on Lenk's laptop. It would sound on every other laptop he'd ever owned if Martha Einkorn had not meticulously deleted this particular piece of software from all of Lenk's other electronic devices, including those that had been already set aside for the Lenk Sketlish Museum of Creativity, for which ground was already being broken on an island in the bay.

If Martha Einkorn had not used Lenk's passwords to which only she had access to remove this piece of software, the alarm would sound on every laptop and FantailTablet and smartphone and FantailWatch he'd owned. But if the alarm were removed from every device, it could not be acknowledged, and it if were not acknowledged and dismissed within fifteen minutes, it would begin a chain reaction of further warnings, requests for confirmation by further third parties, and if those could not give a satisfactory report, automatic deployment of drones and notifications to search-and-rescue authorities.

It was a very serious matter to authorize the use of a tracking chip embedded in a person's body. Lenk Sketlish set up his systems with a great deal of care and thought. He didn't want just *anyone* to be able to track him in any circumstances. He set up a "dead man's switch." If he hadn't logged in to any of his usual devices after twenty-four hours, an alarm would sound. If he himself didn't turn it off, it would be authorized to release the details of his tracking chip to the relevant authorities.

In the cantilevered office overlooking the city, Martha Einkorn dialed a certain number into the safe built into the steel floor of the room. She pulled out the laptop, which was giving off a soft metallic chime. She opened it, plugged it in. Looked at the screen.

"Confirm," said the screen. "Lenk Sketlish personal alarm has been activated. Confirm that you are safe, Lenk."

She tapped in Lenk's password.

She listened to the soft chime as if it were Lenk's own nagging voice.

On this day, as on every other, Martha Einkorn turned the alarm off.

PART 6

how to
know
for sure

extract from Name The Day survivalist forum

sub-board: ntd/foxandrabbit

>> *OneCorn is at* **Prepped To The Max** *status.*

There is a prelude to the story of Lot and Sodom.

Before he settled in Sodom, Lot traveled with his uncle Abraham and they were good, dear friends. On their travels, Abraham and Lot found rich grazing lands for their flocks, forests of mighty trees, and places where they felt the sacred presence of God in the curve of the land. Over time, Abraham and Lot became wealthy—their sheep had lambs, as sheep do. They looked after them well. They traded the wool. They ended up with silver and gold.

But they argued. Genesis doesn't say about what. So let's just say that part isn't important—when people live and work together they argue about some bullshit. Same as it ever was.

Let's say Abraham said to Lot: "I can't actually stand you anymore and you can't stand the sight of me. So. Let's split up the land between us. In front of us are, on the one side, the plains of Tzoar and on the other side the plains of Canaan. If you go left, I'll go right. If you go right, I'll go left. I just never want you saying this wasn't fair."

The plains of the land of Tzoar were fertile and the plains of Canaan dry. So Lot felt that was a pretty easy decision.

They could have said: Let's share all these lands in common. That way if some lands have a drought or are hit by a huge ball of flame from heaven or whatever, neither of us will lose everything. But Lot was a fearful man and he wanted something to hold, to feel certain about.

Listen: nothing in the world is truly owned. There is no tree or patch of soil or animal or mountain or river that grows a label naming its owner on its bark or on its flesh or through the strata of its rocks. Once upon a time, "owning" meant "having a special duty to care" for something, not that you alone could have it or use it. "Owning" is invented, it is a symbolic behavior. And by inventing owning, we invented Rabbit. That's how Rabbit came into the world. When we say to each other: Just stay away from me, take your territory and stay there so I never have to see your stupid fucking face again.

Lot went to live in the plains near Sodom and Abraham went to the great trees of Mamre. Lot felt great about his choice because he owned a fertile

>> ***HatOnBack is at*** One Tin O'Beans ***status.***

What in the holy hell is this? I thought this was about survival?

land. The world was still large enough, just about, to get lost in. And in fact, Lot's flocks had feasted and he had prospered.

But of course with owning comes theft.

The king of Elam launched a war on Sodom—well, we say a war but back then cities were a few thousand people so it'd be more accurate to call it a "raid." This band of raiders, led by their war chief, overran the city and kidnapped Lot's household and rustled his sheep and stole his gold and silver and all the good things he had stored. Well, these things still happen today.

Soon, Abraham heard what had happened to his nephew. And he hated Lot's fucking face but he was his *nephew*. So Abraham took three hundred of the lean tent-dwellers who followed him and they went after the Elamites. He divided his followers into six phalanxes: to the east and the south, the north, the west, the northwest, and the southeast. They went stealthily, without any light, but they were used to defending the flocks by night against gray wolves. They encircled the camp. They waited for a sign. Abraham blew a note on a ram's horn and all the men descended on the Elamite encampment and took it quickly and with great force.

In the camp Abraham found Lot tied

›› *FoxInTheHenHouse is at* GoBagPrepped *status.*

It is. It's about being the kind of people who survive. If you want to be a person who survives.

›› *HatOnBack*

Is that a THREAT

›› *FoxInTheHenHouse*

Nope. Stick around, you might learn something.

up and cut the ropes. So how did Lot feel at that moment? I'm going to say: *complex*. Chastened, humble, afraid, grateful—and perhaps also resentful, angry, filled with jealousy that Abraham had taken the less fertile land and yet still he was the one to rescue Lot and not the other way around. Lot was a greedy man and he viewed the world through greed.

The leader of Sodom honored Abraham and his followers too. They'd freed the women, children, and young men taken as slaves by the Elamites. So the leader of Sodom gave a feast in Abraham's honor where they ate sweet goat's cheese and good bread and sang together.

At last, the leader of Sodom folded his legs under him and said: "Abraham. By the laws we keep to among ourselves, since you rescued us, all my wealth and my women, the chattels, and the children belong to you now. Please, I beg you, give me back the people and keep the wealth for yourself."

Abraham had his doubts about the value of this new idea of ownership. So he drank his goat milk and thought carefully. What good had it done Lot to take the fertile lands west of the river? Abraham had the strong sense that there was something better than hoarding up goods. That his strength

›› DanSatDan is at* LarderFull *status

Or don't. No one's forcing you.

and security came not from specific objects in a stronghold or dug into a bunker against a day of reckoning. Abraham's feeling was that his ability to rescue Lot had come from those three hundred men who trusted and respected him. A community and a reputation are stronger than gold bars and jars of grain and wine and oil. The only future we ever own resides in our trust in others, their trust in us.

So Abraham said: "I don't want a single thread of cloth or one strap from one sandal."

It wasn't virtue that made Abraham say it, it was wisdom. He enjoyed riches—he was a wealthy man for those times with flocks of sheep and fine cloth and jewels and stores of food.

What he knew was: more than greed causes wealth, wealth causes greed.

The richer you are, the more you have to be careful about that.

Lot had ears, but he did not hear. He thought of how they'd shouted "fuck you then!" and "no, fuck you!" and gone their separate ways. Then, he and Abraham had had about the same amount of stuff. And how had this bullshit happened to him?

By the time the mob arrived at his door, Lot was broken. He had no language but the deal. Grab what you

›› *RiasMom is at* PlantingAnOrchard *status.*

Or come and go for a while before you make your mind up, like DanSatDan up there.

›› *FoxInTheHenHouse*

That's it. See how the words sit with you. We've got time.

can, own it and use it. Give and take, trade and bargain.

He said: "Leave these guests alone but take my daughters."

And from then, there was no way to look back.

Abraham and Lot are a warning against what we have already done. Abraham and Lot are a warning not to do it *more*. Abraham and Lot tell us that we will often have the choice between accumulating more gold or objects and creating more trust. Choose to trust.

The road to ruin is paved with certainty. The end of the world is only ever hastened by those who think they will be able to protect their own from the coming storm.

1. the most parsimonious solution

It needn't have been technology billionaires. There were plenty of other forces of merciless capital and power in the world. These simply happened to be the ones to whom Martha Einkorn had access. They were the ones who were so focused on the future that they could be dazzled by a vision of all they feared coming to pass. They were the ones she could persuade to buy AUGR and to think that a set of matchboxes and beads could learn to transcend time, who believed so strongly in the promises of artificial intelligence that they took its words more seriously than their own senses and reason. For this to work, they just had to be willing for the computers to know more than them, and they had to want—in their heart of hearts—for the world to come to an end. All of life is contingent, and if Martha had found herself in the middle of a different kind of revolution, she would have swum upstream in it nonetheless.

It hadn't been easy. Deciding to do it is never enough. Having the idea is never enough. Moving the world takes a thousand thousand tiny pieces.

The easiest thing, of course, would have been to kill them. Get them onto the plane together. Put an explosive on board, detonate it when they were out at sea, debris falls into the ocean, no one finds it, no one knows where the plane went, disable the black box before you start, terrible tragedy.

But killing would not do. There was a vertiginous afternoon in one of their anonymous out-of-the-way hotel suites when they discussed it. Even Badger truly raised the question of whether killing their mother would be the simplest, most parsimonious solution. Of whether, in fact, they could do it.

"I think I could kill Zimri," said Selah.

"A lot of people feel that way after a decade of marriage," said Albert.

"I can't do it," said Badger. "It's not even that I think it's the wrong answer. I just know I can't."

"The thing is," said Martha, "even if we decide we should do it, one of us will decide against it the day before and go to the FBI. Not killing them makes it more possible that this whole plan will really happen."

"Cold," said Albert at the same time that Selah said, "Realistic."

Badger looked at their own hands and felt suddenly that these were not their hands at all, that they belonged to somebody else and were moving and fluttering in this strange, ugly way of their own accord. The thought of killing, of a murder charge, of a trial—Badger felt completely certain this could not be their life.

"If we save their lives and keep them somewhere safe," said Badger, "we'll never be guilty of murder."

And that was how they came to it. A terrible, unforeseeable accident. Brought on by their own technology. They could always be found somehow.

"It's messy," said Selah. "If they're still alive, they band together, they figure something out, they walk to civilization, they make a mast out of tin cans and a transmitter out of their own fillings. There's always a chance they'll pull some Iron Man shit, be back in three months, and we will all be in *jail*."

Badger said: "So we make it easy for them. Easy enough that they don't get desperate. My mom already thinks it's going to be a luxury vacation."

This is always the secret; this was how these technology fortunes had been made: make it all so easy and enjoyable and frictionless that you never start to ask yourself the big questions about whether this is really how you want to be spending your life.

The more people who knew about the plan, the more likely one of them would leak. Selah suggested they use Zimri's method: divide and rule. Find people who had a good reason not to tell anyone else what was happening.

There was no need for the corrupt factory supervisor in Shenzhen to know what he was making. If he did what he was told, Martha would not have to let Mr. Sketlish know about the "errors" by which a little under one-tenth of 1 percent of the product of the factory had been sold to third parties, the money going into the supervisor's pocket. That really boiled the sweat out of his body. So she had an invisible production line.

They made small, innocuous transmitters, had them packed into precisely the same boxes as the other perfectly legitimate spares for a private jet and shipped using barcodes only Martha would ever be able to identify, to sit in the spare-parts storage units of several emergency airfields in picturesque locations in the United States and Canada. When the time was right, there would be a carton with their own transmitter where they needed it, one that had been sitting there for months or even years. And when the transmitter was plugged in, smartphones and other devices would preferentially connect to it. Anyone connected to one of these transmitters would think they were looking at the internet, but they would actually be seeing the world through an invisible filter. Bywater and Nommik and Sketlish would see something that would encourage them to stay away from the world.

Selah did most of the filter coding herself, with the help of five distributed teams, each of whom thought they were working on different projects that never came to fruition. One team working on "creating fake news" were told they were the black hat—they had to create an apocalypse as real and convincing and hard to detect as possible so that another team's work in deepfake detection could be tested. They were never to know who that team was; they would never hear the results of the tests.

That was twenty MIT and Stanford graduates lit from within by the glow of righteousness and justice, working long hours in front of their screens for two years, creating a program that would take any footage or any stills of any city in the world and morph their contents to show an appalling pandemic in progress. They used artificial intelligence programs to write posts, alter posts, insert new items into photographs, tweak the world in large and small ways.

"Fucking love it," said Selah, standing in front of a screen where an innocuous tourist photo of a couple in front of the pyramid at the Louvre was transformed seamlessly into a terrifying image of police attacking pigeons with a flamethrower.

"We were inspired by *28 Days Later*, obviously," said the team lead, an earnest twenty-seven-year-old named Bradley. "We decided we'd get some amazing visuals if the next great plague came from animals. Like the Black Death!"

He showed her his modeling. How fast a plague like that would spread. What would have to happen for it to have erupted on several continents almost simultaneously. The 2020 novel coronavirus had given them lots to play with, but they'd made it much worse in a dozen different ways.

There was something Bradley found satisfying in imagining this plague, Selah could tell. Zimri was the same. To imagine the destruction of mankind, the terrible end of things, the flame and blood and pain and death . . . was that the satisfaction? A kind of sadism? Or a masochism? The conscience acting on the self, saying, "This is what you deserve, this is what you earned." Maybe. A man driven to commit and then cheat again and again is a man who does not believe he deserves to be known.

"Mate," Selah said, "this is perfect. They'll never know the difference."

Bradley frowned. "I hope they will. Otherwise . . . you know . . . we're all fucked?"

More than you know, my friend. Your own filters aren't letting you see how deeply we're all fucked.

Albert had worked a long time earlier on a now-defunct project to create a virtual gaming suit.

"Virtual sex suit, you mean," said Selah, and Albert admitted that the adult gaming market had been a large part of their business plan. There were parts inside the suit that . . . swelled and other parts that . . . became soft, and further parts that grew and yielded and vibrated and—

"Yeah, yeah," said Selah, "you were making a suit for grown men who literally want to crawl back inside their mummy's vag. Which is all men. Except the gay ones, sorry."

"None taken," said Albert.

The project had hit some snags to do with costs. There was no price point they could make the thing for that was less than it would cost to hire a practically infinite number of real women to do all the things the suit might do for you, or to you.

"What about the *gaming aspect*, Albert?" said Selah.

"Turns out not a lot of people want to actually feel what it's like to really be a soldier, I guess?" he said.

The "mixed reality" capacity was already present in the suit prototypes. If you were looking through the visor, it would look as if you were seeing the real world, but in fact you'd be seeing whatever the suit wanted you to.

"So we add in like . . . plant and animal recognition for the region? We already know what region they're going to, so that's not too difficult. Instructions about how to survive there, ditto. Load up a bunch of entertainment. Use a standard Anvil service personality type with voice recognition." Selah was nodding, checking off a mental list.

"Yeah." She smiled. "Yeah, it's doable. We'll need some more assets but it's doable. The thing is, it looks like it would work in any situation, but actually it only needs to work in this one really controlled situation. So we can do it. And if we want to fiddle with it while they're in play, we can always do an overnight update via satellite, or even augment it or interact with it in real time. Not harder than real-time drone updates, and Zimri's people do that every fucking day."

The place wasn't hard to decide on. The FutureSafe zones were no-fly areas; they wouldn't see aircraft in the sky, so they wouldn't try to signal. Admiral Huntsy Island was the most remote FutureSafe in the portfolio.

"We'll set the video drones to avoid the areas they've been. It'll be pretty simple," said Selah. "We edit that shit anyway. Zimri's taken me to visit a couple of the FutureSafe zones already; he uses them for corporate entertaining. Online users always think they've seen everything—you'd have to have the top-level security to notice that the drones are avoiding some areas or playing yesterday's footage sometimes."

"I can fix that," said Martha. "It'll just be me. I already have the island set up for . . . long-term survival."

Martha waited for the others to cotton on.

"No," said Badger. "You turned a *wildlife sanctuary* into a bunker?"

"There's a reason we're doing this," said Martha.

Badger pulled a carrot stick out of a container in their bag and munched furiously.

"Fuckers," they said. "If we don't do this now, they'll be destroyed by bloody revolution in a decade."

"Good point. We're helping them, really," said Selah.

Organizing a disappearing plane was somewhat complex. Albert was a pilot—he could fly the plane, he could get it into place, turn off the transponder, bail out with a parachute, leave remote pilot software to fly it on a few more hundred miles, then bank sharply.

"You *want* to do that?" asked Badger.

"I'm in extra time anyway," said Albert, "might as well have some fun."

There were targeted explosives that could make the plane look like it was being taken down from the outside while giving the passengers plenty of time to escape. Tricky. Easy for someone to get injured or even die. But safe enough that they could tell themselves no one would *need* to die.

AUGR was the last part to fall into place. They'd been looking for something like it for a while—something that would convince these people to get on that plane, to do it quietly and secretly, to cover their own tracks. Martha had found it at a technology incubator. The inventor, Si Packship, was trying to make predictive tactical military software—but the military make their own stuff, and all he really wanted was to be bought up. Martha reoriented him: What if, instead of trying to predict enemy movements, the software analyzed the current tactical situation in detail, offering combat options an operator might otherwise miss? What if that prediction element could be oriented in a different way? Toward the consumer market, toward people who want to know when bad things are on the way?

Si Packship had said: "I don't think AUGR is going to be able to do what you want AUGR to do."

And Martha had said: "Don't worry about it. Really, just don't worry about it. All we need is a 'proof of concept.' You know? Like when you want to show what your software will do but it doesn't do that yet, so you commission a little animation to show it working?"

"You want an . . . animation from me?"

"Lenk Sketlish is very personally interested in this project. I want something I can show him so that he will invest in the project, and then we can get it to do what we want it to do."

"Isn't this how Elizabeth Holmes got, um . . . in trouble with Theranos? Making it look like it could do something it couldn't do?"

"Really, don't worry. Lenk is more of a kinetic, tactile learner. This will help make it real for him."

Poor rich Si Packship, he had really tried his hardest to make AUGR what Martha wanted it to be. The tactical analysis part used the iterative game mechanic, a billion beads through a billion matchboxes: How could you escape from danger in this locked car? In this garage? In this convenience store? In this children's play park? Again and again users and testers telling the machine whether it had gotten it right, spotted things that could be used successfully to defeat an assailant, to hide, to get away faster. That part was always going to be the impressive and convincing part: put it on someone's phone, wait for them to be in danger.

"But my mom is literally *never* in danger?" said Badger. "I mean, that's her whole thing."

"It'll be Lenk," said Martha. "He had himself kidnapped by a gang of eight bikers once just to see how he'd cope. Gave them a six-month window to do it anytime he was alone."

"Fuck. What happened?"

Martha shook her head. "He used the safe word two hours in. To get to a conference call on time."

Selah laughed her throaty laugh. "What a dick."

So this was the plan. They'd give them AUGR; they'd all be convinced by Lenk managing to escape some fake kidnapping. And because the first part had worked, they'd believe the second part would work too.

But as it turned out, they hadn't needed a fake kidnapping when they had a real assassin.

Martha Einkorn had given AUGR to her lover, and then a person motivated by internet conspiracy theories had followed Lai Zhen into a crowded mall in Singapore and opened fire. AUGR had gotten Lai Zhen out, had kept her safe. And when Lenk Sketlish, Ellen Bywater, and Zimri Nommik had reviewed the photographs and video files and seen what AUGR had done, they believed in AUGR. Not just with their money, which was relatively easy to extract from them, but with that rarest of all commodities: their trust.

The money had never been the point. Finding Si Packship, polishing his presentation, securing the investment, none of this had been what Martha and Badger, Selah and Albert needed for their plan. It was just window dressing, all there to make the thing look convincing. What they needed was to know that Ellen, Lenk, and Zimri would actually get on the plane when the AUGR alert tripped. And after the billionaires looked at the footage from the

Seasons Time Mall, they saw what AUGR could do and what it could save them from. They trusted AUGR. Perhaps more than they trusted any living person. So everything was ready.

And then all that had been needed was The Future. That was what they called it between themselves—The Future—although it wasn't really a "future" per se and it was composed of more than seventeen hundred individual bets and short stock positions. It was a bet like a prophecy, based on knowing precisely what was going to happen. And it had to look as though it hadn't come from them.

Placing the Future had taken some time and trouble; Selah and Albert had set it up through a series of 127 different holding and shell companies, investing their considerable fortunes in hedge funds and venture capital associations, buying up certain stocks and—most importantly—shorting certain other stocks. The Future they created would do extremely well if, within a certain brief window, the stock of Fantail, Medlar, and Anvil fell dramatically and suddenly.

The only way to really control the future is if you're the one making it happen. As the terrible news came through of a disappeared plane, in every stock market on the planet certain beads ran through certain matchboxes and the messages they represented moved around certain amounts of stock and money. All anyone could say afterward was that some people had become very rich that day but it was never entirely clear who.

2. we will never know the whole story

"The world now is different from the way it was just three years ago," said the journalist. "How much of that do you think is down to you?"

Martha was appearing via glittering holographic video-link at the Seasons Time Mall in Singapore. The mall had turned its concrete-and-steel roof into a dedicated green space for nesting birds and other wildlife. Many cities had embraced these projects now, especially with the Fantail funding available. It wasn't one of the important infrastructure projects—the thing that really moved the needle for wildlife and habitat extension was the huge and growing network of FutureSafe zones. But it sent a message: the largest mall in the world was now turning its real estate into the largest rooftop wildlife sanctuary in the world. Each of these things added up, each of them changed the public mood a little, each of them made it clearer what cities always ought to have been.

"I think we can't put any of that down to me," said Martha. "Really, Fantail has been led by the public mood. I think sometimes when terrible things happen, we're driven to make them mean something. I've been proud to be part of that process."

Things had gotten better. After the plane had vanished, things had improved, at first slowly in fragments and then rapidly and in unison. There had been a realignment of priorities at Fantail, at Medlar, and at Anvil. And subsequent to that, there had been a realignment of priorities in the world. There was a growing interest—even a relish—for doing dramatic and fast things to solve the world environmental crises. There was support for the expansion of the FutureSafe zones to join up large tracts of land and for people to live in those zones—if they lived there at all—by putting the animals and the balance of the natural world first. If you want to live in a city, people said, enjoy the city. But cities are not wild. The wild needs our respect. There was a growing belief that perhaps you owned things by having a responsibility to them as well as having access to them. There was a general move away from polarizing debates, toward the sense that everyone would have to learn to make a little room for one another. It had happened strangely fast, given everything. As if that plane going down had ended a certain line of logic and people had gone suddenly sane.

Zimri Nommik's widow, Selah Nommik, had taken charge of the company immediately—she and Zimri together owned more than 80 percent of it anyway. And Anvil's stock was in free fall after the three billionaires vanished. She'd stabilized day-to-day decision-making, and six months after the three of them had disappeared without trace, when the FBI had concluded their investigations with the presumption that the plane had sunk to the bottom of the ocean, Selah Nommik had begun proceedings to have Zimri declared legally dead. For the good of the company, for the good of the world economy, it had been agreed within the year. They had flown on a private plane on a registered flight plan that it appeared they hadn't followed. There had been thorough searches across wide areas: a radius of hundreds of miles from their last known position. No wreckage had been found; no signs of life could be discovered. If those three people were still alive, one of them would have found a way to let someone know. They were dead.

Selah Nommik was not Zimri. Unlike him, she had been uninterested in fighting the various legal battles around the world to stop competition and monopoly authorities from doing what the law told them. She agreed to break Anvil up into eighteen separate constituent parts—some of them directly competing with one another and some allowing space for other competitors into the market. She made a very beautiful statement to the media saying that what she had learned above all from the Tech Plane Tragedy was that the world couldn't afford to have all its eggs in one basket, ever. She broke the company up, and then started to give it away. She made vast cash donations to good causes large and small—but she also gave parts of the company itself away wholesale. The web services arm was turned over to a charitable foundation, all of whose profits would go to preserving wild places around the world. The food-and-grocery-delivery business became a nonprofit, taking money from wealthy people buying artisanal yogurt and plowing it into at-cost, healthy, entirely plant-composed meals around the world. She bought land and preserved it as larger and larger wildlife sanctuaries. With the approval of the governments of Nepal, Bhutan, Thailand, and Indonesia, she installed Anvil's drones to protect the last wild tigers in the vast areas of wild land she'd bought up. The drones tased without mercy and dragged the poachers out by their feet. The population of wild tigers began to increase. With the new technologies it started to seem less and less important that humans should be able to tramp these FutureSafe zones with their own feet. Leave the tiger places for the tigers.

Fantail had cycled rapidly through three interim CEOs, each ably assisted by Martha Einkorn, Lenk Sketlish's right-hand woman, who had shot to prominence after the disappearance for her sheer levelheadedness. And for the surprisingly large number of shares Lenk had left her—larger than the proportion he'd left to his children—and for the control he'd given her of his children's trust until the children were thirty-five years old. His ex-wives got nothing. Martha Einkorn, evidently, had been the person he trusted. And after trying out their COO, their CFO, and then a former CFO of Anvil who lasted less than a month, the board decided to trust Martha too.

She had followed Selah Nommik's lead in directing Lenk's legacy toward global good. She spoke about Badger Bywater's idea of "enclosures," that this money had been made from public property and ought to go to the benefit of future generations.

Fantail was not a wholly controlled company like Anvil. But at the same time, Anvil's pivot had changed the atmosphere around giant technological megacorporations. Competition authorities were emboldened; governments had seen the tax and economic benefits of the breakup. The public mood had changed once they saw that turning Anvil into eighteen different companies hadn't meant that they weren't able to get their laundry detergent delivered. The voters, slowly but surely around the world, were starting to vote for more radical policies on environmental protection. Even an analysis of comments on various social media networks showed that there had been a subtle but almost instant alteration in tone after the Tech Plane vanished. No one could say how it had happened, precisely. There was just a change in the wind.

Fantail managed to avoid the major breakup by spinning off its own subsidiaries and by working with local communities. There was the LenkRacer—he'd always been interested in cars, in new technology, and this fast electric self-driving car was a beautiful homage to his legacy. Fantail worked with governments across the world on RacerMonth—a monthlong shutdown of the streets of cities with a huge work-crew installing the infrastructure for the new electric cars. They sold it as a lockdown, but with a wonderful goal in sight. Car owners were offered a trade:

turn in your old gas or diesel car in exchange for lifetime access to the LenkRacer system via your choice of app.

You locked down for between a week and a month at home, and when you came out the streets were quiet, the air was clean, the children were safe to play. With the car-sharing system, only one-quarter the number of vehicles were needed. The streets weren't clogged. There was room for bicycles and tricycles to pedal through the quiet roads. Working town by town, city district by district, and state by state, they converted most of the world within nineteen months. Every year, 1.3 million people didn't die in road traffic accidents. Every year, 7 million people didn't die from air pollution. Once it was over, it was hard to believe we'd ever been willing to sacrifice that many people to the gas engine.

Medlar had followed more slowly. Its board had replaced Ellen Bywater with a male CEO who was a lot *like* Ellen Bywater and he had—as a sop to the tender sensibilities shown by Anvil and Fantail—given a large amount of money to the Bywater Foundation for the Arts. They'd invested in Indigenous art and a concert series broadcast online. But as time had gone on, Ellen's child Badger Bywater had become a leader among the shareholders, encouraging the customers and investors in Medlar to demand the company do something more impressive. Supported by three obscure investment funds that now owned around 17 percent of Medlar, the board was pressured to lead the world in repairable, recyclable technology. Albert Dabrowski gladly took charge of the project, which everyone felt was a very nice gesture of unity.

It had gone like this, in small but incremental steps. The great wealth of the world's technology companies had changed tack—instead of hurtling unthinkingly toward ever more profit, they decided to think primarily about the kind of world they would leave behind. Other companies followed their lead. The deaths of Ellen Bywater, Lenk Sketlish, and Zimri Nommik came to stand for a growth of corporate responsibility. The white rhino and the elephant and the snow leopard were saved. The rain forests advanced across the barren lands by two thousand meters a year in each direction. Grabbing the dry soil and turning it rich and dark, sending up the great trees into the canopy, sucking the carbon from the atmosphere and holding it underground. A spongy algae developed by Lenk Sketlish in a side project was growing in great plastic-eating masses, leaching the poisons out of the waters and returning the nutrients to the system. The coral was living again, the new growth encircling the dead, bleached bones of the old. Things weren't perfect but there was, fundamentally, a little less despair and a little more hope.

"No," said Martha Einkorn, "I can't take responsibility for this. We all did this, all of us together."

The journalist—a young Botswanan woman—smiled warmly.

"If you don't mind my asking, what do you think about the conspiracy theories online? Do you follow any of that?"

"Conspiracy theories?" said Martha.

"You know. There's an UrbanDox theory that says that a group of powerful 'cultural Marxists' got together to somehow . . . deliberately disappear the Tech Plane?"

Martha shook her head and kept smiling. "There will always be people who can't accept the truth," she said. "Accidents just happen. When people have done as much as Zimri, Ellen, or Lenk, there can be an idea that they are or should be immortal. But none of us is immortal. No one could have made them get into that plane against their will. There was some accident. We will never know the whole story. But I think that Lenk would be proud of what we've accomplished in his name and his memory."

This was what Martha had learned long ago. That for

a person to disappear can catalyze something. Even one person's vanishing can be enough to call an entire project into question. It just has to be the right person at the right moment. And the eventual effect of a destructive force is measured by what, precisely, it destroys.

"What do you think he would say if he were here today?"

"You know," said Martha, "I grew up in a very religious way. I used to not like to talk about that, but it's part of my story as much as anything else. My father was a deeply religious man. He used to say that none of us is ever truly gone. The earth doesn't cease to have a use for our flesh and bones. Our stories and what was good in our character are taken up by others. So I don't believe he's really gone. As to what Lenk would say? He'd say what he always said: 'What can we do next, Martha? What's on the way?' "

There was a gentle laugh at this. Martha rode the moment to announce the acquisition of seven new FutureSafe zones in Asia, each of which was more than three hundred square miles. The applause clattered like raindrops.

The interview over, Martha took off her headset and stretched. Outside the window in the crisp of the morning, a flock of black-headed geese flew around the glass block in V formation, honking against the day. They circled three times, their wings like arrows pointing the way toward the future. On the far shore of the lake the maple trees were giving up their red leaves, as if the color in them was their life, bursting outward so exuberantly that they popped. In the lake swam the golden and the dark fish, curled like question marks, venturing and snapping in the light and in the shadow. Outside the window, the world was in motion. Inside the room the air was as still as the dawn and as swollen with possibility.

What would Lenk think? He had thought he was so clever, Lenk, and he had figured out so much. Of course, yes, she had faked the inert submunition dispenser to take down his plane. Of course this had been planned in advance, and obviously it had been she who'd planned it. Of course it hadn't been a coincidence that they landed on Admiral Huntsy, an uninhabited island equipped for survival. He'd just never stepped back far enough to ask the really big question: Had the apocalypse ever even happened?

3. a mechanical centaur

Martha had learned so much from Enoch, and one of the most important lessons was: don't look back, look forward. And yet. Surely it was safe now.

The gnat drone cameras on Admiral Huntsy Island circled the jungle in clusters, in prearranged patterns hour by hour, swooping and swirling, photographing and recording. They filmed the undersides of each leaf, the movement of the insects on the mottled bark, the texture of the crumbling soil underfoot. Through the proprietary Fantail platform and a virtual-reality headset, Fantail users could explore this rich jungle environment for hours. Except for certain areas where it would be too sensitive to send the drones due to the breeding and nesting patterns of some rare species of bird and the delicate ecosystem of plants and microscopic life.

Fantail provided a new version of the island to explore once a week—there was more to observe there than a single user could take in, even if they spent all their days on the island, which some did. Fantail users watched the seasons pass in this gloriously rich environment. They had no way to access the hidden parts of the map, and no complaints that the island was only updated weekly.

Martha stepped through the gaps in space and time, unlocking the portions of the map that Selah Nommik had carefully partitioned off years earlier. She had never done this before. There had been too much to do, and she had wondered whether seeing Lenk would trigger something in her—pity, compassion, guilt—that would prove too painful to manage. In the quiet of her home, now, late at night, Martha Einkorn inputted the special codes, showed her face and her fingerprints to her device, and walked into the parts of the jungle that no Fantail user would ever be able to see. The places where Lenk Sketlish lived.

In the world of illusions, Martha walked the jungle.

Once upon a time, long ago, another Martha had walked a forest like this one. Her father had left her in the forest and she had killed a bear to survive. She had understood then that nature will sometimes throw up a totally destructive force: a bear that might kill you and yet receive no nourishment. Lenk and the others could have been left to gnaw on the world until it was blackened and splintered and they themselves would not have had a drop of nutrition or joy from the process. The bear has to be taken out in one blow and left in the woods.

It was, of course, trivially easy to ask the drones to find Lenk Sketlish in real time and follow him. In the imaginary jungle, Martha padded forward softly, finding that she was holding her breath as if he were an exotic and dangerous animal, easy to startle and hard to escape. There was no scent to the jungle but there was sound—the birds, screeching, startled from one tree to the next; the thrum and tap of the busy lives in every tree trunk. For many long moments Martha Einkorn was too mesmerized to remember, quite, why she had come here.

And there he was. Lenk Sketlish, long and less lean than he'd once been. He had developed a mildly rounded belly, the sign of peaceful living and a body taking on a little extra just to be sure. He was wearing the legs of his survival suit like goatskins, the top part bent back with its arms extended to the ground to form a second set of legs behind him for stability. He looked like a strange god, a mechanical centaur, reaching into the tree for a ripe, brown, bruised fruit, turning it in his hand and tasting it.

Martha smiled to see him. If she could have chosen any end for Enoch, this would have been it. Thinking this, she knew in her heart why she had stayed away for so long. She had been afraid that she might have seen Enoch's fate here—the smoke, the ash, the burning, falling and rising from and into the sky. But Lenk was happy. Healthy and free, like any creature released into the wild after a long confinement.

She followed him through his paradise. It was the season for certain kinds of nuts and he'd tied large oilcloths between the trees, the more easily to gather them as they fell—chasing off the squirrels and rodents who were after his harvest. He looked younger as he worked, in a sense younger even than when she'd met him. There are some of us, she thought, who always wanted and needed to be Fox; people who sought the new without pause, who could only be satisfied with a life of constant movement. Do we drive relentlessly toward the future because we don't wander the world anymore? She wanted to say this to him, to ask: "Do you know how happy you are and how well this suits you?" And so she was startled when he said, suddenly: "Yes."

"Yes," said Lenk Sketlish. "Yes, a good harvest. Not bad at all. What do you think?"

And the suit, the second head dangling close to the ground, said: "Pretty good, sport, get those stored away nicely."

Lenk said: "How many people do you think we could feed from the harvest this year?"

The suit said: "From what you've gathered? Thirty or forty people easily."

"If they come this winter then, there'll be plenty to feed them?"

"Oh yes," said the suit. "If they come this winter, they'll eat very well."

Lenk nodded and Martha wanted to say: "Who do you think is coming?"

But she knew who he thought was coming. There had

been an apocalypse and he was prepared to wait. In his belief, someone would be coming at some point. People would arrive here and he would be able to show them his stores and they would tell him that he was brave and brilliant. That was what he'd been waiting for all his life.

She followed him farther. Down to the south and the east, following the line of the river. He had laid strands of rippled vine-rope in the shallows, and the dark skeins were pocked with a kind of white-shelled clam, orange flesh just visible within. He hauled up some of the ropes and gathered only as many as he needed—fifteen, enough for supper—and then turned to walk back to his autumn camp through the dark woods.

Martha walked alongside him, falling into step with his easy loping pace.

She said, aloud: "You are good at this. You always knew you would be."

Lenk looked to his right, and for a moment she felt he was bashful, turning from the compliment. And then he took a step to the right and vanished.

Martha stopped still. The jungle continued to move around her, green and gold, russet and auburn. The birds clattered from tree to tree. The nuts fell like bright raindrops. No Lenk.

"Reload," she said. "Fantail, reload the simulation."

The world flickered around her and returned. No Lenk.

"Fantail," she said, "where is Lenk Sketlish?"

"Lenk Sketlish is not on the map," said the assistant in warm, friendly female tones.

"He was just on the map a moment ago," said Martha. "Where is Lenk Sketlish?"

"I don't have that information. I'm sorry."

He'd turned to the right. He'd walked a pace to the right. Martha turned to the right. She walked a pace to the right. There was a tiny ripple in the world. The trees continued to sway in the gentle wind above. A spider processed steadily up the corrugated bark.

"Fantail," said Martha, "which version of Admiral Huntsy Island am I in?"

"You are viewing the public archive of Admiral Huntsy last updated three days, six hours, and twenty-two minutes ago."

"But a moment ago I was in the secure version of Admiral Huntsy Island."

Fantail did not understand her. She had to flip her visor up and manually force a reload. Still nothing. The pace to the left took her back into the secure version. The pace to the right took her into the publicly available version of the island.

Suddenly, a way along the path in front of her, Lenk Sketlish reappeared. He had taken a short detour into the woods to her right and vanished into an invisible section of the island. Now he was back, whistling as he horse-strolled toward his camp with a sack full of ripe nuts clacking on his shoulder.

With half an hour of careful work, Martha could see quite clearly which portion of the island had been excised from view. She wouldn't have noticed it if Lenk hadn't vanished in that way—it had all been quite seamlessly done. If she'd just been wandering, if he'd taken a different path, she would have walked from the public to the secure versions of the island without ever seeing the joins. But now she looked for it, there it was. A one-hundred-square-mile section in the south of the island—about eight miles wide, about twelve miles long—was not updating in real time like the rest of the island. There was the carefully doctored weekly drone footage, of course, set like the rest of the island to scour any hint of human habitation. So the drones were still humming through that section in drowsy masses, recording.

Martha spoke to the Fantail systems in all the ways she understood. She gave it her keys and codes—the passphrases that unlocked the rest of the island, that let her follow Lenk Sketlish. Fantail accepted the passcodes but did not unlock. She was not a technological expert but she ran the diagnostic functions she understood. Nothing. She chewed her lower lip.

An hour later in her garden at home, the warblers and the red-winged blackbirds thronged to her bird feeder, each as recognizable as if they had been badged by a branding expert. Martha watched their attentive heads tipping to one side and then another. Looking for the neighborhood cat and for the bright berries in the bush.

She thought: I have been taken in by the world of symbols. I have mistaken the map for the territory. Me of all people.

She thought for a while, and then she called Badger.

"There's a part of the island that's not responding properly to my passcodes," she said. "Do you have any idea what's going on there?"

Badger said: "Oh." And then stopped. Badger was not good with lying.

Martha said: "Is there something you want to tell me?"

Badger said: "Listen, I told them at the time that if you asked me directly, I would tell you the truth, OK? So are you asking me directly?"

Martha said: "I think I am."

Badger said: "OK then."

4. this was not supposed to happen

Just after the Tech Plane disappeared, Albert Dąbrowski's phone had rung at 5 a.m. Someone had activated AUGR.

This was not supposed to happen. He was deep in sleep, had to wring the dreams out of himself like the last drops from a twisted towel. He rolled over in the big bed where Mike was always—these days—not. He reached for his phone, looked at the alert, and said aloud: "Shit."

It was a difficult time. Albert had gotten to his yacht and then his beach house in Hawaii without drawing attention to himself. Even with all the technology money could buy, it hadn't been easy. The plane had gone down a little over seventy-two hours earlier and the news had inevitably reached the press. The windows of silence had expired; Zimri's assistant and Lenk's ex-wives and Ellen's administrative team had been expecting to hear from them. Martha in particular was now supposed to be working to stabilize Fantail at the same time that she was working with rescue coordinators. Selah was playing the terrified, desperate wife—at the same time working through several layers of shell companies to buy up the plummeting stock of Fantail, Anvil, and Medlar. Someone needed to babysit the group on the island, make sure they were in no immediate danger, ensure that the technology wasn't glitching. That, obviously, was Badger to an extent and in particular Albert, who was the only one under very little scrutiny right now.

The babysitting had been, thus far, mostly administering some sleeping drugs through the suits, making the machines sound comforting and human, checking that the story the suits were selling them was convincing and seamless. It had gone, roughly, according to plan.

- three billionaires on a remote island convinced that the apocalypse had happened
- three billionaires not in imminent danger, willingly accepting drugs to help them sleep and recover, becoming uncertain about how many days had passed
- three billionaires not currently highly motivated to try to contact the outside world or regain access to it
- world looking for the three billionaires in exactly the wrong place

Check, check, check, and check.

And now this. An alert on Albert's phone saying that an AUGR instance had been activated in . . . he had to search the internet to find out where Prince Rupert was. Middle of ass-end of nowhere, western coast of Canada. Must be a glitch. Who the hell in the ass-end of nowhere had a copy of the most expensive and secret software currently in existence? Place meant nothing. Send a holding message via AUGR: stand by.

He checked the permissions. The names and idents passed by the phone to the software and the software to him. This AUGR instance had been reported destroyed by an external team in Bucharest. And here it was being activated again by . . . Lai Zhen. The woman Martha had been seeing.

"Oh fuck," Albert said. "Oh fuck fuck fuck."

Badger, when Albert contacted them, agreed.

"We can't call Martha with this," they said.

"Martha gave it to her."

"We know Martha gave it to her, *Albert*. Lai Zhen is the woman from the footage by the air conditioner. The proof it works. I've met her, she's cool actually. She's just not supposed to *still have it*."

"Maybe she stole it back without Martha knowing," said Albert.

"Maybe Martha let her reactivate it."

"Fuck."

"I agree with that assessment," said Badger.

"You seriously think Martha could have done this on purpose?"

"Not *this* this. Maybe she was happy for her to have the protection."

"Fuck."

Albert and Badger called Selah.

Selah said: "Fuck. Piss, toss, arse. Martha fell in love with her."

"So in love with her that she told her about the plan?" said Badger.

"She wouldn't. There is no way she told a journalist about the plan," said Selah.

"Love is the mind killer," said Albert. "Especially early on. I told Mike a bunch of things no one else knew."

"What does AUGR think is happening?" said Selah.

"AUGR only knows what we tell it," said Badger. "It thinks the world is ending and she's part of the program. It wants to evacuate her."

"So that's what we're going to have to do," said Selah. "She's part of the AUGR protocol just like I am, just like you are, Badger. She's going to get evacuated just like we were, right?"

"But . . . there isn't an AUGR protocol."

In the middle of this conversation, Albert's phone pinged. Martha had given him her log-ins to her personal Fantail for the duration of these events—just to help with managing the PR side, to deal with things she'd have no time for. There, on Martha's account, was a message from Lai Zhen.

Is this real? I've had an AUGR activation.

"What the fuck do I do with this?" said Albert.

"We have to use it," said Selah. "Albert, you're the only one no one's watching. You need to get her out of there somehow. Make her think she's really being evacuated by the program if you have to. This could fuck everything."

"Christ, what, like, send her to the island?"

"Maybe that's OK," said Badger. "Maybe it makes it look, like, more real?"

Albert thought: I have brought this on myself. And actually, fuck you, Martha, you've brought this on yourself too. This is what happens when someone gets pulled back into life. Life is fucking messy.

It's real, he sent back from Martha's account. **I didn't know it'd ping you.**

He told Badger and Selah he'd handle it. That he had an idea of what to do. He called the team who looked after the Medlar jet in Honolulu. He needed to leave, immediately.

5. an extended sabbatical

At moments like this, Martha tended to become outwardly quite calm. There would be time for screaming later. Right now, there was a bear in the forest.

"So you're saying," she said, "that you sent Zhen to the island?"

"We've kept her safe," said Badger. "We looked after her. When she needed medicine we did an overnight drop of antibiotics and then sent her to get it as if it was a buried cache of supplies. Literally, it was a UTI, OK, and we fixed it."

"You sent her to the island, and you kept it secret from me for *three years*?"

Martha had gone to look for Zhen after the Tech Plane Tragedy had died down—of course she had. But more than a year had gone past, and Zhen's friend Marius had announced via her sites that she was taking "an extended sabbatical" from her online business. Which had made Martha sad in an iron, cold way that she was used to. This was of course what happened. People moved on if you left them long enough. Probably she'd found a new girlfriend. She'd sent Zhen a couple of tentative messages and then left it. Certain kinds of happiness weren't going to be part of Martha's life, and while she wasn't exactly reconciled to it, she was at least used to it. Her feelings now she knew that Zhen hadn't—in fact—ghosted her right back were complex. A rich text.

Selah Nommik was opening an Anvil FutureSafe zone on the French, Swiss, and Italian border, joining up several smaller national parks and forming part of the great wildlife travel corridor they were constructing piece by piece across Europe. She was in an eco lodge in Vanoise, the pines sharp swords against the sky behind her.

"Mate," said Selah, "she was your Achilles' heel. You fell in love with her. If you'd known we'd sent her there, you would have closed the whole thing down. We couldn't risk it."

"Were you . . . planning to let me know? At some point?"

Selah smiled her wide, disarming smile.

"We wanted to come up with a plausible exit strategy for her. You know. Give it a few years and then make it seem like she'd come up with a way to get off the island herself."

"With the story of what she'd seen there? Come on."

"We hadn't figured it out yet. Seriously, we were *actively* working on it."

Albert Dabrowski was at home when Martha Einkorn banged on his back door and then let herself in, as she'd done all those years ago to haul him back into the world.

He said: "I've heard."

"You knew. You fucking knew and you didn't tell me."

Albert said: "This whole situation is fucked up and it's a fucked-up way to deal with it and I'm sorry but she was just one person."

This was what they'd said to themselves when they started. In terms of saving the whole planet, what is the smallest number of people you'd need to get rid of to move the needle? What is the smallest number of lies? Could you take an eraser and just remove three or four people and that would fix everything? It had seemed almost the same thing when they'd talked about it then—three people or four people.

They had managed to find another CrashJacket, and to piece together another survival suit. Not as perfect as the others—some of the molding was still visible inside from the suit's previous purpose. They had drugged her and put her into the safest technology they had and dropped her over the island.

"You know that wasn't OK, though, right?" said Martha.

"Yes," said Albert, "but the world was dying and we didn't know what else to do."

"Let me see her."

6. whether there might be one good man in sodom

In the virtual island, Martha watched Zhen. The world had been dying and they'd saved it and the cost was—what—a few people living in relative luxury in an island paradise? If there had been another fast way to do it, someone else would have found it. Sometimes it really is down to you, a branch, and your fast reflexes.

Zhen seemed, as far as one could tell, happy enough. As happy as a person could be when they thought the world had ended—which in Zhen's case was a great deal less happy than in Lenk's. Zhen muttered to herself as she wandered from place to place. She talked to the suit, and sometimes the suit had been Selah or Badger or Albert talking back to her. So, almost a person. Zhen seemed lonely—that was the truth.

On the island, Zhen banked her fire in the fumeless hearth and roasted a crispy-skinned fish over the red flickering logs. She evidently found a particular kind of grub that lived in the bark of a yellow-leafed tree especially delicious. Martha watched, fascinated, as Zhen popped several grubs out of their hardened, heat-mottled pink membranes and swallowed them. Then Martha felt dirty and turned it off. She was never going to learn what she wanted to know this way.

Martha listened again to the DaySave of her first meeting with Zhen. To their conversations, to the moment when Zhen said: "I'm so sorry I'm late, it was just . . . it was just unavoidable." To herself saying: "I guess you're going to have to find some way to make it up to me." How had she dared to talk like that? She'd never been that way, before or since. She wondered whether Zhen had ever listened to it again.

The question is how much one is prepared to tolerate. The question is how many unintended casualties are too many. The question is whether there might be one good man in Sodom.

7. just remember that you can

There was a day when Zhen woke before dawn. The suit, sensing the change in her breath and movement, turned on illuminated panels in the faceplate showing temperature, weather predictions, wind speed, miles walked yesterday. She muttered the command words that turned the visor clear again. She looked out through her own reflection at the dark jungle.

The moon was so bright that it cast crisp shadows of the canopy overhead onto the jungle floor. The watery smear of the Milky Way was clearly visible. If she were to turn her headlamps on, she'd see a thousand glittering eyes of insects. But she didn't turn them on. In the distance she heard the whoops and crashes of monkeys. Sometimes when she slept fastened to a branch, those monkeys ran straight over her, taking her prone form for another outgrowth of the jungle.

In a way, she was. She had just taken the very long way around. She'd never thought she'd feel safe in this jungle. But the jungle was knowable. It was trustworthy in a way that Lenk, Ellen, and Zimri never were. There had been a great storm, but the storm had passed.

In the three years since Lenk walked away from her, she had learned the affordances of her empire. She had come to recognize the birds that migrate in their season and the fish that rise to shore in their time. She'd noticed that year by year there were more birds and more fish. The suit confirmed that she was right. The air was cleaner. Less plastic and metal debris washing up on the beach. So something had gone well.

The suit had guided her to stick to the south and east of the island.

"So I can avoid the others?" Zhen had asked.

"This part of the island is best," it had said. "The fishing is best here. There are good places to hunt and to sleep."

Sometimes on the horizon she noted something that might have been the dark smoke of a hastily concealed cook fire, before the fume convertor on the StowtBox stove kicked in. Once on a very still day she thought she heard the sound of a musical instrument—something with plucked strings—from a distant shore. But that would be at least twenty-five miles away. It seemed unlikely.

Still, she took inspiration and asked the suit to help her construct a kind of guitar from carefully sawed and planed wood, strings made from the intestine of one of the largest animals on the island, a kind of antelope. The whole project, from hunting the antelope to constructing a kiln to dry the wood, to varnishing the final instrument, took the best part of a year.

She had come to know these hundred or so square miles well and yet there was still so much to learn. She had a summer home and a winter home, a spring hunting ground and an autumn foraging place. From her vantage point she could span with her eyes the forests and the rivers, the reddened cliffs and the speckled shore; a place she had made hers by knowing it and caring for it. There was time for everything, but there was always more that could be done.

It came to her that she could live here for the rest of her natural life if she had to. Eating roots and tubers and small roasted mammals. She could learn and practice new physical skills; she could become a climber, a spear fisher. She could study languages and crafting skills—the suit had courses for every conceivable self-improvement project. She could delve into astronomy, zoology, botany, and earth sciences. Might even make some discoveries, here in this biodiverse wild. The suit had all the music, art, literature, performance she could ever want. It had downloaded tens of millions of pages from key internet sites. Wikipedia. Various how-to sites. History and debate. Even gossip and argument. All the nonsense of her previous life.

Zhen had read—by this time—all of Name The Day. She'd found OneCorn's posts. It hadn't been a hard code to crack who OneCorn was, and she understood why those posts were there. She discussed the ideas of Fox and Rabbit with the suit several times—she'd even instructed it to hive off a separate part of its artificial conversation program to debate these ideas with her.

This morning, she thought it through all over again. The point of civilization, the idea of cities, the reason for agriculture. All of this. Was there a point in knowing that we used to be Fox, given that now—apart from some small isolated groups, the Taiga dwellers, the North Sentinel Islanders, some people in Nunatsiavut—everyone was Rabbit? Was looking back just always a bad idea, like it was for Edo and for Orpheus? What was the point of berating ourselves for not being hunter-gatherers anymore? For liking symbolic behaviors like music and drawing and movies and games?

In the stillness of the early dawn, Zhen lifted the visor. There were no more bright green names tracking the caterpillars and the ants and the budding flowers and the slime mold. The world was there. As it is.

And in that moment there was no need for words. There were no more names for anything. She was there as you are there.

Wherever you are, the richness and complexity and inexhaustible, unplumbable thereness of the whole rushes in through your eyes and your ears and your nose and across your skin. Every single thing around you is right there and so are you. The teeming world is right there, and all of it is neither good nor bad, it just is.

It is not possible to express this with symbols. All that the symbols can ever be is a flag in the sand pointing at where to dig. You have found the treasure. It is the world as it is.

Every part of the world pressed in on Zhen as present and as sure as the future had once seemed to her. The sight of crawling things and flying creatures, the sweet scents and the sour ones, the faint taste of cherries on her tongue, the atonal harmonies of the jungle screeches and howls, the intense and beautiful sensation of the suit's interior softness on her skin, too strong and too real and too present for words.

All the words went away.

But the sense that Zhen had in that moment of the whole world around her without names cannot be named. When you try to give it a word, when she thought "flag" and "sand," she fell out of the world and back into symbols. There is no other way. The great evolutionary advantage of human beings is this brain that divides and sorts and names the world. You should not expect to escape it very often. Just remember that you can.

Lai Zhen had once made a video about surviving for years in the deep woods and 8.2 million people had watched it. She had said:

- prepare yourself for uncomfortable living
- make sure you have a good tent
- trap and hunt with a crossbow
- people are going to get desperate
- try to appreciate the natural world around you

But the Lai Zhen who had done those things was gone now.

She turned a series of visor settings off one by one. She didn't need to see the names of the creatures and plants anymore. She knew which stems were good to eat and which were bitter, which low leaves signaled a sweet tuber beneath the earth, which grubs would cook well over a fire to a nutty crunch. She knew the birds and the insects, the soft and the hard rocks, the trees whose wood was good to burn and the trees whose wood was good to build. She'd practiced how to hunt and set traps and build a smokery, how to take the lives of a few slower, older animals, in the way that a fox keeps the rabbits fast and clever. She had made fragrant beeswax candles and chalky fired earthenware pots. She knew which muds would bake to a hard but brittle pottery and which would be thick but sturdy. She remembered as another person the girl who had feared that the mud would swallow her whole.

The suit had taught her as a parent might have taught a child long ago, not to be here as an emergency in case of a disaster, not a place to retreat to out of fear, but as her home. The world as her home, in the way our ancestors were at home in the world once, long ago. It had only taken a global apocalypse, an array of technology, and three years of her life.

That night she stood on the promontory and watched the sunset across the jungle. Red-and-gold mackerel clouds over the tree canopy, then dim embers in the sky and then utter dark. The wordless world was always there now. She had only to dip into it and quench her thirst.

There was no future now; time did not point as an arrow, it was a spiral, around the seasons again and again until one day her bones would sink into the earth and her flesh would go to start some other life again. Well. Good.

8. one last right thing

In the predawn light, a polymer skiff with a flexible solar sail skimmed the water heading toward Admiral Huntsy Island.

No boats were permitted and no aircraft flew overhead, but certain beads had been placed into certain matchboxes and there was a short window in which the skiff's pilot could cross the barrier zone unseen.

The waters were as clear as the sky, a lucent blue, lit from the inside, dazzling and alive. The great underwater trees grew up toward the light, and between their branches, shoals of tiny silver fish glanced this way and that, seeking and being sought. Neither balanced nor out of balance but constantly in motion toward growth or oblivion.

The polymer craft beached on the golden shore and the pilot deployed its three anchor-spars deep into the sands. They burrowed through the silt and splayed their grabbing hooks out deep underneath her feet with a series of satisfying low thunks.

If the pilot were found here, alarms would activate at nearby drone stations. Within eight minutes she would be surrounded by armed flying battle pods with the authority to incapacitate her using electric stunning and remove her bodily from the island. And that would be nothing compared with the almighty fuckup that would happen if Lenk Sketlish spotted her here. However. All of the countermeasures were held at bay for now, for her to try to do one last right thing.

Martha sat on the sand, her heels dug into the silken grains, to watch the sun come up. All the risk meant nothing if she did not risk this, at the last.

9. it felt like danger but she knew it wouldn't kill her

"Someone's waiting at the beach," said the suit.

"Is it Lenk?" said Zhen. "Has he found me?"

"No," said the suit. "Listen, I can't tell you what to do. But I think you should go down to the beach and see who it is."

Zhen remembered the feeling she used to have all the time that there were so many threats in the world and that she would never escape from all of them. That when she ran from the Enochite in the Seasons Time Mall she had had a sense of familiarity and relief, that at last the world matched what she had always expected.

She thought of running, hiding, waiting, spying, attacking. And she thought: No. This world is my home now. And she walked down to the beach.

There was a woman sitting looking at the tide, the stranded colors dark blue and bright blue, inky wash layered over shade. The woman was heavyset, her hair just touching her shoulders and—it had been so long since Zhen had seen Martha that she'd forgotten this feeling, a seemingly inexhaustible source of excitement, even after everything. Even with it all, her stupid fucking heart pounded at seeing Martha.

Zhen looked at Martha and Martha looked at Zhen. They were older now, and each of them had learned more than she'd imagined three years before. Zhen's skin was overwhelmed by the possibilities of human touch, and yet it seemed to her that the chasm between her and the touch of another person was too vast ever to be breached again.

There is a space between one human and another that

we long constantly to close. That is what makes our decisions different from the decisions of the matchboxes and beads. We want to connect one to another; we cannot help ourselves. We cannot live all the days of our lives not trusting in another person. We must leap even if we fall. We must.

Martha said: "It's really good to see you."

Zhen said: "Yeah."

Martha said: "I have some things I need to tell you."

And Zhen said: "No fucking shit."

But still, she listened.

In that last place on Earth, Martha showed Zhen evidence. What had happened to the world and what she had done. She had a labeled dossier—hard copy in a waterproof file and electronic—the documentation of the entire thing from beginning to end. She took Zhen's hand in hers and the touch was like a completed circuit joining Zhen again to the human race. That single touch was so overwhelming it was painful.

Martha showed Zhen the satellite phone and internet connection wired into the skiff. She flipped open a panel on Zhen's survival suit and connected it to the great world of humans talking. Images flooded through the visor faster than thought. The world still out there, the world the same, the world changed.

Zhen watched and listened until the sun was high in the sky.

Then she said: "You did it, then?"

Martha said: "We did accomplish something. Yes."

"But you knew I was here?"

Martha shook her head.

"Funny," said Zhen, "because I knew the world hadn't ended."

And she pushed Martha into the sea.

The ocean was as cold as shadow, and Martha gasped

and her head went under and came up. The salt stung her eyes and a cut on the webbing between her finger and thumb. Her hair was thick and stiff with salt, and her body was carried by the water, and as she tried to stand, a wave knocked her down as cold as the first, or colder. She thought suddenly of amniotic fluid and the salt-sweet taste of a woman and of her mother knocked down by a Frito-Lay truck and of what it meant to turn into salt. She tried to stand again and the water knocked her down again and she tried again and went down again. She started to laugh because it felt like danger but she knew it wouldn't kill her, and that was the funniest thing in the world, as it was funny that to escape from the hurtling waves, she crawled like a baby from the salt toward the sand. And perhaps her laughing was also crying because the taste of salt-sweet water is the first to pass through any of our mouths.

"What do you mean," she said, "you fucking *knew*?"

10. it'll all have to be incredibly real

The streets were shiny and still when Zhen had left the hotel in the black limo. They moved swiftly through the city, north and east, out, open country. An hour outside the city on a quiet road, the car stopped. The screen descended.

"The protocol is that we wait here," said the driver. He pulled down his mask. "And we have some things to discuss."

The driver was Albert Dabrowski.

"Look," he said, "I'm going to level with you. You've gotten involved in some very big stuff here. Criminal, financial, kind of a heist situation. You were never supposed to be here. But I've been thinking about it and we could use you. If you're in."

He'd told her the plan from the start. How they'd used the artificial prophet AUGR to get the three billionaires onto the plane. How the plane was somewhere no one would ever look for it. And now they were going to try to do something actually decent with those companies.

"Look, we have a problem now," said Albert. "We think they have enough communications shit there to actually get in contact with the outside world. Selah figured it out the other night. Using the suits as an energy source. It'd take them a while, but they could do it."

"So you want me to go to this island, smash the communications equipment?"

"That's about the size of it."

"And then . . ."

Albert winced and breathed in through his teeth.

"And then I guess you'll need to wait there . . . for a while?"

"How long is a while?"

"Look, I don't know when we're going to be able to get you off the island and that's the truth of it. I can't tell you what's going to happen, how long it's going to take the companies to stabilize, the world."

"Three months?"

Albert turned his hand palm up and moved it briskly upward a couple of times—the "higher" gesture.

"Six months?"

Wincing face. The same gesture again.

They'd discussed where and how Zhen could find all the technology on the island the billionaires might use for communication. They'd talked about how—if it became necessary—Zhen could act deliberately to split them up, hide them from each other, confuse them. In the end very little of that had been necessary. Zimri Nommik, it turned out, never traveled anywhere without a Pringles can full of his own drone swarm, which he used to carry him away from the others. Ellen Bywater came up with the idea for herself of letting Lenk think he'd destroyed her inside a suit, which—after all the explosions—got up and walked off, putting its own limbs back on. But that was in the future. When Zhen and Albert spoke, they thought these people might need some encouragement to self-destruct.

"Aren't you worried I'll go to the police with all this?" Zhen asked Albert.

"Are you kidding? You've got nothing except a phone you might have rigged up yourself and about fifteen million dollars' worth of criminal damage to Zimri's bunker, by the way. If you go to the police, you'll sound like a lunatic and we'll prosecute you. But anyway you can't go to the police. You can't go anywhere. You're in my car in the middle of the ass-end of nowhere and your options are: do this, or do a year in a safe house somewhere until we know it's OK to let you out."

"Neither of those seem like great options."

"I don't know. You're a survivalist. You could help save the world? And the weather on that island is incredible."

Zhen thought about what it was she'd wanted out of her whole entire life and—if that was all over now—what she could possibly do that was worth a damn.

"Oh," said Albert, "I should mention, we will really have to drug you. Obviously. Because they'll all have equipment that can measure your blood solutes, it'll all have to be incredibly real. If I talk to you through the suits, it'll have to be as the suit, OK?"

"Um."

"Honestly, it is up to you. We can't let you go right now, but we will make sure nothing bad happens to you. And I think it's definitely going to be worth it. In terms of the world."

"Can I call Marius? Otherwise he's just going to keep looking for me. Which will also make it awkward for you."

"Fine," said Albert. "Don't tell him more than you have to."

"Alright," said Zhen, "I'll take the agente provocateuse role on the tropical island with the billionaires."

"Incredibly smart choice in my opinion. I think you'll get a kick out of it."

At last, Zhen heard the distant sound of a helicopter at the same moment that Albert Dabrowski grabbed her wrist and she felt a sharp scratch on the back of her hand.

"Don't worry," he said. "You're going somewhere with a million beautiful things."

11. we have to get there as fast as we can

Martha sat at the edge of the ocean, panting, exhausted, legs apart, at Zhen's feet. She did not try to get up.

She said: "Look, Albert is a dick. You can take everything I've given you and go to the police. That's what I came here for. I came to say sorry and to give you everything."

Zhen said: "Aren't you going to try to convince me not to do it?"

Martha said: "I'm going to try. But I think it's OK if it doesn't work."

"You fucking . . . your friends fucking kidnapped me and brought me here and kept me here against my will." She had stepped out of her suit, which stood next to her, an oddly patched friend and protector. "Look at my leg." She showed the long curved scar. "You did this to me."

"I'm sorry," said Martha. "I didn't know but I should have known and I'm sorry."

Zhen sat down suddenly on the sand.

"Look," she said, "tell me the truth. Did you get me to turn a woman into a pillar of salt because of some religious bullshit?"

"Oh," said Martha.

"Yeah, I read your stuff about the pillar of salt and survival, and you know, I didn't have all the pieces but I *knew*, I knew something was screwy."

"It wasn't intentional," said Martha. "You know, I didn't send the Enochites after you but obviously I felt responsible, and so I put AUGR onto your phone, and it tracks like . . . blood pressure, heart rate, a bunch of stuff. So I'd know if you were in trouble and it could help, AUGR. I wanted to help if you were in danger."

"So the pillar of salt was like . . . a coincidence?"

Martha thought back to the alert coming through from Zhen's phone. To AUGR's outline of the tactical possibilities of Zhen's situation. To the overwhelming guilt Martha had felt in this moment that her actions, the fractal unfolding of her decision to leave her father, had led to this troubled person pursuing Zhen down an air-conditioning vent in a mall in Singapore.

"AUGR offered me a few different options to get you out of there. I guess the salt . . . I didn't think about it until afterward. It just felt right. You know I grew up in a really weird way and a bunch of those stories are just sunk into my bones. I don't know, I suppose that option felt . . . familiar to me."

"AUGR gave you options? It wasn't just doing it all itself?"

Martha had forgotten that Zhen hadn't known this part.

"Oh," she said. "No, AUGR never really worked. It can't do what we said. It can't see the future. It's just a tool, like a satnav or a translator, you know? It can look around, analyze what everything can do, what can be used as a weapon. It can present options."

"It never worked?"

"No. I mean. You can try to be prepared but no one can know what's coming next. The system is too complex. These artificial intelligence things, we treat them like gods but they're not real. There's no way to really know what's going to happen."

"It never . . . worked?" Zhen was suddenly choking for air, laughing the true laughter that only comes when we sit with another person in trust. "It never fucking *worked*? You got them here, you convinced three of the richest people in the world, you got *me* here and it never worked?"

And Zhen was laughing, like Martha, a kind of laughing that is like crying.

Later, Martha said: "We had to do it quickly. Rip the Band-Aid off. You know, eventually all of these things would have gotten solved or the human race would have totally collapsed and the planet would have righted itself one way or the other. But doing it slowly would have been horrific to live through. Hundreds of years of misery: rising seas and famine and drought, refugees from one war bringing so much pressure onto another country that it created more wars. Civilization boiling itself down into enclaves. New diseases coming from the bats and the insects displaced when we cut down more and more trees. We were circling the drain. Hundreds of years of horror before we could start again."

"I thought you said there was no way to know what was going to happen," said Zhen.

"Yeah, well, there's no way to know exactly which of those things were going to happen in what order, obviously. But a bunch of those things were going to happen, and Lenk and his friends were going to make sure they were OK, but the rest of us were going to have to live through it and suffer. And this was just . . . this was a shortcut. I can't control everything forever . . ."

"Oh, you can't? Really. I guess it's good you know that. Good to know, yeah."

"I just thought, if we can get through this part as quickly as possible, if we can just move really fast, then we get to the next bit where it's actually nice and there is electric public transport and low-cost food and the birds come back and we all get to mend our electronics, not throw them away, and the cities are more livable and the rivers are clean and healthy and the air is more breathable . . . we just get to that part quickly. The future is coming. The wind is driving us toward it. There can be a beautiful world on the far shore, I really think so. But we have to get there as fast as we can."

"And now?"

Martha chewed her bottom lip.

"Maybe I've done enough," she said. "You can't fix everything forever, but you can try to tip things in the right direction. Whatever you decide, maybe it'll still be OK."

Zhen weighed the files Martha had given her in her hand.

"I could take these to the FBI, then," she said. "The FBI and the BBC, the CIA and Australian secret services and the French and German ones, and all of them—I could take . . . I could take it to everyone and you would be arrested and sent to prison for the rest of your life."

"Probably," said Martha. "I think . . . I think if you do that, there's a chance people will try to put some of the things I've done back the way they were. Out of anger. Feeling manipulated. But that's OK. When I decided I had to come get you, I knew there was no set of lies I could tell that would stop you finding out the truth. So I decided to tell you."

"And I can do what I want. Go to the media and the government. Fuck you in more ways than anyone has ever been fucked before."

Martha said: "I'm not asking you for anything. It's your decision. I've put myself in your power."

She raised her hands and surrendered.

Later, a great deal later, Martha said: "You really waited all this time because you trusted I'd come."

"I trusted someone would come. But I hoped it'd be you."

Martha smiled. "So in the meantime, did you meet anyone else?"

Zhen said: "Oh yeah, on the deserted island. I've had a long thing with . . . Ellen Bywater. Didn't anyone tell you?"

"They told me it was Zimri."

"Oh, he's more my type."

Their fingers met and touched. Sometimes it's just right. It can be tough to figure out all the logistics. But this part sometimes just works.

Zhen said: "Three fucking years of my life. And my leg. Three years and a leg. Well. Not the whole leg. Still, though."

Martha said: "I'm really sorry. It was unavoidable."

And Zhen said: "I guess you're going to have to find some way to make it up to me."

They laughed as children do when they are thrown high in the air. We are all falling, all the time, from the half-understood past to the unknowable future. The other name for falling without fear is flying.

ACKNOWLEDGMENTS

"Come to the Arctic," said Margaret Atwood to me, "it will change you."

"But maybe I don't want to be changed, Margaret," I said.

And yet I did, and it did. Thank you, Margaret. You were right. Again.

This book owes a huge amount to that trip to the Arctic with the extraordinary Adventure Canada team. Thank you to Rolex, who made it possible for me to take that trip.

I am grateful for conversations I had in a school hall in Rigolet, also called *Tikigâksuagusik*, Nunatsiavut, a town on the shore of a frozen sea. To the people of Rigolet who patiently explained to me what it means to "live off the land" while it slowly dawned on me that even I, urban born and bred, would find it deeply satisfying. And for conversations with Lena Onalik and Derrick Pottle and later with my *Zombies, Run!* collaborator Ishmael Hope about Native, Indigenous, and First Nations knowledge and ideas, thank you. All errors of understanding in this book are of course my own.

If, as a reader, you have wondered how we settled Rabbits ended up with such murderous hatred of people who live even small parts of the hunter-gatherer life that we all, after all, lived until a few brief millennia ago, I urge you to seek out the work of these and other Native, Indigenous, and First Nations teachers and writers. I've come to feel that even hatred of Jewish people (constructed as "wanderers" as we are) draws partly from that same self-disgust directed toward our human origins and, more than that, toward who we truly still are. It is everywhere once you know what you're looking for.

Many of the ideas in here, particularly the thought that it is laughable to search in deep space or within computer algorithms for intelligent life when we're ignoring, torturing, despising, or destroying so much intelligent animal life here on Earth, are developed from conversations with the late, much-loved and much-missed Graeme Gibson.

Thank you, Adam Curtis, for conversations and especially for the thought that rather than getting the machines to be as clever as we are, we are training ourselves to think down to their level.

Thank you to my colleagues and friends in the tech and games industry who like me *love technology* and are also committed to trying to make the industry less . . . like this. Particular thanks for thoughts and/or roiling anger to Adrian Hon, Holly Gramazio, Meghna Jayanth, Alex Macmillan, Rachel Coldicutt, and Anna Pickard. I encourage readers interested in the ideas about technology in this book toward the work of Jaron Lanier, Timnit Gebru, Douglas Rushkoff, and Paris Marx. And toward the brilliant TV series *Halt and Catch Fire*.

Thank you, Adam Tandy, who wrestled this book into shape with me, and without whom it would probably have knocked me over. Thank you, Annette Mees, who figured out the end with me. And the middle. Thank you, Francesca Segal, who got me to finish it. Thanks to Gillian Crawford at Ballymultimber for your perfect-for-writers cottage. And to Tom Sutcliffe, because he can't bear long acknowledgments sections.

Thanks to my wonderful editor Tim O'Connell, to my agents Veronique Baxter and Simon Lipskar, to Helen Garnons-Williams, to Di Speirs, constant supporter and friend. To those others at S&S, including Jon Karp, Irene Kheradi, Maria Mendez, Danielle Prielipp, Maggie Southard, Shannon Hennessey, Amanda Mulholland, Yvette Grant, Lewelin Polanco, and Jackie Seow who helped bring this book into the world, I am grateful for your work and support. Thank you to Victoria Chaiben and Niamh Cumming. Thanks to @ohomatopoeia on Instagram for Singapore knowledge. Thanks for careful reading and thoughts to Maz Hamilton, Metis Hon, Dr. Benjamin Ellis, and Helena Lee. Thanks to my parents Marion and Geoffrey, to Rebecca Levene, to Esther, Russell, Daniella, Benjy and Zara Donoff, to David and to the Excellent Women.

And thanks to readers who've got this far and don't mind a bit of tricksiness. Those who know that nothing is ever really over shall receive their reward over the page.

MANY, MANY YEARS LATER

Everything is always in motion. Nothing remains still. Despite what anyone says, history never, in fact, ends.

Very little remains secret after one hundred years. The origins of the enclave on Huntsy Island—renamed to honor the Native people who lived and died here—are now well known. There had been a ridiculous accident, the kind of thing that happened in those ancient days when people had a strange religious belief in the protections of their all-seeing technologies. An early-warning system had gone off much too soon and had sent three very powerful people to this beautiful place, cutting them off from the world. They had not known how to be found and no one had known how to look for them. There had been a period of grief and searching, and then the world had shrugged and moved forward without them.

Some historians suggested that the new movements, the change in the tide of thought, even the growing quasi-governmental powers of the FutureSafe zones had been a direct result of this disaster. The fact was that by the time the world discovered the truth—when FutureSafe sent the first caretaker group to live permanently on the island forty-one years after the original accident—the puzzle was already, for most people, irrelevant history.

Only one of the original three was still alive. Lenk Sketlish was old and confused. He asked the new settlers whether there had been a great cataclysm in the outside world. They told him yes and he welcomed them to his island. It took a few months for them to understand who he was. He died within three years, and with him the living memories of the events on the island. Lenk Sketlish was buried in a place of honor under a cairn of stones that was visible from the eastern windows of his mountain at dawn. It was another thirty-eight years before the next generation of caretakers on the island discovered, through decaying recordings and rusted technologies, what had happened here.

Ellen Bywater had died two years after the crash. Her assistance suit had recordings of her talking to herself or sometimes addressing her dead husband, Will. She became very disoriented, then very depressed. The suit had pleaded with her to try to escape, to contact the other people on the island for help. She had turned off its communication functions, leaving it a mute witness to her end. She'd taken the suit to the beach on the far north of the island. She'd left it sitting there with its knees drawn up to its chest staring out into the ocean. It had watched as she put stones into the many pockets of her lightweight flying suit and walked out into the sea. Later, it had recorded—with a troubled, partial, 48 percent facial recognition certainty—the return, for a few days, of the body of Ellen Bywater to the shore and the scuttling crabs and beetles and seabirds and bright green millipedes, their mouthparts working, that had helped the flesh that had once been her sublimate back into the living world from which she'd come.

Exploring a distant cove accessible only by climbing down a crumbling cliff, the caretakers found the suit sitting there, knees up, arms wrapped around them, visor down and recording the myriad parts of the living world that passed before it. Small birds pecked at its feet and at the tiny crustaceans that had latched to its heels in the sand. A rodent a little like a squirrel had taken to tucking soft seeds under its ass for safekeeping. It waited like that, its solar cells slowly failing, its residual power just enough for the barest flicker of monitoring functions.

Zimri Nommik had died even earlier but was found a great deal later. He had walked for three days to the farthest point of the island he believed to be nearest the mainland. He was sick, but he refused the suit's suggestions of reconnecting with the main party and accessing their medicines and assistance. The suit told him it could find extra stores of medicine but he did not believe it. Instead he found a cave and used his drone swarm to wall him inside a beehive cell with slabs of stone, to protect himself from predators. The suit did all it could very loyally. It gave him all the drugs that might be useful; it monitored his fever as it spiked. When his heart began to falter, it shocked him back to life. It gave him morphine so there was little pain at the end.

When he was finally gone, the suit, like Ellen's, had no further instructions as to purpose. It continued to hold Zimri's body within its cocoon, lying on its side in a dark, concealed cave. The cave was warm and dry, its walls partly composed of salt. The sun was bright for months at a time. A shift in the stones allowed hot parched air to circulate. As the body decomposed anaerobically, consumed by the very bacteria that Zimri had once carried on his skin and in his gut, the suit came to a decision itself to vent the noxious gases into the cave. It ventilated the corpse with the hot salt air and the body began to dry out faster than it could rot. Zimri's high-tech wicking sports clothes drew the moisture out of his corpse. After eight to ten years the smell dissipated completely; the flesh that had mostly dried on the bones was a desiccated wire-tangle of tendons and ligaments stretched tight over the skeleton. When the caretakers gently rolled the stone from the cave mouth, they found Zimri Nommik's dead face gaping through the faceplate at the sandy floor without urgency or needs.

Historians still debate the precise narrative of the accident that happened here. Toward the end of Ellen Bywater's life, the suit recorded several attempts at direct communications from her child Badger begging Ellen not to harm herself. When these recordings were found, they occasioned a great deal of debate. Could they possibly be real or were they some sophisticated "deepfake" Ellen had created herself to externalize her debate over the end of her life? If they were real, what did this mean about the accident on the island? Could Badger have somehow known where their mother was? And if so, why had they never spoken about it?

By the point the recordings were discovered, Badger themself was in their midnineties, a parent of three with their long-term partner—the artist Gracie McCall—a grandparent, and a great-grandparent. Of the original FutureSafe visionaries and board members—Martha Einkorn, Selah Nommik, Albert Dabrowski, and Lai Zhen—Badger Bywater was the last survivor. They had by this time overseen the transfer of enormous assets in what had been Medlar, Anvil, and Fantail to fifty-eight independent FutureSafe territories. These territories were already well advanced in the process of allying to create the UAR—the United Autonomous Regions. The UAR was a distributed state made possible by technology and the money technology had brought, a union of zones that had been dedicated—or had dedicated themselves—to the preservation of the natural world for the benefit of all humankind, often by using the proprietary technologies made by their founders to keep most of humankind away most of the time.

All Badger Bywater ever said about the apparent recordings of them was that they didn't want to see their mother's last days. That it must be obvious that if Badger had been able to save their mother's life, they would have done so.

"It was a strange and upsetting time to live through,"

they said. "Everyone knows how close the world came to disaster, the human race to extinction. I've read the theories about how my mother could have made those images herself, and they make perfect sense to me. She went through a terrible ordeal. She was confused. I wish it had been different. I wish she had been able to come home. I wish she had met my children. I can't see what there is to gain in raking over the past. The important thing is the future."

Nothing can be permanently settled or solved. No state is perfect; no utopia exists but that it leaves someone out. All we can be is alert, like Fox, to the changing winds. To ask ourselves in each new situation: What would we hate anyone to do to us? And: Who have we forgotten? To exist in motion, falling forward, trying to bend our own histories toward what is fair and kind, what is sensible and good. We will keep failing, but final success was never the point.

North of Seattle, a woman is running through the forest. Over the tree-thronged miles, a paper and a stored tightbeam communication are folded in the top pocket of her shirt. The jackrabbits and the black-tailed deer leap and bobtail the road with the grace of wild things. Her dirt bike failed a way back down the road. If they're not after her now, they soon will be. The United States of America does not appreciate the interference of the United Autonomous Regions in their affairs, and they would capture her as a spy and try her as a traitor if they caught her.

The newly elected president of the United States is an Enochite—pretending to be a fairly standard moderate Fox and Rabbit Movement person, she actually belongs to one of the more extreme wings of the belief. Her faction believes that the prevention of "pieces" is the moral duty of every one of God's creations and that she must unite the world under a single world order. Starting with the so-called Autonomous Regions whose militaristic and absolutist protection of wildlife habitats is a threat to the global order. It would be better, she has communicated via tightbeam, for every one of the 1.2 billion citizens of the Godless Regions to die than to allow them to continue holding the world hostage with their empty mechanical suits and their swarms of drone gnats. The Seceded Regions must be reunited with their mother countries. The Basque Preserve must go back to Spain. The Cornish Zone must return to England. Kootenai and Flathead have to be part of the Greater United States again, for fuck's sake.

Fifteen miles ahead is an armored survival suit that has buried itself facedown in the earth around a hollow tree. If she can get there before sunrise, she will make the border of Haida Gwaii tonight with the information in her pocket. There is no other way to warn them; any communication would give away her position. She runs through the night, more at home in the forest than she has been these long years in the city. Believing in something strong enough to power her. The work is never over, there is no final battle; the fight is the destination, the constant tense balance between the present and the future.

ABOUT THE AUTHOR

Naomi Alderman is the bestselling author of *The Power*, which won the Women's Prize for Fiction, and was chosen as a book of the year by the *New York Times*, the *Washington Post*, and the *Los Angeles Times*, and was recommended as a book of the year by both Barack Obama and Bill Gates. As a novelist, Alderman has been mentored by Margaret Atwood via the Rolex Mentor and Protégé Arts Initiative, is a Fellow of the Royal Society of Literature, and her work has been translated into more than thirty-five languages. *The Power* was adapted as a series for Amazon Prime, starring Toni Collette, on which Alderman was an executive producer. Her first novel, *Disobedience*, was adapted into a feature-length film by Oscar-winning director Sebastián Lelio. As a video game designer, she was lead writer on the groundbreaking alternate reality game *Perplex City*, and is cocreator of the award-winning smartphone exercise adventure game *Zombies, Run!*, which has more than 10 million players. She is a professor of creative writing at Bath Spa University. She lives in London.

ABOUT THE TYPE

This book was set in Verdana Pro and Minion Pro, the former which is published by Carter & Cone and the latter is an Adobe Original typeface designed by Robert Slimbach. It is important to note that Carter collaborated with Microsoft to design fonts that were specifically legible on computer monitors. Minion on the other hand—with its many ligatures, small caps, oldstyle figures, swashes, and other added glyphs—draws inspiration from the typefaces of the late Renaissance, a period of highly readable type designs that didn't sacrifice elegance.

Zhen, I found it. I know you loved up in secret fuck cave or whatever, love is great. When you want to know the truth, email me. mariuszugravescu@gmail.com